M for Mammy

Eleanor O'Reilly

TWO
ROADS

First published in Great Britain in 2019 by Two Roads
An imprint of John Murray Press
An Hachette UK company

1

Copyright © Eleanor O'Reilly 2019

A CIP catalogue record for this title is available from the British Library

Hardback ISBN 9781473672352
Trade Paperback ISBN 9781473672369
eBook ISBN 9781473672383
Audio Digital Download ISBN 9781473672390

Typeset in Plantin Light by
Palimpsest Book Production Ltd, Falkirk, Stirlingshire

Printed and bound in Great Britain by Clays Ltd, Elcograf S.p.A.

Hodder & Stoughton policy is to use papers that are natural, renewable
and recyclable products and made from wood grown in sustainable forests.
The logging and manufacturing processes are expected to conform
to the environmental regulations of the country of origin.

Hodder & Stoughton Ltd
Carmelite House
50 Victoria Embankment
London EC4Y 0DZ

www.tworoadsbooks.com
www.hodder.co.uk

For Brian and Ella – with all my love

All I know is a door into the dark.
Outside, old axles and iron hoops rusting;
Inside, the hammered anvil's short-pitched ring,
The unpredictable fantail of sparks –

Seamus Heaney

CHAPTER I

Jenny

A Good Day

by Jennifer Augustt

'Would ya ever come out from in under the stairs and go round to your sister's or go out for a walk or do somethin' else for God's sake?' Da says.

Silence. Ma's in under the stairs again.

Ma cries and prays a lot when she's in under the stairs. She cries and prays a lot when she's not in under the stairs, too. She says, 'Jesus Christ' all the time but Da says Holy God doesn't give a F-word about us and Ma tells him to watch his feckin' language and does he want Jacob's first word to be a F-word?

Da says he doesn't care so long as Jacob has a first word and Ma scrapes the muck off the plates and slams the dishes in the sink and Da tells her that her brother Uncle Patrick was always weird and that there's none a that kind a thing in his family. Then Ma says stuff about Da's cousin Mickey who ended up in jail for refusing to speak at all to the judge who found him guilty a not talking. Then Da tells Ma her sister, Auntie Eleanor, is for the birds completely and that her nephew, the one with the tyre marks still on his back and his head after a bin lorry drove over him in the back lane, definitely has something serious wrong with him too.

Then Da goes down the pub with Uncle Michael for a drink which must be a big one coz it takes him four and a half hours to drink it. I think Uncle Michael must be on the spectrum too because every time I see him he asks me how old I am and what class I'm in now and I see him once or twice every week when he comes to take Da down the pub.

Sometimes Ma goes mental when Da goes down the pub and sometimes she doesn't even know he's missing at all. When she does notice he's not watching *Neighbours* or not out in the shed, fixing things that aren't even broken with other bits a broken things that need fixing, she says, 'Where's your daddy?'

But if you say nothing sometimes she forgets. Sometimes she doesn't though. And then the next day Ma and Da don't speak for ages and the quiet gets real big and Jacob sits staring at his fingers which are always moving even when they don't need to be moving and he's there with his moving fingers thinking about nothing and he sometimes sits like that forever coz he doesn't know time like when he wakes up in the middle a the night and he doesn't know it's not day he only knows *Peppa Pig* isn't on the telly and neither is *Thomas the Tank Engine* and then we think there's going to be even more trouble but then we remember *The Simpsons* must be on some channel some-where coz *The Simpsons* is always on some channel somewhere, even if it is the middle of the night.

I think Da might be on the spectrum too coz Da doesn't know time either when he tells Ma he'll be back in an hour but he doesn't come back for four and a half hours and he says, 'Sure it got too late for comin' home early.'

'Autism's a disorder,' Ma says.

'Autism's a bastard,' Da says.

Autism came to live in our house one Wednesday in February when Jacob was still just a baby. Ma says he got in through the kitchen window we'd left open for the cat and he took Jacob away. Granny and Da thought Jacob was deaf coz he didn't smile when you sang 'Hickory Dickory' or when you played Peep and he didn't look at you when you called his name and Ma started to cry when the nurse in the clinic said she thought Jacob was definitely deaf. Ma told her Jacob wasn't deaf. She knew he could hear. It wasn't that. Then Ma cried again when the doctor the clinic nurse sent her to see told her he thought that Jacob was deaf too. Ma said he should stop telling her about all the things Jacob would never be able to do and that he wouldn't have to go to a special school in Dublin on a special bus. And Ma was right all along. Jacob wasn't deaf.

Autism could have come for me but Ma says autism prefers boy babies.

'That's a pile a shite,' Da says.

'Look at the stats,' Ma says.

Da says there was no such thing as autism in his day. Then Ma says words like 'epidemic' and Da says words even worse than F-off. Then Ma storms out of the room and Da shouts that she should have a medical degree by now and if she put as much time into looking after herself as she does into chasing causes and cures then we'd all be better off and it's like they're two people talking different languages like when Granny shouts at the French students she keeps in the summer coz she thinks they're stupid and deaf not just foreign and French and they don't understand each other at all.

Jacob puts his hands over his ears and rocks backwards and forwards or he walks round in circles. Jacob doesn't like shouting or storming out of rooms. Words and shouting get very confusing for Jacob. It's kinda like the different words tumble and jumble when they join together to become shouting and it's like Jacob's thoughts tumble and jumble into sticky scrambled things that get stuck in his hair and then in his brain and then he gets frightened and starts tapping the walls or scratching the telly. His eyes roll round in his head and he makes funny noises that don't sound like words, they just sound like funny noises, and then it's like everything in the whole universe is happening at once. This is called a 'meltdown'.

'Da, I'm starving!'

'Right, kiddo. Get your coat. We're goin' to Luigi's,' Da says out real loud. 'Your Ma can just stay in under the stairs.'

So, I get me yellow anorak and stand in the hall and Da wrestles with Jacob coz he won't put his coat on.

'Ah now, don't get upset, it's freezin' outside,' Da says.

So, I tell Da, Jacob will only wear his Spiderman coat this week so there's no point trying to put that green jacket on him. Da grabs Jacob's Spiderman coat and bundles Jacob inside and then we think we're ready except Da forgot to put Jacob's gloves, the blue ones on the string, inside one arm then round the back of his head and down the other arm and Jacob knows they're missing so he looks up into the sleeve of his Spiderman coat to see if he can find his blue gloves that are missing but I know he won't find them and Da knows he won't find them coz they're hanging on the end of the stairs.

'Ah sure, it's not cold enough for gloves,' Da says.

Me and Da and Jacob go round the corner and past the Pizza Hut and cross the zebra crossing and past the play-ground to Luigi's.

We haven't been to the playground for ages. The last time we were there it was full of people and when we came home I heard Ma telling Da that the playground's the loneliest place in the whole wide world coz in the playground there's lots of children the same age as Jacob and that makes it harder for her to pretend to herself that Jacob's fine and not different and not special and you feel even worse, Ma said, when you see the other mothers playing with their children and sometimes she wishes it was their child who was different or special or silent and not her own child and she said she knows it's wrong to think like that about anybody and you wouldn't wish it on your worst enemy even though she loves Jacob so much her heart hurts and then her head hurts to think that maybe she'll be the only one to ever love him like that and what if she wasn't there to love him? Who'd love him then?

'Sure, I would a course,' Da says. 'Do ya want a cuppa tea?'

But Ma didn't want any tea. She just kept going on about how sometimes she even hates those other mothers for having painted nails and nice arching eyebrows and for having time to have their hair coloured or to get a false tan or for having the energy to go to Zumba or yoga or even the energy to smile or for having perfect children or for being happy all the time but sometimes she can't help it and she hates herself for hating them like that and for even thinking like that about anybody else and the more she thinks about it the more she wants to rip their stupid eyes out with their stupid painted nails or smash their stupid smiley faces off the swings or crush their stupid tanned legs in the see-saw or mangle their stupid highlighted heads in the roundabout and then Ma said the more time she spends in the playground the more angry and jealous and bitter and sad she becomes. So we don't go to the playground anymore.

I think Ma must be on the spectrum too coz she doesn't

like going anywhere, anymore, and she doesn't like people anymore either. She doesn't like hugs or kisses except if she's teaching Jacob Huggie-Kissy-Bye-Bye on one of her 'good' days. But even on her good days she looks sad and she doesn't see that a real grey skinny face has slipped down over her lovely happy old face like one a them Halloween masks in the Two Euro shop with the worn-out elastic that doesn't even keep the mask up on your head. And she doesn't tell us stories or even read any of the books I get from the library in school with me on one of her 'bad' days and sometimes I even have to bring the books back to school even though I don't even know the story inside them coz reading on your own isn't the same as reading with Ma when she does her fairy-tale voice and tells me and Jacob about how stories are the thing we need more than anything else in the whole wide world coz we remember each other through stories. And I think Ma is right because I think that's what I miss most of all on the bad days coz Ma's stories always make everything better again, no matter what.

Sometimes Ma screams about her lost baby boy, even on one of her 'good' days, but then I tell her Jacob isn't really lost, he's just somewhere where we can't find him or hear him or tell him how much we all love him even when he's just sitting over there on the couch. Ma goes mental then and goes back in under the stairs. This is called a 'meltdown' too.

Luigi's shiny and sweaty in his white vest and scary tattoos and his big hairy belly hangs out over his pants and he looks like he eats more chips than he sells and he doesn't speak very good English. He forgets words and sometimes says the wrong words or he looks under the counter like he's trying to find the words he needs to say a sentence or he looks up in the air waving his arms about hoping that the words will fall out of the sky and into his mouth.

'Ah sure, he's not the full shillin',' Da says.

Da sat beside Luigi in school when they were little, when Luigi's name wasn't Luigi, when it was just Tommy Doyle.

I sit beside Jane-Anne Comerford Smyth in school. She was my best friend in the whole wide world till last Tuesday at twelve o'clock when she told Kylie Murphy that Jacob's a 'spa'. So I told Jane-Anne Comerford Smyth that she's a 'spa' and then I stabbed her in the arm with me pencil and she started to cry like a cry-baby and then she told Teacher and Teacher gave out and said I was a disgrace and that we don't allow behaviour like that in our classroom, now do we? Then Teacher told me to go see Sr Mary Assumpta up in the office.

Sr Mary Assumpta up in the office is the boss nun. Da says she's like 159 years old in Nun Years. Nun Years are different from human years. Da says nuns live longer than people do. It's like when they're born they look like they are about thirty but then everything slows down, so they never really look older than sixty-eight no matter what age they are. Every Nun Year is equal to about twelve human years or something like that. Da says there's even a Nun Year Converter online to work out the age of a nun.

I think Sr Mary Assumpta looks like Marvel out of *The Untouchables*. And she is untouchable too coz no one ever heard of anyone ever touching a nun or stealing one either and I think even that if she was moving at 800 miles an hour and suddenly hit a wall that wasn't there a minute ago she still wouldn't be hurt coz she'd be protected from the bang by her big holy force field and she'd just bounce back and be fine and she knows everything about you like Holy God knows everything about you but she's not

friendly or all forgetting like Holy God is. Sr Mary
Assumpta forgets nothing.

When I went into the office it was like there were these
big dark clouds inside in me head and I couldn't think
through them. Then something happened to me breathing
and I forgot how to do it. My arms and throat started
shaking, my hair started leaking and my tongue got stuck
to the top of me mouth. I tried to remember if breathing is
in through your nose and out through your mouth or if it's
in through your mouth and out through your nose. But I
couldn't remember. So I just kinda pushed all the air in
and out through all the holes in me face all at the same
time which doesn't really work coz I still couldn't catch my
breath and when it got into me mouth it just fell straight
back out again and me nose didn't even know the breath
was even in there in the first place.

Sr Mary Assumpta was sitting behind her desk with her
'I know what you did' face that she puts on whenever
you're in trouble and I have to tell her what I did even
though she says she already knows what I did anyway.
Then she says I'm a disgrace and we don't allow behaviour
like that in our school, now do we?

Then I said, 'Why can't Jacob come to school here?'

Sr Mary Assumpta starts looking at the wall behind me
like there's a picture of some faraway place she wants to
go to on it, even though there isn't, and she says school
isn't the place for little boys who won't speak and there's
no room for him here anyway and I wonder how she
knows Jacob can't speak and why there's no room for him.
He's not very big.

Then I tell her he's really good on the computer, and
she says, 'Lovely. But remember we have a cake sale and a
coffee morning and we sell ribbons and collect phones for
Autism Ireland every September and we do shoe boxes

and hampers at Christmas and Trócaire boxes at Lent and
sponsored walks and minutes' silences for all the other
unfortunates in the world and we should feel good about
that, Jennifer, now shouldn't we?'

Da sits me up on Luigi's tall steely cold-on-the-bum
counter so I can see all the food pictures lit up on the wall
behind Luigi's humungous head and then Da bends down
to get Jacob but he's too busy looking up the sleeves of his
Spiderman coat for his missing blue gloves that are
hanging on the end of the stairs at home. I tell Da it's
okay coz I know what Jacob wants for his dinner. I get
chips and a jumbo sausage in batter and Da gets a batter
burger and chips. Jacob gets chips and chicken finger balls
even though he's not allowed chips or chicken finger balls
or chocolate or sugar or yogurts or nuts or strawberries or
ice cream coz he always gets sick when Ma knows he's had
anything like that but he never gets sick when me or Da
sneak him nice things and Ma doesn't know.

The smell of chips is everywhere and it's the loveliest
smell in the whole wide world. It's warm and salty-hot and
cosy and it gets into your tongue and your teeth and into
your eyes and up into your nose. It even gets into your
hair and your socks and then your mouth waters coz you
think you're really starving even if you're not really
starving at all and you only just had your dinner about an
hour ago coz the smell of chips always makes you feel like
you are starving and like you haven't eaten for about 100
years and it seems like you've been thinking about the
chips and waiting for the chips for about 100 years too
and then you think you're going to die a the hunger if you
don't get some chips right away. And Luigi's chips can
only be eaten outta soggy brown-paper bags, shiny with
greasy see-through ripped-open sides, on one of Luigi's
sticky-top tables with loads and loads a salt and as much

vinegar as you can squeeze out of the bottle and before you put the first one inside in your mouth you blow softly on it like you're telling it to Ssssh and then you look at the great big-fat-lovely-yellow chip like it's the first chip you've ever seen in your whole life and it's warm and it's thick and it's the loveliest taste in world. The chip is crunchy and big between your finger and thumb and sometimes it's so hot it burns your finger and your thumb but you don't mind coz it's the loveliest taste in the world.

And the hungry rumbles inside in your tummy wait for the first bite and then your whole mouth feels like the luckiest mouth in the world. And the three of us just sit and look at our chips and it's like Luigi made these chips only for us and nobody else and there's nowhere else in the whole wide world that we'd rather be except here coz this is what it's like to be happy even if we're just happy for as long as it takes us to eat chips.

We eat real slow and when the last chip is gone we lick our fingers, one at a time, trying to make the taste last forever but we know it can't last forever. Then Da goes back to thinking about Ma and I go back to thinking about Jane-Anne Comerford Smyth and Jacob goes back to thinking about his favourite missing blue gloves that really aren't missing coz they're at home hanging on the end of the stairs.

Then we remember it's Tuesday.

Granny comes every Tuesday and squints up her eyes and looks at Jacob like he's something that just fell off the side of the moon and landed right there in our kitchen and she says things like, 'Musha, some a them grow out of it,' or 'Ya wouldn't think to look at him now, would ya?' or 'Mrs Murphy down the road was tellin' me her sister's son is handicapped, too.'

Then Ma throws her eyes nearly up into her hair and

sighs out real loud and chews her bottom lip like she's starving and tells Granny she just doesn't understand. But Granny says she reared five all on her own, so she thinks she knows a thing or two about children and then she reminds us all how lucky we are coz we're not starving or Protestant or living in Africa or up above there in Butlins. Then Granny tells us all about Posh Spice and who's dead and about the weather. Ma gets even more angry and bites even harder on her lip but Granny pretends not to notice. And Da says a curse word even worse than the F-word and Granny pretends not to hear. I'm really, really sure Granny's on the spectrum coz she's always pretending not to notice or hear like the time she said she was having a special Mass said in the Holy Rosary Church, up the road, for Jacob, and would we come and Da was standing behind her shaking his head and sticking his fingers down his neck like he was getting sick and Granny could see him in the mirror on the back wall but she looked away anyway.

Ma says, 'Of course we will,' and then Granny says she offered up a novena to St Anthony that morning coz it was a Tuesday and that's the only day of the week that he works and coz St Anthony's the saint of lost things she thought he might be able to help Jacob find his lost voice. Da laughed out real loud and Granny says she doesn't know why he's laughing coz there's more chance of Jacob finding his voice than there is of Da finding a job and then Da says F-off with his mouth but not with his voice and he thought Granny didn't notice, but she did. Then Granny said that Posh Spice did have a boob job and Mary Fitzpatrick died and that there's plenty a work out there for anyone willing to get up off their fat arse and that we're in for a cold spell for the rest of the week but that the weekend will be milder.

So, we just sit in Luigi's looking out the window and we wait till seven o'clock till the coast is clear and Granny's gone off to bingo.

When we get home the house is all dark and there's only Ma sitting there on her own, in the kitchen, talking to Lonely. Lonely's our fish. Not our dog. We got him instead of a dog.

I can remember one day before last year Ma says to Da, 'Autism speaks loudest when Jacob's most silent.'

'That's a pile a shite,' Da says back to Ma. 'Let's get him a dog.'

Ma says over her dead body are we getting a dog and does Da not remember the cocker spaniel who ate the little girl's head off on Sky News?

Da says, 'That's ridiculous, cocker spaniels don't eat little girls' heads off,' and Ma says Da's ridiculous if he thinks he's going to bring some flea-bitten mongrel into this house but you could see Da was already training the dog in his head – making him sit and stay and roll over and be good for Jacob.

So, Da went out and bought us a goldfish instead of the dog Ma wouldn't let us get and we named him Lonely.

I think Lonely's on the spectrum too coz he doesn't ever notice our flat noses pressed against the plastic bowl or the smell of fish fingers in the kitchen coz he's too busy swimming round and round in circles and he doesn't come back or look at you when you call him. Ma says that's coz he likes the peace of his underwater world and that the water stops your voice from travelling and so his ears don't hear and that's why he's silent forever but Da says, 'That's a pile a shite. Lonely doesn't hear ya coz he's a fish and fish don't have any F-word ears.'

Sometimes I think Jacob's like Lonely in his own underwater world of silence with no voice and no friends and no

one to talk to except Super Mario and Baby Luma. Baby
Luma first finds Mario sleeping in the planet that houses
the Gateway to the Starry Sky after he's blasted outta
Mushroom World and then he helps Mario save Princess
Peach from Bowser with the Spin move he uses to break
crystals and attack enemies and further his jumps. In the
end Baby Luma dies saving the universe from a black hole
and you never have to look him straight in the eye coz his
eyes are at the side of his head. Jacob likes eyes at the
sides of heads coz then he doesn't have to do the eye
contact thing Ma makes him do even though he hates it.
Jacob doesn't like looking in eyes. I hope someday Jacob
can find his way out of the Starry Sky and come back to
the sitting room where we'll be waiting for him on the
couch and I hope that when he comes back we'll understand him a little bit more and help him a little bit more so
he doesn't always have to try learning things all on his own
and he'll see just how much we all love him. Da says he'd
gladly swap places with Jacob and save him from that big
F-word black hole called autism.

Ma blames herself and the injection for the measles. Da
blames 'those fuckers up in Dail Eireann with their big
flashy cars and their big budget cuts'.

Ma goes to healers and magic-card-readers and people
with crystals hanging outta their heads, wearing sandals
with socks instead a shoes. Da says they're all money-
grabbing bastards and goes out to the shed or goes down
the pub with Uncle Michael.

Da gives Ma a bag a chips, puts on the lights and the
telly and Jacob goes up to his room to get his Nintendo. I
hear Jacob coming back downstairs and I know he's
already playing Super Mario coz I can hear Mario running
and swimming in the Sparkling Waters of the Fourth World
but then I hear a thump a bang and a thud thud thud and

a crash and a smash and a falling falling falling like the falling's never going to stop. And it's like we all stop breathing. We're all real still and not moving in the frozen kitchen coz we're all too afraid to go out to the hall. Then suddenly the silence stops and the music on the telly starts blaring again. The microwave beeps. The clock tick-tocks. Da's can splish-sploshes on the floor. Ma's chip falls under the table. And then like the house is on fire we all move all at the same time and we're all screaming at the same time, too. We all push past each other out to the hall. My leg goes before Da's but Da's arm goes before mine and we get stuck in the door. Then Ma's whole body shoves us both outta the way and it's like she shapeshifts out to the hall. Then we see him. Jacob's Nintendo's broken into millions of pieces right at our feet.

'Fuck!' Jacob says from the top of the stairs.

Ma's eyes fill up with tears, but she doesn't cry. Da's mouth fills up with words but he doesn't speak and then Ma looks at Da and Da looks at Ma and then for the first time in ages they smile at each other and then they smile at Jacob and me.

Jenny stands in front of Mrs Nicholson's desk looking at all the red marks on her upside-down copy. There's big red X's and circles; deep, angry-looking red lines; red words float over blue words, spilling out between the margins; red arrows joining red circles and ugly exclamation marks, straight up and cutting, announcing themselves with the disgust of being forgotten, making silent little screams on the page.

'Where do I start?' Mrs Nicholson nods hopelessly, her red pen hovering over Jenny's best handwriting, all joined up and slanting slightly forward, the way it's supposed to. 'Just look at this. We never say *I would a,* now do we?' The red pen marks are so deeply cut into Jenny's copy that their naked impression is minted into the next page and the one after that. There's more red now than blue; big-searching question marks having upside-down meltdowns. 'We don't want it too long, now do we? Shorter is better. It was only supposed to be two pages. We have rules about homework, now don't we?'

Jenny watches Mrs Nicholson finger-lick through her story. She doesn't know why there's so much tut-tutting and head shaking going on. Jenny thinks it is a good story and she liked writing it. In fact, Jenny is sure this is the kind of story that would win in a story writing competition. She might even win a bike, for first prize, or enough money maybe to buy a bike.

But Mrs Nicholson keeps on tut-tutting in time with the side-to-side shaking of her head and she looks like she's going to burst into flames any minute. Jenny imagines her exploding and then splatting all over the walls, sticking to the ceiling and dribbling back down again to make more hellish little squiggles before she seeps into the floor and disappears forever.

'Oh, now, I don't think a granny would Ever say that, now do You?' Mrs Nicholson's finger falls on Granny's *arse*. Jenny hopes she didn't notice Da's *shite*. She thinks about Granny and what she'd say to Mrs Nicholson about red pens if they ever met. 'Your sentences are far too long, though I do like the bit about the chips.'

Jenny stands up slightly taller. She thinks she might smile.

'But this is all wrong here.'

The half-smile falls off the bottom of Jenny's face.

'Where?'

'This bit. Who is telling the story? How would You know what your father is thinking, here, in the café, or the little boy either?'

'Coz, I just know. That's my little brother Jacob.'

'*Coz!* There's no such word. Nor is *outta* a word or *kinda* for that matter either!'

She looks like she's decided not to burst into flames after all, but to set fire to Jenny instead. Jenny smells herself smouldering. The burning in her neck shoots up into her face.

'We need to work on full stops, now don't we?' She scribbles more upside-down red words on top of Jenny's upside-down blue words. Mrs Nicholson slams Jenny's copy shut with a slap and a bang. 'Maybe we should try to listen a bit more and follow my instructions!'

Now shouldn't we? Jenny says inside her own head. Jenny picks up her copy.

Mrs Nicholson brushes imaginary crumbs off her blouse.

'Now, Jane-Anne, this Really is Wonderful. The Day You Saved the Kitten. Lovely. Just Lovely.' Mrs Nicholson makes all the capital letter sounds in her voice sing across the room.

Jane-Anne smiles sweetly at Jenny as they pass, between desks.

'Definitely one for the Winner's Pile!' Mrs Nicholson chirps.

Jane-Anne opens her eyes real wide like she can't believe all the good capitals in the air. 'SPA!' she whispers to the back of Jenny's head.

Iliona Reszczynski, the little Polish girl with the biggest eyes Jenny has ever seen, shares an understanding little half-smile with Jenny as Jenny moves closer to their shared desk. Jenny, quietly and without being noticed, places her copy upside down in the square metal bin at the back of the room and then sits back down on her chair.

'GOOD IDEA!' she imagines Grammar Girl saying to Punctuation Panda up there on the wall. But then she remembers what Mrs Nicholson said about Not Knowing.

Annette

Big flakes of cold night fall through the air, settling on the gate of number six in the middle of the row. It's a tired gate, useless really. The latch is old, sitting on years of coloured paint hardened into flat bubbled patterns. No longer white nor grey or cream. No-colour gate, it drags over concrete, eating further into the half-circle fossilised into the path. It stops along the midline of the half-circle. It doesn't open. It doesn't close.

Together they pass through the gap, leaving the sleeping house behind. The house getting smaller with each step they take. Then it is gone.

It is a habit now to stop at every tree, reach out little fingers to feel warm wrinkled bark beneath threaded ivy, spongy silver-green moss. Annette leans in beside him. A gentle pull and tug underneath works a piece away from the base. The damp earthy smell sticks to her fingers, darkening her nails.

'Moss grows on the side away from the sun. Moss likes the dark.'

They walk on into the night. A small sprinkling of light crystallises in one small corner of the sky. A small wind blows under the white of a new moon. Annette looks up into the stars.

'The night sky is really just a very big shadow,' she tells Jacob. 'Don't ever let it make you afraid. The darkness comes when we turn our backs on the sun. So really, we block the sun's light ourselves. We make our own darkness each night.'

She doesn't know how she knows this or why she's telling Jacob. But she does and she is.

Like the moss, Mammy? she almost hears him say.

Yes, baby. Just like the moss, she almost says back.

Hand in hand they feel their way along the path, blue-black lonely shapes in cold winter hats.

'*Estrella* is the Spanish word for star.' She tries to roll the *e* off her tongue. But she can't. Too short and crispy, it stays stuck behind her teeth, silenced and diminished by the louder *a* that widens her mouth into a bigger capital shape. Then she thinks maybe it's the *r* she should be forcing her tongue to roll out, like all the rolling-Spanish *Sesame Street* tongues and brown eyes. '*Entrada* means entrance.'

Yes. It's definitely the *r* pushing her mouth open – widening, raising, reshaping her tongue – making it flick off the back line of her top teeth. But still the broad *a*s, bigger than they should be, swallow up the lesser *r*. Her lips pull apart like an old wound, the word pulsing in red beats behind her eyes.

'*Salida* is exit.'

Salida is green. *A* is the most important shape there – louder than all the other shapes, taller than all other sounds. It's always the *a*, no matter how small. *A* always feels too big for her mouth, too loud, like it needs to be shouted out into the dark. Just to get it out. Get it gone. Annette would have liked to have learned Spanish, liked to have taught it to her children. Looking up into the night, she wonders what's the Spanish word for moon?

There's a gathering of thick-branched naked trees all round the sentinel red railings beginning and ending in another gate, a pointy multi-coloured gate. Closed fast and padlocked. A watching cat folds itself deeper into the darkness. Tinfoil eyes stealing the last coloured light. Grimy scraps of withered leaves stick to the soles of their boots, making everything tacky and wet. The ground rots away under their feet.

But Jacob knows where the secret place is, the space that buckles open like an invisible split, just wide enough for shoulders and a head and careful little feet. He looks up.

She looks down.

Are the trees very sick, Mammy?

No, they're not sick, baby. Just waiting.

For leaves?

Yes, sweetheart. For leaves.

They pause, waiting for each other. They have learned patience and silence. Annette hums a tune inside her head. There's a basket shackled to a tree, a little wind blowing. Somewhere a cradle is rocking, a bough breaking. It's just a song she remembers about a swinging baby, falling into the night.

Then with one step Jacob slips further inside the darkness, like he's being unborn. Annette, holding a bar in each hand, breathes in through her nose, out through her mouth, scrunching her belly button back in line with her ribs. There's a tingling in her spine, a faint little shudder like a distant memory of falling from a great height. Flexing fingers, grinding teeth, she remembers again his perfect little face the first time she saw it on a cold October morning five winters ago; the smell of his little baby head resting in the palm of her hand or in the space under her chin. His first smile. His first tooth. His first step. Ten fingers. Ten toes. Each one counted, re-counted, recorded. His locked tight little jaw. She looks away feeling again the tears that gathered at the back of her eyes, the wobble of her chin. There's a pull in the soft, fleshy space between her thumb and her forefinger. She feels a widening gash, though she can't see it, a trickle of blood. Tongue and lips work together cleaning it, kissing it away. Breathing herself taller she turns to the side, making herself fit.

The silence inside is fierce, washing the playground like a flood. It gushes through the bars, settling in corners, behind the tower, under the swings. She can hear it roaring in the trees reaching over, in the empty slide bearing down. It drips out of the sky on to the soft playground floor, growing in the darkness, like a shadow eclipsed. It's in the swings and the shape of the roundabout and in the grass. She can taste it. Annette breathes it into her lungs and feels it might drown her. It runs down into all the empty places inside her, like rainwater. It settles in her hair and on the trees and takes her shape and their shape and all the earth is wet with it. Like an endless black dampness creeping up endless black walls. And silence has a smell like the inside of a press, locked and musty, stale-tasting rank moisture; the air is thick with it. And when it hits her it feels like the slice and cut of a knife across and deep into her stomach, ripping her away from herself. It's the loneliest pain in the world. There's no beginning and no end to it. It just is. Twisting and tightening, like thick clothes-line rope stitching her back up again and again and again. And no one is there to say sorry for causing it or to ask if she's okay. No one wants to look at it and tell her that it's not her fault, she's done the best that she can and that he will be okay, that he will, one day, say *Mammy*, in a voice of his own. No one's there to hear him.

Annette releases her stomach. Muscles push up-ways and out. She winces silently, rubbing the dimples that pucker her back. The air is cold. Each breath dusted in white.

She looks for her shadow in the darkness. It's beside her, watching up from the ground, elongated and thinner, her head a new distended alien shape.

'Centre yourself. Breathe. Feel your attachment to the earth,' the Chinese acupuncturist, with the smallest hands she's ever seen, had said in the free one-off special she'd queued for in the shopping centre last Thursday.

She closes her eyes. Breathes in slowly. Waits. And breathes out. She feels her mind beginning.

The night's silence shakes into little pieces and falls into the ground. All around them the round-up noises of the day squeezing in through the bars chase the silence away. Doors click-clack shut, tight against the dark and the morning and the drill of more waking hours. A car alarm screeches from somewhere and nowhere at the same time. A lonely bark, not like anything really, falls into the yellow-orange of a faraway light. Bottles rattle in a crate. The homeless man on the steps of the broken-down cinema on the corner rustles through yesterday's news, reading stories to keep him warm in the dark.

He comes here every night after a day of nowhere walking. Annette knows the shuffle of his tired feet. Taking off somebody else's shoes, he rubs sunken eyes, settles into the ground. Annette thinks of her own father now and slowly through the gloam she sees him again standing beside her on the other side of the road. Her hand reaches towards him, fingers stretching through the darkness, as though to touch him once more before he is gone. He has October-coloured teeth, a chain-smoker's squint. Annette can hear his knees cracking. His knees always crack when he stands up or sits down. And she is there too, smaller, holding his hand, his old bike between them.

The bike was blue. She remembers now. The day was hot. Too hot. They pushed the bike over the tracks into an evening of sand dunes and sunshine; shiny wheels turning rhythmically, a ting-a-ling bell and magic looping pedals; the tide on its way out washes all trace of their footprints and tyre tracks from the sand; a song without any words is hummed behind the call of a cuckoo. Her father opens a bag of Scots' Clan, offers her the bag; a creamy chewy chocolate dressed up in two tones – the taste of a memory melts into her mouth, and she smiles at the thought of another. Then he'd lifted her up and together they'd made the bike move seamlessly, like oarsmen treading the sea.

A single swing squeak creaks back to life.

Jacob pushes his little legs out for ups, pulls them back in for downs. Falling up-ways then down-ways again. Falling, flailing, flying, grabbing at stars. Little Moon Boy. But nobody's there to see. No one watches the shadows of tinkling chains, the swish-whish of air. Annette thinks of all the pulled curtains and flattened blinds in all the dark sleeping homes on the street, missing the little-smiling sounds swinging into the night. And she hears all the unspoken sounds between them. They have a quiet way of coming and meeting each other in their own wordless way. They don't have to talk to know.

I love you, Mammy.

I know you do, baby.

Annette counts to ten, only getting to five because ten is too far away so six becomes only four to go, seven only three, eight only two and nine means there's only one more before she gets back to one again. Then she'll be there. It's quicker that way. It's cleaner. Easier to manage. Her mind likes to know she'll get back down to one again before she ever gets to ten. Then she can begin over. Ten is the end.

'If he doesn't speak by the time he is ten,' the doctor had said.

Ten is the end. There's nothing after ten – only more silence, more silent ghost-screaming into the dark. Time will tell.

'Jacob, promise me that if you ever get lost or if ever you can't find Mammy that you will come here. Come here to the playground. Somebody will find you here.'

All about them the daylight sounds of running hopscotching feet jump and gurgle with laughter waiting to be heard, tomorrow. Morning buggies and bums will stop for pause, a moment's rest. Chatting mothers hush crying babies back into a sleep that has not yet happened. Little legs and scraped knees clamber up climbing ladders; toes push down and up see-saws, now standing silent; runners rub against slides in head-first bursts of yellow hats and freezing fingers. Jacob's feet will run with other running feet, tomorrow; arms outstretched in twirling-whirling circles, he'll win the game of tomorrow-playground chase. Tomorrow he'll be first to the top of the ladder. There'll be no pouting mouths, no pointing fingers, no throaty coughs, no pity under their faces. Annette will call Jacob over and tell him to take off his gloves and to be kind to the silent little looking-down boy over in the corner.

'Go and ask that little boy if he'd like to play,' she will say.

'Okay, Mammy.'

His words will rise like balloons. And he will make his way over to the forgotten little boy in the Spiderman coat. He will take him by the hand. He will swing him on the swings, pushing him gently in the small of his little silent back. They will be dizzy from the twirling roundabouts and swinging swings but he will hold that little boy up straight, squaring his shoulders, until the world settles back down again. Then the little boy will smile a silent *thank you*. And Annette will smile over at Spiderman's mother, alone on the bench, and she'll feel that woman's pain in her own heart and in her own head just as if it is her own.

CHAPTER 3

Jacob

Mammy says there's nothing in the house. *Not even a loaf.* Loaf is another word for bread like jacket is another word for coat. Jacob knows lots of words inside in his head. *Nothing in the house* means it is Tesco time now.

Daddy says he'll go but Mammy shakes her head and gets up and gets dressed.

'I'll take the kids with me. Won't be long,' Mammy says.

Jacob looks out the back window of the car. There's the church with the coloured-y window and the big angel with the white-crying face that looks like he's going to jump off the roof and into the ditch any minute and there's the field where the sometimes horses sometimes stand looking out over the wall and the garage that used to sell petrol and cars but now it only sells coal and gerbils and Christmas trees at Christmas. Jacob likes seeing all the things outside the glass. And then they are there.

Jacob loves the red of the word Tesco. The way the redness reddens against the deep purple-blue of the night. Big letters floating over blue dashes. Tesco looks better in the dark. The big windows are yellow like butter. But the sign isn't red and shiny like it should be. It is harder for Jacob to trace with his finger. Something is wrong. The sky is too blue, cut across with too many wires. The wires aren't there at night.

The car stops. Jenny opens her seat belt. Jenny reaches over and clicks Jacob free. Mammy counts to five, then backwards

again. This is a rule. A rule is the same as a law. Jacob presses
his face against the glass, cupping his hands round his eyes to
stop his own reflection looking back in at him. He's looking for
the darkness that should be falling down out of the sky. But it
is not coming. The letters are all stuck on sticks – all ups and
acrosses like the lollipop roof on the second little pig's house.

I'll huff and I'll puff and I'll blow your house down.

Jacob likes the way Jenny leaves all the spaces for big breaths
when she's pretending to be the wolf.

Mammy usually takes him at night, when Jacob gets up and
there's nothing to see on the telly. Most times they are the only
ones there. Holding hands. Being okay. Saying nothing. Mammy
lets a big breath out of her mouth. She takes a band off her
wrist and ties her hair up in a knot at the back of her head.

'You ready to get out of the car, Jacob?'

Jacob tap-taps his knees.

Mammy opens her door stepping into the picture outside.
Mammy smiles in at Jacob through the window. She sticks out
her tongue. Jacob's eyes fix on her forehead. Mammy says foreheads are as good as eyes if you don't want to look into eyes.

Mammy opens the door and takes Jacob's moving fingers into
her own. Jenny goes to pick out a trolley. It's a long path to
Tesco. There are lots of shoes. Black shoes. Brown shoes. Red
click-clacking high shoes. There's even a pair of wellies. Two
trainers push pedals round and round turning silver circles over
the grey on the ground. A pigeon picks at a stone, his sideways
eyes rolling. Jacob spots a twiddle stick. A tiny bit of lost tree.
Darting forward his middle finger jumps up and down on his
thumb. Little enough jumps, just tiny spaces apart. A foot stops
and stumbles. Another foot presses down on his hand.

'Jesus Christ!' falls out of the mouth way up high in the air.
'You okay? Jesus. I'm sorry.'

'It's okay. Don't worry. He's fine.' Mammy grabs Jacob,
brushing down his clothes with her hand.

Jacob straightens up, the little bit of twig rolling between his fingers. Mammy closes her hand around Jacob's. They stay on the path. Mammy says the left and right words like she always does when they have to cross from one path over to another.

'Yes, Ma. We know, Ma.' Jacob hears Jenny behind the trolley.

They wait till the wheels of a green car roll past. Jacob can only see two wheels though he knows there are two more on the other side. He'd be able to see them if he were already standing on the path over there near the crisp bag that's all scrunched-up reds and yellows. Jacob looks for his toes. They're inside his runners. He's wearing his Sunday socks. And his Sunday underpants. It's Sunday today. No bus today. Today is a car day.

The smiling man inside the door nods at Mammy. Jacob knows the man's face and the man's boots with all the laces, but he doesn't know the man.

'Should be okay. Quiet enough today.' The man's half looking at the little screen under his belly, half looking at Mammy.

'Thanks, Tom.' Mammy checks the pink square in her hand. It has a sticky line across the top at the back. That's for sticking it up on the fridge. 'Right so. Lettuce.'

Jacob knows where the lettuce is. But it's too high up. Mammy checks the numbers on the front of the packet and puts the bag down on the bottom shelf. Jacob reaches over and puts it into the nearest corner of the trolley.

'One avocado. Four bananas.'

Avocados are under pears. Jacob loves avocados. Jenny loves ice cream. Jacob's not allowed ice cream. Jacob can pick up the avocado without any help, but Mammy needs to squeeze it first. Mammy likes pressing things with her fingers. This is important like a rule or a law is important.

'Perfect.'

Jacob places it at the other end of the trolley. Jenny counts to four and points to the bananas. Jacob puts them in opposite the lettuce. There has to be enough empty space between them. This is also important.

'Oh, and bread. Don't let me forget the bread. I didn't put it on the list. But there's not so much as a crust in the house.'

Crust is like loaf. It is another word for bread. But they are not near the bread. This place is cold and humming and sharp. It's very white. Something is wrong. The bread is way over there. Past the noise. The noise is growing now, getting bigger. It was grey and far. Now it's white. Bright, blinding white. Moving closer. Jacob drops his twiddle stick moving his arms up and down through the noise. Breaking it up. Making it smaller. The lights up in the sky start flicking and buzzing. Buzz. Buzz. Flick. The buzzing and flicking stick to his fingers. Jacob drags them along the cold shelves. Mammy says now she wants yogurts and butter in this cold place.

But bread is next, Mammy. Bread is next.

Mammy's face is in front of Jacob's. Mammy holds the two sides of Jacob's head.

Bread, Mammy. Bread. Bread. Bread, Jacob wants to scream, but the words are like shadows. Jacob cannot catch them. The noise is too big, and his voice is too small and nobody is listening.

'Everything's goin' to be okay, sweetheart. Mammy's here. Don't worry, baby. Don't worry.'

Mammy takes her hands away from Jacob's head. She rubs his shoulders. Her knees make a big crack. Mammy gets taller. Mammy's face gets smaller. Further away. There's a squeaking wheel behind him. A mobile phone screeching. Jacob reaches out, but everything falls through his fingers like water. There's a pain, even bigger than himself, growing inside all the noise; it's in his toes and his elbows, inside and outside his head all at the same time. There's more noise now. Burning noise all over the air.

Mammy, I'm on fire, someone is shouting.

Jacob pulls at his jeans. Little fingers ripping the burning away. The shouts are inside him, pushing at his belly, trying to get out through his skin. He takes a thousand pictures all at once. He's going to burst. He falls to the floor beside the humming fridges curling himself into a ball. His little body lies between the cheese and the milk trying to stop the everywhere shouting that's coming from him, coming for him. Mammy's hand rubs the back of Jacob's neck. Mammy smells closer. 'Come on, sweetheart. Up. It's okay. Itsokay. Isokay.'

The squeaking wheels are coming. Stop. Turn around. Go away. Feet step to the side, getting faster.

'Ma, let's go home.' Jenny's words come from somewhere over Jacob's head.

'No. This is good for him, ya know.'

More words stick into other words.

'Jacob, I can't remember where the bread is. Can you find the bread, Jacob? Show Mammy where the bread is?'

Mammy wants bread. There isn't a crust in the house. Crust is another word for bread.

Jenny gets yogurts and butter.

Bread is next. Bread is next. He knows, he knows where the bread is.

Jacob's eyes close on the colours. The yellow-pink is still there inside his lids. Jacob feels the burning again. Burning colours eating his eyes. Mammy stands him back up, dusts the marks from his knees, kisses his head.

Bread is next.

Jacob opens his eyes. He sees the metal music playing all over the air. The sounds in the sky. Beeping scanners. Rustles moving along on a belt. Squawking children. Stomping-shouting-running feet. Clicking doors. Scratching bags. Laughing mouths. All the noises fall down into him, melting together, scorching his skin, sticking to his scalp. With twisting fingers, he holds on real tight to his hair like he's afraid his brain's going to fall out on the floor or his ears are going to fall off the side of his head.

'Ma? Please, Ma?'

'Stop it, Jenny. This is good for him. He needs to know where everything is.'

'He does know. He knows, Ma. This isn't "good" for him! Please, Ma, please.'

'It is!'

'Ma, look at him.'

'Jennifer, please.'

'But, Ma—'

'I said stop it! What if he needs to go shoppin' himself? One day, when he's bigger.'

'What?'

'I won't always be here, you know. He needs to be able to do this himself.'

'Ma, he'll never be able to do this himself. How would he even get here?'

'Don't you ever say that again! Do ya hear me? Don't you ever let me hear you say that again!' Mammy bites down on her lip like she's starving. Starving is like hungry only starving is worse. Mammy holds Jacob's hand real tight leading him along past all the boxes and bottles and crackers and broken-down packets into more noise, red-coloured noise full of loud-shrieking shapes. Then Mammy stops. 'Here we are, sweetheart. Will you get the bread?'

There's a coin on the floor and little piles of white growing taller under a shelf where the sugar bags lie down looking at the bits of themselves they're leaving behind on the tiles. Mammy squeezes the bread with one hand but uses her two hands to give it to Jacob. Jacob looks for the place where it should go but the middle of the trolley is blocked. Jacob holds the bread in the air. Jacob doesn't know what to do. Jenny takes the yogurts and butter out and holds them up so Jacob can see. He lets the bread sit in their place. Jenny carries the yogurts in one hand, the butter in the other.

'We need eggs.'

Jacob takes the sound and smashes it down into a single noise, trying better to hear it.

Mammy, I know. I know where the eggs are. Mammy, I know. I know, Mammy.

Mammy looks up in the air for a sign. Jacob roots behind the back of his eyes: Rice Krispies, Coco Pops, smiling monkeys, Sugar Puff monsters, green frogs and a tiger. Then eggs. Eggs are next. He doesn't remember this place with new things in red bottles. All the colours fall out of strange corners, hissing lights. Triangles split open into lines. Circles dance around squares. Squares stick into the corners of Jacob's eyes, like needles.

'Over here.' Jenny's head peeps through the shapes.

Mammy pours him like water against the slow creeping dark. 'Here we go, sweetheart.'

Out of the corner of tired eyes Jacob hears the dimples on the green boxes. Little clumps of green noise. A big yellow-brown smell sticks to his face, sliding into his ears. Jacob scratches it off. Claws it away. Scratch. Scratch. The big eggy-fish smell creeping towards him slips into his mouth slicing his tongue.

Mammy, get it off. Cut it out with the big knife on the man's stripy apron. Mammy. Mammy. Mammy.

Tongue flicks against teeth. Head banging on air. Bang. Bang. Bang.

Eggs.

Falling, falling.

Split. Splat. Plop.

Mammy. Mammy. Mammy.

Jacob bites down hard. Mammy cries out, closing her eyes. Holding her wrist, she counts to five, then backwards again. Jacob's body is gone. Washed away like the little girl on the telly. Mammy falls on to her knees. There's a tear behind Mammy's eye. Jacob tastes its salty falling.

Split. Splat. Plop.

Thump. Thud. Thump. Thud.

Black boots get bigger. They're coming. Laces in V-shaped criss-crosses grow upwards from shiny silver holes. Two big arms with square fingers lift Jacob up into the sky.

'It's okay. Hush now. Hush.'

The burning stops. Mammy looks up from the floor. Jacob looks down from the sky.

'Let's get you all home.'

'Thanks, Tom.'

Jacob looks over Tom's shoulder as the trolley gets smaller and smaller. Mammy holds Jenny's hand. When they turn the corner, the trolley is gone. The big doors swish open like magic. The air outside is quiet.

CHAPTER 4

Annette

March brings a new freshness to the morning light, sharpening the shapes and colours of things. Ten o'clock tingles a cold yellow-white; the breeze sharp-blue, and too cutting. It looks like summer at the bottom of the garden but the roof casts a long, lonely shadow of dark purple-grey, throwing a chilly apex on the ground, splitting the morning into light and half-light, nearer the house.

Everything still belongs to winter, though the worst of it is over, it's still all confused, so confused, so confusing, she thinks to herself.

The air, unfriendly and cold, adds muscle to the iron-rod, ice-cream pain, behind her left eye; a sudden screaming stabbing between pockets of wind. She pulls her shoulders up around her ears, sinks her head down into the neck of her jacket.

The spring will bring shorter nights, longer days. Maybe even a word.

She wanders down the garden and stops. Left or right? This way or that? Does it really matter? Won't she end up in the same place anyway? Doesn't she always? To the right, the cherry-blossom fingers reach for pink, stretching themselves into the light and the promise of fleeting-papery flowers. She knows the lonely-loveliness of watching it, watching itself fall, like pink snow, through the kitchen window.

But everything is as it should be, apparently. Karma. That's what it's called. She revisits her free, on-line Tarot reading. She had typed in her name and her question and picked three cards from the stretched-out digital line. The *Past* card hadn't revealed itself. She was asking about the future. The other two, The King of Swords and The Hanged Man, both upside down, had told her that nothing in this world happens to you that you do not for some reason or other deserve. It could be from a past life, they had even inserted her name – *Annette, you are responsible for your own happiness and your own misery.* It's a bit like an inheritance you leave to yourself, really. It's all about balance – apparently. Left and right.

Half of her stands in the brightness pouring down from the sky. The other half stands in the cold shadow of the roof. A dark stripe splits her body into yellow and black.

She looks at the border of daffodils along the back fence, half remembering a poem about tossing heads and fluttering breezes, dancing victorious proud trumpets and stars in a never-ending line.

She remembers the daffs at her father's funeral, though she doesn't remember him dying. She only remembers him dead, in a coffin in the parlour, where he was laid out in his best Sunday-blue suit. Not that he had ever worn it on a Sunday or any other day, as far as she can remember. But it was the only suit he had and that's what it was called. The blinds were fully closed; the curtains pulled tight; the dark-holy smell of candles congealing the air, serving it up in heavy slices. All the saints with their unmoving-moving eyes and the pulsing Sacred Heart, with his finger of warning and his head to the side, watched over him from the wall. John Paul tick-tocked from his clock in the corner. All the sounds of time counting down.

People came in and out of the room, capturing in their ramble all the mystery and silence of death. How could he have been here yesterday? Out in the garden digging and dying? Not here today? Here and not here all at once? The space he had filled before empty now except for the box. And where were his feet? His shoes?

But the stillness in the room is stronger than their moving and mumbling. Their awkward sympathies, murmured little silvery sounds, seem to fall away and vanish beneath the flowery rug and painted skirting under the weight of the deathly silence and the biggest pile of sandwiches she's ever seen. Before or since.

She can still see the yellow skin, stretched like parchment over his face. It is the colour of wallpaper; dirty, smoky dead wallpaper that needs to be ripped from the walls; his fingers are too long; his dough-white hands, shackled in rosary beads, are still puffy; his eyelids glisten under the big black metal Christ, held fast forever by his hands, on the studded crucifix nailed to the wall. Mrs Murphy, next door, brings vol-au-vents and egg and onion sandwiches made into triangles, with the crusts cut off. She's sure it was Mrs Murphy – no one else on the row had ever even heard of vol-au-vents. But Mrs Murphy was *different*. They hadn't liked *different* back then.

She thinks of the girl she used to sit beside in school. The girl with no hair. It must be thirty-five years ago now. Fiona Byrne. The girl with the hat. That was her. Fiona Byrne. Sr Mary Rose had really hated her. Annette still feels like scratching when she thinks about Fiona Byrne and her no hair under her hat. She scratches the back of her neck, her shoulders shiver. She does little head shakes. The hat was woolly with stripes. And Fiona wore that hat for a whole year. Then the hat came off the following September and she had hair once again, but she would always be bald as far as Sr Mary Rose and the girls in the class were concerned. She would always be poor and dirty and different. She would never sing in the choir or be picked to go on messages.

They still don't like different, she supposes. *Different* then meant being apart, meant having notions. *Different* means something else now. Something different yet the same. Mrs Murphy had been *different*. Annette doesn't know why but there had been something other in Mrs Murphy. Rolling eyes, knowing glances and cutting sneers were exchanged when her *and who does that one think she is* fancy vol-a-vents, on a proper Willow pattern plate, had appeared in the kitchen.

She remembers the Willow Tale her father told her every time he drank tea, cast forever in blue and white delft, kiln-baked in Annette's earliest memories. The glazed little legend was one of his favourites. It was the only Willow cup in the house. He'd show her the little blue man and the little blue woman running away over the little blue bridge, shaded by the wavy overhang of the big bendy-blue willow tree. Tracing their shapes with a delicate finger she'd strained to hear their running blue feet, to feel the wind flowing whitely beneath their curling motionless flight, way up there, far away from the yard, enclosed by the big blue-crookedy fence. Then she'd touch the cold shiny-blue feathers of the lovers soaring way up high over the blue apple tree Annette knew would never lose its apples. And he smiled every time he told her the story, wrapped around the little blue cup in his hand, hardened by fire and set into shape.

Mrs Byrne, from number three, brings tea bracks and fairy buns and even more sandwiches, cheese and onion ones with brown sauce. There's no threat in that. Nothing different. Brown sauce doesn't have notions. It seemed like everyone calling brings sandwiches, just to feed all the other people bringing sandwiches, on plates all smelling of cling film. And they all stand around saying what a beautiful corpse he is and how he would have loved all the sandwiches and the cakes and the fuss and some of the men standing beside the wilted-yellow wallpaper roses or hovering around the good-front-room door tell her they are *sorry for her trouble* and some of the women standing beside the coffin say the rosary behind clacking beads and bent heads. And some of them cry.

Then later on after plenty of whiskey and sandwiches and tea Jackie Doyle or the Bull Redmond, she can't remember which one, calls on her father to give them a song – forgetting he was dead – but then remembering again makes the sign of the cross and slips out to the kitchen for a fag, where her mother, very busy being very busy, is boiling the kettle and cutting the crusts off the sandwiches with crusts and giving orders about milk and sugar and going over the *arrangements*.

'There'll be a piper, of course,' she said.

Annette had never understood why and she'd never asked either. The sound of bagpipes has always made her want to cry.

'March is the month for daffs and pipes,' her father used to say.

He had always filled up too, though she had never actually seen him cry, at the St Patrick's Day Parade just as soon as the long call of the pipes came marching down over the hill. She hears it again now wrapped inside the big brooding silence of the garden. Though she can't see them, yet she sees that same sorrowful sound, lonely and beautiful all at once, flow over the fence and gather around her feet. There's a primal drone resonating in the grass, the broken pots, the cherry-blossom tree. There's that one same note staying constant behind all of the other notes and it is unlike any other sound.

On her left stands the clothes line, brilliant in blue-white flapping sheets. Annette moves straight ahead. It's easier that way.

On hands and knees, she picks at the bits of winter still left on the ground. Her hand is cold, drooping downwards. She straightens her back, sits her bum on the backs of her folded-up legs, stretches her fingers, rubs her wrist straight and looks up into the sky. Squinting into the light through dark-flicking lashes, Annette sees flitting and darting at the side of her eyes.

Pins and needles tickle her feet.

The swallows are back, growing their nest. They're early this year. Their half-finished mud bunker sticks to the wall, just under the eaves of the half-triangle of the roof. *Grand Designs,* she thinks to herself and smiles up at the emerging cup of the nest. The robin appears from nowhere again – little black eyes, like bullets, watching her from the side. He bobs and taps around the garden. He is always alone. Annette rubs the sides of her head, the bridge of her nose. One swallow flies off as the other flies back, each taking its turn kneading, shaping, filling in cracks. They will do this all day, all summer. Then they too will be gone.

They should all be yellow, she thinks, looking down at the daffodils she had planted with Jacob last Halloween. She can see the two of them again, back then, on the other side of the winter, planting bulbs in a place where maybe a springtime-word might grow. But some of the flowers are washed out – translucent-magnolia, cloudy-white and anaemic. Some are orange. Some are white. Some are orange and white. Narcissus, her mother calls them. Is there a plural for that? Like Narcissi or Narcissium? She checks the little plastic label still stuck in the ground.

Cyclamineus Daffodil. Narcissus Cyclamineus in brackets; Cyclamineus Daffodils have nodding blooms with strongly reflexed perianths and long cups. Flowers in late winter or early spring. Flowers come in a wide variety of shades like red, orange, yellow, green, white and pink.

The words get too small in the light, turning into painful squiggles through painful eyes.

Narcissus fell in love with his own reflection and then he drowned when he fell into a pond trying to kiss his own face. Someone turned him into a daffodil. She doesn't remember who. There was a girl too. She's sure there was a girl. A girl left with nothing, only her voice. Echo. That was her name. She's sure that was her name. She was in love with Narcissus.

Annette remembers Sr Mary Rose – or was it The Hanged Man? – warning her:

'Those who consider themselves too beautiful will be punished by God. *E-TER-NAL-EE*. Let there be no mistake about that.'

Daffodils. Echoes. No voice. A nun. A Hanged Man. Let there be no mistake about that.

A sudden flash of white sears the corner of her eye. All the yellows fall into the ground. Golds, greens and pinks. There's a girl in a sparkly dress. A boy in a Spiderman coat. A child with no hair. Two or three others she knows but can't name. There's a man lying face down in the garden, a shovel at his side. Younger versions of older people mixed in with strangers she doesn't know, or she's forgotten. But instead of helping her they start to pass slowly, their edges fading, like ghosts in some sombre parade.

Whispering sounds wash into each other. Hush. Hush.

More pins and needles seep up from the ground. She is too heavy on one side. The pain in her head screeches through her so completely it has no beginning now and no end. There's burning. Burning, like candle wax melting into her eye, a hot poker gouging at the socket, the face-stinging spasms scorch and sear their way even to the parts she can still feel – down into her fingers and toes and into the small of her back, like some explosive current firing its way through her; a parasite wrapping itself around her whole body, eating its way right to the top of her skull with clotted fangs, her breath shortening in suffocating rasps and rattles. She tries to scream out to the shadow people, but, turning their backs, they move steadily on.

The cake, she remembers. The image burning.

His shoes. She tries to find them again, to fix them; to paint over the greying scuffed toes. But she still sees all the marks she cannot coat in colour.

The candles are melting. The shoes gone.

She sinks into the ice-cream pain. The robin hops a million

miles away, through prisms of light. *Come back.* The navy leather is still cracked and lined. The magic pen isn't magic! *Don't leave me. Again.* It pretends to make them better. It doesn't. Time either speeds up or slows down. She isn't sure. *Come back. Count to ten.*

What time is it? She can't see her watch. It was here a minute ago.

If she could just know the hour or the minute; hold on to the numbers, the sounds in her hand, just until the children come back with Daddy. *One.* She reaches out to grab the ticking-away seconds she can't find. *Three. Four.* That's all she has to do. *Five.* Just hang on to the ticking and tocking. *Count to ten.* Catch the falling numbers. The children will be here, outside all the pain. The children will be here needing dinner, baths, lunch for tomorrow, stories for bed. *Six. Eight. Nine.*

If she can just hang on. *One. Two. Three.*

She watches a stranger, paler version of herself, *Four,* her right hand pushing out into the foggy air, grabbing something she cannot see. A stranger's voice bursts behind her eyes. *Five.*

The earth is too close. The sky too far away. *Four.* Another flash. Another dull rumble. *Five. Four.* Another fall into a dropping face, a failing hand. *Three.* She's too heavy. Heavy now and light. Too light. Left or right? *One. Two. Three.* Does it matter? *Three. Four.* What time is it? *Seven. Eight.* Catch falling numbers falling away.

A voice, a thick-tongued thing deep, deep inside and outside all at the same time tries to push *help me* words out through a broken half-mouth. Her head falls to the side. *Nine.* She keeps grabbing the nothing she tries to hold on to. *Eight.* Shifting into a different space, a new time with new numbers floating out of her reach, it is impossible to know where anything begins or ends. The numbers out in the world now are lost at the end.

Is there an end? A beginning? A time? Where is Kevin? Where are the kids? There should be someone. Something. Someplace.

Some time. There is no place. No candle. No cake. No card. No word. No time to tell. There should be the other half of a mouth. There is blood. There shouldn't be blood. There shouldn't be blood.

The colours drain away, seeping and leaking from the garden. Then everything is silenced in white air.

CHAPTER 5

Jenny

When Jenny arrives home from school, she's starving. The front door clicks closed behind her as she walks into the sweetness of warm cakes and sugary apples that's pouring out of the kitchen and into the hall. The smell of baking drips out of the air on to her tongue, without her even having to open her mouth. She stops suddenly just to taste the smell.

She can hear the tap rushing water into the sink, the clank of a tray on another tray, the rattle of plates, behind the door. She thinks she hears herself smile, she can't be sure. Ma must have remembered. Ma hasn't made buns or a cake for ages.

Jenny hangs her coat on the end of the stairs, throws her bag down in the corner. She knows Ma will go mental but she just can't wait. She'll put her bag away later.

'Ma, are ya makin'—?'

But the kitchen is so full of Granny when Jenny pushes open the door that she finds herself pausing for a moment and wondering if there's enough room in there for the two of them.

'Ah, hello, pet. I'm just makin' an apple crumble for afters,' Granny says, like this is something she does here every day.

'Where's Ma?'

'And, hello to you, too! How are ya, Granny? I'm grand, Jenny, thanks for askin'! And how are you today, pet?'

'Fine. Is Ma not here?'

'No, pet.'

'Where is she?'

'Isn't she just gone away for a little while for a bit of a rest.' Granny says it like it's a question Jenny should know the answer to. 'So, then I thought to myself, sure while I'm here anyway I may as well just make a nice apple crumble. For afters. There's nothin' like hot apple crumble for afters,' Granny says, clearing off the kitchen table and putting a cup in the sink.

She takes the sharp knife Ma says they've Never Ever to touch down from the rack and stands in the light of the window, washing the blade under the hot tap. She looks out at the big cherry-blossom tree in the garden while she's wiping the knife clean. Then she puts it back in the high-up rack again, where Ma always keeps it.

'Gone away? Where? Where is she gone?' Jenny asks the back of Granny's head.

'Dublin. How was school?'

'Fine.'

'Did ya learn anythin' new today?' Now Granny's down peeping into the little yellow window in the front of the oven.

'No. Why is she gone to Dublin? Why is she gone today?'

'This crumble's almost done,' Granny says, like it's a big surprise. 'And now, may I ask what was it you were doin' there all day so? Sure, ya must a learned somethin'?' Granny's standing up straight again now, looking round for something else to dry with the tea towel in her hand.

'I didn't! When will she be back?'

'I don't believe that! Nothin' at all? Real soon, pet. Real soon.'

'No. Will she be back for dinnertime?'

'I'm not sure. I don't know. Do ya want to help me make some a them chocolate-chip muffins ya like while the oven's still hot?' Granny, spotting something else that needs doing, is already halfway across to the other side of the kitchen.

'Will she be back before bedtime? I got *The Prisoner of Azkaban* for us to read.'

Granny hangs the tea towel on the hook, opens the fridge, takes out the butter and cuts a small square off the side. 'Ah, I don't care what them ads say about not believin'! Ya just can't beat real butter!'

Then she's back at the cooker again, melting the butter in a frying pan she must have pulled out of her sleeve. Turning the heat down to make the sizzle sounds quieter, she takes Ma's big baking bowl out of the press. She wipes all the dust off it.

'Would ya ever bend down there like a good child and get me the flour outta the back a that press? Me knee's playin' up somethin' awful today. Must be the weather.'

Jenny gets the flour and the baking powder and the sugar and the vanilla stuff and all the other things Granny asks for, out of the press.

'Why did Ma not tell us she was goin' or say when she's comin' back? Why did she have to go today?'

'Jesus. Eggs!' Granny shouts out, like it's some kind of emergency. 'Would ya ever run down to Lizzie's there, like a good child, and get a half-dozen? Sure, didn't I forget all about the eggs!'

'Is it coz Ma and Da were fightin'?'

'Nobody's fightin', pet. Sure, won't she be back before ya know it? Hurry up now! Or the shop'll be closed!'

'But it's only after school. It's only early.'

'Now, ya know how that one is. She could just take a notion and shut up early.'

'Will Ma be here when I come back?'

'No, pet, she won't.' Granny stops, like she's going to say something else, something she has to think about saying. Her mouth opens then closes again like she's changed her mind back to saying nothing at all. The nothing words creep up the walls, like invisible spiders.

Jenny can feel a secret rising in the kitchen.

'Now, scat!' Granny finally says after the minute of nothing.

Jenny grabs her coat back off the stairs and runs down to the shop on the corner. The big door is hard to open, and Jenny can never remember if it's a push door or a pull door. When she pulls it gets even heavier. She pushes instead and falls into the last bit of a sentence still hovering in the air inside. The women in the shop stop talking when Jenny appears. There is no sound, though Jenny can still see the words *stroke* and *ambulance* floating in the lights up over her head.

'Ah, Jenny, how are ya, pet?' Lizzie asks, looking down at Jenny from over the top of her glasses.

Lizzie's glasses are divided into two different parts with a little glass line running across the middle bit of each lens. The reflected light curves in under her eyes making yellow-block shapes on her cheeks. There's a gold chain running down from her ears then it disappears in under her helmet hair.

'Good, thanks.'

'And how is Jacob?'

'He's good, too.'

'Haven't you grown?'

Jenny wonders why older people always tell you things about yourself by asking you questions.

'Haven't you gone the image of your mammy?' another voice says, from the side.

'How's school?' Lizzie says, straight away before Jenny can say anything to the *image of your mammy* question-answer.

'Good.'

'Good. Now, what can I get you?'

'Eggs please, but I'll get them myself.'

Jenny wanders down past the newspapers and Coke cans, past the bread and the fridge, right down to the back of the shop. She can hear whispering behind her though there aren't any more words.

She bends down low to take a box of eggs from a shelf that is so near the ground Jenny wonders why they didn't just leave the eggs on the floor. She takes the other way back past the biscuits and birthday cards and the biggest Kinder Egg she's ever seen. The women are talking about the weather and the clocks going forward when she arrives back at the start again. Jenny places the eggs on to the counter.

'That'll be one fifty-nine please, pet,' Lizzie says, looking at the box through the bottom half of her glasses.

Jenny realises she doesn't have any money, but she roots her hands into her pockets anyway. She doesn't know why.

'Granny didn't give me any money,' she says, reddening through her cheeks. 'I'll go and get some and come back then.'

'Not at all, child. Don't you be worryin'. Sure, tell Mae-Anne to drop it in next time she's passin'.'

'I'll be real quick.'

'I wouldn't hear of it, pet.' Lizzie passes the egg box from her side of the counter over to Jenny. She places a Twix on the top. 'Oh,' she says, 'I nearly forgot.' She takes a Kinder Egg out of a small box on the counter. 'And that's for Jacob.'

'Thanks,' Jenny smiles.

Lizzie gives her a wink.

'Bye,' Jenny says, as she moves towards the door.

Does she push it or pull it? She can't remember. Just then, a big man swings the door open into the shop with an open hand and very strong arm and Jenny passes right under his big-strong arm back outside on to the street.

She passes the shop where nobody goes anymore. She thinks she remembers going in there with Granny one time when she was small, but she's not really sure. She looks at the broken letters over the door. She remembers Ma telling her all about the two men behind the big wooden counter like they were characters in a book she was writing, just for Jenny.

'They were identical! They even wore the same clothes! And at first I thought there was only one Mr Boyle but then one day when we went in there were two of them, exactly the same, leaning over the counter talking,' Ma told Jenny, one day on the way home from school.

Jenny remembers the red skirt she was wearing and the long white socks. Her shoes were black and shiny, and Ma carried Jenny's bag up on her shoulder and held Jenny's hand.

'It wasn't a big shop,' Ma said, as they stood looking at the *Closed* sign on the door. 'But it was long, like a hall, and everywhere you looked things were hanging on nails or sitting on shelves or packed up in boxes. There were Jelly Alien Babies in pink and blue plastic prams and holy statues with flashing halos and flapping wings. There were Holy Communion dresses on a rail out the back and holy tea towels and St Brigid's crosses and all sorts of fishing rods laid out on one of the glass shelves under the counter. Toasters and kettles and bicycle pumps stood side by side on the long shelf up on the wall behind the two brothers. There were packs of cards and silver vases and shiny diamond earrings on a stand in the corner. Pots and pans dangled from hooks in the ceiling and a big blow-up crocodile float was tied upside down on a nail just inside the door. And you could find everything and anything in that shop and we spent more time rooting though boxes and crackling plastic wrapping than we did actually buying anything at all,' Ma said, laughing as she gave Jenny's hand a little squeeze.

Then they continued on towards home.

The windows have big sheets of wood in them now, no glass except the bits in the corners and there's a big broken gate across the front door. Jenny places the eggs down on the flaking old window ledge while she's opening her Twix. It's a sad-looking place. She takes a bite and chews slowly, picks up the eggs and carries on towards home.

The old man with the shuffling feet is sitting in the doorway of the house where nobody lives anymore. It's beside the dead shop. The net curtains on the windows are ripped and grey. One of the windows is broken. Jenny wonders if maybe this is the man's house and that maybe he's lost his key. His wife is probably out in the back garden, putting the clothes on the line, so she doesn't hear him. Jenny watches the woman behind the house bending forward with her two arms stretched out as far as they can go, holding the end of a big white sheet in each hand and using her chin to keep it up in the middle. There are clothes pegs in her mouth. The children running around are shouting and laughing. There are two boys and a girl. A big yellow dog bounces behind them, his pink tongue hanging sideways outside his mouth. Then the old man makes a tired sigh and Jenny knows really that this man has no house and no key and no wife and no children and no other clothes except the yellow-green jacket he always wears, every day of his life, even in summer. She looks down at the folded-up man on the step, at the walking stick by his side, wondering what it is that has happened to him. He looks down at his feet. His shoes are odd. One is black with laces. The other one is brown. It should have laces too. But there's nothing where the laces should be. Jenny can feel the colour of his favourite jacket bounce off her face. It's so bright and so yellow-green Jenny bets she would be able to see it from the moon, even if she was standing with her back to the earth, with her eyes closed.

'Would ya like a bite of Twix?' Jenny hears herself saying, before she's even got time to stop the words falling out of her mouth.

The man says nothing, though Jenny thinks she feels him smiling behind his beard. It definitely moves a little, grey whiskers parting around his mouth. His shoulders drop closer to his knees. Jenny puts the eggs down on the path and removes the other chocolate Twix finger. Leaning forward slightly, she holds it down to the man, close enough so he doesn't have to reach far. His old, old hand trembles a little as his fingers close around Jenny's small gift. His head shifts forward ever so slightly.

'Thank you, Jenny,' he whispers.

Jenny picks up the eggs and moves on. She wonders how the old man knows her name. She doesn't know his name. Maybe he has magic powers, like Dumbledore, and that his beard just needs to be washed and fluffed, and eyes that should be twinkly behind half-moon glasses and a wand. Maybe he is here in disguise.

In a new version she's just now imagining, the old man hasn't lost his keys at all. He had been able to get into the house, but when he did, the children were not playing chase and the dog was a cat this time. A marmalade cat with only one eye. The dog had probably attacked the cat and they had given the dog away to a farmer in the country. His wife wasn't hanging clothes out on the line either. How could she be? She had been sick for a very long time. That's why the man had gone out in the first place. He had gone to get the doctor. He had been in such a rush that he'd put on two odd shoes. The doctor is a tall man in a white coat and he lives just down the road. He told the man he would be up just as soon as he'd finished bandaging the leg of the woman sitting in the waiting room. The woman is old. Her leg is purple and too fat. She doesn't have any teeth in her mouth. Her teeth are wrapped in a piece of tissue in her pocket.

'Please, Doctor, come quickly! She's not well. Not well at all,' the man says, closing the door of the doctor's office and heading off back home again. And he's here now sitting on the step waiting for the doctor to come. He has sweets in his pockets for the children.

'Well now, aren't you just like lightnin'!' Granny says when Jenny comes back into the kitchen.

'I forgot the money,' Jenny says, handing over the eggs.

'Go ta God, child, so ya did. My fault, pet. Don't worry. I'll pay Lizzie on me way home.'

'Will the shop not be closed?'

'Not a fear a that. Sure, Lizzie's too cute to be closin' early now she's the only one doin' the Lottery this side a the town.'

Granny lets Jenny crack one of the eggs at the side of the bowl and quietly they watch it slithering down and then remaking itself back again into its proper shape, before settling comfortably on to the top of the flour. Granny gives Jenny the wooden spoon. Holding it straight Jenny stirs, gripping the spoon at the top. Granny's floury hand moves in below Jenny's. Together they mix yellow into white, changing everything in the bowl into something new. Granny pours the milk in slowly. Jenny stirs all the time, folding and shaping everything together. The baking powder sprinkles off the spoon into the bowl and it is gone. A few drops of vanilla will do.

'What's a stroke?' Jenny asks.

'Will ya lift that up, pet, like a good girl, till I wipe down the counter?' Granny dusts off the flour making it sticky and heavy. Then with a wet cloth she washes it down. 'Feckin' sticks to everythin'!' she says, looking back into the bowl. 'Jesus, didn't we forget the cocoa!'

They both look down at the creamy-white lump they've created.

Granny makes a little laughing sound with her voice, but her eyes are not smiling. Her eyes are glassy and wet. She slips her finger in behind her glasses, pushing them up in a tiny jump, and runs it along the little red line at the bottom of her eye. She does the same on the other side. 'Would ya ever get the cocoa, pet? It's over there by the toaster.'

The little red can is light, but it feels as heavy as the secret in the room.

When they're finished Granny puts the muffins in the oven and puts the eggs into the fridge beside all the other eggs in the fridge.

'The long evenin's will be here soon enough and mark my words, everythin' will be a bit brighter then,' Granny says, to nobody really.

CHAPTER 6

Annette

Half-open eye squint   At light.

                    Too Bright Lights eating Spooning out
eyes for more

Burning. Candles. Charring to nothing. Red embers.

Incinerated face.

          Unseeing closed eye. Closing on Empty Darkness.
Empty. Too empty. Deep.

Voices in

          muffle

                    mumble   screaming   whispers.

     Things happening   out   of   sight

               Doors and feet

Hands making ready

          Not yet.   Just yet.

Crash down crushing Pain Rushing in beating skull Throbbing
inside Eye.   Dark.

               One side black heavy unfeeling

Other peeling away

Face closing in too close to open eye
smothering drooping face.

Like Daddy.

'Doctor   Betts.'

Blood Smells rotting in death. High there rung upon bars.
Curtains. Creeping. Seeping. Leaking to nothing and back.

Purple organs

Wither and Die

'Hear   can   You   me?'

Lights flicker eye open

Sound.   Name.

Faceless Too big.

Too-big shouting sounds louder
piercing. No Face. Feet Thumping. Pens clicking between
reason and light

Numbed pulse beating. Rise to Fall. In and Out.

'You are.   Hospital.   You –   haemorrhagic

stroke.

Metal Clip. Aneurysm – Cerebral

Craniotomy

Bulging

Risk

Rupture

Rupture run.

Away.

Drifting on tides Ebb and Flow Far away.
Water tightening lifting Down.
Stealing lost colour – lost unremembered face Forgotten.
Names in upside-down smiles Spiralling downward to
blackness where born Everything is

born.

Was Born. Ten. Left under coloured-in Words of Red.

'Annette, finger follow you finger my?'

Scratch itching memory scrape scratching inside

clawing eating Strings of yesterday unattached.
Broken – hanging loosely in darkness Now or before or not.

Before then—

Then Screeching under lid of Locked Box – clear rasping – cold ground deathly blue Face. Daddy.
No Teeth.   Ripping under wood. Clay clawing fingernails growling – growing brown grooved channels of skin. Daddy.

Shrinking hair.

Daddy.

Chink chink. Spade sinking into gravelly Muck soaking up sounds
Gone.

Closing throat.

Stinging dark, blinding. Silent moving.

Name in stone.

Daddy.

Hanging ivy hovering. Strangle turned soil – damp claggy clay sifted. Shifted.

Ready.

No handle.   Voice. Escape.

Clawing through earth calling recalling screeching crying.

Grass Taking Root overhead.

Jaws rotting around yellowing teeth.

Vanished Dust – blown away Rain.

Back. Back again. Up Up Up. Rise and Fall. In and Out. Over. Under. Release.

'Annette,   squeeze   hand can?'

Big lips smile forming questions framing soar light.

'You   feel   palm pinch?'

Solder drips   falling   ground.

Outside lying down self looking up into light
colours of white. Ceiling splitting open in freshness new.

New white. Brilliant pain.

Not this

staleness inside mouth.

Moved or moving, weightless wave hauling, pushing. Up.
Up past voices hushing, machines beat, beat beeping. Fingers
press hard, parting face. Splaying wide eyelids. Stepping back.
Forward again.   watching from behind searing
eyes wide   arm strokes sweep in air.

'Leaking.

Blood.

Brain.'

Annette half   seeing. Entire. Little pen light moving
shaking eyes. Fading away face. Near and far.

Frozen arm.

Frozen leg.

Not cold.

Warm. Too hot-warm.

Candles   Ten

There and not.

Here and there.

Feather jaw. Powder pillow down.

Something's happening.

A shoulder yoked.   A side disremembered.

No feeling. Arm, leg, jaw Eye   There and not
there.

Searching lines. Drawn down covered body. Trapped
failing parts of something other

Gone away   Far.

Another clipboard. Another pen.   Words
drowning in silence and pity savouring numbers over and under
lines.   Plummet down hung just by
rumoured foot.   Too far away for more
words Other words whispered under dry thick tongues
shadowed complete like secrets small.

'Damage. Left.   Some.

Right   Hemiparesis'

Still white. White still face hovering over sheets

starch   crisp   white.

New for now face.

New now eyeless stare.

Scratch-scratching pen

Writing words.

Make her again   New again new.

New picture Now.

Floating down arm. Floppy-sinking arm Flat or Empty
Drowning Displaced weight falling away.

Dark hair on heads bowed over. Reflect.

Dragged out long roots pushing up dribble sounds

from the soft mulch of slow mouth.   Words
echo sending back Now stranger's voice.

New now voice. New now sound howling

against lost things rhyming to set darkness echoing.

Wielding dead arm heavy stump toppling into side feeling
Left or right?

No more choices. Not now.

Is it night? Day? Something in between fog and grey

searching for window glass of light in dark

of tick-tocking clock inside

Tick.   Tock.   Tick.   Tock.

Shoulder slumped. Head hanging. Eyes water. Mouth sours
tasting itself green bile.

Outside a mouth moves through gloaming sounds.

CHAPTER 7

Jacob

Mammy's gone. Not here. Granny's here. Granny smells like Mammy. But only sometimes. Sometimes means not all the time. Not like the time on the clock. Just the time in between. In between times Granny smells older than Mammy like she's been inside the press longer. The circus is here too.

Granny says *bringing* tomorrow. Tomorrow is not today. Today can never be tomorrow. *Ing* things happen today or tomorrow. This is a rule. *Will* things only happen tomorrow or later today. But not *Now*. *Now* things are different. *Now* things are heavy and strong. *Walk* is a now thing. *K* is strong. *K* looks strong like it can't fall over. *Sit* is a *Now* thing too. *T* is very strong, carrying a big bar on its head or through its neck if it's only small. *Watch* is *Now*. So is *Talk*.

Mammy says, 'Tomorrow Jacob *will* talk.'

Yesterday Granny *brought* Jacob to Tesco. Today Granny is *bringing* Jacob to the park.

Park means to stop your car. Park means a green place with seats and trees too, where Jacob can eat Smarties and sit on the man's bench.

Tomorrow Granny *will bring* Jacob to the circus. *Ing* and *Will* are the rules about today and tomorrow things.

There are lots and lots of rules about yesterday, today and tomorrow.

The circus wasn't here yesterday. The circus is here today. Granny will take Jacob to the circus tomorrow.

The big stripy tent with all the yellow lights grew up like grass, in the field beside Tesco, during the night. The circus is here. Jacob has never seen the circus. Now today is tomorrow but really it is still just today. Tomorrow is somewhere else – far away. Like Mammy.

It is very dark inside the tent and it smells like the ground outside when it has been raining for a long time. But this is inside. It is not raining. Looking back, Jacob sees the outside, where he was just a minute ago, vanish into a triangle of light laced up to the top of the tent. Chips and popcorn smells and a pink-sugary sweetness, making his tongue wet, creep into the back of his mouth and up inside his nose. The smells swirl round Jacob's feet and all through the air and they are so warm Jacob feels like Mammy is giving him a big pink and white marshmallow hug.

Tesco has big pink and white marshmallows in bags. Aldi doesn't. Mammy went away.

There are small twirling colours spinning in circles, reds, blues, greens and yellows, lighting up the darkness and the hair and eyes of the children waving them around. Some children with sticks are holding up candyfloss heads.

Something's wrong. Something's not right. Jacob can't see the rules.

The rules are gone, Mammy. No rules here.

The big tent swallows up all the noises and voices and carries them away.

Jacob looks up in the sky.

There is only one voice here, Mammy.

It is a big voice. The biggest Jacob's ever heard. A voice with no mouth and no body.

The voice is nowhere and everywhere – all over the air. It comes up through the grass and into the seats. Jacob can feel it in his shoes. It bounces out of the lights. It lands on Jacob's head, falling up from the floor and down from the sky.

'Welcome, ladies and gentlemen, boys and girls.'

It is a ghost voice with no beginning. And no head.

Ghosts wear sheets.

They are very white.

'Prepare to be amazed, astonished, astounded.'

There are red and gold curtains.

Up in the tent sky Jacob can see poles and ropes, chains, nets and lights hanging like the web of a spider, hiding silver, under the rain. Then the dark gets darker. The voice gets louder.

There is blue music coming from somewhere Jacob can't see.

A big round light shines on the curtains. The curtains open. A woman with a big tall black hat and sparkly legs moves into the light circle and floats into the bigger ground circle at the bottom of the steps. The woman's voice is too big for her small lipstick mouth. Her cheeks are all jumping sparkles. Her teeth are very white, nearly blue, like the circle of silver light she's walking around in. She flings her arms wide open and everyone clap-claps.

Jacob doesn't clap-clap.

Granny clap-claps.

Jenny clap-claps too.

The lady steps outside the circle. A man steps in. The man throws hula hoops and balls up in the air all at the same time and they move around the air in a magic-circle line passing through his hands, back up and then down again.

There are horses, jumping and white with big plumy feathers on their heads. Fluffy-white feathers with sparkles. Jacob likes the way the sparkles make everything bright and happy like jumping-up-and-down smiles.

Smiles are happy.

Happy is a smiley yellow head Mammy stuck up on the fridge. Mammy sticks Jacob's pictures up too. But that was before yesterday. Yesterday Mammy *stuck*. Tomorrow Mammy will – *be back*, Granny says.

But Jacob knows it will never be tomorrow. It will always only be today.

A spinning woman hangs by her teeth up in the sparkling sky. A skating-round-in-circles man spins her round and round like a magic silver wheel. Round and round. A clown with a big round red nose and strange-looking feet that don't really fit him throws a big yellow cream cake through the air at another clown-man with a flower in his hat. The clown and his flower hat look much bigger in the big shadow-shape up in the sky. Jacob follows the round circle of blue light into the corner of the ring.

The shape of something grows rectangular-black. It is a box. A magic twinkling twirling round box. There's a girl in the box. A man in a cape cuts off her legs spins her around and puts her legs back on.

Ta-daa.

Clap-clap.

The cape man cuts off her small head, spins her the other way and puts her head back on again too. He closes the door on the big magic box. He makes big cape circles with his arms. He opens the box. The girl is gone. The man closes the door again, spins the box around, opens the door. The girl is back.

Ta-daa.

Clap-clap.

Another girl with gold-yellow hair makes birds out of tissues she finds up inside her glitter-gold sleeve. The gold-yellow girl throws them up in the blue air with big wide-open glowing arms. They roll and glide like swimming birds floating on the wavy air. There are rabbits, white ones and brown ones and black ones with red eyes, bumping and thumping out of her hat. There are small white dogs hopping and dancing and jumping through hoops. There is a man rolling rings of yellow-orange fire up and down his big strong arms. Up in the sky there's a swinging man swish-wishing across the lights. He does big pushes with his legs, and then slow-falls, upside down, hooking his knees round the bar to do upside-down swinging. A flying pink candyfloss girl catches his hands and hangs like a Christmas bell in the winking ceiling.

Then just like magic they are all gone.

Everybody clap-claps into the empty air.

All the no rules go round and round in Jacob's head behind his rolling round eyes.

'Roll up. Roll up. Face painting and pony rides for all.'

Ms Rabbit can only do tigers. Jacob looks for orange faces with black stripes. He sees a butterfly girl with blue wings opening up her face and a cat girl with black spots and whiskers. He sees Spiderman, Superman and Batman with black wings where his eyebrows should be but he doesn't see any tigers. Jacob likes tigers, but he likes zebras too. Zoe Zebra has black and white stripes.

'Do ya want to get your faces painted?' Granny says to Jacob and Jenny.

'Jacob wouldn't like that,' Jenny tells Granny.

'Course he would. Sure, doesn't everyone want a shot at bein' somethin' else?'

'He wouldn't, Granny. Jacob only likes bein' himself.'

'And he's right too,' Granny says over Jacob's head. 'But sure, isn't this just like dressin' up? Would ya like to be Superman, Jacob?'

But Jacob knows Zoe Zebra's face is really just all white. Zoe Zebra has black stripes. She doesn't really have white stripes at all.

Granny holds Jacob's hand as they move through all the seats. There are lots and lots of feet running and jumping – some are just standing and not moving at all. The lady at the table has silver sparkly shoes. The heels of her shoes disappear into the ground.

'And who would you like to be today?' The silver shoes wiggle.

'What about Superman or Spiderman?' Granny says down on to the top of Jacob's head.

Jacob wants to be a tiger.

'Oh, you would make a brilliant little Spiderman,' the lady says, sitting down, and her shiny heels come back up out of the ground. 'Let's see now. We'll start with some red first.'

Tigers are orange. Tigers aren't red.

'Then a black web and white eyes.'

Tigers have black stripes.

One leg crosses over the other. One shoe is higher now. It dribbles off the end of her foot. 'Do you like Spiderman?'

Jacob's finger taps the top of the table. Tap tap tap. Jacob cannot see any tigers. Tigers are big cats. Jacob has a cat. He doesn't have a dog. Jacob's cat isn't a tiger. It is just a cat. Jacob's cat is called Cat. Jacob is Mammy's Little Happy Cat.

The lady's fingers gently pull Jacob's face out from his chest and up to the sky. Her finger and thumb make a V at the bottom of his chin and up around his mouth. The lady has red lips. She is smiling at Jacob. There is red paint on a brush. Jacob can't see any orange. He can't move his head. Tigers are orange.

Jacob tries to wriggle his body, but it's stuck to his head. The lady has long shiny-red nails.

Tigers have black stripes. They don't have orange and black stripes. Sometimes the stripes look like triangles. Sometimes they look like lines.

The lady has sparkly triangles at the side of her eyes and on her cheeks. They sparkle like the fairy dust Jenny makes.

Tigers have whiskers. Sometimes whiskers are black. Sometimes they are white. Black is the opposite of white. Big is the opposite of small.

Mammy says Fat Thin Up Down In Out Happy Sad Over Under Open Closed Fast Slow Cold Hot Black White Big Small.

Whiskers are never triangles. Whiskers are always lines.

Jacob feels the brush pushing flatly against his cheek. He closes his eyes. He can feel all the shuffling feet trapped under the big tent sky of the circus. The air is full of new sounds and whispering smells. The trap-trap of the pony passes and is gone, then passes again. Jacob listens for the sound of a tiger, but hears none.

'I just love the rumble and roar of the circus,' Granny says to Jenny.

'Is she nearly finished?' Jenny says back.

'Why don't you get a butterfly or a fairy, Jenny?'

'He doesn't like bein' touched near his head.'

Jacob opens his eyes to find the word *Rumble*. Jacob likes the word *Rumble*. It's quiet and loud all at the same time. It feels nice inside his head and it sounds nice too when Granny says it into the air.

RUMBLE

Jacob thinks all the letters in rumble must be big and they all must be friends. Frog and Toad are Friends. Peppa and Zoe are Friends. Friends hold hands because they are friends. Not because they are falling over. Jacob thinks all the letters in RUMBLE hold hands in a big line together. They are in the right place. The best place. They are strong and still holding hands even after Granny has said them all in one word that is gone. But Jacob can still see it.

R is the first letter in the line. U is next. Jacob thinks about Bob and the alphabet train. M was hiding behind the lamp-post. B is M's best friend. L is next in the letter line. E is last. Jacob doesn't think anybody can hear E. L just likes having E there. Bob finds E. E is yellow. Yellow is Jacob's favourite colour. Jacob wonders if there are other words where the letters are so happy together.

'You really do look like Spiderman,' Jenny says to Jacob, taking his hand and leading him back to his seat.

Granny gives Jacob a cream cracker out of her bag. A man breaks a big brick with his head and then uses his head to push a big car. The man's legs are white. His hair is too long. He has a big silver belt. He doesn't have a shirt or a jumper.

Another man with white legs ties a rope to the strong man's ear. The strong man pulls another car close to the edge of the light with his ear. Then he lies down and the first man drives over him in the big car he'd pulled with his ear. The man gets up off the ground and a lady with white sparkly legs and sparkly feathers sticking up out of her head gives him a big silver bar. The man holds it up with his two hands and lifts it up over his head like a big T. Two ladies in red sparkling dresses jump out of the darkness and they do funny hop-ups and grab on to the bar. They spin around and pull themselves higher and sit up on the bar. There's one at each end. The man holds the bar and the sitting ladies up in the air.

Granny claps. Jenny claps too. Everybody's clapping.

Jacob puts his hands over his ears.

Granny takes another cream cracker out of her bag. 'Here, pet,' Granny says, handing Jacob the square cracker with all the little round holes in it.

Jacob looks at the cracker. He thinks about his hands. Jenny's hands move over his, covering his ears.

'It's okay, Jacob. Itsokay. Isokay,' Jenny says.

Jacob looks at Jenny's butterfly wings. He waits. His hands fall away from his face. He tap-taps his leg. He shakes his head. He looks at his feet. His lace is open. Granny gives Jenny the cracker. Granny bends down. Granny makes rabbit ears. 'Over, under, around and through, meet Mr Bunny Rabbit and pull. How are you?'

But Mammy says that the rabbit was sad. His ears were too long. He tripped over them all the time. One day a fairy landed on the bunny's head. She lifted up the bunny's ears and crossed them over like an X.

Jacob doesn't like X. X doesn't sound happy. X is an angry sound. *Angry* means not Happy. X is in *Vexed*. X is too loud except when it's in *Fix*. Then *F* is louder.

Mammy puts one ear through the bottom of the X and she pulls the rabbit's ears up together. Mammy makes each ear into a loop. Mammy makes another X like before. That was before yesterday. Before yesterday she put one ear under the X and pulled again. The bunny lived happily ever after.

But this is today. Yesterday is gone far away. Like Mammy.

Granny pushes down on the front of Jacob's shoe like she's looking for his toes. Jacob's toes are inside his shoes. Jacob knows they are there. Granny can't see them. Jenny breaks the cracker in two bits. One bit for each hand.

CHAPTER 8

Jenny

Granny arrives in the kitchen, of course, just as Jenny is picking the black bits off Jacob's fish fingers. Five minutes earlier, and they wouldn't have been burned. Ten minutes later, and they would have been eaten, burned bits and all. Either way, Granny wouldn't have known, and Jenny could have saved them all from what happens next.

'What's that smell? Where's your father?' Granny asks, madly waving her hand up and down in front of her face.

She doesn't wait for Jenny to answer. Granny looks busy today. Well, busier, if that's even possible. Today, Granny looks like she has a very important job to do and by the way she's moving and the way she's asking questions, Jenny knows that, like it or not, Granny's job will be done, and quickly too, *come hell or high water*, which is one of Granny's favourite sayings. It can mean a good thing, like, *come hell or high water, we'll get you that bike* when it sounds like a big promise, or it can be used for bad things like, *you'll get that homework finished by seven o'clock, come hell or high water*, when it really means *and if you don't there's goin' to be big trouble!*

Jacob and Jenny sit at the table and wait. Jacob eats his fish fingers. Granny is in the sitting room now, shouting over the noise of the television.

'You listen to me, Kevin. I'll not tell you again! Those two children are out there eatin' burned fish fingers and God knows what else and it's not good enough. Not good enough at all! Do you hear me?'

Before Da has a chance even to speak, Granny is back in the kitchen again, huffing and puffing, shuffling and tut-tutting, but not really saying anything at all.

'Ah Jesus, Mae-Anne, I'm doin' the best that I can here,' Da says, coming in through the kitchen door and trying to catch Granny's words as quickly as he can, because Da knows that if they are left up in the air like that with nowhere to go, they'll just get bigger and angrier and tumble down on him later anyhow, crushing everything and everybody in their way. And today it is Da who's in the way.

Granny looks all around the kitchen. Her eyes stop when she sees the big pile of washing, still wet, on the counter. 'Well now, Kevin, if I agreed with you there, we'd both be wrong, now wouldn't we?' Then she takes off her coat and heads for the line with an armful of washing. 'Isn't it an awful pity now altogether, that stupidity isn't painful,' she says, on her way out to the yard.

'It's not been feckin' easy, ya know,' Da says, shaking his head behind Granny's shape, dazzling outside in the sun, and sticking his two fingers up on each side of his nose pretending he's scratching his cheeks.

Jenny starts to laugh. Da starts laughing too, but then, like he suddenly remembers where he is and who is there and all the reasons why he shouldn't be laughing, he stops. Jenny stops laughing too.

'There's great dryin' out today. I'll be back this evenin' with me stuff,' Granny says when she's finished hanging the clothes up on the line. 'And just remember, Kevin, those who laugh last, think slower. There's goin' to be changes round here! Big changes! Come hell or high water!' And then she is gone, just as quickly as she had come, leaving Da and the children to wonder which will come first, hell or high water, and to work out exactly what it all means; if it will be good, like a present, or bad, like the homework, this time.

A few hours later Granny is back in the kitchen again, like she has just fallen out of the sky or grown up from the floor. She didn't ring the bell or knock on the door. Nobody saw her coming. One minute, she isn't there. The next minute, she is. Jenny's at the table doing her homework when Granny appears like a genie out of a bottle. Jenny looks across at Jacob, like Jacob knows how Granny managed to get into the house or out of the bottle. But Jacob's not telling Jenny. Jacob just keeps on humming and twiddling a sweet wrapper in his moving, up and down fingers.

'Nothin' good ever came out of a dirty house,' Granny says, as though something terrible was going to creep out from in under the table and out the back door.

Then she peels off her coat and goes into the sitting room. Dropping her pen, Jenny follows Granny inside.

'I'm movin' in. Now! And there's to be no debate about it, either,' Granny says, over the noise of the TV.

'No need for that, Mae-Anne,' Da says. 'But thanks anyway.'

'The state a the place. But sure, no matter how near your coat is, your flesh is always nearer.'

'What exactly is that supposed to mean?' Da says, like Granny's mental, but Granny is already back out in the kitchen by then.

'How did *she* get in?' Da says to Jenny, like maybe she knows Granny's secret.

Jenny shrugs.

'She's the very same as one of them Wall-Crawlers and I would bet any money she can set things on fire with her mind, too,' Da says, in a little voice, his fingers held straight, like a fence covering his mouth, just in case Granny can see through walls, too.

'Isn't it a pity now, ya didn't think a the milk earlier and I only just passin' the shop?' Granny shouts from the kitchen.

'That woman,' Da says, pausing after *that*, just to make sure Jenny knows exactly who *that* woman is, 'is way more annoyin' than Twitter! Except, unlike Twitter, there's no fuckin' word limit on *that* woman! Excuse my French, but I swear to God, one of these days, *come hell or high water*, I am goin' to kill her!'

'Mary Boyle says her Martin's been promoted and he's even got a company car – imagine that, and there's you sittin' on your arse watchin' *Home and Away*,' Granny says, walking back in with a tea towel in her hand.

'It's *Neighbours*, actually!' Da says, but Granny's already gone back out to the kitchen again.

Da sits back in his chair, looking up at the words Granny has left, floating up over his head, like they were going to stay there for a very long time, just hanging around in the air.

'Will ya be stayin' long?' Da shouts from the corner.

'As long as it takes!' Granny shouts back from the kitchen.

'To do what?'

'Whatever needs doin'.'

Then Granny comes back into the sitting room again, takes her apron and her yellow washing-up gloves out of her bag, opens the buttons on the sleeves of her blouse, rolls them up, and pulls and stretches the gloves nearly up to her elbows.

'You goin' to take out me tonsils, Doctor, or do ya want me to bend over?' Da says, laughing out real loud.

But Da looks frightened.

'I see ya didn't put the Sellotape back where ya found it?' Granny says, ignoring Da completely, and looking down at Jenny and pointing to the drawer under the TV. On her way around the sitting room, she picks up cups and crisp bags and shoves an old newspaper up under her arm. And then she disappears, once again, into thin air.

Jenny puts the Sellotape back in the drawer where she found

it, and she's just about to go back to her homework when Granny appears again, and, this time, she turns off the telly.

'Hold on there now, just one minute!' Da says. This time he isn't laughing.

Jenny escapes, back to her long division. But just as she sits down at the kitchen table, Granny arrives in behind her again. Jenny's starting to wonder if there's more than just one of her Granny. Granny divided by two. Or four. Or twelve. She might have a twin, an evil twin, like Bart Simpson's evil twin brother Hugo, who was chained up in the attic like an animal and fed a bucket of fish heads once a week. Jenny tries to imagine the Hugo version of Granny. Hugo Granny is bigger than Granny, even though they are both the same height. She plays bingo too, but she cheats and often steals from the old ladies sitting beside her. She's been living in a hideout under the ground that she dug with her bare hands since she escaped from the attic. Mind control is her favourite game, and she throws words around like knives with razor-sharp edges that can actually cut you and leave a scar. And there's always creepy music wherever she goes, that's how everybody knows that she's coming. And it's always dark when she arrives, too, even if it's only just dinnertime. Jenny remembers Da going around the kitchen saying, *No, I am your father,* all the time, when he worked out on the computer that Darth Vader was his evil twin. And Jenny remembers how Da had explained to her that Darth Vader had actually been a good guy, but that he had turned to the dark side because his mother and wife had died, or else he went there to stop them from dying, Jenny can't be sure, but she knows he only went bad because everything in his life was going bad too.

Granny starts sorting all the plates into big piles; one pile for big plates, another pile for small plates. The bowls are next, and then all the pots. She separates the knives from the forks and the big spoons from the small spoons, setting them in groups on the counter. She puts the sugar back in the press and the butter back in the fridge. She throws the empty Rice Krispies box in the bin and then she rinses out the last bits of coffee stuck to the bottom of the jar, and there's so much clinking and clanking and bashing and banging that Jenny can't even hear Jacob's humming anymore.

'What do you think you're doin?' Da shouts, following Granny out into all the noise.

'Well, I'm not one for sittin' round doin' nothin' like you. I'm gettin' your house in order!'

'What do ya mean by that?'

'What do ya think I mean? It's hardly feckin' cryptic I'm bein'.' Granny wipes all the counter tops with a cloth and says something about slaumin' and strealin'. She tut-tuts her head from side to side. 'I offered up a novena to St Blaise this mornin'.'

'Good for you.'

Then, suddenly she's over at the cooker scrubbing and scraping, like she's trying to make it disappear.

Jacob rocks backwards and forwards on his chair. Jenny tries to divide 200 by fifteen.

'I saw a programme on the telly. A documentary, actually. It was all about how he made a boy somewhere in Spain grow his leg back again even after some doctor had cut it off him. It took him two years to grow it back but when he did it turns out that it was the same leg that they'd cut off a him in the first place,' Granny says.

Jacob puts his hands over his ears. He is still rocking. Jenny carries over the five and tries to work out how many fifteens there are in fifty. Then she just leaves all the fifteens where they are on the page, changes sides, and sits over beside Jacob, where she has a completely different view of the kitchen.

'No way?' Da says, 'Really?' rolling his eyes around in circles till he is nearly looking inside the back of his own head.

'It even had the same bite marks still in it from when a Alsatian dog attacked him when he was three and it still had all the same marks the chickenpox had made on it when he was only two and a half. So, I thought maybe he could fix Jacob, too.'

'Well now, that's the last thing Jacob needs, an extra feckin' leg.'

'Watch your language! And aren't you just great at the sums now too, all the same!' Granny says, and she turns on the taps and big fluffy white bubble-foam grows up over the sink, like it's something magical coming out of her fingers. 'And maybe while you're at it you could count up on your right hand the number a days you've worked in the last three years.'

Jenny can see Granny's face in the black window in front of her and she knows Granny can see her, too.

'Ah sure, maybe I'll give Jude a go too while I'm at it,' Granny says then, into the blue-black-window shape of Da.

'Ah sure, why not? If you're on a roll,' Da says, but he doesn't mean it.

'St Jude is the patron saint of Lost Causes.'

'Yes. I know who he is. But Jacob is Not a lost cause,' Da says real loud and real slow, like he wants every word to mean something very serious, but especially the *Not* because he definitely said the *Not* with a capital N.

'I know he's Not! I Wasn't thinkin' a Jacob!' Granny definitely uses a big N and a big W.

Da folds his arms tighter across his chest. 'Don't go to any trouble on my account.'

'It's helpin' them children with their homework is what you should be doin', and not sittin' around here all day feelin' sorry for yourself. God knows, many's a man that destroyed himself through self-pity and for what, I ask ya? For the want of somethin' constructive to do! And would ya not pick up them toys there, before somebody trips on them and breaks their neck!'

'Ya know, Mae-Anne, as usual, you are right. This is My House,' Da says, with all his capitals standing tall, like soldiers getting ready for battle.

'And These are My Grandchildren!' Granny says and there are so many capitals fighting around in the air, bouncing up and down and bumping into each other, that it seems like there isn't enough room in the kitchen for them all.

Jenny rubs Jacob's arm and his rocking slows down, becoming more of a little sway; his humming softens.

'Oh, 'tis true what they say, all right! A mother with a purse is better than any father with a plough team,' Granny says, nodding her head like she was agreeing with something only she knows about, but she's making so much noise clanking and banging plates and pots that Da doesn't seem to hear her. 'There isn't Even so much as a sliced pan in the press and, sure God help ya, you're so Feckin' Busy watchin' *Home and Away.*'

'I Was Watchin' *Neighbours!*'

'I see Johnny Dempsey workin' above in the garage. But sure, I suppose You'd be too Grand and overqualified for Anythin' like that,' she says to Da's face in the window.

And it's like all Granny's capitals join together in one big strong line, and they push Da back out through the door, his face disappearing from the window. Jenny can only see his back now, as he picks up his jacket off the end of the stairs, and says that he's going off for a walk.

CHAPTER 9

Jenny

Dear Ma,

Granny brought us to the circus and it was brilliant and Jacob came too. He even had his face painted, Ma, and he didn't even have a meltdown or anything. And do you know what else Granny did? She moved into our house last week, to mind us. Granny says that Da doesn't 'have hands to wipe his own backside' and Da says that Granny's 'an awful pain in the arse'. And, Ma, he says he knows he's not supposed to use bad words like that, the ones he says are his French words, but he says that sometimes he just can't find any other words, or that the right words haven't been invented yet, when it comes to him trying to describe Granny.

When you went away Da had to mind us all on his own but he's just not as good at it as you are, Ma. He was always burning the toast and scraping the black bits into the sink, but they always ended up on the floor anyway even though he was trying to get them into the sink or the bin. And he did that every single morning except on Saturdays. On Saturdays I made Rice Krispies for me and Jacob. Then we ran out of Rice Krispies.

And the tiles in the kitchen got real crunchy from all the bits of scraped toast and it stuck to our shoes. And there were never any matching socks.

Da says, there's 'some fucker' of a sock monster living in our washing machine. Da says that's the French for 'big hungry beast'.

I hope you are feeling better, Ma? I got The Prisoner of Azkaban out of the library but I'm going to wait till you come home so we can read it together. That'll be good, won't it, Ma? Granny said I should write to you, coz the battery in your phone is broken and that they don't allow phones in the hospital anyway. Granny says they don't allow people into the hospital either coz they might make the patients in the hospital sick. But I told Granny that the people in the hospital are already sick and that's why they're in the hospital.

I am good. So is Jacob. I do letters and words with him every evening coz Granny says we can only have the computer for fifteen minutes every day. Granny says computers google your brain and sure isn't that why everyone is so fat! Granny says fatness is nothing to do with anything at all except eating all the wrong food and sitting in front of the telly all day long pretending to play football or tennis, when really we should all be out on our bikes or kicking real balls into real goals.

I read Jacob a story every night, too, before bed. We're reading Biscuit Bear at the moment, and Jacob really loves it. Remember I used to love you reading that to me, too, Ma, and do you remember the time we made Biscuit Bear cookies and we used Smarties instead of currants, for Biscuit's eyes? I wish we could do that again, Ma. Jacob would really love that. Maybe we will when you come home. And Granny says you'll be home before we know it.

And, Ma, you wouldn't believe all the stuff Granny brought round to our house. She brought all her photos of Grandad and the Pope. She brought her own cups and saucers, the blue ones with the birds and the tree, and she *brought over her butter dish and milk jug. She even brought her own Hoover coz ours is still making funny noises, Ma, and it's not sucking up anything at all. Granny moves stuff around all the time. She drags anything she doesn't like the look of out to Da's shed. She fixes broken things and some things that aren't even really broken like the clock on the oven that just blinks orange zeros all the time. But we like it like that, because when it's always zero o'clock it means we always have loads of time before we have to go anywhere. And I swear, Ma, she rubs the windows till the glass is squealing and she scrubs all the floors so the whole house smells like the swimming pool and she polishes everything so hard that everywhere you look your own face is always looking back at you. She checks how much sugar is in the bowl and how much toilet paper there is under the stairs and if we need milk for the morning.*

And she put a statue of Jesus dressed up like a princess in a big fancy red dress in the window over the front door. He's got a blue crystal ball in one hand and only two sticking-up fingers on the other hand and he's got so much Sellotape round his mouth and his neck he looks like he's been kidnapped and if he says one word about who took him he'll be killed right there in our hall.

'What's that?' Da said, when he saw him for the first time, and Granny explained to us that he's called the Little Child of Prague and that he's in charge of the weather. Da took him down off the little shelf he was on and asked Granny what was wrong with his head. Of course, Granny went mental and we all thought she was going to have a meltdown or maybe something worse and then she called Da a 'heathen'. A heathen is a person who does not belong to a widely held religion (especially one who is not a Christian, Jew or Muslim) as regarded by those who do. I

googled it and that's what Google said, and I think it means that Da doesn't believe in God, or something like that, anyway. Then, Ma, Da tells Granny that the Little Child of Prague must be crippled with the weight of the big crown on his head. So, Da put another bit of Sellotape round the Child of Prague's wonky neck and he put him back up in the window again. I think Google was wrong about Da.

And, Ma, Granny always leaves her teeth in a glass on the back of the toilet and Da says he swears them teeth have eyes and ears too and they just give him the willies and the sweats every time he opens his pants or sits down to do his business.

Ma, who is the old man in the yellow-green jacket and odd shoes who lives in the broken-down house beside Lizzie's? How does he know my name?

We miss you, Ma.

Love,

Jenny

Jenny folds the pages in half and runs her pointing finger and thumb hard along the middle to make a crease. It still doesn't fit in the envelope. Opening it again she folds it over on itself three times, flattens it along the new crease lines and turns the end over, doubling it up on itself. She pushes it into the envelope Granny got from the drawer. It still bulges ready to explode. Jenny straightens the packet, forcing each corner down until the whole thing is flat like it should be.

'What address should I write on the front? Where will I send it?'

'Don't you be worryin' about that, child. Sure, can't I give it to her tomorrow?'

'But I'd like to post it.'

'Okay so, I'll stick it in the postbox this afternoon. Have to go to collect me pension anyway.' Granny zips Jenny's letter safely away in the secret back pocket of her bag.

'Granny, when can we go to see her?'

'Soon. Here, do you want a sweet, pet?' Granny says and hands Jenny a Milky Moo.

Jenny untwists each end but the line down the middle where the wrapper wraps over itself is welded to the sweet inside. She thinks about the old man on the steps with the sweets still in his pockets for his children. He is bringing them to the cinema later, when the doctor is gone. She wriggles the wrapper away but there's still lots of milky-white stickiness forcing it back together. She tries to peel it off in small bits. But the small bits get smaller and smaller. He will buy them all popcorn and drinks when they get there. She removes what she can, then puts the sweet into her mouth anyway, and sucks at the last bit of paper, separating it from the sweet with her tongue as it comes away.

CHAPTER 10

Jenny

'Ya have to tip your pretend hat, if ya see a magpie,' Jenny tells Jacob as they watch the stripy loner in the front yard.

She touches her forehead, goes through the motions of taking off her imaginary hat, which must really be a cap because of its very long pretend peak.

'Then ya Must ask him how his wife is – Mrs Magpie,' she says, giving the big M of *Must* more time, making it slow and important. 'Or else ya can just close your eyes and pretend ya didn't see him at all coz if he's all on his own it means that Mrs Magpie is dead.'

Jacob traces the V-shaped wobbles of the fence made by the rain on the window.

'And ya hope that when you do open your eyes again that you'll see him with another magpie, maybe his sister or his brother. It doesn't really matter as long as there's more than one. Granny says it's really important that ya don't see only one coz one is for sorrow but two, well, two is for joy.' Jenny turns from the magpie and watches Jacob watching the rain shapes and moving colours.

When it's raining the street is so quiet it seems like Jenny and Jacob are the only ones living there.

The quiet splish-splosh of rain is broken when Da comes into the room with a screwdriver in one hand and blood falling out of the other. Da is dancing and hopping from one foot to the other like his shoes are on fire. He says something about his hand and whisper-shouts out a whole load of curse words in a big long line, some of which Jenny has never even heard before, like he's trying out all the curses in the world to see which one is the best and the loudest and which one can make him feel better enough not to have to look for any other curse words instead. Finally, it seems Da decides 'Bollox' is probably the best so he pushes all the others back out through the door and just keeps on saying it over and over.

'Bollox. Bollox. Bollox. Bollox.'

'Da, what's wrong?' Jenny slips off the couch and faces back into the room.

'Fuck. Shit. Bollox.'

'Da, you're bleedin' all over Granny's floor.'

'These are MY FLOORS!' Da snaps at Jenny. 'This is MY HOUSE.'

Jenny looks around. The house is so full of Granny's stuff sometimes it's like they've moved in with Granny, not the other way round. And because Granny's the only one who cleans the floors now, she thinks they are hers.

Jenny goes out to the kitchen and gets a Peppa plaster for Da. Then she hears Granny in the sitting room screaming at Da about how she's just hoovered and wiped all the floors.

'What in the name of God have ya done to yourself now?' Granny says to Da.

'I was doin' a job!'

'Well now, that'd be a first!' Granny goes off to the kitchen again passing Jenny on her way back.

'What were ya doin', Da?' Jenny enquires.

'I was rewirin' the plug on that stupid feckin' lamp by Her bed!'

'Come out here ya feckin' poultice ya,' Granny screams from the kitchen.

Da goes back out to the kitchen. Jenny goes back to the window where Jacob is watching the rain and waiting.

Annette

Stale Clean air tasting mouth.

Flicking lights daytime white. Yellow night. Round round over under back.

Falling words harden in Shapes of Sharp colour. Melting splashes Sound dripping drips down. Like candles

Melting away Morning sheets Evening Colder.

Clattering Rolling trolley back. Eyes inside sleep. Slipping backward hands.

Silent window Blue

Swirling inside red

Thumb pressing head Press squeezing finger.

'Good. Central response.'

Sticking. Prod. Poking stabbing pen. Eye light. Blink and Roll.

Open. Close.

'There's definitely more movement. Watch.'

'How long, Doctor?'

'Hard to say, Mr Augustt. Every patient is different. Her surgery went well, as you know. No more bleeding. Just taking her time. You just have to be patient, I'm afraid. But the signs are very good for now.'

'But it's been so long—'

'There'll be ups and downs, of course. She'll have good days and she'll have bad days. Just try to stay focused on the good days, Mr Augustt. Let them encourage you all.'

Heft. Hoist. Haul.

Hurt sealing Mark.

'It is slow, I know. But every day there is a slight improvement. Talk to her, Mr Augustt. Keep her updated on her life. Patients respond best to familiar voices and family news.'

'How?'

'Keep it simple. One thing at a time.'

Flame out inside and burn open wound. Fix. Heal. Ooze inwards. Bleed. Cut. Crushed. Peel away. Searing Light fade bleared name and feel. And Feel even numbness. Feel. Smell and nod blinking eyes yes. No. One. Two. Two. One. Deep down things Waiting

Twitching to

tighten.

Rise. Fall. Lead of fingers. Foot in stone. Unremembered now Heaving Storm.

Look. Looking Here.

Long Last fingers sipping sheets Growing nails scrape

scratch.

Swinging hours swirling light dark. Now. Not now. Before after shackled feet. Severed tongue. Bald cry. Far away seashell ear listening in no bottom Frothing drowned faces. Faraway Names. Fly away beneath words watery sky. Bruising rocks purple knees. Dentist dust mouth. Moulded Stuffed Cotton. Marbled teeth.

Forming shapeless words dissolving tongue in teeth.

Bracelets. Flower names four corners of colour.

Wall beside.

Yellow-white egg flickering over grey faces coming.

Back go nothing.

Changing darkness of Dark head in light pacing. White shape remembered close.

Easy.

Soft here in face.

'Annette, can ya hear me, love?'

Tap-tap root and up. Voice in shadowy echoes

Echoing hand.

'I fixed the Hoover.'

Touch fingers. Smile

cry into eye.

Dissolve.

Melt away this dark sleeping thing.

'And I cleaned out the shed.'

Burning moving-waking Mouth sealed up sounds of red sky.

Bloody seeping drawing flame in tongue name.

Waking up limbs in eye of faces wringing an ear.

Have. Hold. And listen to clouds souring grey. Remember steady air before swing. Swallow and Fall dappled night of now.

'Love, I have to go home now. Back to the kids.'

Morning noise Clatter make fall to Begin.

'Good morning, Annette. I'm back on today, for my sins. Dr Betts tells me you're making great shapes altogether, now, so you are! He's just gorgeous, isn't he? And I hear yesterday was a good day. We'd better get you sorted before he gets here on his rounds. Wouldn't want him to think we hadn't made an effort, now, would we?'

Fly. Buzz and tickle feet. Nose. Flick Blue-Green Bottle. Disappear. Back no word sound fuzzing circle air.

Good

Day

Bad

Days

Begin to End in beginning.

'Feckin' flies this time of year.'

Eating egg fly. Feasting flesh tickle suck inside soft pink Dead Larvae eyes eating skull Inside Out.

Inching hatching gnawing at bone slack jaw.

'And don't you be worrying about your hair, Annette! That'll come back. I've seen it before. Think of all the time you'll save! And all the money! Now that's better.'

Finding sounds in lost eye. Sideward glance smoke. Disappear. Clumps on pillow.

'So, have you any news for me, Annette? I know you must be missing them kids like crazy. And I know it's hard for you right now. But I promise you, things will get better. That Dr Betts is nothing short of a miracle worker! Sure, it's like Lourdes in here, so it is! Wouldn't mind a cold bath with him though!'

Open back skin flicking light

Side watching fly

There and not.

Waiting eye open. Little suck sucker creep in to Burrow and crawl. Slink deepen in spew milk to purge

Blinking eye. One. Two.

'Ah, there now. Now we're getting places. A boy and a girl, isn't it?'

Once down. Back. Look. Writhe to slither.

'Me too. Lucy, she's my eldest. She's eight going on seventeen. And Daniel, my little boy, is four and three-quarters. The three-quarters bit is very important to them at that age! But God, is he hard work, let me tell you! I think boys are all the same though. Lucy was easy but Dan, well Dan is an Antichrist. Had he come along first, there would never have been a Lucy! You just couldn't be up to him. But sure, good or bad, we wouldn't swap them for the world, now, would we?'

Down. Up. Again. Birthing to breed swapping worlds.

'How about we try propping you up a bit? For the lovely doc!'

Close. Open.

'He shouldn't be long now. How about a little freshen up? I always feel better after a wash, don't you?'

Into thumb curling word not spoken. Shake. Quiver past unsounding pitch louder shout. Wring. Toll bellow Bell.

'Ah now, would you look at that! Thumbs up is it? Blinking not fancy enough for you any more then? Sure, you'll be doing Beyoncé for us, by the end of the week.'

Lift sheet making more white. Wash clean and new. Soft water slinking over just barely skin. Gentle long gentle smooth soak sponge kissing clean.

Wipe better me away.

New shining clean window. Clear clean to see. Sink into light feeling touch to smile in eye placing lost mouth lying fresh in new child. Pain loosens.

Boy. Girl.

Between bed and

new time candle stories.

No cake or

Head rub in Happy breath places.

Open closed teeth make porridge.

Treats and. Fairy Sunday. Saturday slippers morning pyjamas.

Toes. Nails. Cut-cut-cutting swiping smooth tumble dry swab little feet thump thumping. Landing. Middle bed. Flicker breath finding toes in thighs back. One. Nothing separate. Together feather skulls in velvet foreheads reaching feeling empty never born to die before brown eye and blue searching up.

Ma

Mam

MAMMY

Mammy

'There now. Isn't that better? Let's move those toes. Come on. I know you can do it.'

Slow tremor writhing shaking louder. Jerk away. Contract. Shaking outside splay splatter toes.

'Don't worry, Annette. That's to be expected at this stage. Your muscles can go into a type of spasm of involuntary movement. Very promising sign, actually.'

Boy. Girl.

Name empty not. Freckles remember look see.

Girl. Boy.

First and next who now.

Under faces grasp to reach shining red letters fade away. Fall find again to say Love in Name.

Boy.

Girl. Boy.

Name.

Girl.

Boy.

Crush and wring to pulp. Break leak flit away broken phantoms. Smoke curling blue air.

Names trickle bleeding red.

'Ah sure, would you look who's here now. Better by far than any auld doctor and earlier too!'

Smiling sad smile

Shuffling

Shoulders heavy in clothes creasing.

'Sorry I didn't get in yesterday, love. I had to stay with Jacob while your mother took Jenny shoppin' for new runners.'

CHAPTER 12

Jenny

Dear Jenny,

I hope you are being good for Granny? I miss you so much and Jacob too. I am feeling much better now, thank God, and sure the doctor says I'll be home before you know it.

The food here is good, except sometimes it's a bit cold.

Granny says you are doing very well at school and that you are a great help with Jacob. I believe you went to the circus and that it was great fun and Jacob even had his face painted like Spiderman. That's marvellous news, now, altogether.

Isn't it great that Granny is there to mind you and keep the place tidy! I know your daddy was trying his best but sometimes a house just needs a woman for everything to run smoothly. And I do know that Granny can be difficult at times. She can get vexed but remember her bark is worse than her bite and believe me she adores you both and would give you her last breath if you needed it. She just worries about us all, maybe too much at times, but that's what mothers do, Jenny, they worry. So now, you leave the worrying to me and Granny and we'll sort everything out and things will be back to normal as quick as a dog can lick a dish.

*My phone is broken. The batteries fell out, so that's why I
have not called you and Jacob. And Granny is right, you
know, they can't let too many people into the hospital on
account of the bad flu going around, but sure with the
bright evenings here now, that'll be the end of all the
winter colds and coughs.*

*Keep helping Jacob with his letters and words and
remember Granny is right about those computer games
and eyeclouds and things. Really, they should all be
smashed, and children should be out playing football and
chase and not stuck in corners eating crisps and melting
their brains.*

*I think you were asking me about the homeless man in
your letter. I don't know who he is. He just kind of arrived
a couple of years back. Where he came from, nobody
knows, and well, Jenny, there, but for the grace of God,
go I. I don't know about him knowing your name though,
but he's a harmless poor soul and you don't need to fear
him. I've never heard tell of him uttering so much as a
word.*

Give Jacob a big hug from me. Tell him I love him.

I love you, Jenny, and I'll see you real soon.

Love,

Mammy

Nobody has ever written Jenny a letter before, not even that
French one Teacher made Jenny write to when they had to do
Pen Pals in school. Jenny had told her all about Ma and Da
and Jacob and about Jane-Anne Comerford Smyth. She had
told her that chips are her favourite food. She had even told
her all about Luigi's. She'd asked all the questions Teacher had
put up on the board: does she like living in France and what's
it like living in a foreign place; Jenny would like it and maybe
she could go over for her holidays; has she ever been anywhere

else instead of France, Jenny has not. Jenny had been very excited about the idea of receiving a posted letter back, all the way from France. But it had never come. Jane-Anne said it was probably because of the picture Jenny had sent of herself with the letter.

And Jenny cannot remember the postman ever knocking the door before to say he had *a special letter* to deliver. He usually just pushes letters and brown envelopes in through the letter box.

'Did ya get a letter?' Granny asks from the doorway into the kitchen.

'Yes. It's from Ma. Ma wrote me a letter.'

'Ah, did she now? She said she was goin' to all right, when I was up there on Monday.'

'Granny, why can't we go to see Ma?'

'Sure, amn't I killed tellin' ya! They only allow visitors durin' the week, when you are at school.'

'But Ma says it's coz of the flu.'

'And she'd be right, too.'

'Can we go durin' the summer holidays?'

'Ah go ta God, child, won't she be long home by then.'

'Can we go, if she's not home?'

'Mark my words, your mammy Will be home.' Granny definitely uses a big W for *Will*.

Jenny reads the letter over and over, again and again. She keeps looking at the writing that isn't Ma's. It's too scratchy and skinny. It's not right at all.

'Granny, this isn't Ma's writing,' Jenny says, even though she doesn't want to say it out loud, in case she's right and there's been some awful mix-up and this letter isn't for her at all.

'Ah Jenny, did I not tell ya about her arm? She hurt it up there in the hospital. I think she tripped. Anyway, isn't she only havin' to use her other hand, for the moment just, while her right arm heals.'

Jenny smiles down at Ma's strange squiggly writing and even though it looks different, like it's going to fall over the line any minute, Jenny can hear Ma's voice in every single word.

CHAPTER 13

Jacob

Granny smells sad. Like she's tired and not the right colour. Granny is very white like she's silver. There are big dark circles round Granny's eyes. Jacob likes circles.

Granny's eyes are blue. But today they are grey like all the blue fell out into the teapot. Granny's making tea. Tea takes a long time. Granny stands looking out the window. Granny is singing a song with no words. Jacob likes the Mm-mm of the sounds. Granny is waiting. Jacob sits at the kitchen table, making a picture.

When Mammy draws *sad* the yellow head has an upside-down smile. *Happy*'s smile is up-ways like a big U. A straight-line smile means *thinking* or *not sure*. A wibbledy up and down line means *angry*. *Angry* is the same as *vexed*. Granny says *vexed*. Mammy doesn't.

Jacob draws a big circle like the one round Granny's eye. O is a circle. He colours it blue. He can't colour it white. White is not a marker colour. Blue is. He draws two small circles inside the big blue one. He colours them black. Jacob draws a small triangle under the black circles. A triangle is like a square with one side missing so two of the sides fall into a V. He colours the triangle black like the circles. He draws an upside-down U for the mouth.

The kettle bubbles and spits on the counter. Jacob likes the round shapes and colours of bubbles. Granny puts some of the kettle water into the teapot. Then she throws it back down the sink. She does it again. This time she doesn't pour it away. Granny puts tea bags into the teapot. Granny puts the teapot on the top of the cooker. Granny stands at the cooker watching the teapot.

Jacob draws a triangle. This is the body under the big blue-circle head. He colours it yellow.

'How's about a nice cuppa for our elevenses, Jacob?'

One arm sticks straight out of the triangle body like a branch. So does the one on the other side. One leg is longer than the other.

'And a coconut cream?'

Jacob hears the rustles and flicks of the packet. He throws down his marker. Runs over to the centre of the kitchen. Granny pulls the packet open at the top with two hands. She pulls back the plastic. Just like magic pink and white fluffy biscuits slide out on a noisy, flat tray.

'Now, Jacob, what do ya say? Yes please?'

Jacob's fingers rush at the biscuits.

'Ah. Ah. Now, what do ya say?' Granny pulls the biscuits away.

Jacob points at the biscuits, looks up at Granny. Granny's glasses are back. Her eyes don't look small any more. Jacob points again. Then looks away. Granny hands Jacob a biscuit. Jacob smiles at the biscuit. The biscuit is round. Circles are round. Ovals are not. Jacob doesn't like ovals. The biscuit is white. White is not a marker colour.

'Well, I suppose Rome wasn't built in a day, child, now was it?'

Jacob pushes the biscuit into his mouth. He uses two hands for this. The biscuit is big. Jacob's mouth is small. It is inside his mouth. Then it is gone. *Mammy is gone.* So is the biscuit. He points at the packet again.

'Just take small bites. There's no rush, pet.' Granny hands Jacob another biscuit. It is pink.

Jacob takes a bite. He looks at the bit left in his hand. It is not round. It is not a shape any more. Like the moon when the man takes a bite out of it because he is hungry.

'Good boy.'

Jacob likes the way the soft bit sticks to the roof of his mouth. The other bit falls into his teeth.

Granny puts the biscuits up high in the press. They look smaller. She closes the door. She brings her cup and saucer over to the table. Jacob stands watching the press waiting for the biscuits to get bigger and come back down into his teeth in small bits again. Granny pours a cup of tea. Jacob hears the brown colour pouring like water in an upside-down U.

'Why don't you come back and finish your picture? It's lovely. There might be another biscuit, if ya do.'

Jacob roots for Super Mario in Granny's bag. Super Mario is gone like the biscuits. He moves back from the centre of the kitchen. *Centre* is like *middle*. But *centre* is stronger. *Middle* sounds like it's sleeping. *Middle* is grey without any shape. *Centre* has sides and corners. *Centre* is more important.

'And sure, maybe we'll go to the playground in the afternoon, when Jenny gets back from her little friend's house. Would ya like that, Jacob?'

Jacob draws a square, a big one in the centre of the page. He draws two smaller squares inside and a rectangle under the squares. He puts a cross in each of the smaller squares. A cross is two lines. One line goes up. The other line goes across the centre of the up line. He draws a small circle in the rectangle. Granny takes one of Jacob's markers and stands up straight like a pencil. She moves behind Jacob and writes MAMMY over the round blue head in Jacob's picture.

'Ah, I know that ya miss her. We all do. But she'll be back in two shakes of a lamb's tail. Can ya copy the letters, Jacob? Can ya write *Mammy*? M. M for Mammy.'

The word does a dance on the page. All the colours come

together in the letter shapes moving in and out of each other, swirling round like flower-feathers. Orange turns into yellow, red into pink and back into red again, green goes blue and indigo and violet like all the rainbow colours falling into the sea. Jacob draws a rainbow like an upside-down U up in his sky. Under the rainbow he draws a man with buttons like tears.

Granny finishes her tea and rattles back to the sink. Jacob draws a small square girl and a shapeless boy. There is a dog with big teeth and rabbit ears standing at the gate snapping up from the page. The gate doesn't open. Raindrops fall down from the rainbow into the yellow flowers he has carefully drawn behind the house.

CHAPTER 14

Jenny

'Let's play hide-and-seek,' Iliona suggests, but Jenny's not sure how that will work in a square yard that's wide open and flat, like a desert, and surrounded by a wall to stop them all spilling out on to the road, and that they're not allowed to climb over.

Jenny scans the big space, stretching her eyes, searching for somewhere she might hide. Iliona has already turned her back. She has her two hands held tight over her eyes. She's counting to ten.

Jenny runs to the top of the yard where Jane-Anne has lined up some of the girls from their class. Jessica Maguire is at one end of the line. Courtney Jordon is at the other. Between these two stand the others, hopping from foot to foot, hoping to be picked.

Jenny doesn't pass them. Instead she turns to the left and races towards the big plastic grey bin in the corner. She crouches down behind it, steadying herself with the slightest touch of her fingers on its dirty curving sides. She keeps her head down. She thinks about Jack peeking out of the pot just as the giant comes back into the kitchen with a basket of golden eggs in one hand and a sick-looking chicken in the other. The giant screams at the hen to lay a golden egg and then he goes over to the press and pulls out a golden harp with the face of a sad young girl stuck to the side. Jenny can see the big coarse black hairs growing out of the giant's nostrils.

She can almost smell his stale breath in the warm stench drifting out of the bin.

'Play!' he screams at the frightened harp-girl and the harp begins to play a gentle tune while the lovely face sings a sad song without any words.

Jenny has never heard anything so lonely as the harp-girl's voice.

When she has been there long enough for the song to be over and for her legs to wobble a little Jenny dares to peep out from the side of the bin where she expects to see Iliona coming towards her. But there's nobody there. Nobody anywhere. Jenny stands up to check again. She sees the back of the last girl in the line disappearing in through the double doors that will close any minute, now that break time is over. Jenny sprints to catch up and just manages to reach the back of the line as the children shuffle back into their classroom.

CHAPTER 15

Jenny

Dear Ma,

We had a test in school today. I got ten out of ten in my sums last week, even though it was long division and I'm really not very good at dividing things by twelve or fifteen. But today's test was one of our summer tests and it was on all the counties in Ireland. I learned to remember them by the colours in the book. Antrim is orange, so is Cavan. Teacher is from Cavan. Da says that all the people in Cavan are so mean they'd only give you one measle at a time and they'd only be lending them to you at that! He says that's why she's so stingy with her marks. Kilkenny, Laois and Westmeath are all yellow. We went to Kilkenny on our school tour last year, and we saw the castle with the lovely gardens and the big fancy table in the hall, so that's easy to remember, but I've never been to Westmeath or to Laois either. Da says there's nothing much to see in Laois, apart from the cows on the soccer pitch, but he says Meath is a great place. He showed me on the computer a big mad looking grave thing that was built there a long, long time ago. It looks like a space ship. It is a place for burying very old people and there's lots and lots of secret tunnels and passageways inside it. It is called Newgrange and Da says that on the shortest day of the year some people are picked to go there to watch the sun either coming up or going down, I can't remember, but Da says it's like magic because everybody is there to see the longest night of the year ending. So, it must be to see the sun coming up. Da says he's going to take us all to see it, when you are better, Ma.

Dublin, Tipperary and Down are all blue on the map. Da says I could sing to remember all the counties coz he says there's a song written about every county in Ireland but he only knows two. One is called 'It's a long way to Tipperary' and the other one is 'In Dublin's Fair City'. Waterford is red. So is Wicklow. Offaly and Donegal are green. Galway is purple and shaped like a dragon.

Teacher made us all change places for the test. She put me beside Jane-Anne Comerford Smyth and even though we're not friends anymore Jane-Anne started telling me how she doesn't need to know any of the counties in Ireland because her Doddy's cor has Sot Nov, so it always knows where they're going and how to get them there. And so does her Mummy's jeep. Then, Ma, Teacher tells me to stop talking even though I wasn't even talking. And Jane-Anne kept on talking in whispers, behind her hand and she asked me what Sot Nov voice we have in our car and I said that we have Spongebob Squarepants giving us our directions and, Ma, I know it's not good to tell a lie, not even a white lie like that, but I just didn't want her to know we don't have Sat Nav or that our radio doesn't work either. I also said that we have heated seats. And then Teacher writes all the rules of the test up on the board in big capital letters

NO TALKING. NO COPYING. NO LOOKING AT THE BOOK.

And then Jane-Anne says that we should share all our answers and that way, we'd definitely get everything right. It was all her idea, Ma. But I didn't say, 'No.' The first question was to name all the counties in Munster. I knew them all! Cork, Kerry, Limerick, Clare, Waterford, Tipperary. And then Jane-Anne kicked me under the table. I looked up and Jane-Anne's eyes were moving from my page to hers and back to mine again. Her page was empty. So, I sat back, pretending to stretch, so that Jane-Anne could see my answer. Then we had to name all the counties in Leinster and, Ma, do you know how many counties there are in Leinster? Loads and loads. Da made me learn a stupid sentence about them; When We Were Kicking Off Dust Little Light Lizards Crawled Kissed and Marched. The first letter of each word is the same as the first letter of each county in Leinster. Da says there's a special name for remembering things that way, but he couldn't remember what it was. And even though Da's sentence was stupid, it did make me remember them all. Ulster and Connaught were next. Little Snow Men Get Runny was Da's sentence for Connaught. And for Ulster he made up a poem: Ulster's counties in a line, Donegal, Derry, Antrim, Down. Altogether there are nine, Armagh, Monaghan, Tyrone, Cavan, Fermanagh, so let's not frown. And Ma, I was exhausted from all the yawning and stretching. When it was over, Mrs Nicholson told Jane-Anne to collect up everybody's test, and then she told us all to draw a picture of our favourite county and to say why it is our favourite county.

I drew a picture of Wexford, Ma, coz that's where we had the picnic in the place near the castle and you told me and Jacob the story about the little prince who lost his voice but then the little girl with the pigtails found it for him at the bottom of the King's garden and they all lived happily ever after. Do you remember telling us that story, Ma?

Then Mrs Nicholson called me and Jane-Anne up to her desk and she said that it seemed very strange, to her, that both of us thought that Leitrim was in Munster and that

Limerick was in Connaught. And, Ma, before I could say anything, Jane-Anne says that she's always mixing those two up. And she had this really confused look on her face.

'Really?' Mrs Nicholson said, but I knew by the way that she said it that it wasn't really a question at all. It was more like a big shove or a slap, said with a sneaky smile, because it was a Really that didn't believe a word Jane-Anne was saying and it was just waiting to catch her out. But then Jane-Anne said that she had a pain in her tummy. Teacher asked me, why did I think that both of us wrote down that Monaghan was in Leinster and that Meath was one of the newest counties of Ulster?

'Could YOU PLEASE explain that to me, Jennifer?' she said, but she looked like she already had the answer.

So, I told her that I got mixed up with Da's sentences, but this wasn't the answer she was looking for. And then Jane-Anne said that it was all the M sounds that made it hard to remember, even though it was my turn to answer. Then Teacher went mental and her voice went real high and she said that one of us CHEATED. That one of us COPIED the other one's test, and that she wanted to know WHO it was. Ma, I could see all Mrs Nicholson's capitals ganging up against me. And they were so high up over my head I felt like I had shrunk and wasn't my right size anymore.

Jane-Anne told Teacher that she had been trying to hide her answers with her left arm around her page, and she even showed Teacher how she had done it, by putting her arm around her make-believe answers, so I couldn't see. And, Ma, she was so good at telling Teacher about how She Hadn't Cheated that I started thinking that maybe it had been me doing all the copying. But it wasn't, Ma, I swear.

Teacher said I was a disgrace and that's not how we behave in this classroom, now do we? She gave me all the counties to write out five times each and then she told me to get back to my seat. Iliona Reszczynski put her fingers on my arm and said she knew it was Jane-Anne and not me, who was telling all the lies. Iliona is my new best friend now. I've been going over to her house a lot and her family is very nice. She is Polish and she has a little brother too. We are going to stay friends forever. Her Ma invited me over to their house for a sleep-over next week and we are going to watch DVDs and have a midnight feast, if Granny says it's okay. Iliona and me are probably going to stay up all night talking and telling each other all our secrets. She says she will teach me some Polish words. That's going to be great isn't it, Ma? Iliona and me will be able to talk to each other in school and Jane-Anne or nobody else will know what we are saying. It will be like a secret language, just for us.

I had to bring The Prisoner of Azkaban back into school, Ma, because we are only allowed to keep books for two weeks. But I didn't read it, so I wrote my name down on the Borrowers' List again and now I still have it for us to read when you are better.

And, Ma, I asked Da why we don't have Sat Nav, when I got home from school, but he said that getting lost is the fun part of any journey and it's the best way to find out where everywhere is, even the places you've never heard of, like Monamolin, and are not going to anyway and would never go to, even if you knew they were there, like Carnew. But with our system, Da says, we'll know the whole country before we get to the place we're actually going to, and sure isn't that where all the adventure is?

Then Da says that you are the only Sat Nav we need, and that we'll have you back soon enough anyway.

Granny says dinner is ready and that this isn't a café she's running. I better go.

I love you, Ma,

Jenny

Jenny runs down the stairs straight into the shepherd's-pie smell that's making the whole house feel a lot more like Granny, and less like Ma, every day.

'Granny, do you have a stamp?'

'I do, to be sure. I always have a stamp. Ya never know when ya might need a stamp,' Granny says, and her head is so far inside her bag Jenny thinks she might fall into it.

She pulls out balls of crumpled-up receipts, two short green pens that look too short to be pens and are more like pencils that have been pared halfway down, a comb, rosary beads, a bin tag and a notebook.

'Ah, here we are,' she says, like she's just found an old friend right there, sitting at the bottom of her bag.

She hands Jenny a stamp.

Jenny carefully peels it away from the shiny cream paper on the back and then, she doesn't know why, she drags it along her tongue. The stamp sticks to the tip of her tongue and it tastes like Sellotape does when she can't find a scissors and has to bite it into small bits.

'Ya don't need to lick it, child!' Granny says with a little smile.

'I know.'

'Sit down there now for your dinner. Did ya wash your hands?'

'What's Ma's address?'

'Oh, give it here, child. I'll be passin' the post office tomorrow. I'll send it off for ya then.'

Jenny slides the letter across the table. Granny takes it up and slips it in between the book and all the other stuff in her bag.

CHAPTER 16

Annette

Half man-woman face now looking into smiles saying too much and not enough. Under pale masks in pity cast. Lying down statues on graves.

'You're lookin' better today. Much better today, thank God. Bit a colour back in your cheeks, love.'

Talking eyes flicker over moving up and down lips suddenly shutting to pretend everything is okay. Better. Feeling the shrivel pink-paper skin cover her now. Feels Mother's kiss. Cold hand on too hot-warm forehead.

'Are ya a bit hot, love? I'll open the window. A bit a fresh air will crown ya, love.'

Too hot air. Fresh. No more perspective. No words for curing.

'Isn't that better now, love? Sure that bit a fresh air will crown ya.'

Planed-away stare seeing down deep inside. Paring back
to all that is left. Now. Broken. Painted back in for watching.
The checking eyes.

'I brought ya some flat Seven-Up. Your daddy swore by it
too as a cure for all and every ailment. And some chicken soup.
The food in these places is always freezin'. Definitely, there's
more colour in your cheeks today, love.'

Colours in cheeks. Come to visit. Check. Sit. Smile. Flat
Seven-Up. Straws for sucking. Ice-cream buckets. Plastic spoons.
Soup. Knickers. Books in bags. Flicking pages to read back
black words telling stories to feed babies. With no hair.

Photographs. Pictures to remember who what where
before now. Before colour. Before when.

'Ah now, Annette, would ya take a look at this? Do you
remember that day, love?'

Seaside. Blue-breaking waves. Green umbrella. Feel it like
Braille etched into eyes. Sky pushing clouds over end of world's
edge. Wool blanket in patches. Buckets. Chicken sandwiches.
Nets catching crabs, pointy fish.

'Do ya remember the day we took that, Annette? Would
ya believe I found it under your stairs, at home, when I was
doin' a bit a cleanin'? I can see you and your daddy there like it
was only yesterday. Surely ya can remember Seamus and all the

sunburn? Like a lobster he was. God above, but do ya remember how much you all loved a day on the beach?'

Shouting slow questions.

Words in faces known or not falling into sea picture. Tide washing away now.

'How are ya feelin' today, love? They're treatin' ya well here anyway. I can see that. Sure you'll be home before ya know it, love.'

Propped up. Slumped down. Listening to hear words. Shuffle feet slide beside her. Up corridors. Down. Open doors and mouths close to keep sickness in. Inside. Deep. To smother over a bad head foggy with blood. Swirling. Gushing blood leaking. Swollen pain sludging in scraped-away scooped-out skull. Too big for fitting burst open like boil pus seeping through.

'The kids will be made up to have ya home, love. We all will. They'll be on the holidays in two weeks and sure now, don't ya know they can't wait. I'd bring them in to see you, but I think it might be a bit soon, yet.'

Creeping around like spiders webbing. Weaving words and names in glue globby thick. Lance to drain away what to know or to make new again. Better new. But they knew. Remember the thread. Spools spinning back and forward to return her. To safety. Candles.

'Do ya know that poor divil sleepin' rough, love? He's always around. Always on the cinema steps. Quiet man. Never says a word to nobody. Not like Mad Paddy Nugent, who's still standin' outside the chemist's, wavin' his arms and screamin' at the trucks goin' by. But, I suppose, Paddy's not had it easy either. He came outta one a them homes, an orphanage, I suppose it was. Anyway, I passed the poor divil, on the cinema steps, he was, the other mornin' and do ya know what? We had a right chat, so we did, and it just struck me that at the end a the day, aren't we so lucky we all have each other. No matter what else happens, when you've got your family, you'll be okay. And you will be, love. I promise ya that.'

Ripped. Stretched. Gouged to shape. Tortured angles. Splay open. Cut to pieces re-formed on canvas white sheets inhaling stained up there ceiling. Flickering on burning cake. Faces and darkness move in. Out. Move away. Just in case.

'You're lookin' better today, love. Definitely, you are. Definitely. I'll bring the children for a visit soon. Real soon. I will, love. I promise.'

CHAPTER 17

Jenny

Dear Jenny,

That young Comerford Smyth one didn't lick it off the ground, you know! Sure, that child couldn't be anything else, but a sneak. You just ask your daddy. He could tell you a thing or two about that one's father! And, do you know what, Jenny? So were all belonging to her! Cheats and liars! The whole lot of them! Her grandfather Jim Comerford was the crookedest man ever to walk on two legs. He turfed his own brother out of the house when their mother died, and he had his own father put away in the mental hospital, up above, in Newcastle. He never got out. And Jim Comerford's children are no different. Full of airs and graces, mind you, but would rob the sight out of your eye at the same time. And as for that mother of hers. Well now, she was never anything but a cheat and a liar, like all them Comerfords that had gone before her and the whole town knows it. So, she's got it on both sides. Her grandmother was Janice Smyth and she was the nearest thing to a tinker you'd ever meet. That one smothered her own mother with a pillow to get at the will. And we all know what a crook that father of hers is! A real cowboy if ever I've seen one! Amn't I killed telling you, what's in the dog comes out in the pup!

You don't mind her, Jenny. Sure, won't you be on your

*holidays real soon? In the meantime, you just keep doing
all your work. And don't mind that teacher one either. I feel
like going in there and giving her a piece of my mind.*
    I hope you and Jacob are helping Granny.
    Love,
    Mammy

Jenny can't believe Ma didn't use the word 'Disappointed'
with a big capital D, not even once, even though Jenny did
nothing wrong, well, not really. Ma says 'Disappointed' with
a capital D when she's really annoyed; when she's so annoyed
she can't find any other word. 'Disappointed' is the worst
word in the whole wide world and it means so many things,
not just disappointed! The way Ma says it, means she's
ashamed of you; or it means, *I had such high hopes for you and
you let me down – I'm so disappointed in you;* sometimes it can
mean, *I thought you were better than that but you're not. I know
that now.* And worse still it can mean, *You have made me sad.*
Making Ma angry is not as bad as making her sad. When Ma's
annoyed she shouts and screams but then she gets tired and
she forgets but when Ma is Disappointed, with a big D, it
takes much longer for her to forget. Sometimes Ma just goes
under the stairs for ages and sometimes she is just very quiet,
for a very long time. Jenny Hates the word *Disappointed.* She
Hates the word *Pants,* too. Granny says *Pants* instead of
Knickers. And *Slathers.* She really hates *Slathers.* It makes her
feel dirty like she'll never get washed and the funny thing is
Granny uses it when she's talking about cleaning. And Jenny
Hates the word *Fudge* – it's too heavy and seems to stay in
her mouth even after she has said it. But most of all, Jenny
Hates the word *Left* because it doesn't even know what it
means, except that *Left* means *Not Right.* It can mean *Gone
away* or it can mean *Stayed behind.* How can one word mean
the opposite of itself?

Jenny folds the letter back along the fold lines Ma made to get it into the envelope. She smells the paper and touches it. She puts it into the drawer she keeps for special things. It sits in perfectly beside *The Prisoner of Azkaban*.

CHAPTER 18

Jenny

The days get longer and warmer and the mornings are bright even before it's time to get up, but still Ma doesn't come home. Granny closes the curtains in Ma's room every night and opens them up again every morning and she runs her hand down over the quilt, to flatten it out, even though it's still flat from when she flattened it yesterday morning. She checks for dust on the windowsill with her finger and she sometimes just stands in Ma's room for ages taking in big breaths like she's breathing Ma back into the house. Da doesn't sleep in there any more either. He says the room's just too big without Ma.

Sometimes Jenny pretends Ma's still at home but she's just in another room. If Jenny goes into another room and Ma's not there, she pretends she's just gone upstairs or into the kitchen, and when Jenny calls her she sometimes pretend-hears Ma saying she'll be back in a minute, so she follows Ma's voice upstairs or out into the kitchen, but when she gets there Ma has moved off again, maybe to the bathroom or out the back yard. Jenny follows her all round the house again and again and even though she can't catch her she knows that she's there; somewhere. She's just hiding.

Granny sends Jenny and Jacob out in the garden all the time now. She says, 'Shoo, now the fresh air will crown youse,' or 'And what do youse want to be sittin' like two lumps on the couch for on such a fine evenin'?' when she needs them out of the way and she needs them out of the way all the time now because there's no school for the summer and Granny says she has 'a million and one things to do and havin' to entertain you two makes it a million and two.'

Jacob likes the swing in the garden and the way his shadow moves up and down when he kicks his legs in and out to go higher. Jenny likes pushing him and listening to his happy giggles and watching his feet disappear into the shadow when she pushes him real high. Then he laughs when they see his feet coming out of his shadow again, just like magic, when the swing swing-swongs back down.

Jenny tries to show Jacob how to swing himself higher, in case someday maybe she's not there to push him, by lying back a little bit while he's pushing his two legs out real straight to go up and then sitting up straight again and pulling his legs back in to come down but Jacob just keeps kicking his legs, like scissors cutting the air, and he thinks it's all just a game.

And sometimes when Jenny gets fed up trying to get him to swing by himself she tries to teach Jacob a song or a new word, like Ma used to do, and sometimes his mouth moves but there's no letter shapes or word sounds coming out. He just opens and closes his mouth a lot. But Jenny knows he is listening and trying real hard and she knows he really, really wants to say something because he pushes his tongue upside down and makes little noises and snaps with his teeth.

'Don't worry, Jacob. The next time a word comes into your mouth it *will* come back out again too and we *will* all be able to hear you. Even Ma will hear you the next time.'

Then one Friday evening, after Granny has run them both out of the kitchen again, Da's shadow-shape appears beside them, filling up the grass space – much bigger than theirs.

'Did youse get shooed out, too?' Da asks with a grin.

'Yes.'

'Right so,' Da says. 'Fall in. Let's get goin'.'

'Where are we goin', Da?'

Da turns from the children and opens the shed door. The light pushes past him making everything in the darkness look warm and golden inside. A bit like the cave in *Aladdin*.

'Get offa that swing, soldier. Stand to attention,' Da shouts from somewhere inside in the cave and even though they can't see him now, Jenny knows he can see them.

Jacob gets down off the swing and they run into the shed after Da, but the stinking smell of something horrible, creeping out from inside, pushes them both back out into the yard again. Jenny's eyes start watering, and something from deep down in her stomach rushes up into her mouth and she has to swallow it real quick before it turns into something else, something bigger that might fall out of her mouth and all over her shoes. Jacob takes in big breaths of air from the garden and shakes his head and wriggles his shoulders like he's cold even though he can't be cold because it is the summer. But the smell seeps into the garden, sneaking around the grass, dripping off the tree. It sticks to the washing on the line. It's like the smell of rotten eggs and sour milk, mixed with something very dead and something very warm. Waving her hand up and down through the air to stop it wrapping itself around her face, Jenny looks back in through the swinging-open door and the sticky-heavy dark, but she doesn't see any treasure. As her eyes move around the space behind the door, a small reflected bounce of blue-silver draws them to rest on something strange hanging from a hook in the ceiling. Squinting inside she sees that the strange hanging shape-thing is a chicken.

There's a big chicken hanging down from a hook in the middle of Da's shed, she says to herself, just to help her understand what it is she is seeing. *And it looks like it's moving even though it's got no head.*

Jenny tries to make sense of the scene. But then she realises that the chicken isn't really moving at all. It's the skin that's doing all the wriggling and changing. The chicken's just hanging there dead, dressed up in a moving maggot suit. The little grubby white maggots are real busy bumping over each other, like they're blind with no legs but with a very important job to do and they probably are blind with no legs and it is them that's doing all the moving and making the headless chicken look like it's alive even though it looks like it's been dead for years, too. And they're slipping and sliding and slithering their way in and out of the purple-pink plucked chicken skin and some of them fall into the bucket down on the ground.

'Ah, Da, what's that?'

'That's me pet chicken Ernie. Me little maggot maker.'

'Where's its head?'

'Over here. Do ya want a look?'

'NO!'

'Ernie's helpin' me out. Helpin' me grow bait. Don't ya go tellin' *Twitter* nothin' about him! Do ya hear me? He's our little secret.'

'Granny says we're not allowed to call her Twitter.'

'Oh, does she now? How does she know I call her that?'

'Granny knows everythin', Da.'

'And what else does Granny say we can't do in OUR OWN HOUSE?'

'Well, there's a whole list a things up on the fridge.'

'What list?'

'The list Granny wrote out and stuck up on the fridge.'

'When?'

'Last week.'

'I haven't seen it!'

'Well, it's there and you better read it. It's very important, Granny says.'

'Important? What's so important about it?'

'The rules!'

'What rules?'

'The rules on the fridge!'

'So what's on this famous list of rules then?'

'Well, number one is, Granny's not to be called Twitter.'

'She's been called a lot worse, believe me. Number two?'

'We've not to drink milk outta the carton. Only the tinkers do that. And we're not supposed to say *poxy* or *manky* coz they just sound like words only the tinkers would use too.'

'Go on.'

'Always put the crayons back in the box.'

'Fair enough.'

'You can't make someone pull your finger before ya fart.'

Da laughs.

Jenny counts the rules up on her fingers.

'Six is a really important one, Granny says. Ya can't record anythin' she says and put it up on the Internet, like those girls did on their poor ma when they pretended the dog ate the ham at Christmas and the ma went mental and started cursin' and makin' a holy show of herself and everyone in the country seein' it.'

'Oh Jesus don't be puttin' ideas in me head.'

Jenny holds five fingers open on her left hand. The thumb on her right hand is up too and so is the pointing finger beside it. The other three are tucked into her palm.

'I think seven is that we have to go to Mass, every Sunday.'

'Fat chance a that happenin'!'

'Eight is about talkin' to an adult if you feel afraid or worried. But she copied that one off the Childline poster in Tesco. We've to remember that Granny is not our cleanin' lady. That's number nine.'

'Did she write them up on tablets a stone?'

'What? She wrote them on the sheet she stuck up on the fridge.'

'You've got to tell me number ten.'

'That one's about Ma. It's the most important rule of them all, Granny says. Ya can't stop talkin' to Ma every day even though she's not here coz no matter where she is she can hear ya.'

Da turns his back to look at his chicken but Jenny knows by the fall of his shoulders he's thinking about something else and it's like there's a big bit of trouble skittering around inside the back of his head. Then he bends down, picks some of the baby maggots out of the blue wriggling bucket and goes back inside in the darkness inside the shed-cave.

Jenny and Jacob go back to the swing. Jenny hears Da banging around, moving things and bumping into other things.

'Atten-chun,' Da suddenly shouts out from the shed.

Jenny and Jacob glue their heels together and stand up real tall beside each other in a line. They know this game. Jenny pushes her arms so far down past her bum she nearly falls backwards into the bin. Jacob tries to copy Jenny. Then she takes big massive breaths into her nose and squeezes her chest out so she looks a bit like a turkey in the dark shape of herself in the grass. And she holds her head up so high it feels like someone's pulling her nose off her face with a Hoover. Jacob, head down, walks off down the garden.

'We're off on adventures,' Da says. 'Squad will turn to the left in file.'

'Where're we goin' to, Da?'

Jenny uses the toes on her left foot and the heel of her right foot to twist the rest of her body around to the left. She stamps down her foot real hard to keep herself from falling over. Jenny knows she has to be careful with this bit.

'Forward march!' Da shouts in his big army voice.

To do the *forward march* Jenny brings her left leg up so high she nearly kicks her own head in the face. Then she stamps back down on the grass with the same leg and she makes a V with her feet.

'Where's the adventure, Da?'

'Up at the lakes, soldier. I'm takin' ya fishin'. Where's Private Jacob?' Da screams out from one of the shadowy corners of the shed.

'He's down at Ma's flowers. Are we goin' now? This minute?'

'Yes, if ya hurry up.'

'What about our dinner? Granny's goin' to go mental.'

'We're goin' to Catch *our* dinner. You leave Twitter to me!'

'You've not to call her Twitter, Da. That's rule number one.'

'Sorry. I meant Moses.'

When Da does appear out of the shed his eyes are red and shiny in the sun.

'What's wrong with your eyes, Da?'

'Feckin' smell a dead chicken!'

Da's wearing all the green clothes that make him smell like he's made of wet grass. He's got the biggest wellies in the whole wide world, growing up over his legs like ivy. His jacket has a million pockets but no sleeves and there's a knife and a hammer and a scissors peeking up from one pocket and a Mars bar and pen squished into another pocket. All the zips have feathers. He has his fishing rod in one hand and a big bag of wriggling fishing maggots in the other.

'Come on, soldier,' Da shouts down the garden at Jacob.

Jacob pulls the heads off some of Ma's daisies and clutches the little, broken, white petals in a tight fist. Skipping forward on tippee-toes, he dances up through the grass.

'Now. Back to business. Squad will turn to the right in file. Right turn. Left. Left. Left. Right. Left.'

Jenny knows she's supposed to use the heel on her left foot and the toes on her right foot to twist her whole body around to the right but she's so mixed up about her toes and her heels and her left and her right that she just turns her whole body the other way around real quick but then loses her balance and plops down on top of her own shadow in the grass. There's a plane flying past the sun but it's too bright-white to look at. Jenny closes her eyes. She can still see the searing, yellow-white spots scraped and burning into the back of her soft eyelid skin.

Da laughs. 'Private Wibble-de-Wobbledy. Ten-hut!'

'Where youse goin'?' Granny shouts out the kitchen window.

'We're goin' to catch our dinner,' Da shouts back at the glass.

'No. You. Are. Not,' Granny says, making each word into a sentence. '*You* of all people should know not to promise a fish until it's caught. Dinner will be ready in ten minutes.'

Da marches at the front with Jenny behind. Jacob follows Jenny around the side of the house, through the side gate and into the front garden. Crazy Billy, from next door, is in his front yard too, pretend fishing, like always. Da puts his hand up which means they're to stop.

'Catch anythin', Billy?' Da asks.

'Only the attention of arseholes,' Billy says with a smile on his face.

Billy always looks like he's smiling even when he's not. He's either got too many teeth in his mouth or he thinks smiling is the only thing he's any good at.

Then Billy slides his head to the side and flicks it, forehead first, at a strange man and woman standing just outside the Augustts' front gate. The woman looks frightened. The man looks like he's got somewhere real important to go in his suit. The woman's mouth is pulled right across her face, like an elastic band she keeps stretching tighter and tighter to make it look like she's not frightened at all. But Jenny knows that she is.

'Jesus is here. He is with you. He has come again, invisibly,' the man says to Da and hands him a little picture across the half-open gate.

'Invisible me hole! He's inside in my fuckin' kitchen, in drag,' Da says back to the man. 'And he's a big fuckin' auld woman of a man.'

The man looks at the woman and the woman looks back at the man, like they can't make up their minds if they should stay or go. The man decides to stay. The woman isn't so sure. She moves back away from the gate.

'Is this him?' Da says, looking at the picture.

'Yes. Jesus was just a man, just like you and me, when he lived among us,' the man says, looking straight at Da.

'I think they've got the wrong fella altogether,' Da says, showing Billy the picture across the wall. 'What do ya think, Billy? He looks nothin' like me!'

Billy nods his head.

'This is a gift from God,' the man says and he nods at the woman.

The woman roots in the bag at the man's feet.

'Jesus doesn't blow-dry his fuckin' hair like that! Doesn't he not, Billy?' Da says, passing the picture back to the man.

Billy shakes his head.

'Jesus Christ, Jehovah, there's better photos of him than that. Ya must a caught him on a very bad hair day,' Da says, winking at Billy.

The woman looks up from the bag, like she's just heard some new news she hadn't heard before.

'Surely be to God, Jesus is more rugged than that. Isn't he, Billy?

Billy smiles at Da.

'Jesus is more like a Job or a John the Baptist or one a them other long-sufferin' poor bastards in the Bible. Ya know the ones I'm talkin' about, surely? He's got a big wild-lookin' heretic head on him. An outlaw with holes in his hands and trouble in his eyes, who rides into town once a week from the desert, on the back of a donkey, covered in locusts and settin' fire to all a them bushes that can talk.'

The woman seems to freeze halfway up the man's leg. She lets out a little 'oh' like it's a tiny fart she's been trying to keep in, but it gets out anyway and then her elastic lips snap back to her nose and give her a shock. Her mouth falls open like she doesn't even know her face isn't smiling any more. She takes a book out of the man's bag and hands it up to him. 'This is the word of God. The word of Jehovah. The Kingdom message,' the man says, and he seems to grow taller as he hands the book over to Da, like he's giving him a really expensive present that could break any minute. Da hands it to Billy. Billy throws it back over the wall on to the path. The woman bends down and picks it up and hands it back to the man.

The man takes a big breath into his nose, 'The righteous will enjoy paradise on earth in a restored Garden of Eden where there is no sickness, old age, death or unhappiness.'

'Did ya hear that, Billy? They're goin' to restore the Garden of Eden. Clean it up a bit. Put out all the fuckers that shouldn't be there. The old, miserable, sick ones can just fuck right off!'

Billy smiles at Da. He doesn't look at the strange man and woman at all.

'Jehovah can save you at Armageddon – you must believe,' the man says, stepping back a bit from the gate.

'Would ya ever come in outta that, Billy!' Billy's Ma screams from somewhere inside in their house. 'It's only Tuesday. Sure, we won't be needin' them fish till Friday.'

The woman looks at the man. The man keeps looking at Da.

'Tell ya what,' Da says, opening the gate, 'why don't ya go on ahead inside. I'm only havin' a laugh. We'll have a nice cuppa tea. Me mother-in-law's inside in the kitchen there. She'd love to hear all about Jehovah and Armageddon and all a that other stuff and sure we'll be back in a minute. We're just nippin' out to get the milk.'

The man looks like he's just got ten out of ten in his spellings, he's that happy. He looks over at the woman. She looks like Teacher just told her to go see Sr Mary Assumpta up in the office. But she pulls her smile back across her face again anyway, and they both squeeze themselves sideways in through the gate and walk up the path behind Da to the front door. Da opens the door and they follow him inside. A few seconds later Da bolts back out of the house.

'Run!' Da shouts in his army voice.

He picks up his rod and his bag and throws his leg over the gate. Jenny grabs Jacob by the hand and pulls him through the small space between the gate and the wall. Da flings everything into the boot.

'Who were those people, Da?' Jenny asks when she's settled Jacob into the back seat.

'Jehovahs,' Da says, like it's a curse word.

'What are Jehovahs?'

'A Jehovah is a sneaky little bastard who tries to worm his way in under your carpet and take over your mind and change ya into another Jehovah.'

'Like zombies do?'

'Ya, like zombies do – but these mad fuckers, excuse my French, are more dangerous, harder to get rid of. They think they have to make more Jehovahs to get into heaven. It's a bit like a vampire suckin' blood.'

'Why do they think that?'

'Coz some other mad Jehovah told them that only somethin' like four a them can get into heaven. The more people you bite and bring into the gang, the greater your chances.'

'Will they try to turn Granny into one a them?'

'Not when they spot her horns and big cloven hoof under the table!' Da turns on the radio. But it doesn't work.

When they get to the lake everything is quiet again.

'Ah now, this is more like it,' Da says, taking all his fishing stuff out of the car. 'I'm feelin' real lucky today.'

They walk over to the lake together. Da opens his fishing bag and takes out a lunch box full of the chicken-maggots from the shed. It used to be Jenny's lunch box but when she got too old for *Hello Kitty* she gave it to Da for his worms.

'Ya have to hold the rod between your fingers and thumb,' Da says, fixing the line. 'And hold it delicately, like you're holdin' a child. Ya can cast the line out on your own or with some help if you're small, but the cold smell a brown trout, the squelch and slap on the bank and the brightness when it twists and turns at your wellingtoned feet, will make ya feel big.' Da takes a little worm out of the box. 'And ya must always put the hook in the middle a the maggot and not through his head and keep your eyes open when you're hookin' him even though ya feel sorry for him coz although he doesn't scream ya know his wrigglin' and squigglin' must mean he's in pain.'

Jenny looks down at the maggots. The little maggots are clean and white, but they don't have any heads.

'Da, how do ya know which end is the head?'

'Ya let them go and see which way they move. The end that goes forward must be the head, unless they decide to walk backwards, arse first, kinda way. But they rarely do that unless they're on to ya and they're tryin' to trick ya into thinkin' their arse is their elbow.'

'Do maggots have elbows?'

'Do chickens have teeth?'

'I don't know. Do they?'

'Course they do. How else could they fish or play hurlin'?'

'Chickens?'

'Maggots!' Da laughs.

'They look a bit like Rice Krispies or little fat crawlin' fingers,' Jenny says, feeling them wrinkling themselves into her ears, up under her nails. Her whole body does a little shiver dance.

'I suppose they do,' Da says.

Da puts one on to the hook and throws the hook and the maggot into the water and nobody talks for a really long time. Jenny looks down at the rippling versions of themselves, looking back up at them from the water.

The three stand, for a very long time, in a lovely shared silence but then Da breaks it apart.

'Ah, the wind is all wrong.'

'Is it?' Jenny looks around.

'And there's too much of a glare on the water.'

'Da, you said that the last time, too.'

Jenny takes Jacob off for a walk to the top of the lake. She looks up at the mountains, lying like the shoulders of a big strong man stretching his arms out on every side. And he's holding the lake. He's minding it. And the small scraggly trees at the ends of his arms are like reaching out hands and fingers that'll never meet and the noises of the wind are everywhere, and you can never get away from them until the mountain man's hand sweeps over the water and makes everything still. Jenny picks up a stone and throws it bouncing across the water, splishing and sploshing and making giggle ripples that push off each other just before they disappear. Jacob smiles, like the half-circles left by the stone, but Jenny can never really be sure that he's smiling for now or if it's just a left-over smile, one he's forgotten from yesterday or the day before. After a while they get a bit bored throwing stones.

It's nice here.

Jenny hears Jacob's words stolen away by the wind.

It's quiet.

'Yes, it is quiet here, Jacob, isn't it? Will we go back and check on Da?'

Okay, Jenny.

Jenny loves the way she hears Jacob say her name.

Do you think he might have a fish?

'I hope he does have a fish, Jacob. I'm starving. And that would make him feel real proud, like he's a winner.'

Let's go and see.

'Okay so, let's go and see.'

Jenny takes her little brother by the hand and they run back to Da.

'Catch anythin', Da?' Jenny crosses the first two fingers on her right hand – she's hidden it up behind her back.

'Nope. Must be them feckin' maggots. But next time, kiddo! Just you wait and see. Let's head back to the car.'

Da picks up his rod and his box and throws them back into the boot. They climb into the car and Jenny clicks Jacob back into place. She looks at the back of his little head, looking out at the trees.

'Da, we're starvin',' Jenny says to the back of Da's head as he clicks himself into the front.

Da looks around and he looks frightened, like a little boy who is lost in Tesco and he can't find his mammy. His da is gone, too.

'Jesus Christ, I forgot all about your dinner. I'm so sorry,' Da says into the back of the car. Da pulls the squished-up Mars bar out of his pocket and hands it to Jenny. 'That's just for starters.'

Jenny sees a tear running down the side of Da's nose. She un-clicks her belt and pushes the top half of her body between the two front seats. The gap is so small she can hardly breathe. Da gathers her into himself like he's never going to let her go and Jenny can feel a type of shudder she has no name for, wrapping its arms around them both. In the end it's Da who lets Jenny go and says the something they need to make them both stop feeling sad about the thing they don't want to talk about anymore.

'Your mammy's goin' to get better, ya know. It's not, it's just—' Da loses his place in the sentence and drags the back of his hand across his face. 'I promised ya fish! Didn't I?' Da says, like he's just remembered something else he forgot.

Jenny slumps in the back of the car looking up at the sky. It's all pinky-red dashed with silver. There are long golden clouds, mixing with evening light, behind darkening trees.

On the way home, Da stops at Luigi's and gets fish and chips. They eat their dinner in the car.

CHAPTER 19

Annette

Yellow lady coming going over under back and not. Stays longer now time for this. Come to speak. Sounding words out. Doctor lady. Here to help. With pen and black book for writing words not spoken. Square book with big letter reading open on bed.

'Annette, this is a huge improvement. Really it is.' Little word line falls from pink moving up down in out doctor lady mouth.

Not this. This mouth. Dry. Barren. Black book opens. Turns. Scribble. Scratch scrawl.

'Let's try it again, shall we? Can we do that, Annette?' Pen tick-clicking on doctor white teeth. Bottom. Top teeth close down. Little space. Left for clicking. Ticking. Tick talking face like white silver heart shape remembered. Changing shape in coming-going in-out moving head. Look. Up. Look. Down. Doctor writes scribble scrawl.

'It's all about practice and, of course, patience.'

Smiling. Patient. Waiting. Patient. Smiling for smiles. Waiting for patient.

Something inside moving. Black creeping thing. Quick. Creeping dark inside thing scurries crawling soundless in falling-down mouth. All over legs push tickle down. Up to move sudden forward and back again. Sudden up. Sudden down.

'So let's try it again, Annette. Once more. Take your time now. JEH-nee.' Pink mouth doctor pulling lips over white teeth.

Black body heavy falling pushes down pulling-up running legs. Clipping in silence to fill up empty mouth.

'JE-NEE.' Half mouth half slow half opens. Close. Gums crawl back. Pull away over red gums hard. Leave fright. Off-white teeth too big.

'Excellent, Annette. Well done. Now can you try to say JAY-Kub?' Pink lips purse.

Stick spindle flicking legs clogging breath break forwards and back. Side to side. Light stabbing skitters in dripping mouth. Glue-filament spit congeals to choke on teeth loosened.

'JA-CAB.'

'Well done, Annette. Well done.'

Wide back. Push out teeth. Make way for standing fangs. Leg-long knees quiver in cracks then patter to scurry creep creeping thing deeper. Perfect! Doctor lips smile in nod up-down head. End rangy hairs stretching forward move to bend quick terrible flicks. Fangs click-click-clicking. A million sightless eyes watch twitching. Sudden scuttles under tongue to lurk laying silent eggs.

JE-NEE.

JA-CAB.

JA-cob.

JeN-nE.

Tasting names on tongue. Swollen. Hold them to savour. Remember. Save for later.

'Well, Annette, you can say the two most important names in the whole world now. Isn't that right? Well done.' Doctor lady turning page. Open book. Pictures. Colours. Letters big. Smaller words. Pointing pink nail to follow sound moving in lines. Lipstick smile. 'Annette, can you give me the word?' Tip. Tap.

Word shapes rising. Floating up to wide open mouth. Snow White. Wicked old witch shrivelled black. Remember. Remember. Remember. Sore in voice. Dead or sleeping for kisses in glass box sealed. Wide triangle sound rising in back of ripped throat. Green. Red poison drains away shredding tongue. Open mouth falls shut swallowing back silent sound. It is gone. Burned away glowing white.

'AP-pel.' Yellow lady's eye searching something in fade-away face. 'Say it after me. Take your time now. There's no hurry.'

'AP-L.' Breathe out broken rasps. Wicked old mirror witch is back and darkness swallows running away child chasing huntsman.

'Excellent. Now, Annette, can you point to the yellow ball, for me, this time?' Turn page. New picture shapes turn. Colours mix changing names. Sounds falter. Unsure. Lost.

Yellow lady waiting patient. Mouth spider sleeping. Yellow colouring in smiles on cold fridge. Finger moving over triangle blue and heart shape red, over green square to find yellow sun. 'Well done. Now can you say BA-LL? Ba Ba B is for ball.'

'BA-ll.'

'Good.' Scribble scratch lady book with pen. Finger lip touching tongue to turn over page. Lipstick smile. 'Now let's try C. Ca Ca. C is for cat. CA-at.' Tapping nail tap tap tap picture. 'CA-at.' Softer now. Whispered out *t* so t.

'CA-KE.'

'Well, yes, C is for cake. Good. Good. Good. Can you say CA-at? If you can say CA-ke you can say CA-at, Annette. This is great. Really great.' Smile.

'CAND-LS.'

'Candles? Yes. Candles! Very good, Annette, Excellent. Now can we try CA-at?' Smile.

'Ca-t.'

'Excellent.' Scribble scratch lady writing book into turning pages. 'D-og.' Finger tap tap tap. 'Do you have a dog, Annette?' Smile.

'CAND-LES. CA-KE. JE-NEE.'

'Well now, isn't that wonderful, Annette? Making sentences already. Super! D-og.'

'D-Og.'

'Very good, Annette. Now let's try the next one.' Finger tap tap tap. 'E-gg.' Lipstick smile.

Humpty egg falling. No eggs. No. Cake not making for candles new. All gone horses of king sitting on walls. Egg crack. Broken. *Gone into flowers. Forget.* Throat burning too hot fire. Scratch away. Tear out. Breath shouts.

'Annette, are you okay? Can I get you anything? A sip of water maybe?' Standing up lady pouring water. Jug. Plastic cup. Straw. Sucking water halfway. Stop. Again better. Higher. Higher. Higher. Scribble. Scratch. Write for later. 'You can do it, Annette. Take a good hard suck up. This is great for strengthening those muscles.' Smile.

Water rising and release into mouth feeling its freshness burst like spring raw. More run run away. Escape back away. Down dribble straw back into cup.

'Well done, Annette. I know it's hard, Annette, but you've done very well today. And each time, each day it will be that little bit easier. Baby steps, Annette, baby steps.' Lipstick. Smile.

CHAPTER 20

Jenny

Dear Ma,

I hope you are feeling better? Granny keeps saying she's going to bring us up to see you, real soon, but she never does. She says anyway you'll be home before we know it. But she's been saying that for months and months. She says that you are very busy with all the doctors this week and that maybe next week would be better.

Me and Iliona went swimming on Monday. It wasn't very hot. The sky was grey-white and milky all day. But it wasn't cold either. The water was freezing at first but then after a while it was okay. And it's worse if you stand around waiting for the waves to splash you so cold your whole body goes stiff for a minute and your arms fly up round your ears. It's better to pretend you can't feel anything at all and just take a big breath and jump in. Iliona's ma was with us. Her name is Anna and she has lovely red hair. She doesn't like the cold water so she just sat on the beach, with their dog Olaf, watching us and making sure we didn't go out too far. Ma, can we get a dog?

On Tuesday, it was raining so Granny took us to The FunZone, but she said that's the last time she's ever going there because she says that place was designed specially for kids to kill themselves stone dead in, what with all a them feckin' balls and slides and floatin' windows. On

Wednesday morning I met Iliona in the park. Her little brother Kristoff was with her. And, Ma, he is very sick. He is in a wheelchair and he looks very yellow. He can only half talk out of the side of his mouth, but he smiles the biggest smile I've ever seen when Iliona sings 'For The First Time in Forever' for him. It's like his wheelchair falls away and he floats up out of it, he's that happy. He is seven. But he still wears nappies and he can't go on the swings, so we spent the whole morning telling him stories to make him laugh. Then we brought him to the shop, to get ice cream. He loves ice cream. Iliona says that's because it's soft and cool and that helps him eat it.

Oh, and Auntie Eleanor got a new car. She brought me and Jacob out for a drive on Friday. Well, it's not really a car. It's too big to be a car, and it's not really a jeep either. It's too small to be a jeep. Auntie Eleanor says she thinks it's called a Crossover or something, but she's not really sure. It has black windows you can see out through from inside, but you can't see in through them from the outside and it has the biggest sunroof I've ever seen, like the whole roof bit is made of glass and it has two little televisions in the back, attached to the backs of the front seats. Imagine that, Ma! Nobody is allowed to eat in it, not even Saidhbhe. Ma, Saidhbhe can speak Spanish! A woman comes to their house every Wednesday to teach her. Even in the summer time! Granny says that is just ridiculous and would Auntie Eleanor not just lay off and let Saidhbhe be a child a little bit longer. Auntie Eleanor says that she thinks Saidhbhe is very clever. Granny says that every mother thinks their child is a genius and that if she's such a brilliant genius she'll still be a brilliant genius when she's finished being a child! Auntie Eleanor made a secret face at Granny, and then, when Granny was busy, she took me and Jacob and Saidhbhe out for a drive in her new car. She said she'd *love to be a teacher. I can't imagine Auntie Eleanor as a teacher. Can you, Ma? We all went to the playground and Jacob had a brilliant time there. We all did. Saidhbhe kept trying to walk up the snake slide, but just when she'd get to the top, she'd flop down, and slide backwards on her bum to the bottom again. And Jacob can go across the little bridge thing, all on his own, Ma. The three of us went on the roundabout and we were on it so long that we got dizzy and everything kept spinning round and round even when we got off. I hid up in the tower for Hide and Seek, and Jacob found me after only about a minute. He was the first one up the ladder, when we had a race. Auntie Eleanor took loads and loads of photos to show you. But my favourite one is the one she took of Jacob on the swing. He's laughing so hard that his eyes are just like slits and the whole bottom part of his face is just his wide-open mouth and all his teeth. And I was pushing him, but you can't see me, in the picture, so it looks like he's swinging all on his own. It's brilliant, Ma. Auntie Eleanor says she's going to get it framed and bring it up to the hospital for you. And you will just want to keep smiling when you see it.*

But, Ma, the really best part of the whole afternoon was when we were coming out of the playground. We met Jane-Anne and her cousin Elizabeth, and Auntie Eleanor made sure that they saw us getting into her car. She started calling my name and pointing over across the road, to where the car was parked, pretending that I didn't know where it was, and she was just showing me, and she was so loud that everybody who passed started to look around to see where it was, too.

Auntie Eleanor says she's going to bring me and Saidhbhe and of course Iliona to the North Pole to see Santa at Christmas time. I asked her if Jacob could come too and I said that he would love it and that he'd be no trouble at all coz I would mind him. Auntie Eleanor says she'd love to bring Jacob, but she'd be afraid he wouldn't like the plane and that his ears might hurt. She says it's something to do with going up so high but that we could bring him back a brilliant present. So, I decided then that maybe Jacob should stay here with Granny instead coz, Ma, I wouldn't like Jacob to cry with a pain in his ears. Iliona will be fine. She's been on lots of planes. Sometimes she goes back to Poland to visit her granny on a plane.

Her granny's name is Alsa Reszczynski and she lives up on the side of a mountain with lots of goats and some sheep. They have little tink-a-ling bells round their necks, so they can't get lost. She makes cheese and sells it in her village. And Iliona says it snows a lot on her granny's mountain. One time when she was there she said there was so much snow that the whole place looked like the little world in Granny's snow globe. They couldn't leave the mountain for weeks but Iliona said it was so beautiful that nobody cared about going any place else. And when you went up higher and looked back down at the village it was magical, like a fairy tale. The houses are made of wood and they are built in the shape of triangles and they glow fiery-orange against the dark blue night sky. So Iliona won't mind the cold in the North Pole too much either.

Da says he wishes Granny lived up the side of some feckin' mountain in Poland. But then he says he'd feel bad for the poor old goats.

And, Ma, do you know what Lonely did on Thursday? He jumped out of his bowl and splatted himself on the ground. I was in Iliona's house, but Jacob was here. He found him on the kitchen floor, and Da says it was just in the nick of time too, and that Lonely wouldn't have made it one minute longer if Jacob hadn't rescued him and given him to Da to put back in the water. He is smaller now than

he was before the big jump, and he is a different colour.
But Da says that happens to fish in the summer. The
sunlight causes them to change from orange to yellowy-
gold and because of the heat they don't eat so much and
so they lose weight and they look smaller. And Da thinks
we believe him. He looked so excited about all the
changes and the sunlight and stuff that I think he started
to believe the story himself so, I didn't like to tell him that
this new fish is not Lonely!

Ma, Granny says your right arm is still a bit sore. I hope it
feels better soon.

I love you, Ma,
Jenny

Jenny picks up the book lying beside her on the bed and studies
the strange-looking creature on the front cover. She can't decide
if it's a dinosaur dressed up as an eagle or if it's a dragon that
thinks it's a flying horse. But, certainly, there are bits of horse,
dragon, dinosaur and bird all together in this beast. And Jenny's
not sure if it's feathered or made out of steel. She's not sure if
it's scary or cute. She can't even decide on the colours washing
through it as browns turn to greenish-blues which then turn to
greys and back to browns again. The big front claws of the
Dragon-Horse-Dinosaur-Bird look ready for anything that
might fly up at it through that dark night of the full yellow-plate
moon. Harry and Hermione are clinging either to the neck or
the head of the thing that's made up of so many other things.
Like a mongrel, Jenny supposes. Da says a mongrel is a dog
with no real class of his own. He might have the brain of a
sheep dog with the heart of a terrier and the coat of a whippet.
He's a bit a one thing and maybe quarter of another so he's
not really any breed at all unless you come up with some stupid
fancy name for the poor little fucker like Labradoodle or
Cockapoo or Puggle or Schnoodle and sell him and all his pups

off for a fortune, to some eejit who thinks it's cool to have a designer dog with legs that are too short for the size of his body or with not enough room in his face to breathe properly. Jenny thinks Harry Potter could definitely have a Puggle or Schnoodle!

She reads her letter out loud to Harry and Hermione and they seem to agree that it is a good letter. A letter Ma would like. Then she arranges the book and the letter beside her on the pillow and lying down, she rests her hand on them both, feeling Ma almost there with her again, the two of them lying together on top of her quilt, reading side by side in the yellow glow of the lamp, drifting off into a world of magic and spells and adventure. She hears Ma's voice and the sound of her breathing in the silence they used to fill out together, here, in Jenny's room.

Tomorrow she'll give Granny the letter to post off to Ma.

CHAPTER 21

Jacob

Jacob sits on the couch tap-tapping the screen.

'Get that thing away from your face or your eyes'll go square! And then ya'll go blind!' Granny's words rise and break, like tiny falling crystals over Jacob's head.

More words flash on the screen. The words are red. They are big words.

'ENTER THE MUSHROOM KINGDOM,' Jenny tells Jacob.

Jacob presses ENTER. Dit dit dit dit dit dit.

'Ssssh. Keep it down, you two!'

The big green turtle swallows Mario. Mario is dead.

'MOVE CURSOR ON MARIO,' Jenny says in a big voice, looking at more big words on the screen.

'Jenny, not so loud,' Granny says, like she's shouting a big whisper.

Jacob touches the button. The button is small. Mario stands up. Jacob makes Mario run with his pushing-down finger. Dit dit dit dit dit dit.

'Another five minutes now, Jacob. Then I'm takin' that thing away.'

Mario's white glove smashes Granny's words into the mouth of the plant with the big yellow teeth. Pow. Pow. Pow. Mario walks across the screen. Jacob tap-taps the screen.

RETURN. NEW GAME. SELECT.

Red and white spotted mushrooms grow up from the ground. Jacob watches the twisting-round circles at the bottom of the screen. Jacob hands Jenny the game.

'You want to go back to the beginning?' Jenny presses the button in the corner.

START AGAIN.

The screen is black. The words on the screen are white. Jenny tells Jacob all the white words on the black screen.

THERE IS A PROPHECY IN THE MUSHROOM KINGDOM.

IT SAYS MUSHROOM KINGDOM WILL FALL AND RISE AGAIN.

THIS PROPHECY WAS LONG FORGOTTEN BY ALL THE MUSHROOM PEOPLE BECAUSE NO EVIL CAME UPON THEM.

UNTIL BOWSER SHOWED UP.

> KNOWING THE PROPHECY
> PRINCESS PEACH SURRENDERED.

> THE KINGDOM FELL
> INTO GREAT SORROW.

Jacob tap-taps his press-button finger into his knee.

'Pick the Koop!' Jenny points at the spinning turtle-circle on the screen. Jacob presses the green circle. The turtle spins.

'Granny, can I go over to Iliona's house for a while? I'll be back for me tea.'

Bang. Bang. Bang. Mario boxes. The green turtle head falls down into white smoke. Mario flies through all the green and orange colours. Down. Down.

'You surely can – will reduce the noise if nothin' else. But why don't you ask her round here for her tea? You're always over there. They must think you don't have one to look up nor down at ya! I'm sure she's a grand little girl.'

Green thing. Mario falls on to the green thing in the orange sea. Red thing. The red thing opens its big black mouth to eat Mario. Dit dit dit dit dit dit. Mario runs into the red thing's eyes. Splat. Jacob laughs.

'I'll ask her, but I don't think she'll be able to come. She has to mind her little brother. I'm going over to help her. Her ma's in work.'

Mario jumps on a cloud. It is white and moving. The white-moving cloud goes inside a big black circle. Mario gets smaller. The circle gets bigger. Mario is gone.

'Is that the little child in the wheelchair? God bless him.'

Mario is back. Mario jumps up and down on the cloud in the blue mushroom sky. Clang. Clang. Clang. Clang. Jacob makes Mario break through a face on the castle. Smash. Smash. The face breaks into small pieces. The face is gone.

'How did you know about Iliona's brother?'

Mario falls on the red floor. There are two grey clouds on the wall behind Mario's head. They are not happy clouds. They have upside-down smiles.

'Ah, sure don't ya know it was Lizzie, below in the shop, who told me. Sure, doesn't that one know everything about everybody and what she doesn't know she makes up! She's only happy when she's spreadin' gossip. Course ya'd never know a thing about her own though, cute enough. She knows that child's family, I suppose, through the shop.' Granny looks into the corner.

Jacob makes Mario run into the centre of the screen. A yellow thing with red hair runs into the centre to get Mario. The yellow thing comes from the other side. Jacob bang-bangs. Mario bang-bangs. The yellow thing bang-bangs.

Jenny turns to Jacob. 'You be okay while I'm gone?'

Mammy is gone.

Mario hides behind a big yellow knee. Dah. Dah. Dah. Dah. Dit. Dit. Dit. Dit.

'I won't be long.' Jenny's voice is small, like Mario. Jacob stares at the screen. 'Don't let him punch ya like that, Jacob. Stand up for yourself!'

Bang. Bang. Bang. Too late. The yellow thing throws flashing orange balls. The twirling orange balls hit Mario. Mario turns into something else. The cursor flashes.

'Right. Now that's enough a that for today.' Granny takes Mario away.

'Next time we'll get him, I promise ya, Jacob,' Jenny says.

Jenny touches Jacob's knee. Granny puts Mario into her bag. Jacob goes to the window. It should be blue like the sky. It is grey like the upside-down Mario-clouds. Jacob squints into the light.

Where's Mammy? Tap-tap.

Daddy is asleep in the chair. His mouth is hanging open. He's making little breath sounds in his nose.

Mr Magpie where is your wife? Tap-tap.

'Sssssh!' Granny holds her finger straight like a pencil at her mouth. 'Your daddy's tired.'

Tap tap tap. Jacob's finger presses the window. Jenny is getting smaller outside. Then Jenny is gone.

'Do you want to do a jigsaw, Jacob?' Granny looks for the box. 'How about this one?'

Jacob tap-taps the window. Two-finger tapping is sometimes better than one. Mr Magpie is back. Jacob scratches the top of his forehead. Mr Magpie is black and white. Sometimes the black turns blue and green. Then it is black again. Mr Magpie stands in the grass looking for something he can't find. He folds his wing hands up behind his back. The lost thing is in the grass. Jacob tap taps the window. Mr Magpie tap-taps the ground. Mr Magpie looks up and all around then tap-taps some more at the ground. Tap tap tap.

'Jesus, Mae-Anne, what time is it? Ya should a woke me.' Jacob hears Daddy making words and sentences behind his back. Daddy yawns.

'So now it's suddenly my fault you're sleepin' in the middle a the day!' Granny makes words and sentences too.

'But I wanted to head up early this evenin' before she gets too tired. Where's Jenny?' Daddy's sentences are longer than Granny's.

Mr Magpie stands on the side of Jacob's red frisbee. It is upside down in the grass so Jacob can't see the stars on the front. The stars are all gone into the grass. Mr Magpie hop-hops around the side and dips his beak in to drink the water inside. He looks up and around. Then he dips his beak down and in again.

'She's gone round to her friend's house. That little Polish

girl. Ilione, or somethin' like that, she calls her.' Granny's words and sentences take longer to say.

Another magpie falls into the garden. Her feet land on the grass. She folds her black and white arms behind her back.

'What? Again? She's always there these days. I've never even met the child.'

'Grand bit a distraction for her all the same. She needs that at the moment.'

'I suppose she does. Anyway, I'd best be off before the traffic.'

'I've put two clean nighties in a bag and some underwear. It's on the hall table. Tell her I'll be up Friday, please God. What about your dinner?'

'I'll get a sandwich when I'm there.'

'Suit yourself.'

Mr Magpie bob-bobs his head. He flicks his long tail up and down. He throws up his arms like he's going to fly away. But he doesn't. Daddy gets smaller. So does his voice. Daddy waves at Jacob from the end of the garden. Then Daddy is gone.

'Jacob, can you find Thomas's head? I can't.' Granny holds one jigsaw piece up in her hand.

Mr and Mrs Magpie nod and bob at each other. Mr Magpie has a drink. Mrs Magpie looks around. Mrs Magpie puts her beak into Jacob's frisbee. Mr Magpie looks around. Jacob looks around. Granny looks under the couch. Granny picks up another jigsaw piece. She turns it around in her fingers. She finds a place for it on the floor.

'Ah, give us a hand, Jacob! Ya like this one.'

Jacob does a circle around Granny like a big silent O. He goes back to the window. Tap tap tap. Mr and Mrs Magpie are gone. Something's wrong. Something's not right. Jacob tap-taps small circles around on the glass.

'Ah, now we're gettin' places.' Granny finds another eye for Thomas's face.

Mr Magpie is back. He stands in the garden, with his hands

behind his back, looking at Jacob. Jacob scratches the top side
of his forehead, dips his head into the glass. Granny feels around
on the mat for Gordon's green carriage. Granny takes off her
glasses. Granny rubs her eyes. Granny puts her glasses back
up on her nose. Jacob circles around Granny. Jacob likes circles.
Gordon is bigger than Thomas. Thomas is blue. Gordon is
green. Mr Magpie is black and white. Sometimes he is blue
and green. Mrs Magpie is gone. Granny makes a bridge for
Thomas. Granny finds one side of Thomas's smile.

'Oh God don't ya just hate when there's a piece missin'?'
Granny searches the floor. Granny turns the box upside
down. Granny tap-taps the top. Jacob makes a bigger circle
around Granny. Jacob goes back to the window. Mrs Magpie
is back. She changes into violet and green. Her tail is long
like a dark rainbow. Mrs Magpie looks sad like Granny. Mrs
Magpie looks up in the air. Granny looks under the mat.
Jacob looks out the window.

The telephone ding-a-lings in the hall. Granny gets up off
the floor.

'Jesus, this knee is givin' me awful trouble this weather, Jacob.
I'll be back in a minute.'

Mrs Magpie hops up on to the window outside. Granny's
voice is smaller now. Mrs Magpie's eyes are yellow. They are
round like small holes at the sides of her head.

'Hello.' Granny's voice is different.

'Ah, how are you?'

Jacob tap-taps the glass. Mrs Magpie opens her mouth like she
is going to talk.

'I was in yesterday but that young one was there. What's her
name?'

'Aye, that's her. Nice girl. Must have missed you.'

'Not so bad now, thank God. Ah, it's slow going but she's getting there.'

'That's right.'

Mrs Magpie closes her mouth. She looks sad.

'No. Not yet.'

'Ah, yes, a few words now, thank God. Mind you, it's very slurred. She gets a bit confused. Like one minute she knows you and the next she's not too sure. She has good days and bad days, I suppose. It would rip the heart clean out of you to see her.'

'Yes. That's true. Fell out in clumps.'

Mrs Magpie tap-taps the window.

'They don't know. Could be the shock or the treatment. It's rare but it can happen, according to the doctors anyway.'

Jacob tap-taps the glass.

'Something about the immune system. Could be permanent. But please God, it won't be.'

Mrs Magpie lowers her head.

'Very agitated at times. She's frustrated. Sure, ya can imagine yourself.'

Jacob touches his hair.

'She's usin' the walker. Just a few steps now but sure it's some-thin' I suppose. She gets very, very tired. The doctor, though, said that was to be expected.'

Mrs Magpie has long feet. She has curling-up-and-under toes.

'Well, this is it.'

Jacob tap-taps the window. Jacob wriggles his toes.

'Ah, they're all very good to her there, all the same.'

Mrs Magpie tap-taps the window.

'No. Kevin's just gone. I'll go Friday, please God.'

Mrs Magpie opens her mouth. She makes a sound but it is not like talking. It is like squeaking. Or laughing.

'No. No. They're all right. Jenny's grand, really. She misses her, a course she does, but she's tough and she's strong and sure doesn't she have that little friend of hers to play with. Bit of company for her, ya know. It's poor Jacob I worry about more. He's so lonely lookin'. He misses her somethin' terrible. He's very, very close to her. Ya know yourself now what little boys are like about their mammies! Sure isn't she the anchor in his whole life! He's lost, really he is, without her.'

Granny is talking. Granny is not laughing.

'Ah, sure I know.'

'Sure, wasn't I the same with me own!'

'I believe poor Sarah Hennessy passed durin' the night. God be good to her. I was only talkin' to her at ten Mass last Sunday.'

'True enough. Sure, ya never know the minute.'

Mrs Magpie looks around.

'How is poor John goin' to cope on his own without her? The poor divil.'

'Really? No, I hadn't heard that now.'

'He did not! When? I don't believe ya!'

Mr Magpie is back.

'Ah, sure isn't an inch as good as a mile to a blind horse and isn't time the father of all truth!'

'That's right. He was.'

Mr Magpie tap-taps the grass.

'Sure, he wasn't much use to her when she was alive. And her beatin' her way up to the chapel every morning before goin' to clean for Fr Timmons and him lyin' home in the bed.'

'Oh, sure, now, don't I know. Don't be talkin' to me.'

'Ah now, there's never smoke without fire!'

'I will, of course. Thanks, Lizzie. God bless.'

Granny is back. Mr Magpie is gone.

'How about we have our dinner soon, Jacob?'

Mrs Magpie hops back down into the garden. She is smaller now.

'It's your favourite!'

Jacob tap-taps the window.

'Will you come out and help me set the table?'

Mrs Magpie looks up in the sky.

'And I have ice cream for afters. With chocolate sauce.'

Mrs Magpie tap-taps the grass.

'Ah, Jacob, ya know, pet, I'd cut the tongue outta me own mouth and give it to ya along with every word I ever knew, too, if I could, child.'

Mrs Magpie is gone.

CHAPTER 22

Jenny

'Ah, ya can see the evenings slippin' away all the same,' Granny says. Her face is a dark cloud and she says she can feel the winter creeping into her bones – 'like an auld fox sniffin' for hens in the night', especially into her bad-knee bone.

And Granny is right. Jenny watches the night coming a bit earlier and then a bit earlier each day. There's a taste of something bad in the air, like something that might slither and fall out of the dark and change things.

It's nearly time and Jenny hates it. The rain has stopped. The sun is shining. There's something awful lying in the bottom of her stomach. The strawberries are all gone and so are the swimming togs. Every day feels like Sunday night and there's nothing Jenny can do to stop it happening.

Everywhere she looks there are mothers getting their children's hair cut or they're buying long socks and grey skirts and sticky-white labels and colouring pencils. The whole world is getting ready. The Minnie Mouse lunch boxes are all on the top shelf in the Two Euro shop and the hurleys and runners are all back in the sports shop window again. Tesco have put all the uniforms out at the front of the shop where the long flowery dresses and bikinis were last week. The Coke and the Fanta are gone, replaced by millions of copies with forty pages or eighty pages or 120 pages, 'If you're really bright,' Granny says, all covered in plastic. Even the telly won't let her forget.

Every time Jenny turns it on there's a stupid song or a stupid voice telling her all about little Emma and her €4.29 skirt. Little Emma's mum is busy packing little Emma's half-price Petits Filous and crayons and smoothie into her new Minnie Mouse lunch box. And when little Emma's not smiling into the sitting room, it's little Sean, in his €4.25 pants, staring out at her instead. And his mum is busy packing his *one euro for six pens* and his half-price Cheesestrings into one of his *two for the price of one* Thomas the Tank Engine school bags. Sean and Emma's mums buy loads of €2 tissues, in nice coloured-y boxes, to wave their little ones off. Granny says she can't Wait till they go back.

Even Supervalue and Lidl send things in through the letter box, with *Back to School Lunch Box Ideas* they think are great. There's pitta breads with sweet corn and tuna stuffed inside and tortilla wrap things with ham and cheese and tomato and loads of other things shoved into the middle, that nobody would ever bring to school for their lunch even if their ma was here to get up at seven o'clock in the morning to make fancy things like that. The Kellogg's chicken is going to give everybody free books and free day trips to castles if they go *Back to School*, too. In England!

And then Granny says, 'Let's cover them books!' and she takes out a roll of wallpaper from her bag. 'I had it left over, from the sittin' room. No use lettin' it go to waste!'

Jenny looks at all the flowers and tries to imagine her copies and books covered in little bits of Granny's front room. Jane-Anne's copies will be colour-coded with smiley face stickers showing off her name.

'What about the clear stuff in Cut Price?' Jenny says, feeling the sponginess of Granny's walls between her finger and thumb. 'Ma always used to get that for our books.'

'Right so, pet,' Granny says, putting the thick wallpaper flowers back into her bag.

Granny rolls the contact paper out on the table. She has the scissors, the roll of wallpaper and the Sellotape at the ready. 'Just in case this feckin' contactin' business doesn't work,' she says looking down at the books suspiciously.

She studies all the little red squares on the papery back of the clear plastic and placing the first book down upon it, she seems to count, with her fingers, the number of squares to the side and the number she needs from the top and from the bottom. She cuts along the lines and uses both hands to flatten out the curling-up sides. Trying to pull the paper bit away from the clear sticky bit isn't as easy as it looks. Starting at the corners she tries to find a way to separate them. But she can't no matter how close she holds it up to her face. Eventually she just bites into it and rips one away from the other, throwing the paper part on to the floor and, using both hands, she holds the clear bit in place on the table.

'Put that book down, now!' she shouts, like she's either saving a life or going to kill something.

Jenny quickly places her maths book down on to the clear plastic, but Granny's hands are still in the way.

'Move your hands,' Jenny says.

'I'm tryin',' Granny answers, but the more she tries the more the clear stuff sticks back to itself, doubling over and making itself into a new shape that will never fit. Because it's not even a shape now. It's definitely not the big square she cut out in the first place. It's an almost shape but that won't do.

Then Jenny tries to separate the contact from itself but the more she peels and pulls the more it seems to resist and curl in on itself again. The stickiness just transfers on to their hands and when Jenny does finally manage to flatten it and smooth it over it just creases and crinkles even more, making little bubbles and pockets of cat hair all over the front of her book.

'Jesus Christ, who invented this stuff?' Granny says. 'The divil himself!'

So, Jenny goes back to school because Granny says she has to but it's not *Grand* or *Lovely*, like Granny says it'll be and it's not like she never left the place and she'll be delighted to see all her little friends again either.

When Jenny arrives in the school yard, Jane-Anne is picking out the people she wants for her best friends this year from the line that she's made. The most likely to be chosen are at the top, the least likely at the end. Beth Malone cries when Jane-Anne tells her to sit down because she's too fat.

Jenny stands to the side and waits for the bell. When Mrs Nicholson opens the door, she looks different. She smiles at the children and welcomes them back to school.

The morning passes slowly.

After little break, Mrs Nicholson has to go out for a minute, to meet a new student who has just arrived late. The children whisper names and make guesses about who or what it may be.

'Sssssssssh,' Jane-Anne says, with her pointing finger covering her lips and tipping the end of her nose. 'Teacher left ME in charge, so No Talking!'

Jenny doesn't remember Teacher leaving anyone in charge. She looks at all the confused summer faces around her. No one says a word.

Jane-Anne stands up at the board and asks everybody where they went on their summer holidays. She tells them all about Mickey Mouse and Thunder Mountain and about all the jewels and gold in Cinderella's Castle in Disneyland.

'So where did you go?' she asks, and everyone looks round the room, like the question is a ball bouncing from wall to wall.

Jenny knows those faces; everybody is hoping they don't catch Jane-Anne's ball and that she's aiming at the person behind them. Jenny sees all the heads lowering. Carrie Doyle roots for nothing in her bag and she doesn't find it.

'I'm talking to You!' Jane-Anne says in her new teacher voice. 'You with the funny head lice haircut.'

The whole room seems to sigh with relief. The walls buckle then straighten. All the heads look round and smile crooked smiles, like sorry smiles offered up for Jenny though they're not sorry, at all. Jenny knows. Not one bit. Smiles that try to stay small because too curved would show happy mouths – too many teeth. But still they smile, even though they don't mean to.

Jenny thinks she's going to get sick.

'I went to Timbuktu for three weeks with my family,' Jenny says, sitting up straighter, but as soon as the lie is out in the room she can feel it sticking back on to her cheeks, making them red and hot and she can't control it anymore.

It spreads into her neck like an awful disease and leaks back into her tongue again. Her brain feels thinner, like it's empty even though it's boiling over with pictures and words she can't grasp. Why hadn't she said somewhere else, like Westmeath or Wexford? Wexford is nice. It's the bum bit of the teddy bear map of Ireland, on the wall. It is blue and its little tail juts out into the sea and it is long enough to go for a holiday in. Why had she lied such a big stupid lie about a place Da made up, to trick Granny when she says, 'And Where Were You?' And there are lots of castles in Wexford. She could have stayed in one of those castle hotels she's seen on the telly. Her room would have been right at the top of a tower. That's the most expensive room in the hotel but she doesn't mind because when she walks in, she sees how beautiful it is.

'The photos will be brilliant!' she would have said, looking out at the blue-sparkling river, beneath her window. Then she would see the four-poster bed. 'Isn't it magnificent?' she would have whispered to Jacob. 'Look at the velvet curtains and matching velvet quilt.'

But Jacob would have been too busy opening the box of

chocolates on the velvet pillow. 'Look at all the chocolates!' Jacob would have said. 'The fairies must have left them here for us!' Jenny would have known that it was the maid who had left them, but she wouldn't have told Jacob that. 'How did the fairies know we were here?' Jacob would have asked, holding up his two hands, like he had an invisible ball or an invisible apple in each one.

There's a fire in the big fireplace in the room, not because it is cold outside, it's not, but because castles always have fires, even in summer. There are so many logs stacked up in the corner that the woodcutter would have been exhausted.

'Let's get ready,' Jenny would have said, 'we're going pony-trekking with Ma in a minute and then we'll be playing tennis on the court, down there, just under the balcony.'

'But I thought that was a blue-sparkling river?' Jacob would have said, like he's just remembered what was outside the window and it wasn't that!

'The tennis court is beside the river!' Jenny would have said, sounding funny and excited and a little bit embarrassed. 'And then we are meeting Da for dinner, when he's finished playing golf!' Jenny would have explained everything to Jacob, so he would have known what to expect.

'Da? Playing golf?' Jacob would have laughed, spitting bits of chocolate all over the golden stripy wallpaper. 'Now I know you are telling me stories, Jenny!'

And the two of them would have sat up on the bed together, imagining Da playing golf, and eating all the chocolates left by the fairies.

'Oh really?' Jane-Anne says, ripping their holiday apart. She looks like she's just won a big shiny bike or a holiday for four in Jenny's Castle Hotel for coming first in The Father Fennell Essay Writing Competition, she's that happy.

'Yes. Really,' Jenny says, looking away and then back again. Her voice feels bigger and louder than it should. Her teeth are sore. Everything inside her body falls down, like when you put your foot through an imaginary step in your sleep and you jerk forward into the air. And her insides slither down further past her tummy, into her knees, before she feels the choking vomit, which is welling up in her ankles.

There isn't a sound in the room. Everybody else holds their breath like they are just about to go underwater so there's more air for Jenny's voice to fill up. And she wants to stop talking but she can't.

'It's really nice and warm there and the people are lovely and so is the beach. And my whole family came, and we stayed in a lovely hotel on the beach and we only wore bikinis for the whole time we were there and flowers in our hair, coz you have to do that – it's so hot.'

As Jenny recalls her holiday abroad she starts to feel the sun on her skin; she smells salt in the air. The words come out of her mouth so fast it's like the wildebeest charge in *The Lion King*. And the words stick together, making pictures. Jenny colours them in with more words and they swirl around over the other children's heads. Jenny tells them all about the elephant she befriended and the terrified zebra she saved from a sabre-tooth tiger. Of course, there were all the fancy dinners and jeeps too and just when she thinks she's finished then over the cliff come a whole pile more wildebeest words and lies about camels and baby giraffes and treasure and pirates and snakes.

She tells Jane-Anne how she was made princess of the whole island on the second day they were there. She catches sight of herself in a gold dress with glitter straps, sitting on a throne made of leaves and coconut trees. She wears a flower crown in her hair. Later she'll have to go to funerals and parades and stuff and wave at the crowds who have come a very long way just to see her. But she doesn't mind. She's the judge of the parade. Everywhere she looks there are lights in the trees and reflected in dancing colour shapes on the water. The women are shaking their hips and dancing in swirls. They have pink grass skirts that rustle and flick, coconut bras, black feathers in their hair. They are so happy with the flower bracelets round their wrists and their ankles that they don't even seem to notice the dancing men, with yellow snake hats, forming larger dancing circles around them. The men move like coloured birds, twisting and spinning in the light. They wear orange, square-cut shirts shimmering with beads, and white satin pants to their knees.

The room lets out a little gasp. It is tiny, but Jenny can hear it. The children straighten up in their seats, waiting to hear more of her story.

'And on the third day,' she continues, 'we went on a safari. It was in the jungle. We had lunch straight out of the trees; oranges as big as footballs, bananas and pineapples that were so sweet the taste stayed in our mouths for days afterwards. Just after lunch we were getting ready to go when we heard something rustling in the bushes. The driver took out his gun and told us all to stand back because it could be a wild beast, like a hungry lion or tiger looking for food. But I saw a small foot just under the rustling bush and I told the driver not to shoot. There were two very brown eyes staring out at us from the middle of the bush and a little hand grabbing and clawing its way through. I went closer. "Don't be afraid," I said to the eyes, "we won't hurt you." The bush opened in the middle, just like somebody had pulled down a zip, and a small boy appeared. His dark hair was down to his waist. He was very dirty and he growled quietly, showing us his teeth. When I tried to touch him, he jumped and tried to run away but Da caught him. He scratched at Da and tried to bite him but Da wouldn't let go. "It's okay. Itsokay. Isokay," Da kept on saying, over and over again. Finally, the boy stopped fighting and kicking. We asked him what his name was and why was he here, out in the jungle, all alone. He didn't answer. He couldn't answer. He didn't have any words. Then he took Da by the hand and led us through the trees, down a long winding path to a river. We walked for hours and miles, deep, deep into the jungle. When we got thirsty, we drank from a place where the water swirled in a small pool. "This is the home of the Aswathy People," the driver said. They are a warrior tribe who worship crocodiles and can only count up to two. "We must not stay here!" he said. When we did stop we were standing at a cave. "Tigers," the driver said holding up his gun. The boy pointed to the cave, then to himself. He lived with the tigers. Right there, in the middle of the jungle, this little boy lived in a cave with tigers. There were green leafy plants creeping and crawling around the rocks, above the entrance, and flowers, that looked so pink in the sunlight, it hurt our eyes to see them. Da lifted him up. "Don't worry, son," Da said, and we took the boy back to our hotel on the beach. He spent the rest of our holiday with us and we taught him new words and sentences. Da taught him how to play poker and we called him Stretch Wilde. Then one morning the owner of the hotel, a very rich man, said that he would love if Stretch Wilde would come to live with him and his wife. They didn't have any children of their own and they fell in love with Stretch the first time they saw him. Stretch is just like their own son now and they are all coming over here next year on their holidays.'

'Wow! Isn't that just a lovely story! And such a happy ending, too!' Jane-Anne says, breaking the spell. 'Why don't you come up here so and show us all on the map where Timbuktu is, exactly?' Jane-Anne points to the big coloured map on the wall.

Jenny drags her whole body up through the desks. Each step sounds much louder and feels much heavier than it should. All eyes follow her to the top of the room. Jenny prays she doesn't trip or wet her knickers or fart. She looks up once at the others. Heads turn to the side, down to the floor. Some look up at the ceiling or out through the window or they study the signs and charts on the walls, as though they have never seen them before.

Sarah Flynn squints and struggles to read big bright red letters, like they are too far away.

BULLY FREE ZONE is spread across a square patch of the wall. There's a big kid with black hair snarling at a small kid with standing-up frightened hair inside a red circle with a line cutting across it, like a NO PARKING HERE sign. Even Grammar Girl, with her curled-up ends and sun-faded face, up high on the other wall, looks away. Jenny has no idea what to do next. She tries to make herself smaller by folding her two shoulders in and up around her neck like a scarf. Maybe she'll just disappear, like Violet in *The Incredibles* or like the Cheshire Cat does in Wonderland. Something sharp seizes the back of her throat and for a moment she's back in her seat watching herself, like a ghost drifting and rattling up to the board. Her breathing goes only one way. She's pushing air out through her mouth but there's none coming in to replace it. Her eyes, stingy and dry, blur over in a burning fog. She can barely see the map.

Jenny stands at the top of the room and stares at all the colours of the world. The purples and pinks, yellows and reds, the dark greens and light greens, just fall and fade into each other, in the middle of all the blue. There is just so much blue. She can't even see Ireland and there's no arrow to say, 'You are here.' But then, just like magic, the colours seem to fade. Timbuktu lights up, in the lilac of Mali, in the head part of Africa, and the rest of the world plunges into the sea.

'Here it is. This is Timbuktu,' Jenny says, standing taller than she has ever stood before.

Carrie Doyle starts breathing again. The row behind her does too. Sarah Flynn smiles broadly, as though Jenny has just found something Sarah had lost and had spent ages and ages looking for, and she's saying, 'Thank you.' Molly Bergin leans against Sarah Kelly and giggles behind her hand. They both look up at Jane-Anne and the shock that covers her face, like chickenpox.

'Were you going to bury your mother in all that sand because it's cheaper than buying a grave?' Jane-Anne spits at Jenny, as she stands watching the room. Jane-Anne is counting faces. Remembering names. Smiles fade. Breaths fail.

'What?' Jenny asks, not understanding what Jane-Anne means, but not waiting for an answer either.

And just like her hand is not her own; like somebody else is moving it, telling it what to do, it reaches out and grabs Jane-Anne by her hair. Jenny watches herself again, this time in slow motion, pulling at Jane-Anne's long, golden curls. Pulling. Pulling. Pulling. Jenny's fingers twist in through the ends of Jane-Anne's hair, strands of it tightening around her fingers. She yanks harder. Jane-Anne's head is pulled back. Jane-Anne twists herself around, pushing Jenny to the right with her arm. Jenny can't hear a thing, even though Jane-Anne's mouth is wide open, and Jenny can see that she's screaming and screaming and screaming. Jane-Anne keeps silent screaming. Jenny keeps slow-motion pulling and pulling. She wants to stop. But she can't. She doesn't know how. Her fingers twist harder. Then Jane-Anne's hand grabs at Jenny's hair. The two of them locked together now in a tangle of squeals and shrieks. Jenny feels the tight pull near her scalp and the quick release as three or four hairs, maybe even more, are ripped from her scalp. Jenny sees more hair falling in broken strands than there actually is, but that makes no difference at all. Jenny tries to unravel her fingers. But she can't and the more she tries the more knotted they become. Jane-Anne twists and turns. She's nearly up to her elbow in Jenny's hair. Jenny doesn't know how many times Jane-Anne reaches out her other hand, trying to grab at more hair. Somebody is trying to tell them to stop. Maybe it's Jenny herself, she's not sure.

Then suddenly, out of nowhere, Mrs Nicholson appears, pulls Jenny by the arm, shoves her away with one hand and reaches for Jane-Anne with the other. The muffled buzzing in Jenny's ears snaps and she hears all the noise in the room as it gathers speed before being pushed out through the window by newer shrieks, louder cries, waiting to fill up the air. Jane-Anne is lying on the floor. Jenny presses the sleeve of her jumper up to her mouth and realises that she is shrinking, like the last and tiniest Russian doll in the middle of the set in Granny's china cabinet. She is last. She is alone. 'Jane-Anne, are you okay?' Mrs Nicholson asks, in a new voice Jenny's never heard before.

Jenny cries in the corner. Nobody asks if she's okay. Everyone in the room is looking at her and not looking at the same time. Mrs Nicholson grabs Jenny's arm and pushes her to the door. She puts her outside.

'Get up to the office Right Away. You are in Big Trouble Now, Young Lady. I Don't Care what Else is going on! We Don't allow fighting like that in Our classroom, now Do We?'

Jenny creeps along the hallway up to the office. She slither-sits and waits. She's suddenly so tired she forgets to be frightened. She feels very small now, like the chair is too big. Iliona Reszczynski comes down the hall. She is quiet today. She's got big tears slopping down her chin. She doesn't say, 'Hi.' She just sits down and puts her hand lightly over Jenny's, like she's saying, *Don't worry, everything will be fine*, with her fingers. Jenny tries smiling, but it doesn't work very well. Iliona doesn't smile back. *Today's not a day for smiling*, Jenny thinks to herself, making all the joins in her head.

Mrs Nicholson passes without a word and seeps behind the big office door, like the measles. Jenny hears low voices. The bell rings somewhere up high. Doors open, and the hallway is too bright. Children, in lines, are walked out to the yard, past Jenny. Then the doors close and Jenny sits in the dimness of midday.

Finally, the quiet is broken by the echoing sounds of swift feet coming down the hall. Jenny looks up and sees Granny getting bigger and louder as she gets nearer. Granny's face is like Ma's, but there's something else in it too, something Jenny's never seen before and she's got no name for it. Then she gets scared.

'Right. You. What happened?' Granny says, moving along past Jenny, like she's not even there.

Granny doesn't knock on the office door either. She just pushes it open and stands for a second in the light Sr Mary Assumpta keeps all for herself, inside in her room. Granny puts her hands on her hips and catches her breath. She's all shiny round the edges. Glowing gold, like a superhero, it looks like she's just about to reach into her pocket and pull out her lightning rod or her energy whip before she marches in and does brainwashing and torture on Sr Mary Assumpta.

'Please, Mrs Greene. Do come in,' rings the voice from some place inside the light.

Granny pulls Jenny in behind her. 'Now, what's goin' on?' Granny asks everybody in the room.

'Well, Mrs Greene, We Are Concerned. Very Concerned Actually. About Jennifer.' Sr Mary Assumpta speaks slowly. Her eyes grab on to Granny first. She uses her right hand to introduce Jenny to Granny, like they are strangers and not related so much, that they don't even know each other. Then her grabbing eyes get Jenny.

'Right. What has she done?' Granny's talking about Jenny but she's eye-grabbing Sr Mary Assumpta now.

'Well, Mrs Nicholson, here, was in the room when it happened.' Sr Mary Assumpta uses her flattened hand, this time, to introduce Mrs Nicholson.

Mrs Nicholson nods and clears her throat. Granny, still standing, turns her whole body to face Mrs Nicholson. Jenny doesn't remember Mrs Nicholson being there in the room when it happened. She remembers something about a new student.

'There was a fight,' Mrs Nicholson says, carefully looking around for her words. 'Jennifer quite viciously attacked another student.'

'Attacked? How do ya mean Attacked, Exactly?' Granny says, taking all of her capitals out of her bag. Granny's getting ready.

'Well, she pulled her hair. Repeatedly. And she didn't stop until the other child fainted.'

'Fainted? Oh, Sweet Jesus. Is the other child all right?' Granny says, putting her capitals away.

'She didn't faint—' Jenny says, but nobody is listening.

'Still very shaken,' Mrs Nicholson says, nodding her head, like she's agreeing with something else Granny didn't say.

Granny moves her body around again, this time facing Jenny. 'What have you got to say for yourself, child?'

Jenny can't seem to find any words.

'Jennifer has become increasingly removed from her peers,' Sr Mary Assumpta says, filling in the gaps left by the space of Jenny's silence. 'She has isolated herself from the other students, completely.'

'What? Sure, isn't she only back a couple a hours? And what about her friend, that little Polish girl?'

'Mrs Greene, Jennifer has been excluding herself for some time now. Isn't that right, Mrs Nicholson?' Sr Mary Assumpta asks, sitting back in her chair.

Everybody turns to look at Mrs Nicholson again.

'Yes, that is definitely true. I noticed it particularly in the final term last year. She refuses to mix with any of the other children either out on the yard or in the classroom and specifically asked to be allowed to sit alone during lessons,' Mrs Nicholson says, likes she's just learned the answer off by heart for a test.

'But sure, didn't she spend best part a the summer with her little friend – what's her name? Illione or somethin' like that.'

All heads look to Jenny.

'Who?' Mrs Nicholson and Sr Mary Assumpta say together, looking at each other now.

'Tell them, Jenny. Illione, isn't that her name? The child that sits beside ya?'

'Oh no, Mrs Greene,' Mrs Nicholson says, like she's just solved a big mystery, 'you are thinking about Iliona Reszczynski. Yes, she did sit beside Jennifer, but only for a short time, possibly only two or three weeks. The family moved to Longford, I think it was. She was only here for maybe a month, at the beginning of last year. Lovely child.'

Sr Mary Assumpta is busy pushing buttons on her computer.

'Are ya sure?' Granny says, with a new wrinkle between her eyes.

'Quite sure, Mrs Greene,' Sr Mary Assumpta says, moving her reading finger in straight lines across the screen. 'Iliona Reszczynski with an address at thirty Mews Meadows, attended this school last September, for a total of three and a half weeks. And yes, Mrs Nicholson, you were quite right, she is now attending school in Edgeworthstown. Lovely part of the country.'

'She said we were goin' to have to bury Ma in sand coz it's cheaper than earth,' Jenny says into the room.

Everybody turns to face Jenny again.

'What? What did ya say, child?' Granny bends down and looks straight into Jenny's burning eyes.

'Jane-Anne said so. I didn't mean to hurt her, Granny.'

'Jenny, go on back outside now, like a good child. I'll be out to ya in a minute,' Granny says, standing up straight, leaving Jenny's face behind.

Sitting outside the big closed-up door, Jenny looks at the empty space all around her. She sits on her hands. She's suddenly very cold and the clock up on the wall is too loud. She hears the big hand scratching and straining to one o'clock while the smaller ticking of the other hand passes in circles. Then Granny, drenched in light, appears before her.

'Right,' she says. 'Home!'

Jenny stands up and follows Granny back down the hall.

'You're on a couple a days' holidays, for that! But, you'll have no more trouble outta that one, pet,' Granny says over her shoulder and Jenny wonders if Granny's talking about Jane-Anne Comerford Smyth or if really she has just killed Sr Mary Assumpta and left her lying there, dead, beside the Maltesers and the picture of the Pope who died, right there on her desk.

CHAPTER 23

Jacob

Jacob eats all the apples and bananas in the bowl. He eats all the cream crackers in Granny's bag and all the bits of pizza-cheese stuck to the side of the bin. Jacob looks around the kitchen for the fluffy pink and white biscuits Granny makes like magic come out of the press.

There is a big glass rectangle on the table. Lonely's bowl used to be there. Before. The bowl is not there now. The rectangle is green. Like left-over rain. Jacob can't see any biscuits.

Jacob stares into the deep yellowy-green inside the rectangle. It is very dark, like black, except for the light at the side. Like daytime and night-time mixing together inside the wobbling, up-down water. Lonely is gone.

Jacob goes back to the counter. He opens a drawer. He closes it again. It clanks and rattles. Jacob comes back to the table.

Lonely's bowl is not there now. Not there now is the same as gone. Porridge comes in a bowl. So does soup. Granny puts apples and bananas in a bowl on the counter. Bowls are round like fluffy pink and white biscuits are round. And frisbees. Frisbees are round. Lonely doesn't like soup or frisbees. Lonely likes bowls and swimming.

Jacob goes back to the counter again. He opens the drawer again. He closes it again, louder this time, making bigger clanks and sharper rattles. Something clatters on the floor. Jacob can't find the biscuits. Jacob comes back to the table.

Lonely's bowl has changed into a rectangle. Jacob doesn't like rectangles. Jacob likes circles and squares. And biscuits.

Jacob goes back to the counter. Jacob looks for the biscuits. Open. Close. Bang. Clank. Rattle. Clink. Jacob comes back to the table.

Rectangles aren't circles. They are not squares. Rectangles are too big to be squares. Too pointy and sharp to be circles. Jacob doesn't like rectangles. Jacob likes circles and squares.

Jacob goes back to the counter. He opens another drawer. Open. Close. Bang. Clank. Rattle. Clink. Clatter. The biscuits are gone.

Jacob moves back to the table. There are bubbles at the top of the water. They move along in a line. It is a long line. Longer than the line of a square. Green is not a water colour. Water is blue like the sky. Trees are green. So are frogs. Cornflakes are not green. Cornflakes are orange like balloons. Jacob looks for a frog. Mammy says once upon a time a frog turned into a prince when a princess dropped a gold ball into a pond. Once upon a time is the start. Once upon a time means a long time ago. Before today. Today is now. Tomorrow is not today. Today is different.

Lonely was gold. He lived in a bowl. Once upon a time. That was before today. A bowl is not a pond. A pond has water. It is round like a circle. A river has water too. But a river is not a pond. A river is different. So is a bowl. Granny says the frog had to sleep under the princess's pillow to turn into a prince. Granny puts Jacob's pyjamas under his pillow. That is in the morning. Morning is the start. Like once upon a time is the start. Daddy says he is not sure. Not sure means not knowing the right answer. There was a kiss. Granny is sure. The frog turned into a prince. Mammy said. Mammy kisses Jacob's head. Mammy rubs Jacob's hair to sleep. That was once upon a time. That was before today. That was before now. Today is now. Tomorrow is not today. Tomorrow is different.

Granny takes Jacob's pyjamas out from under his pillow. That is in the night. Night is the end like happy ever after is the end. Daddy says he is not sure. Not sure means not knowing the right answer.

Jacob tap-taps the glass. Lonely comes out of the green. Jacob doesn't see any frogs.

Lonely is a goldfish. A goldfish is not a dog or a prince or a tree. A goldfish is different. Dogs have wagging tails if they are happy dogs. Goldfish don't have smiling tails or smiling mouths. They are not made of gold. Mammy has a gold ring on her finger. Gold is very shiny and hard. Hard is the same as not soft. Soft is different. Like fingers and toes are different. Jumpers and socks are different too. Mammy says different is good. Daddy says different is hard. Hard and easy are different. They are not the same. Granny says different is chalk and cheese. Like a fish out of water. Fish don't have fingers or toes. Jacob looks down at his toes. He tap-taps his finger. He wiggles his toes. He looks back into the rectangle. Lonely fades away. The green gobbles him up. Fish fingers are in a rectangle box in Tesco. It is a cold box. There is a smiling man on the front of the box.

Fish fingers are orange. Like tigers are orange and cornflakes and balloons. Trees are green. Dogs are not green. Green is dark and light. Green is before anything happens. Granny says blackberries are green before they are black. The green man on the traffic light means walking before the red man means stopping. Lonely can't do walking or stopping. Lonely can only do round and round swimming. Round and round. Swimming is not walking. Swimming is different. So is stopping. Swimming is like flying under water. Stopping is not like that.

'What are ya doin' down here on your own, Jacob? It's the middle a the night.' Daddy's mouth opens and closes making lots of sounds. Daddy's arms stretch out like he's flying.

Jacob presses his forehead to the glass. Lonely isn't gold

anymore. Now he is different. Now he is orange like a tiger. Jacob likes tigers and trees and fish fingers.

'I got a new little friend for Lonely. And I got a good-as-new tank. And when I get a job I'll get a brand new one, I promise. One with a proper filter! The whole works!' Daddy's face comes down beside Jacob's. Jacob and Daddy look into the green. 'And we'll get a rabbit!'

Lonely flies through the water behind the glass. Like a rainbow. He is very good at swimming. He flap-flaps his fins up and down, down and up. He flicks his body like an S. He opens his mouth like an O. The O closes again and Jacob can't see the dark orange circle inside Lonely anymore. Lonely gets bigger. He turns orange-red and silver. Now he is different. Like he doesn't know what colour he is. Jacob wants him to be yellow-gold again. Now he is silver-white. Like Granny. Lonely makes another O with his open-closed mouth. Jacob tap-taps with one finger. Lonely gets smaller then bigger again. Jacob waits for Lonely.

'Lonely looks tired,' Daddy says. 'I think it's time we all went to bed. Are you not sleepy, Jacob?'

Waiting is not the same as going away. Waiting is different. Lonely goes away. Jacob doesn't. Jacob is waiting. Jacob squints into the green. Lonely is back. Lonely watches Jacob from the other side of the glass. Jacob tap-taps his window. Lonely goes away again. Jacob doesn't go away. Jacob is waiting.

'I'm tired myself. Tired doin' nothin.' Daddy's face moves away. Daddy's knees make cracking noises. 'I used to have a rabbit, when I was your age,' Daddy says, then Daddy goes away.

Jacob pulls at his ear trying to hear all the sounds that aren't there anymore. Lonely wriggles his body. His head wiggles from side to side. Lonely has no neck. Lonely's head just comes out of his body or his body comes out of his head. Jacob isn't sure if one is different from the other. Lonely swims back into the darkness at the other side of the rectangle.

Daddy comes back. Daddy rubs his eyes. Daddy's shoulders are up too high. Daddy's head is down too low. Like a bird out in the rain.

'I remember buildin' him a little hutch, makin' him a cosy bed to sleep in. I was proud as punch of that little hutch. First thing I ever built on me own. My eyes are itchy with sleep!'

Jacob blinks. Blinking is not sleeping for a short while. Blinking is quicker.

Lonely is back. Lonely doesn't blink. His eyes are stuck on open. Wide open. Like he's just had a shock. Granny says shock. Mammy doesn't. Lonely has big eyes. They are black eyes like burned tinfoil. Lonely is gone. Jacob is waiting. Jacob hums. He tap-taps the glass. Lonely comes back. Lonely is yellow again. Lonely is smaller. Lonely pushes his head into the bottom of the rectangle. He wags his tail. He wobbles his body. Then he is still. Still means not moving or not home yet. Then he is gone.

Jacob looks around for more noise. Daddy is gone. Jacob doesn't like the dark quiet. Sometimes the quiet gets too big and too empty in the dark. Like flying in space or underwater.

The empty space of the room is too big now. Too quiet. Jacob looks for the tick-tock of the clock but it's not there. It's gone. Mammy is gone. Jacob is waiting.

Lonely comes back. He is bigger. He kisses the top of the water. Mammy kisses the top of Jacob's head. Granny puts Jacob's pyjamas under his pillow. Lonely is gone. Mammy is gone.

Now Lonely is back making more kissing Os. He is redder than before. He makes a bubble. Jacob likes bubbles. Bubbles are round like the pink and white biscuits Granny makes like magic come out of the press. Lonely likes Os and see-through tails. Jacob can see through Lonely's tail like it's not even there. But it is. So are his new eyes. Lonely's new eyes are black with gold circles. Jacob's eyes are blue. Lonely doesn't have any ears.

Lonely has fins. Lonely clap-claps his flying fins but there is no sound. Mammy's eyes are blue. Like Jacob's eyes are blue. Lonely opens and closes his mouth like he is talking. Lonely wants to tell Jacob a water secret but Jacob can't hear him.

Jacob pulls at his ears. He hums away the no-noise. He makes bigger taps, louder hums. Tap-tap-hum. Louder. Louder. Lonely is back. Lonely left his shape behind him in the dark green. It is a long way from the dark in the centre to the yellow light at the side. Lonely flies up to the top of the green water line. It is bright like green silver.

Daddy is back. Daddy has a blanket. 'Do you want to come inside and watch a bit of telly, Jacob?'

Lonely changes colour again.

'Sure, we'll find somethin' to watch.' Daddy holds out his hand.

Lonely looks at Jacob.

'Whatever you like. Thomas might be on.'

Jacob looks at Lonely. Jacob puts his finger to the glass. He doesn't tap-tap.

'Ah, come on, Jacob. I could do with the company, to be honest.'

Jacob just presses his finger until the top bit goes white and the bit under his nail goes pink-red. Lonely kiss-kisses the white of Jacob's finger blowing him Os through the water. The shape behind Lonely gets bigger. It changes from green into silver-white-gold. It swims and it does head wiggles and tail wriggles and clap-claps with no noises. It makes S shapes in the water.

'Look! I brought down your favourite blanket.'

The shape flaps its wing hands and tail again. Lonely sees the shape. The shape sees Lonely. They look at each other in the light. They make kissing Os. They look happy. They swim into the darkness again. Then they are gone. Jacob looks back at the place where they talked to each other. There is only the drip-dripping like rain in the back of the toilet.

Jacob follows Daddy into the sitting room. Daddy turns on the television. Road Runner meep-meeps.

Daddy sits down on the couch. 'Do ya know what? I don't care what anybody says, I like Wile E. Coyote. I do. I mean who else could skate around and hand glide, all at the same time, and in that heat? And would ya just look at that blueprint, Jacob! Look! A blueprint is like an idea, drawn on a page.' Daddy puts his feet on a cushion. Daddy doesn't have any socks. 'And he can build anything! Anything at all. Look at that! He's only gone and built himself a flying helmet out of handle-bars and a ceiling fan!'

Jacob sits down on Mammy's chair.

'And he's a trier. He is—'

Jacob tap-taps on Mammy's chair.

'Ouch! Ah Jesus, and how was he to know they'd be testing Scud missiles, there, in his desert! Oh, but, I know how ya feel, Wile E. Blows your whole world apart.'

Jacob tap-taps his fingers.

'I suppose you're just lookin' for somethin' ya can't seem to find. Maybe—'

Jacob wriggles his toes.

'Ya know, like when they came and closed down the site and put us off. Like we were no good—'

Jacob stands up.

'I remember your man, in the suit, from the bank, standin' there, all business he was, watchin' us, like we were criminals or somethin', orderin' us to pack up our tools. "You've got five minutes," he says. Five minutes! And they marched us off, in a line, like a chain gang. My toolbox fell open. One of them stood over me. There I was, down on me hands and knees, gatherin' up hammers and chisels, and this big fella standin' over me tappin' his foot. Not a word, of course, from Smyth. And now Jenny's only gone and pulled the head off his young one! Jesus! Suspended for two days. From national school! Course they're not callin' it that. *Time Out*, they said. I don't think I've ever heard of anyone bein' suspended from national school. Takes the nuns! Ya know, Jacob, I can still hear the clanking of all me tools fallin' to the ground, the tap-tap of his foot—'

Jacob goes back out to the kitchen. Road Runner meep-meeps. Jacob looks at the two fish in the rectangle on the table. Lonely's not Lonely anymore.

Jacob comes back into the sitting room again.

'It'd be different, ya know, Jacob, if I could travel. Go after the work, like I used to. God knows there's been nothin' round here for so long—'

Jacob waits at the door. Road Runner meep-meeps.

'But I don't want to do that.'

Jacob sits on the couch. Road Runner meep-meeps.

'And that's no life anyway. Away from your family. Buildin' houses for other families? Missin' your own all the time. But they say things are picking up. And I've—'

Jacob moves his fingers. Wiggles his toes. Road Runner meep-meeps.

'I can't sleep meself, kiddo.' Daddy's hand covers Jacob's. Daddy's knees make cracking noises. Daddy pulls the fluffy-soft blanket up around them. 'How's about you and me bunk down here on the couch tonight?'

Jacob climbs into the space between Daddy and the end of the couch. Daddy puts the brown softness under Jacob's chin. He tucks in Jacob's feet. Daddy and Jacob fit together like two shoes that are the same and not different. Daddy isn't wearing any socks.

'I know how much ya miss her, Jacob. There's nothin' worse than missin' your mammy. It's like a big gap in your breathin'. I know. But I'm here, kiddo. I'm here. And I've got meself an interview comin' up in a couple a weeks. But don't you go tellin' nobody about it. Do ya hear me? It can be our little secret, for now.'

Jacob smells Mammy in the blanket. Jacob closes his eyes. Daddy rubs Jacob's hair. Daddy hums. Jacob listens to Daddy's breathing song, feeling the up and down of Daddy's air. Jacob smiles into all the sounds.

CHAPTER 24

Annette

Silent loud screaming swallowed whole inside her making new again names down different corridors. Different doors. Different walls. Annette doesn't know where she is or how she got here. Everything seems forgotten for now then remembered only to be forgotten again. Everything is different here. Different yet just the same moving feet squeaking wheels whispered words. Rattles and clanks ring in through the light pushing through square windows.

Old and new words slip and slide around in her mouth. Some were lost. Others found again for now. Mouth shapes forming words she knows and yet doesn't. Letters growing behind an unspeaking eye scanning new smells she knows to be old. With her good eye she notices the passing blue-green watching lines of wallpaper she has never seen before. Flicking lights hissing. Old now. New hospital walls stripped and made new again with new for now noises.

Echoes of shuffling still outside feet everywhere. Over there. Away. Near or far. Annette isn't sure. Flaking new faces flicker under the yellow light.

'Hello there, Annette,' and 'How are you today?'

More and more questions falling down from the sky. Annette's crumbling tired eye watches. Curved straight-circle lines wind around a corner. Words overhead wax and wane in the warm heavy air. Letters on signs. Pictures on walls.

Moving statues. Doors in burnt colours. Her burning eye reflects.

She tries to imagine a heavy hand lost and too heavy to remember. Unremembered tingling of numbed something there and not. Nothing was before now. Searching for lost-again hand she sees shades of a child warming cold fingers. Pulling at moss on a tree. Burning candles on a cake. And a dog. A yellow dog with an up-smiling mouth lying at the feet of a smoking man. Annette remembers the man but not his name nor his face. Just his shape and his smell. The nameless man leans down to stroke the nameless dog with a strong hand. A kind hand. Then the man scratches the dog's ear. There are toys in a press somewhere in the same room – wooden jigsaws, a little train. Blue or green. She cannot remember. Colours lovely as rainbows in sunshine-rain arching to earth. There and not.

'Annette, we're just going to take you down to the ward now.'

New faces. Voices knew.

'We'll get you settled in then.'

New place smelling old. Different colours of all the forgotten names. Cut off both arms. One. Too. Two remember their faces. Their names to.

'Where am I?' Slowly Annette's words reach out to the pink face of the writing nurse.

'This is the Rehabilitation Centre, Annette. Don't worry, we'll take good care of you here.'

'Where is—' Annette loses the words.

'A move like this can be an awful shock to the system. But this is all good. Dr Betts feels you are ready for our programme here. The confusion will settle, Annette, I promise you. It's very normal to feel disorientated when you have been moved after so long.'

CHAPTER 25

Jenny

Dear Ma,

You have to come home and stop her! Granny says she's going to have a party for Jacob's birthday. And, Ma, I told her we don't have parties here! Jacob wouldn't like it. But Granny says every child loves a party and she says we are going to have Rice Krispie buns and jelly and ice cream and balloons and candles and everything like that. She says she's going to invite all Jacob's little friends from his class in school and that it's going to be great fun altogether. And I told her, Ma, that they are not really Jacob's friends at all – they are just the other children in his class. Granny says of course they are all his little friends and not to be worrying so much and just to leave everything up to her. But, Ma, nobody has jelly and ice cream at their party.

And then I told her how Jacob doesn't like noise or lots of people and how Jacob has never been invited to one of their parties before. Not even one. Not ever. So really she doesn't have to invite them to his party at all. And I said that we should just go round to Luigi's because that's one of Jacob's most favourite things to do. But Granny says Luigi's is no place for a party and what about if some of his little friends don't like chips! I told Granny everybody loves chips and anyway I didn't mean for all them to come, too. I just meant for us to go on our own. Granny says she'll hear no more about it because this is going to be the best party, ever.

But, Ma, what if nobody comes? What will we do then if it's just us and Jacob sitting around in party hats, eating jelly and ice cream and waiting for someone to ring the bell? What will we tell Jacob if no one shows up at all? Or what will happen if everyone does come and Jacob has a meltdown and gets scared?

I said to Granny that Jacob just likes having us at his birthday, but she wouldn't listen, like she never listens to anybody except herself. She says every child deserves a party, like she knows what every child in the whole wide world loves and deserves.

Ma, please tell Granny she's not allowed to have a party for Jacob. Jacob won't like it. Please tell her, Ma.

I love you, Ma, and Jacob loves you too. Will you please come home soon?

Love,

Jenny

Jenny folds her letter in half and slips it inside the envelope. She licks the sticky bit, up one side and down the other. She presses it closed, flattens it and writes *Mammy* on the front. Jenny knows Ma likes *Mammy* instead of *Ma*, though she never says it. Jenny thinks maybe she should start calling her *Mammy*, from now on. *Mammy* is nicer anyway. It's softer and has more m's in it than *Ma* does.

Jenny says it out loud, 'Mammy,' and, like she's never heard it before, she realises that really *Mammy* is just *Ma* and *Me* stuck together, but with a few more letters. But the sound is still the same, 'MaMe.' She says it again and again and smiles down at the word on the envelope, touching it lightly with her fingers.

In the kitchen Granny is ironing.

'Do you have a stamp for my letter?' Jenny asks.

'And what's the magic word?'

'Please.'

'I don't, pet. But put it over there in my bag and I'll see that she gets it.'

'Will you give it to Mammy on Friday, please?' Jenny tucks the letter into Granny's bag.

'Oh, *Mammy*, now is it?' Granny smiles, folding Jacob's vest. She puts it on top of the pile she's already ironed, lying over the back of the chair.

Jenny takes a book out of her school bag and goes back up the stairs.

CHAPTER 26

Jenny

Wednesday 9th October 2013

Our News
   Granny gave Frank, the bus driver, five small yellow
envelopes, with the 'Come to My Party' frog invitations
inside, this morning, when he came to collect Jacob. Jacob
doesn't really like frogs but Granny says Cut Price ran out of
all the Superman ones, so we'll just have to make do with
Kermit!
   Granny asked Frank to give the invitations to Elaine.
Elaine is Jacob's teacher.

Jenny looks up at Mrs Nicholson and wonders if she has a first
name. Mrs Nicholson is very busy on the computer. She's
tap-tap-tapping with her head so far forward she looks like she's
trying to put it into the screen. Every so often her eyes peep
up for a second and her neck seems to get longer as she looks
round the room. Everybody is writing. Jenny can hear pencils
scratching, chair legs scraping and pages turning. Mrs Nicholson
takes her purse out of her bag and goes back to her tapping.
She doesn't look like somebody with a first name, at all, Jenny
thinks to herself. She just looks like somebody who wants to
be taller. But if she did have a first name, what would it be?
She'd never have a name like *Nicky* or *Chloe*. She might have

a name like *Mary* or *Jane*. But somebody called *Mary* would wear knee socks and train-track braces, tied together with pink elastics, on her teeth, and *Jane* would definitely have freckles and pigtails or plaits. Mrs Nicholson crosses her navy legs under her desk. Her tights are wrinkled at the bottom where her foot is pushed into her shoe. She has very short red hair and her teeth are a bit crooked so she's definitely not *Mary. Gertrude*, then? Jenny tries to fit *Gertrude* on over Mrs Nicholson's grey blouse. No. Definitely not *Gertrude. Gertrudes* are grannies, who knit things like scarves and gloves, and Mrs Nicholson doesn't even have a husband and Jenny wonders why everybody calls her *Mrs* and not *Miss*. Jenny decides it must be because she definitely does not look like a *Miss*. Misses are much, much younger and they wear shorter skirts or jeans, and track suits and runners on PE days. Like Miss Kennedy, who teaches the infant class. Jenny tries to imagine Mrs Nicholson in jeans and boots. But she can't. She doesn't even try to put Mrs Nicholson in a track suit. That would never work. Mrs Nicholson has lots of cats. Jenny can imagine her with cats. She talks about her cats when she's in a good mood. And she shows photos of Zim and Tubs to the class. *Dorcas*, maybe? *Dorcas* seems better. The more Jenny looks at Mrs Nicholson the more she thinks she could be a *Dorcas*, if she does have a first name at all.

Dorcas, come in outta that for your dinner. Dorcas, eat up all your peas. Dorcas, would ya ever run down below to the shop for me, like a good girl?

Jenny tries to imagine Mrs Nicholson's mother calling her Dorcas. She can see a woman, but she can't see little Dorcas. Mrs Nicholson would never have been a small girl out playing or going on messages to the shop to buy milk. The more Jenny tries to see the calling woman's face, the more it fades away. Mrs Nicholson would never have had a mother either, Jenny decides.

'Jennifer Augustt, are you doing your work?'

Mrs Nicholson has a small plastic card in her hand. She looks like she's in a hurry. Jenny wonders if being a teacher makes her feel taller?

Yes, Dorcas, I am, Jenny says inside her own head and goes back to her writing.

Elaine said she would put all the names on the front of the envelopes and give them out to all the other children in Jacob's class.

'Course I will,' Frank tells Granny. 'Is the little man goin' to have a birthday soon?' Frank asked Jacob, as he climbed up the steps into the bus. 'And how old are ya goin' to be, Jacob?'

Jenny wonders how old Mrs Nicholson is. She wonders if she's ever had a birthday party with balloons and invitations. She looks like she might be forty-three or maybe she's sixty. Jenny's not very good at guessing older people's ages. Granny says she's still twenty-one and a bit. Da says Granny's so old she looks like she was born in black and white when there was still no colour in the world and no cars and no telly and no Tesco Extra and when your whole family could be dead in a week because of the flu and your neighbours could be dead the next week from all the coughing and sneezing and spitting that came out of your house.

Mrs Nicholson's hair is bright red, like a fox, but that could be a dye she bought in a box in Tesco. Her face is pink, and not grey like Granny's. When she's cross, she presses her lips together and a row of crawling lines appears, like little spider legs above her top lip, and all round her mouth gets crumpled up, like an old hanky.

Happy birthday to you. Happy birthday to you. Happy birthday dear Dorcas. Happy birthday to you.

Jenny tries to hear the children singing, at Dorcas's party.

But she can only hear the tune inside her own head. There are no other voices and she can't find any pictures.

'Jennifer Augustt! I won't tell you again. Get on with your work!'

Jacob walked straight past Frank in the driver's seat, and kept on going down the middle of the bus until he found his own favourite seat. Jacob's favourite seat is four rows back, on the right side of the bus, by the window. Jacob put his bag down on the seat beside him. It was an empty seat. All the other children sit in seats by themselves every day, too. Nobody sits together on the big red bus that brings them all to school. Jacob sat down and looked out the window.

'He surely is. He's goin' to be six in two weeks' time, please God,' Granny told Frank.

'Six! Already? My God doesn't time fly, all the same!' Frank said back to Granny. Both of them looked down the bus.

'Thanks, Frank,' Granny said over her shoulder, climbing back down the steps and back on to the path.

'Not a bother,' Frank said before the two doors hissed and closed in together.

I waved bye-bye to Jacob as the big bus pulled off away from the kerb. Jacob was still looking out the window but he didn't wave back.

'Right so, let's get you to school now,' Granny said to me. 'And when ya get home, this afternoon, we'll make a list of all the things we're goin' to need for the party.'

There's a quiet knock on the door. The children all turn around to look at the new face in the little glass window. The face has a sharp heavy dark fringe and a red lipstick smile. The door opens before anybody is told to get up and answer it. The face has a body, arms, and legs that end halfway down, disappearing inside long purple boots.

All the chairs in the room scrape back away from the desks. Mrs Nicholson bangs down one of her clicking nails on the computer.

'No. No. Please don't get up,' the new voice says from the doorway.

The lady moves her hand slowly in mid-air, like she's patting an invisible head. The half-sitting, half-standing children grip their chairs once again and lower themselves back down.

'Good morning, Mrs Nicholson. I wonder if I could disturb you, for just one minute, please?'

'Of course. Of course. Come in. Come in.' Mrs Nicholson says everything twice, holding up her hand and wiggle-snapping her fingers, like a Garda telling the cars to drive on. Drive on!

The purple boots clip-clop up to the top of the room. The new lady whispers something into Mrs Nicholson's ear. Then they both look down at Jenny. Jenny feels herself getting hotter.

'Thank you, Mrs Nicholson.'

The children can hear the teachers talking now like the sound has just been turned up.

'Jennifer, will you go with Mrs French, please?'

Mrs Nicholson's *will* seems like it's only there by accident. So does her *please*, like it just fell out of someone else's mouth and landed in Mrs Nicholson's mouth because hers just happened to be open at the time. Now Mrs Nicholson must want to get rid of it too, pass it on to somebody else, like it's a streptococcus throat – Granny says that's the most stupid word she's ever heard for *sore* in her whole life – so Mrs Nicholson uses it on Jenny just to get it off her tongue.

Jenny stands up at her desk and waits until the new lady walks back down the room again. She smiles at Jenny.

'Will you come with me, Jenny?'

Jenny steps to the side and follows the lady's purple boots back out through the door.

'Don't look so worried, Jenny. You're not in any trouble. I just thought that maybe you and I could have a little chat. Would that be okay?'

Jenny shrugs. Jenny walks beside Mrs Purple Boots. They are the only two on the corridor. They make their way down to the PE hall. The PE hall is the biggest room in the school and when it's not being used for PE there might be children playing music or practising action songs in there. But today it is quiet. Before they reach the big double doors, they stop at another door that seems to have just grown into the wall. The door is smaller than any other door in the school. It is like the door into a press. Breda, the school cleaning lady, magics sweeping brushes and mops out of small doors like this all the time. Jenny has never noticed this door before.

'Well, here we are, then.'

Jenny wonders why Mrs Purple Boots adds *then* on to the end of her sentence. Is she going to make another sentence? Jenny waits, but nothing comes. Jenny can't think why *then* is better than *now*. *Well, here we are, now. Then* makes it sound like something they have done before now. Like, *They opened the door and went in then* or *They decided to stop then*. *Now* would be better.

The door pushes open inwards and when Jenny steps into the room, leaving the dark corridor behind, she feels like she has just stepped into a story. It is a good story, with candles and colours, like a story she herself would like to have written. The room smells like clean sweets made of fruit and coloured sugar. The room tinkles with light. There is a wind chime somewhere in this room and shiny green leafy plants that look happy, like the ring-a-rosy children smiling down from all the posters on the wall. This is exactly the type of office Jenny would have written about in her story.

'Take a seat.'

Jenny is glad *please* hasn't followed them into this room. *Please* can't be trusted and Jenny never knows if *please* is good or bad.

Jenny stands and looks out the big window. She can see the sea from here. It is only a tiny grey rectangle between the church and the other rooftops. But it is there. Mrs Purple Boots sits down. She swings around on her chair.

'So, where were we?' she asks, like she's forgotten the place in the story.

Jenny shrugs.

'How are you getting on, Jenny? I love the name Jenny. It suits you.'

Jenny's eyes fall down on her jumper and work their way up.

'My name is Mrs French but you can call me Aideen, if you like.'

Jenny looks back out the window.

'Is everything okay in school?'

'Do you speak French?' Jenny says, like this makes any sense at all. Jenny has never met anybody called Mrs French before.

'*Je ne parle pas très bien français.*'

'What?'

'I only speak a little French, I'm afraid.'

Jenny watches Bill, the caretaker, sweeping up all the fallen leaves that cover the yard, like scattered sweet wrappers of different yellows and browns. 'Do you know any Spanish?'

'I know the days of the week in Spanish. I went to Spain, on my holidays, during the summer.'

'Did you? I went to Timbuktu!'

'So I heard.' Mrs French smiles at Jenny.

Jenny sits down. There are books everywhere – small piles and big piles but the room doesn't feel untidy. It feels like a happy room where books in piles seem to belong. Even Granny wouldn't want to move them or sort them out or put them away. There's a big bit of wood in the corner. It looks old – wrinkled like an old man's face. But he's a kind man. A kind old man with kind old wrinkles on his old wooden face. Jenny wants to touch it. She doesn't know why. But she does.

'That's Arthur,' Mrs French says, following Jenny's eye.

'Arthur?'

'Yes. Arthur is a good name, don't you think? A name you can trust.' Mrs French nods her head in Arthur's direction.

Jenny gets up and moves across the carpet. There's no carpet anywhere else in the school. Jenny feels like she wants to take her shoes off. She doesn't know why. She just does. She reaches out. Her fingers fall along the lines of Arthur's face. He's smooth and rough at the same time, like he's happy and sad all at once. Jenny closes her eyes and feels little whispers under his dark skin.

'My dad was Arthur,' Mrs French says, like she's remembering something happy-sad from a long time ago. Her voice feels like it's gone somewhere else, somewhere over the hills.

'You look like him,' Jenny says, without opening her eyes.

'I do,' Mrs French says, like somebody getting married on the telly.

'Mammy says I look like her but Da says I'm a real Augustt. Granny says I just look like myself and that's exactly how it should be.'

Realising all she's just said, Jenny turns around. Mrs French is smiling like she's heard Granny saying this somewhere before.

'Augustt is an unusual name,' Mrs French says. 'Where does it come from?'

'It comes from Da and Da comes from here.'

'Of course.'

For a moment Mrs French seems to be gone again. Jenny turns back to Arthur, strokes his head, which feels warm, and yawns. Just out of nowhere a nice sleepiness wraps itself around her.

'Are you tired, Jenny?' Mrs French is back.

'I don't know. I wasn't, but now I am.'

'Were you up late, doing homework, last night?'

'Yes. Mrs Nicholson says we've a lot to do, before Halloween.'

'Coming up to mid-term is always busy.'

Jenny thinks about last night, and the one before that, and all the other nights put together, when she was busy watching all the chicken maggots again with their crawling-moving skin, eating Mammy. Mammy's asking Jenny to get them off her, but Jenny can't. Mammy's flicking her skin and shouting and screeching and then she parts her hair in the middle and Jenny can see it – a thing, like a baby finger, is stuck into Mammy's head, pinching and sucking and wriggling. Then Mammy shows it to Da.

'Look!' Mammy says. 'Look!' She puts her head down real close to Da's face.

'Holy fuck!' Da says.

'Get it out!' Mammy screams.

'I'm not fuckin' touchin' that,' Da shouts and vanishes into the air.

'I'll get it out, Mammy,' Jenny says.

Jenny always wants to tell her she will do it but it's always one of those dreams where you try to say something, but you can't, and every time Jenny reaches out to Mammy, she just falls down through the air with millions of maggots slipping, like water, through her fingers. And it's always raining in Jenny's dreams about Mammy and even though she can't touch her, Jenny can still hear her screaming from where she's buried underneath the sand. And some nights it's Jenny herself in the ground in a box with no door and no way out. Sometimes there's a gold handle inside the box but it won't open. Other times the handle is silver and it's outside for no reason at all. And she can hear Mammy, creeping through the sand-earth like a lost maggot with no head, and she's looking for Jenny and she's calling her name. Jenny tries to scream out at the top of her voice. She tries to tell Mammy that she's here, inside the box, but her mouth keeps filling up with sand and Mammy can't hear her. Then Mammy's gone and Jenny's left all alone in the dark, with the grass growing up over her head.

'We have a test next Friday,' Jenny says, just for something to say.

'Do you? Oh, I always hated Friday tests when I was in school,' Mrs French says even though she's a teacher.

Jenny turns back around. She can see the woman in the long purple boots sitting before her as she must have been when she was a girl. Jenny can see her, wearing a green and red kilt and a green school jumper, but Jenny bets any money that she didn't wear the right school shoes. Mrs French's shoes would have been bright red or purple and not black, with no heel, like they should have been. And she would have had too many earrings in one ear and too many messages markered on to her bag.

'My daughter never sleeps before a test either.'

Jenny's not sure she likes the news that Mrs French has a daughter who can't sleep.

'She's about your age, too.'

Jenny wonders if Mrs French's daughter wakes up sometimes in the middle of the night holding her head and dream-screaming. Does she sometimes feel wet and hot all at once? Does she think she's still in the box even though she's not? Are the maggots still crawling all over her skin? Do they creep into her teeth and slither round her gums? Does she look under the covers and root through her hair and check inside the pillowcase just to be sure?

'What's her name?'

'Summer.'

'Is that a name? A real name for a person?' Jenny asks, liking this girl more now. Jenny thinks she would have liked to be called Summer.

'I think so. Henry Huggle Monster's sister is called Summer.'

Jenny remembers watching Henry Huggle Monster on the couch with Mammy and Jacob. Mammy used to sit in the middle and snuggle-huggle them both. Of all the things Jenny misses most, it's not being able to snuggle into Mammy. If a genie came out of one of those strange-looking glass bottles, up on Mrs French's high shelf, way up there over Jenny's head, and she gave Jenny just one wish, that would be it – to feel Mammy's arms around her again. Mammy has a way of folding Jenny into herself, like they are joined together as one person. Everything was okay then, even if it wasn't. Jenny can smell Mammy and feel her hair tickling her nose. She takes in a deep breath and scratches her nose.

'It's going to be her birthday the week after next,' Mrs French says, like she's just remembered something she's forgotten a million times. Then she writes a note on a little yellow square and sticks it on to the side of her bag.

'Was she not born in summertime?'

'No. Twenty-fifth of October.'

'So why did you call her Summer then?' Jenny asks the question even though she has never even asked Mammy why she was called Jenny. She wishes now that she had.

'I like the word Summer. It makes me feel warm and happy inside. And outside as well,' Mrs French says, like the last bit is something she's just realised, now, this very second.

Sometimes, just for a minute in the mornings when she wakes up, Jenny feels happy too.

'Granny says a word is just a word but when it becomes a name then it has power.'

'Wow! That is so true. It really is when you think about it.' Mrs French goes off behind the hills again.

Jenny touches the line along another shelf, lower down, on the wall. She reads the names of some of the books; *Harry Potter and the Philosopher's Stone*; *Harry Potter and the Chamber of Secrets*. Jenny counts with her finger. They are all there, all seven of them, changing from purple to orange – all the Harry Potter colours, sitting neatly in a row.

'Do you like Harry Potter, Jenny?'

'Yes.'

'Me too! I've read them all. Twice!'

'These are *yours*?' Jenny asks, like she doesn't believe Mrs French. 'Which one is your favourite?'

'*The Half-Blood Prince.*' The words fly out so fast it's like Mrs French is giving an answer in a quiz she's in on the telly and that there's a big prize for the winner.

'I liked that, too, but *The Chamber of Secrets* is my favourite.'

Jenny thinks about number three, *The Prisoner of Azkaban*, still hidden away in her special drawer, even though she should have brought it back into school weeks and weeks ago. They had only read the first two together, but they will finish them all when Mammy comes home.

'Do you read a lot, Jenny?' Mrs French asks and it's not like Jenny has to say yes because Mrs French's eyes and tight, pulled-back lips are telling her that's the right answer and the only answer she wants to hear. Mrs French asks the question like whatever answer Jenny gives will be okay.

'I used to. Before. But sometimes the words are too big.'

'I agree. Some words are just too big, but they are usually just show-off words and you can skip most of them. Are you reading anything at the moment?'

'Yes. A book in class.'

'What's it called?'

'*The Boy in the Striped Pyjamas.*'

'Oh. I loved that.' Mrs French looks sad, like she's just remembered something else sad and faraway.

Mrs French gets up and moves over towards Jenny. They both stand, side by side, looking at the books. Mrs French searches the shelf with her finger. Her finger seems to know exactly where it is going. It stops at the top of a book. It is a white book. Her finger presses down at the tip and arches up at her knuckle and gently tilts the book out from the shelf. 'Jenny, meet *Anne Frank*!'

Mrs French hands Jenny the book. Jenny looks down at the strange face staring back at her. Anne Frank is only a head, with no body, floating around the middle of the cover and this is her diary!

'I first read *Anne Frank* when I was about your age, Jenny. And I still read her, even now.'

Jenny wonders if Anne Frank has written even more than seven books and that's what's taking Mrs French so long. Jenny searches the shelf for the others but there are none.

Past the seven Harry Potters stand three strange shapes that look like they are melting down on to the shelf. They shine like water on stone; little points of yellow-white reflecting off their heads. They are all the same colour, which is really just creamy-brown, but there are other colours bleeding in and out of the brown which separates them, making each one different as well.

'It is my brother's birthday in two weeks, too. Granny's having a party,' Jenny says, rubbing her fingers down along the first shiny figure, the one with the hat, that looks like a mushroom with the open mouth of a fish.

'Is it really? How old will he be?'

'Six.'

'That's very exciting. I love parties.'

'I hope somebody comes.'

'Of course they will. Everyone loves a party.'

'This is his first party. He's never been to a party before.'

'What's your brother's name?'

'Jacob.'

'Jacob. That's a very strong name. The kind of name that makes you sit up straighter.'

Jenny adjusts her shoulders.

'I had a little brother, too. A long time ago. He died when he was three.'

'What happened to him?' Jenny asks, even though she knows Mammy would kill her for being so rude.

'He was very sick. Do you like my pottery?'

'What was his name? Did you make these?'

'He was called Anthony. Yes, in my pottery class. They're not very good. But I just like them.'

'Granny says only the good die young. Maybe he's a saint now. Granny definitely knows a saint called Anthony. He finds things when they're lost. On Tuesdays. She says small saints can make miracles, too. Was he any good at finding things?'

'I like your granny, Jenny. She sounds like a great character. I can't wait to hear more about her.'

'Will I have to come back here?'

'No, you don't have to, if you don't want to, but I'd like if you did.'

'When?'

'Well, I'm here every second Wednesday.'

'Okay.'

'Have you ever kept a diary, Jenny? Mrs Nicholson tells me you are a brilliant writer.'

Jenny wonders which one of them is lying. She decides it must have been Dorcas.

'No,' Jenny says.

'Will you give it a try? See how it goes, maybe? Only if you want to, of course.'

'Will you want to read it?'

'Oh no, Jenny, a diary is a record of your own personal thoughts. A diary is written only for yourself and not for the rest of the world to see.'

'Okay.'

Jenny closes the door quietly on her way out. She doesn't want anyone else to know about the magic room in the press.

She walks lightly down the corridor, pushing Anne Frank into her bag, and slips back into her own class, hoping no one will spot her.

'Turn to page thirty-two in your maths book, Jennifer, please,' Mrs Nicholson says to Jenny, even though she's writing sums up on the board and she's not even looking at the class.

'Where did you go?' asks Sarah Flynn, leaning over in a small whisper.

'With Mrs French,' Jenny says, like it's perfectly obvious.

'Who's she? What did she want?'

'I'm not sure, really. I think she just needed someone to talk to.'

CHAPTER 27

Jacob

Black. Up and down. To the centre. Across to the end of the page. This is the sky.

Yellow. Round-circle line. Up in the sky. Over the black up and down lines. No lines out of the circle. This is not the sun. It is the moon. The man sleeps under the moon.

Red. Blue. Yellow. Green. Tall lines inside a standing-up rectangle on top of the green up-and-down short lines of grass at the bottom of the page. This is the gate.

'She's not too bad, Stella, considering the size a the bleed. Sure they can do great things now, altogether, so they can. My John, God be good to him, wasn't so lucky.'

Granny's words fly around the kitchen like birds. Jacob follows them with his eyes. Jacob watches how high they soar out of Granny's mouth until it seems like they stop rising and Jacob starts falling instead. Getting smaller. Jacob checks his hand to make sure it's still big like it was this morning.

Jacob stands back looking for more shapes and colours. He follows the lines closely around the page. Mammy says Jacob is getting taller every day.

Red. Down-up lines all the way across the page. A round circle squashed in the centre of the red down-up lines makes the oval shape of the hole in the centre. This is the secret way in.

'And they're hoping to let her out, please God, in a few weeks. She'll be right as rain then. And sure, wouldn't she be better off here, in her own home, with all her own things around her?'

Jacob looks at all the wrong things in the kitchen that are not right. Granny's slippers. Granny's cups. Granny's bucket.

Green. Like an up-ways cloud. Two brown lines coming out of the green join the green to the ground. This is a tree. Jacob draws four trees. One in each corner of the page.

'But now, for all that, they are marvellous people up there in the Rehab place in Dun Laoghaire. There's a whole team workin' with her.'

Apples are green. Apples grow on trees. Cream crackers don't.

'A whole team? Jesus, Mae-Anne, sure that's brilliant now altogether, so it is.'

Black. Two round circles sitting on top of each other like an eight. Triangles. One. Two. One at each side of the top circle. These are the ears. More circles. One. Two. Smaller than the other circles and smaller than the triangles. These are the eyes. Two sideways Vs. One at each side of the small circle in the centre of the top circle. These are the whiskers. This is a cat. The cat is sitting on top of the gate. There are no apples on the trees.

'The Brain Injury Programme, they call it.'

Blue. Up-ways line across and down. Shorter lines down from the line at the top. One. Two. Another line at the bottom joins the two shorter lines together. This is the swing.

'What about the kids? Would ya not bring them to see her, Mae-Anne? Get them ready. Get them used to seein' her again,' the other voice behind the cup says to Granny. This is the voice of the new person in the kitchen talking to Granny. She is not supposed to be here either.

Brown. A circle for the head. Small lines point up from the top of the circle to the sky. A square body with sticking-out lines falls out of the circle. There isn't a neck in between the circle and the square. Circle. One. Square. One. One at the end of each sticking-out leg. These are his shoes. They are different. Different means not the same.

'Musha, Stella, I can't bring meself to do it. I just can't. I keep goin' over and over it in me head. Sure, I have driven meself half mad, but ya know, I can't do it to them. I just can't. And Jenny keeps pleadin' with me to bring the two of them up. And I keep sayin' I'll take them. *Mae-Anne*, I do say to meself, *Ya have to, ya have to*, and I keep promisin' them and then I find some reason why they shouldn't go or why I can't bring them. And it just goes on and on, day after day, week after week, round and round in me head till I can't even think straight anymore.'

'Ah Jesus, Mae-Anne, sure don't I know you're only tryin' to protect them.'

Blue. Colour in the square body. Red. For the sleeves.

'Ah, time will tell! But, Stell, I know I'll have to get them ready. I know it. I do. Just as I know I'm doin' them wrong, keepin' them from her. And God forgive me, but I keep prayin' for her hair to come back. I just keep thinkin' a Jenny's little face.'

'And will it? Her hair I mean.'

'They don't know for sure, but they think that it will. Alopecia Areata they're callin' it now!'

'What about Kevin? What does he think about them goin' up?'

'Ah, ya know, really, he's just like a child himself, God love him. Leaves it up to me most a the time. He's not right without her. He just isn't. If he could only get himself a bit a regular work. Somethin' to occupy his mind. Give him back the bit a dignity taken away by the dole. But he can't think about anythin' clearly at the moment. Only gettin' her home. Sure, doesn't he think everythin' will be grand and lovely once he gets her home again. Happy Ending, Stella, that's all he can manage.'

'Ah, course he does. Sure, aren't we all the same, really? And, please God it will.'

'They'll be delighted to have her home. Specially himself, there.' Granny nods her head at Jacob. 'We'll all have to adjust, I suppose. It's going to be a shock though after not seein' her for so long. I know. But sure at least she's still here, Stell, ya know. And she will be comin' home. Me own weren't so lucky, God love him.'

Upside-down hearts. One at the end of each sleeve. More blue. A blue line goes up one sleeve around the back of the brown circle head and back down the other square sleeve. This is the string. These are gloves. To keep the sleeping man warm.

'Don't I remember, Mae-Anne, God love them. But don't ya know they'll adjust. Course they will. Children are much better at adaptin' than we are. Sure, a child just accepts. But, now for all that, they must be missin' her somethin' terrible. Sure, a house isn't a home without a mother. Isn't he very good, all the same?'

Yellow. Lots of yellow on the top and down the sides of the other circle head in the corner. This is hair. A U for the mouth under the L nose. Pink. Triangle. A big one to keep Mammy warm. This is a coat.

'He's good as gold.'

'And Annette must be missin' them somethin' awful, too?'

Green. Five lines. One. Two. Three. Four. Five. Straight up and down. Five lines across the up and down lines. Six. Seven. Eight. Nine. Ten. Feet go on the across lines. So do hands. Jacob doesn't know why the down-up lines are there at all. This is the climbing frame. Not like the frame on the picture of the black and white man Granny put in the sitting room. This frame is not the same like a dog is not the same as a fish or Monster Munch is not the same as Smarties.

'Oh Jesus, she is. Sometimes I think she's only tryin' so hard for them. Ya know when it seems like she's never goin' to get any better. But she will, Stella, please God and His blessed mother. She will. It isn't for the want a prayers, I can tell ya.'

Grey. Circle. Upside-down U. Long rectangle. Squiggles. No feet.

'I lit a candle for her this mornin' at ten Mass. How's her speech comin' on?'

Red. Rectangle. This is a door.

'Well, now, ya know yourself, she has good days and bad days. But the speech therapist up there is great. Ah musha, she forgets words sometimes. The memory comes and goes a bit, ya know. She talks a lot about John, Lord have mercy on him, like he's still here. Course of them all, she took it the hardest, what with her bein' so young an all. And she'll tell ya a story about him and her goin' down to the beach or diggin' in the garden, with so much detail, ya'd think she was paintin' a picture with the few words she can manage but then she might ask ya what day it is or why she's there at all, like she can't remember the stuff that's just happened, but she can remember her childhood like it was only yesterday. But she mightn't remember that Kevin had been in with her just the day before.'

'And her speech is that good? Sure, that's great news now altogether, Mae-Anne, so it is.'

'Well, now, Stella, sure you remember your own mother, Lord have mercy on her, didn't she have good days and bad days, too?'

'Oh, she did. She surely did, God be good to her now.'

'The speech wouldn't be great now, but sure I know what it is she's tryin' to say to me, even if no one else does.'

'Ah sure, Mae-Anne, I was the same with me mother. I suppose ya just know.'

Green. Small circle circling round and round. Sausage shape under round and round circle. This is a snail on the man's head. The man doesn't have any small circles inside his head circle.

The man has no eyes. The man has no bed. The man is sleeping. The man is not waving.

'What about Home Help, Mae-Anne? Or that Carer's Allowance thing? Surely, she'd be entitled to something? There's feckers all over this country getting free money for nothin'; free prams, free holidays, free houses and the divil knows what else! Surely be to God, someone really deservin' a bit a help should qualify for something? And you can't do everythin' yourself!'

Yellow. Long lines. Up-ways. One. Two. Short lines across. One. Two. Three. Four. Five. The short lines go in between joining the up-down lines. This is the ladder.

'Would ya go way outta that. Sure, won't I be here with her when she comes home? She wouldn't want no strangers and no handouts. Isn't there enough a that around here already! Isn't she me own child? I don't want payin' for mindin' one a me own. My own child. Do ya want another cuppa tea?'

'Ah sure, go on. I will so. I don't have anythin' else callin' me away.'

'What's this, Jacob? Stella, would ya look at this picture. Isn't it great?'

'Aren't you a right little artist now altogether, Jacob?'

'Is that a boat, Jacob? Like a pirate's ship? Isn't it lovely? Stella, isn't it lovely?'

'It surely is!'

'And would ya look at the flag and all the waves? All the lines.'

Yellow. Two bending lines come down from the top of the ladder. Like an S.

'This must be the gangplank?' Granny's finger moves along the S. 'Are they off on adventures, Jacob?'

This is the slide.

'How's your Tricia now, Stell?'

'Still the same. No more I can do.'

Pink. Triangle.

'Where is she livin' these days?'

Purple. Cross line on top.

'I only wish I knew.'

One side of the purple line is up. The other side is down.

'Is she still with your man?'

'Curse a God on it, but don't ya know well now that she is, even though she tells me she isn't!'

This is the see-saw. Orange. Circle. One line down the centre. One line across.

'That's where X marks the spot! Isn't it, Jacob? There must be buried treasure there!'

This is the roundabout.

'Are the pirates goin' to dig up the treasure? Ah sure, Stell, ya can only be there for them when they need ya.'

'When she needs a few bob, ya mean! Usually on Tuesdays, when the dole money's run out. Don't ya know she remembers well enough where I live on Tuesdays!'

Yellow. Square. Smaller squares inside bigger square.

'But sure, didn't he get a big claim outta that accident that time? What's this, Jacob? This must be a picnic blanket! Are these the cups?'

'Course he did. Oh now, I'd say that's long gone. But sure, he's on the sick money now. Drink and drugs don't come cheap ya know, Mae-Anne!'

This is the sandpit.

'Is he still on them auld drugs? I thought he'd gone in somewhere to dry himself out?'

These are the sandcastles.

'That judge made him go. Don't ya know he stayed for a night or two and then him and her got plastered, to celebrate his return. I don't mind the drink so much as the drugs. It's the drugs that's drivin' them all feckin' crazy.'

'Could ya not talk her into sortin' herself out, Stell? Get her a bitta help, maybe?'

Green. Big square.

'Sure, amn't I blue in the face tryin' to talk to her, to get her to come home. Get her away from that fecker.'

Red. Triangle on top of big green square.

'Oh, I could write that book! It's not easy, to be sure, watchin' one a your own goin' down a bad auld road. And don't I know right well! Though it's different with Eleanor. That Karl's a different kettle a fish altogether. Plenty a money to throw around, to be sure, but he's not kind to her. He is not! Course now, she'd never admit that, not in a million years, but a mother knows when things aren't right. But sure, that's a whole other story. Is that a princess, Jacob, with lovely long golden hair? Did the pirates kidnap her? Are they takin' her away?' Granny points to Mammy smiling up at Jacob from the page. 'And that must be the little prince come to save her? I like his hat.' Granny moves her finger away from Mammy and it stops just under Jacob sitting on the swing. 'He's on a big horse I see. Is that the palace?'

This is the playhouse.

'She's lost an awful amount a weight, Mae-Anne. I met her last week outside the bank.'

'Sure, don't I know she's gone away to nothin. But it's him. Always commentin' on her size, he is.'

Up-down line.

'I always thought he was a nice chap, Mae-Anne.'

See-saw. See-saw.

'Oh, don't be fooled by that lad. And sure, I can't say a thing, or I'd be accused of interferin' and now, Stella, you know me. I'd never be one to interfere, so I wouldn't!'

'No more than meself, Mae-Anne. But sometimes I'd just love to give my Trish a good shake and tell her to stop wastin' her life away on that fella!'

'Bring her up above to the Rehab centre, Stell, and I'm tellin' you now, she'd get some land. Realise just how lucky she is to have her health!'

'Sure, Jesus don't I know. Them poor people up there and there's her trickin' around takin' drugs with that tramp! Destroyin' her life, she is.'

Black. Up-down lines. One. Two. One line in the centre joins the up-down lines like an H.

'Well, now, I can tell ya, he wasn't reared that way. Mary Mangan, God be good to her, would turn in her grave if she knew one a hers was carryin' on like that. Brains to burn, they all had. All those Mangans. Didn't she have one a priest? And her eldest boy did very well for himself. A degree, no doubt, from Trinity. Is that the pirates' clothes line, Jacob? Ya'll have to fill it up with all their shirts and pants. That's brilliant, just marvellous. Who'd ever think a pirates washin' their clothes?'

'Oh, Mary Mangan surely was a lady, she was. That Dermot must take after the father. Made an awful hames of himself, too, with the drink. Poor Mary, God rest her soul, had a terrible life with that fecker. The apple didn't fall too far from that tree, I can tell ya that now, for nothin'.'

This is the balance bar. A bar of chocolate is different. It is not the same like cream crackers are not the same as fish fingers. Fish fingers are different. So are waffles.

'Oh now, hasn't the drink been the ruination of many's a man and many's a marriage? And I can tell ya this much, Stella Kearns, if Holy Water was porter my John woulda been at Mass every mornin'!'

Grey. Rectangles. One. Two. Stuck together at the top like a big upside-down V. Orange dots. One. Two. Three. Four. Five. Green dots. Six. Seven. Eight. Nine. Ten. Top dots for hands. Bottom dots for feet.

'Course now, Mary had notions too, Mae-Anne. All them Martin girls had. From the time they were children, Mary had every bronze medal, every highly commended certificate and every feckin' yellow rosette or third place plaque they'd won, for sayin' a bit of an auld poem or winnin' an egg an' spoon race, put up in the parlour window or photographed for the paper.'

Black line. Down. A rope.

'Ah, but sure now, don't we all love to brag about our own, Stella? I can remember our Annette, and she not knee-high to a grasshopper, tellin' all the children on the road about how her daddy had single-handedly saved Byrne's pups, a whole bag a them, from drownin' in the river. Little did she know John had fallen in, he was that drunk; him and Paddy Byrne, Lord have mercy on him, decided, after a bottle a whiskey, they'd have to get shut a them pups by tyin' them into a bag with a rock in it an throwin' the poor little things in the river. Course in the heel a the hunt John, tryin' to be the hero, a course don't you know, let the bag fly into the water and lost his balance. Near drowned himself, too. Is that a tent for the pirates, Jacob?'

This is the climbing wall.

'What happened to the pups?'

'Sure, the two eejits were so full a whiskey that between them they couldn't even tie the knot in the bag properly. Don't ya know sure, didn't the pups swim back to the wall. Then a course himself arrives home, soaked to the skin and full to the gills, with one a them pups tucked up under his oxther and gives it to Annette along with the story of how he'd rescued it! Are they all off campin' on this desert island here, Jacob?' Granny's finger moves from the climbing wall over to the sandpit at the other side of the page.

Jacob stands up. Moves away from the table, brings his hands up to his ears.

'Did youse keep him?'

Jacob rocks backwards and forwards.

'We did. Had him for near on fourteen year. Do you not remember him yappin' every time the gate opened or the bell rang?' Granny stands up. Granny opens the press. 'Jacob, do ya want a cream cracker?'

Jacob stops moving. Granny tries to open the packet. 'Curse a God on it! Who invented these wrappers?'

'Aren't they desperate yokes to open altogether! Wouldn't ya think now they'd be able to invent somethin' better but sure I suppose they're too busy tryin' to send men to Mars to be figurin' out about cream crackers!' The other voice that shouldn't be in the kitchen stands up and gets a knife from the drawer. 'Here, Mae-Anne, use this.'

Jacob looks down at the floor. He keeps watching the shapes in the tiles. Granny's hand holds a cream cracker near Jacob's face. 'Here, pet. Don't you be frettin' now.'

Jacob's head jerks from side to side. He moves his weight from one leg to the other. He keeps watching his feet. The Mm-mm sounds come out of his mouth. He twists his runner into the brown square on the floor.

'Is he okay, Mae-Anne?'

'He's grand. Aren't ya, pet?'

Jacob moves back to the table. He folds the picture up. He turns and walks over to the counter. He puts his picture into Granny's bag.

'Ah now, would ya look at that, Mae-Anne. He wants ya to have his picture.'

'I'm not so sure it's for me.' Granny holds the cream cracker out to Jacob as he makes his way back to his seat. 'Is that for your mammy? I'll make sure she gets it, Jacob. I promise I'll give it to her on Friday. She'll be delighted, ya know. Your mammy always loved pictures and stories, especially them ones about pirates and princesses!'

'Wouldn't ya wonder what goes on inside his little head, all the same?'

'More than you or me will ever know, Stell, I can assure ya a that.'

Jacob picks the cracker out of Granny's hand.

'Ya know, Stell, I remember me own when John died. Their

little ashen faces. So frightened they were, and cold, like they'd been left out all night on the step. I can still see our Annette and she cryin' with her small, tiny body, like there was nothin' inside her but the sadness a the whole world and she callin' out *Daddy Daddy Daddy* and runnin' after the ambulance down the road. Only for our Terry I think she'd be runnin' still. And I can't get that picture outta me mind. And I think a Jenny and himself there and me heart breaks to think about woundin' them like that. A wound like that doesn't heal easy.'

Jacob picks at the brown bubble bits on the cracker.

CHAPTER 28

Jenny

Jenny sits at the kitchen table doing her homework. The smell of liver rises and settles over her head. She leans down, closer to the book, trying to avoid it. It doesn't work. Jenny's eyes water. Her mouth sours with the taste of something awful. Like dread. Jacob sits opposite Jenny. He is drawing a picture. Granny is peeling potatoes somewhere behind Jenny. She can hear the slice of the knife and the flurry of water washing the potatoes clean.

Jenny looks at the last page again. She can't believe this is the end. She closes the back cover over. Jenny waits. The kettle is boiling. Then it stops with a click. Granny rattles the pots in the press. A lid falls on the floor.

'Curse a God on it anyway,' Granny says to the lid, like it has just done something really awful that she's not going to forget about.

Jenny opens the back cover again. Just to be sure. Her eyes move down the page, searching desperately for the lost words and sentences. The ones she knows must be there, somewhere. She's read enough stories to know how they *should* end. Yes, there is always some trouble, even some sadness. But then the children come back home, the princess wakes up, the granny gets her nightdress back and everybody lives happily ever after, except the witches and wolves! She even reads the writing on the back of the book, in case maybe the lost words and sentences, somehow, leaked out on to the cover and escaped. But all she reads there are the things other people and newspapers have said about the book. It cannot end this way. It just can't! Jenny is sure about that.

'Carrots or peas?' Granny asks, without even turning around.

'Carrots please,' Jenny says, not because she particularly likes carrots, but because she particularly hates peas and the way they fly around the plate like marbles, before squishing their soggy wet skins up around the inside of her teeth after they have been caught. And then everything else tastes of peas too. For the rest of the day. At least carrots are quick.

Then, just like the liver smell, Granny appears and hovers over the table. She draws a long triangle, with a smiley face on it, in orange marker, on one of Mammy's sticky-yellow squares. She sticks it on to Jacob's page. Then she peels off another square and draws three green-marker circles. She places the green-circle square down beside the orange-triangle square.

'Carrots or peas?' Granny says to Jacob, moving her finger from one square to the other.

Without even looking at the little drawings, Jacob picks the orange triangle. He taps it with his finger and continues on with his picture.

'Carrots it is!' Granny says, like a big decision, that she is happy about, has just been made and there's to be no changing of minds now either.

Jenny flicks back to page 214. *Chapter Twenty* is marked clearly at the top. **The Last Chapter** is written in thick black letters underneath, like the book is making sure she knows she's close to the end and let there be no mistake about that. Jenny shifts in her seat. She flattens the pages down along the crease in the middle and starts reading **The Last Chapter** again. This time she uses her finger for reading, like she used to do with Mammy when she was little, just to make sure she doesn't miss anything or skip any lines. But nothing changes. '**This is the End,**' she says to herself in big thick black words.

The kitchen is getting hotter and louder and the thickness of all the smells makes the light feel heavy on Jenny's shoulders. Jenny's hands are sticky-wet.

How could the man who wrote the book let this happen? Jenny takes off her school jumper. She had liked Bruno so much and Schmuel too, though she didn't know him nearly as well as she knew Bruno. **He**, she thinks in bold, made the rain and the thunder. **He** made Bruno take off his clothes and his boots. **He** put him in stripy pyjamas. She hates him now – the man who made all this happen. The man who left Bruno holding Schmuel's hand in the dark. Jenny turns the book over to remind herself who **He** is. **John Boyne.** She uses the blackest letters she can find to say his name.

The liver smell hurts Jenny's eyes. It is the strongest smell in the kitchen. As soon as any other smell tries to take over another wave of liver creeps up her nose and down into her throat. It tastes like metal-blood. Jenny gags, like she is suffocating.

'Dinner won't be long now,' Granny says through the smell, pretending it's not even there. But her words just seem to lose themselves somewhere inside the stale bloodiness of the air.

Jenny sits looking at Bruno and Schmuel on the front cover. She runs her finger from one to the other without letting that big stupid fence get in the way. Bruno has dark hair, split and brushed over to the side. Schmuel doesn't have any hair at all. Bruno is wearing a brown tank top and grey shorts. Schmuel is wearing his pyjamas and yet for some reason, Jenny doesn't know why, they look just like the one boy.

'Where's your daddy?' Granny asks as she clinks the knives and forks down on the table.

'Out in the shed,' Jenny says, like there is no other answer to that question and Granny should know it by now, without having to ask.

John Boyne could have put Schmuel's papa out in the shed fixing something. He could have ended the story like that.

'Is all the homework finished now?' Granny asks, leaning over Jenny to put the salt and pepper in the middle of the table.

'Nearly,' is all Jenny says.

And that's the end of the story about Bruno and his family. Jenny takes her pen and scribbles out that line. *Where is the magic?* she wonders. She thinks about Mrs Nicholson – **she** had made Jenny read this stupid book. And Mrs French had told Jenny she'd loved it. They were all in this together, Jenny decides. Jenny would like to take Bruno and Schmuel out of the long room that was too hot and lock **John Boyne**, Mrs Nicholson and Mrs French in. But just at the last minute she takes Mrs French back out again and puts her outside in the rain. And Bruno and Schmuel could have found her out there and she would have known what to do.

Jenny opens the top button of her school shirt. She gets up from the table and opens the window.

'Jesus, you'll get your end. Do you want us all to get double pneumonia or what?' Granny says.

It's always double pneumonia. Granny never says, *You'll just get pneumonia,* like it doesn't even exist unless it is doubled. Jenny doesn't know what pneumonia actually is, but she supposes that when you get it 'double' you must get pneumonia and then get it again, so you must be twice as sick for twice as long. Jenny leaves the window open and sits back down at the table to finish her homework.

'Go on now and wash your hands, like a good child,' Granny says to Jacob.

Jacob puts the top back on his marker. He puts the marker down and goes over to the sink. Granny closes the window. Jenny slides the book back across the table. She doesn't remember putting it over there. She thinks about Bruno and Schmuel running through all the mud and about their pyjamas

stuck to their skin. Bruno wanted to go home. He was afraid
that he would catch a cold out there in all that rain. **John Boyne**
could have let Bruno go home. He could even have given him
double pneumonia and Jenny is sure even double pneumonia
has to be better than being shut up in that loud gasping place
with all of those marchers. Granny dries Jacob's hands. Jacob
comes back to the table, picks up Jenny's book and goes back
around to his own side again.

'I need that, Jacob!'

Jacob takes the top off his marker, sits down and carries on
with his drawing.

Jenny slides the book back across the table. She opens it from
the back and goes backwards through the pages until she reaches
page 206. She uses her finger to find what she's looking for.
She scribbles over the last paragraph on that page. Then she
takes the last nine pages and holds them together with her
thumb and the first finger on her right hand. With her left hand
out flat on page 206, she presses down on the book. Her right
hand tilts the last nine pages down slightly and pulling from
the top, slowly and carefully, she rips these pages away from
the rest. Scrunching them up in both hands she makes a paper
ball. She gets up from the table and throws the ball in the bin.

'What in the name a God are you doin, child?' Granny says,
rushing over to the bin.

'I don't like the ending!' Jenny sits back down at the table.

'But ya can't just go destroyin' a good book because ya don't
like it!'

'It isn't a *Good* book. It's a *Brilliant* book. I just don't like
the end!'

Jenny picks away at the tiny bits of ripped paper still stuck
to the rest of the book. She works them loose with determined
fingers and cleans it all up so well it's as though the pages had
never been there at all, like they had never been written and
never been read.

'So ya said. But you can't just go throwin' away the things you don't like, Jenny. Remember many's a sudden change can take place on an unlikely day.'

'What?'

'Ya can't just go doin' things like that, just because it doesn't suit you!'

'What?'

'Ya can't just get rid of the things in your life that you don't like.'

'I wish I could write a different ending. A better one.'

'Sure, ya can't go doin' that!'

'Why not?'

'Because life doesn't work like that, Jenny!'

'But it's not fair.'

'Fair or not, that's just not how life is. You make the best of what you've got. You don't go around fighting the things you can't change! Now can you both clear off the table please? It's not a restaurant I'm runnin', ya know. The dinner's ready.'

CHAPTER 29

Jenny

Dear Jenny,

I think the party is a great idea. It's something to look forward to, at any rate. And don't you be fretting about it now. Aren't I killed telling you, that's my job? And sure there's nothing to worry about anyway. I'm sure all Jacob's little friends will be able to come and they'll all have a great time. But listen to me now – so what if they don't come? Isn't it nice to give them all an invitation anyway? Maybe some of them have never been invited to a party before either and just think what it will mean to them just to be asked. It's no matter if they can't make it. That'll mean more cake for us. But they'll always know they were asked and that they were wanted. And they can put Jacob's invitation up on their mantelpiece and that might mean a lot to them and their mammies and daddies, too.

Granny tells me you are doing very well now in school and that you are a real little topper when it comes to helping her out and minding Jacob. Your granny is right, as usual, my arm is a bit sore. I tripped over and I hurt it. Black and blue it was, so I'm having to use my left hand instead.

I don't know what I'd do without you, Jenny.

Love,

Mammy

Jenny reads Mammy's letter again. Just to be sure. One more time. Just to check. Each time she reads it she sees that same word light up on the page, like it is the only important word there.

'Us,' Mammy said. 'That'll mean more cake for Us.' Jenny puts a capital on it herself. She uses her finger to steady the sentence.

'That'll mean more cake for us,' she reads it out loud. She tries it with no capital this time. Just to be sure.

Mammy didn't say anything about coming home. Jenny's sure about that. Jenny checks the letter again. No, she definitely doesn't say that she's coming home for Jacob's birthday. It must be a secret. Jenny's face feels strange. Then Jenny smiles, a real smile, for the first time in a very long time. Her smile grows bigger and bigger. Then for no reason at all, she thinks about the video on YouTube that Jacob watches over and over and over.

There are all these children in a big white classroom and the teacher is talking about rainforests and deserts and stuff and then, just out of nowhere, a woman, dressed up in a green soldier's uniform, comes into the classroom, and for a second everybody goes silent but then one little girl in the back row says, 'Mommy?' – like she's just seen someone she thinks she knows but she's not sure so she tries out the name just to see if the person looks around. Then she says it again. But it's not a question this time. The little girl is sure now. She runs up to the top of the classroom and jumps up into her mommy's arms. Her mommy grabs her with both arms and kisses her hair again and again and they stay glued together with kisses for a very long time and even though everyone is so happy they all start to cry, even the teacher. The mommy has been in the desert for seven months and the girl is so excited she can't even talk.

Jenny changes the costumes and the faces. Mammy won't come dressed as a soldier. She will wear her fluffy pink hoodie and her brown furry boots. Her arm will be better. She will wear jeans and her hair won't be in a ponytail. It will be down and much longer than it was. She will look a bit like Rapunzel or Sleeping Beauty after she wakes up. Jenny definitely won't be wearing her school uniform. She will be wearing Mammy's favourite dress – the red one, with the sparkles on it, that she bought Jenny last Christmas. Jenny won't be in school talking about rainforests and deserts and stuff either. She will be wiping Jacob's face or cleaning his hands in the kitchen and they will turn around, both of them at the same time, and they will see her standing in the door. And there will probably be music, playing in the background. Jenny decides it will be 'Can You Feel the Love Tonight?' from *The Lion King*. She thought at first it might be something from *Frozen* but she knows now it won't be because she can already hear the words of 'Can You Feel the Love Tonight?' getting louder from the hall behind Mammy, and Jacob will be so excited that he will talk. He will say Mammy, not like it's a question because Jacob will know, and Jenny will know their own mammy when she comes home again to the party to kiss their hair, and the three of them will stay glued together for a very long time. But no one will cry because Jenny won't let that happen. Jenny makes everyone clap and sing along with the song from the hall and they will all say that it's the best party they have ever been to and then Mammy will bring Jacob up to bed and after she has told him a story and kissed him goodnight, she will come back down to the kitchen, where Jenny will be waiting.

CHAPTER 30

Annette

Between her finger and thumb she holds photographs somebody left on the locker beside her bed. There are two of them. Lost words and names of things or people remembered curdle on the floor of Annette's mind. There is a boy, in one. A boy on a swing.

'Jacob,' she says, 'Jacob.'

There is a man smiling up at her, from the past, in the other. A silent man standing inside a white border framed within the green of a faraway garden, broken only by little yellows, pinks and browns. Annette closes her eyes. Pictures and faces bleed through her to settle in corners too dark for watching. She hears his old voice swelling in her skull then it grows small again, withers and dies like the falling drip of flowers somebody else put on the rattle tin locker. The whole world is here in her good hand.

'Daddy,' she whispers.

Her father, as big as a house to the little girl in the lemon summer dress beside him, is humming a tune. Annette knows this tune, but she cannot remember what it was called. She remembers his stories, dancing through the house with a light rhythm and returning to him again in his chair in the corner; the smell of his cigarettes filling the room; his steel-toe boots outside the back door. He ruffled their hair, took sweets out of secret deep pockets, thrilling them with the crackle of untwisting the wrappers. Then he was gone, face down in the flowerbed, one Sunday morning after Mass; her mother pushing them behind her and calling out to Mrs Murphy next door. She had tried then to remember all the stories he had ever told them, all in that one moment. She saw each of his characters on the grass beside him looking frightened, lost like children afraid of being forgotten. Gathering closer, huddling together, checking they were all there, in the cold shade, where they sheltered. But one was missing. Annette tries now to find her again after so long, the woman in the floury apron with measling shins, somewhere in one of the dusty corners of her mind. The woman with the poker. That was her. She was the woman with the lost child.

The ambulance lights scream. Strange men in grey walk somehow from the sun towards them.

It was a stroke.

CHAPTER 31

Jenny

Tuesday, 22nd October, 2013

Dear Anne Frank,

I hope you don't mind but I'm reading your diary. I wouldn't have read it – Mrs French says that a diary is a record of your own personal thoughts and a diary is written only for yourself and not for the rest of the world to see – but she gave it to me anyway.

I'm so sorry if that is upsetting for you. Mrs French would not like to think that she had hurt you. She loves your writing so much that she is still reading your other books. I like the word 'unbosomings'. I googled it to see what it means. It is a good word, I think.

Yours, Jenny

CHAPTER 32

Jenny

It is Jacob's birthday today. Today Jacob is six. Jenny is wearing her sparkly dress, the red and black one with the bow at the side, that she wore last Christmas. Jenny is ready. All the balloons are blown up and the table is set. Granny is very busy watching the door. Jenny is too.

'Party Bags? What do ya mean Party Bags?' Granny screams. Granny has never heard of party bags. 'Bouncy Castles? What do ya mean Bouncy Castles?' She's never heard of bouncy castles either! Granny's voice gets squeakier, her letters get bigger and her mouth opens even wider every time she says, 'Party Bags' or 'Bouncy Castles'. There's a big annoyed question mark at the end every time too. Her face, getting redder, folds up into itself and her eyes, faded, watery and tired, seem to disappear. She pushes her hand through the side of her hair. 'Why didn't ya tell me Earlier?' she squeals, across the hall, throwing her questions like snowballs, as though it's all Jenny's fault Granny's never heard of PARTY BAGS or BOUNCY CASTLES before and now all the capitals are spilling out of her mouth too quickly and falling down all over her Good Floor, and that's all because of Jenny, too. 'Well, they may go without. IT'S TOO LATE NOW. You get the parcels ready for Pass the Parcel and I'll put the candles on the cake.' Granny's words bite at Jenny like snapping teeth.

Jenny takes the parcels into the sitting room. Granny keeps watching the door, as if by looking at it with such a cross, red face she'll be able to make loads of children arrive on the front step. On time. It doesn't work. Granny looks up at the clock. She checks her watch, goes back out into the kitchen and reads the time off the oven. She shakes her head then stamps back out to the hall and back into the sitting room again. Granny looks at Mammy staring down from the mantelpiece. Granddad is there beside her. Granny turns both pictures slightly inwards, so they can see each other better. 'There now,' she says to Mammy's smiling face, 'That's better, now altogether!' Then she moves over to the window, leans to the side, and pulls back the curtain a tiny little bit, like maybe that's going to work better than staring at the door. It doesn't. 'It's Twenty to Three. I put Two o'clock on the invitations. Where's your Father?'

'Out in the shed.'

'Doin' What exactly?'

'He's workin' on his secret project!'

'Who does He think he is? James Feckin' Bond? Secret Project! I'll give Him Secret Project!' There are so many capitals and question marks and all sorts of other things shooting out from Granny that Jenny lowers herself closer to the ground, to take cover. 'And What are You doin' down there on the floor?'

'I'm hidin' the sweets for Blind Man's Bluff.'

Granny pulls her two hands down along each side of her face, as if to make sure her face is still there, where it should be, on the front of her head. Then the doorbell rings. Granny moves faster than Jenny has ever seen her move before. Jenny runs out behind her.

'You're Late, Eleanor!' Granny spits at Eleanor and Saidhbhe as she walks away from the door, back into the kitchen, leaving them standing outside.

Jenny checks outside but there's nobody else there. Eleanor follows Granny into the kitchen. Saidhbhe wanders around the hall, poking at things that shouldn't be poked at. Jenny closes the front door again and takes Saidhbhe out into the kitchen.

'Mam, I'm sorry. I had Boxilates and Saidhbhe had Spanish.' Eleanor's words run for their lives around the kitchen, looking for somewhere to hide before Granny catches them and stamps them out with her foot.

'I thought that was Wednesdays?' Granny says hoping to catch Eleanor out.

'It is normally, but Ivonne, her teacher, was busy this week, so she changed it,' Eleanor says in a little girl's voice now, a little girl who has been caught doing something she knows she shouldn't do.

'Now, I ask ya, Eleanor, Isn't Everyone just so Feckin' Busy, all the same!' Although Granny's sentence starts like a question it doesn't finish like one. '*Boxilates!* How are ya? Jesus Christ I've never heard such a stupid word, except maybe *streptococcus!* Now that is a ridiculous word! Whatever happened to havin' a sore throat? I ask ya! There's orphans, ya know, Eleanor, all over Africa, in villages crippled by famine and disease and they're that skinny, they're fat! And there's you exercisin' to within an inch a your life and not eatin' because some other feckin' celebrity comes on the telly, straight after one a them ads with the dyin' African orphans in it, and tells you that you too can lose seventeen stone in a week if you only eat one a her shakes a day! Or is it because Karl wants ya like that?'

'How are ya, Nellie?' Da says, with a big grin as he closes the back door behind him.

'And Where were You?' Granny slams the press door and turns around to look at Da with her whole body.

'Kevin, please do not call me *Nellie!* Karl calls me *Ells*. He actually asked one of the company solicitors about changing it. It has to be done by Deed Poll! I never liked *Eleanor* and I absolutely hate *Nellie!*' Eleanor shouts over Granny's slamming and banging, though she looks secretly delighted to see Da.

'Oh, sufferin' Jesus,' Granny says, shaking her head. 'Whatever next! Ells? *Ells!*' Granny repeats the word like she's testing it out. *Ells* does not pass Granny's test. Granny takes a tea towel off the hook.

Da's eyes do a dance. 'Ells? What's all this about, Nellie?'

'Stop it, Kevin! I'm serious! *Nellie* makes me feel like that spoiled brat with the blue dress and ringlets out of *The Waltons* or that stupid elephant that ran away with the circus!'

'Nellie the elephant packed her trunk and said GOODBYE to the circus,' Da sings and then suddenly the song seems to be going around inside everybody's head because that's one of those lines that needs the trumpety-trump, trump trump trump bit, before you can make it stop!

'Oh, whatever!' Eleanor says, breaking the humming noises in everybody's head. She looks like she's planning ways to kill Da.

'She's only thinkin' of changin' her name! Permanently!' Granny tells Da like he wasn't here when Eleanor said it, just a minute ago, and now Granny has to tell Da again or else Granny's just trying to make sense of it herself. 'Don't ya think now, Eleanor, that we've enough to contend with at the moment without all a that kinda nonsense?' she says, and she looks like she's trying to rub the flowers off the plate she's drying in big swooping circles. The plate squeaks.

Granny's really not good at questions, Jenny decides, standing in the doorway watching all the words fighting around in the air.

'Okay, Mam, it was only an idea Karl had, anyway. Forget it,' Eleanor says in a confused voice, or an embarrassed voice, Jenny's not really sure. But she definitely sounds like she's just realised something she hadn't thought about before and now she wishes she had never found the words to explain her idea. So, is it the words or the idea that sound worse? Again, Jenny's not sure. But she decides that she will think about this later on, when there is enough space in her head. Right now, there is not. Right now, there is a big queue of other things waiting.

And Mammy's right there at the top of the line. Eleanor plays with the big box she's holding in her hand. Granny attacks another plate.

Da's eyes are leaping around in his head. He looks like the man who just bought the island on the Lottery ad on the telly. 'It was *Little House on the Prairie*, not *The Waltons!*'

'What?' Granny and Eleanor say, at the same time. Granny suddenly stops moving the tea towel in big, angry-drying circles.

'Nellie Olsen was not a Walton! She was a Prairie girl! Actually, she's written a book. *Confessions of a Prairie Bitch*, I think it's called. I saw her on YouTube. Her mother was Casper the Ghost!'

'Would ya go way outta that, Kevin!' Granny says as her tea towel hand starts moving again. But slower this time, like she's being more careful. 'God now, do ya remember poor blind Mary and her trippin' over herself every time she came down that feckin' big hill at the start?'

'She was!' Da says but nobody seems to know what it is he's actually proving. Is it the bit about Nellie not being a Walton? Or the bit about her being on YouTube? Or the bit about her mother being a ghost?

'Oh, Mam, do you remember us all sitting around waiting for it to come on?' Eleanor says, smiling, like now she's just remembered a thing she's sorry that she ever forgot. 'But it was the smallest one that fell in that cornfield, every Sunday night. It definitely wasn't Mary! I don't remember that little one's name, but do you remember Ma and Pa in the wagon, smiling at the three of them as they tumbled and ran in those plaits? They were all so happy.'

'Well, it turns out that Nellie and Laura were actually best friends in real life,' Da says like he's sharing a big secret. He does a little head nod. 'Apparently that Mary was the real bitch! Alison Arngrim, that was Nellie's real name, said so in the interview.'

'Oh, do you remember the time Laura pushed Nellie down the hill when she was in a wheelchair?' Eleanor says, like she's just shocked herself with what it is she had forgotten she knows. She looks at Granny. 'Why was Nellie in a wheelchair?'

'No, I don't remember no wheelchair. But I do remember her changing her name!' Granny says. 'Ah, that one had notions too! One minute she was Nellie and the next she was Nancy!' Granny says clanking her way through the knives and forks.

'No, that was a new character altogether. Mrs Olsen adopted Nancy,' Eleanor says.

'Did they get her from the Waltons?' Da says, scrunching up his face, in a pretending-to-be-confused kind of way.

'What?' Eleanor says but she doesn't wait for an answer. 'Anyway, Mam, it costs a bloody fortune! Solicitor says it's more hassle than it's worth!' Her words are quieter this time, like she's trying to make them disappear. But it's too late.

'I don't blame Mrs Olsen for gettin' shot a that Nellie! Imagine. Changing her own name! And are you Tellin' me, You're going to Pay Good Money to have Letters Removed from your Own Name? Or is it all Karl's doin'? Not posh enough, I suppose! The Name that I gave to Ya! Jesus Christ! What's Wrong with You?' Granny says, too suddenly and too loud. She smashes the knives in on top of the other knives.

'Ah, I don't know. Like I said, it was just an idea, Mam,' Eleanor says, like she's just brought a size eight dress back into Next because she thought that it suited her, but it turns out now that it doesn't even fit her at all. 'Mrs Olsen didn't get rid of Nellie! Nancy was like a new little Nellie. Mrs Olsen adopted Nancy, when Nellie left.'

'I don't care if she was Nancy or Nellie! It's no reason for You to go changing your Name! And, anyway, Who said ya could do that? Karl, I suppose!' Granny says, slamming the drawer. She folds the tea towel in two and goes back into the sitting room with it still in her hand, to look out the window.

'What do you mean?' Eleanor's question follows Granny around the corner and into the other room.

Da is singing now, 'La, la, la, la la lala la, La, la, la la, lala lala la.'

'Well, I gave ya that Name! Fought Tooth and Nail for it, In Fact! That was My Grandmother's name and SHE was a LADY! Soon as I saw ya, I Thought I knew exactly who ya were! Your father thought you looked more like a Gladys or a Mildred. I should have let him name ya!' Granny's words fly out through the sitting-room door, swirl around in the hall and shoot back into the kitchen.

Da looks at Eleanor, like he's trying to see which name suits her best. Eleanor sucks in her breath so quick, Jenny's sure she can hear it whizzing over her teeth, like she's just had a lucky escape.

'Ah, I'm sorry, Mam!' Eleanor tries to send her words back in the same direction, but they don't seem to make it past the fridge.

'You could definitely be a Mildred!' Da says, nodding his head wisely and pretending to look out at her over his invisible glasses while stroking his invisible beard. 'Gladys works on you, too!'

'Seems I was Wrong!' Granny's words are back, and they have big sticks in their hands.

Just then, before Eleanor can say anything at all, Saidhbhe runs around the kitchen and smashes her head off the counter. She looks up at Eleanor, opens her mouth as wide as she can and for a minute there is nothing but silence and a small, flat pink tongue looking for something to do. Then the tongue curls back, like a big wave getting ready, and Saidhbhe starts screeching without doing any breathing at all.

Da lifts her up and rubs her head. 'You're all right, pet. Bold, Bold Counter!' he says, and slaps the counter so hard that Saidhbhe stops screaming and starts laughing instead.

'Are you okay, baby?' Eleanor asks, before putting the big box down on the Bold, Bold Counter. Then she gives Saidhbhe a kiss on the bit that got bumped. Saidhbhe's bottom lip wobbles again. She buries her head in Da's shoulder.

'I Thought I reared you to have more Sense than that!' Granny's back in the kitchen with her questions that aren't really questions at all.

Da and Eleanor both turn around at the same time to look at Granny.

'What?' Eleanor says again, like she left all her other important words somewhere else and this is the only one left or at least it's the only one she can find right now.

'In fairness, Nellie, now ya could think about doin' the same for poor little Saidhbhe here, while you're at it,' Da says, looking down at the little girl spread over his chest, like a jumper.

'What?' Eleanor's eyes dart from Granny to Da and Saidhbhe and then back to Da again.

'Where are the Rice Krispie buns?' Granny says, to nobody really because this is a question she's really asking herself inside her own head.

'What are you talking about? I love the name Saidhbhe! It's romantic!' Eleanor's shoulders get squarer as she fills up all the space in front of Da.

'Not spelt like that, it's not!' Da says.

'Ells. Ells. I ask ya! Makes her sound like one a them feckin' Kardashians. My Grandmother must be turnin' in her grave right now!' Granny says, like Eleanor isn't even still there in the kitchen anymore. But she is.

'Can't we just forget about it? Please?' Eleanor asks, more Rice Krispie buns sliding past her, on a plate, in the air.

'Well, the poor child will spent spend half her life tryin' to learn how to spell her own name and she'll spend the other half tryin' to spell it out to everyone and anyone she meets. Then she'll have to teach them how to spell it too because no one else in the whole world could make S-A-I-D-H-B-H-E sound like S-I-V-E. Imagine the amount of time she'll have to waste tellin' the young lad behind the counter in X-tra Vision or the Credit Union the correct spellin' of her name so he can put it into his computer to make sure she is who she says she is before he gives her a DVD or a loan – like who'd ever *pretend* to be called S-A-I-D-H-B-H-E!' Da says, like this is something so obvious it doesn't even need a question mark at the end.

Eleanor opens her mouth to say something, but Granny's words come rushing forward like a big tidal wave.

'And just Who do You think You are, Pontificatin' about names?' Granny flashes her glasses at Da and pushes Eleanor out of the space in front of him.

'But you said—' Da tries to say something longer but Granny waves her hand in the air to rub out the rest of his sentence.

'Never Mind what I said! It's what You said that I'm Referrin' to!' Granny snaps at Da.

'I just feel sorry for—'

Granny's big air rubber makes Da's words vanish so quickly it's like he never even said them at all. 'Well, now, You Can just hold on there, just One Minute and Save Your pity for your Own Crowd!'

'What?' Da says, like all his other words ran off with Eleanor's.

'Well, sure, isn't Every Single One of yas called Mickey!'

'What?' Da says. 'I'm not!' he adds, like he's going to win this game.

But Granny's not finished yet! 'Course now there isn't so much as One of them here today, mind you! But sure, they never were what ya might call reliable!' Granny checks her watch. She puts the plate of Rice Krispie buns on the table.

'What?' Da says, looking very confused now and maybe a little bit hurt.

'Well, now, let me see. There's Big Mickey and Little Mickey and Cousin Mickey and Uncle Mickey,' Granny says, like she's reading him the rules off the back of the box. 'There's a Mickey Senior and of course a Mickey Junior. Sure, ya couldn't have one without the other, I suppose. You've a Brother Mickey, a nephew Mickey and Two second cousins who are Mickeys. Your Grandfather was Mickey. And his father before him was most likely a Mickey, too.' Granny looks like she's waited a very long time to say this and now that she has she looks very proud. 'Jenny, will you help me with the Jelly?' she says, taking the big glass bowl of red jelly out of the fridge, leaving all her Mickey sentences behind with Da.

'What are ya talking about, now?' Da says, like he's trying to find his way out of the dark.

'All a them Feckin' Mickeys!' Granny says, shaking her head.

Eleanor bursts out laughing. 'Ah Jesus, Ma!' she says. Then she puts her hand over her mouth to try to stop any more sound from escaping.

'So, what? It's Michael actually! It's a family name!' Da says, but then he suddenly looks unsure, like this news has made him change his mind about something.

'Family name! Would ya ever go way outta that! That's just feckin' well Goddamn Lazy! That's what That is!' Granny says, looking down over her glasses.

Eleanor is laughing so hard her whole body is shaking and Jenny thinks about the time they were in Mass and somebody in the row in front of them let off a big, smelly fart and how Jenny thought she was going to die of the smell and the silent laughing because she knew she couldn't laugh out loud or Granny would kill her. She remembers her head bobbing up and down and her shoulders pushing up into her ears and how she had held her nose and just when she thought everything was okay and just fine, a big snort came out of her nose and her mouth all at the same time and then she panicked because she thought she was choking.

The doorbell rings and Granny races past Jenny, with a smile on her face too, ready to greet the first guests. Jenny runs out behind her.

'Ah musha, come on in outta that, Billy. You're very good for comin'. Come on out to the kitchen.' Granny turns around again and goes back through the kitchen door. Crazy Billy, from next door, goes in behind her. Jenny checks outside. Just to be sure. But there's nobody else there. Jenny returns to the kitchen.

'Ah, how are ya, Billy?' Da says, giving Saidhbhe back to Eleanor again.

'Sit down there, Billy. Let me take your coat.' Granny stands with her arm out. Her hand is open.

Billy looks at all the faces in the kitchen. Then he looks at Granny. Then down at his coat. Then he looks back at Granny again, like he's not really sure what she just said or why she's standing there waiting for something. Billy takes a step backwards, like he's frightened and has decided to escape out the back door.

'Would ya like a cuppa tea?' Granny moves over to the kettle, leaving Billy to decide about his coat himself. Billy watches his boot tracing the grey lines between the tiles on the floor.

'Where's Jacob?' Da asks, looking around the kitchen.

'He's upstairs. In bed,' Granny says, pouring the boiling kettle water into the teapot.

'I'll go and get him,' Jenny offers, getting ready to run. She needs Jacob down here in the kitchen. That's how she's planned it.

'No. Leave him be, Jenny. He'll come down when he's ready. He's tired. He was up most of the night.'

'Why didn't ya wake me, Mae-Anne?' Da says to Granny. This is a proper question.

'I couldn't sleep meself so I was up anyway. Sure, there's no point in us All bein' awake, now is there?' This is not a proper question. This is a Granny question.

Da opens his mouth to say something else but he seems to change his mind and he just closes it shut again.

'I'm just going to bring Saidhbhe up to the toilet,' Eleanor says and goes out through the kitchen door.

Billy very slowly unzips his coat and painfully peels himself open, like a banana with the measles. Billy has put on his Sunday trousers and his going-to-Mass shirt. He folds his coat over in half and places it on the back of the chair in the corner.

'Ya'll have a Rice Krispie bun with your tea now, Billy, won't ya?' Granny holds the plate out with one hand and gives Billy his tea with the other.

The doorbell rings again. Granny hands Da the plate and races back out to the hall. Jenny follows behind.

'Ah, you're very good, Lizzie. Come on inside,' Granny says.

Jenny hears Granny's voice getting tired.

Lizzie, from the shop, comes into the hall with the biggest Kinder Egg Jenny has ever seen in her whole life. Granny and Lizzie go back to the kitchen. Jenny looks up and down the road outside. There's nobody there. She closes the door again and goes back out to the kitchen.

'Well, ya couldn't let a day like today go by without markin' it someway,' Lizzie says, handing Da the big egg.

'Thanks, Lizzie.' Da takes the Kinder and puts it down on the counter. Granny swoops in with more tea and more buns.

'How are ya, Jenny? Don't you look Just Gorgeous. Is that a New dress?' Lizzie, moving closer, puts a Twix into Jenny's hand. She gives Jenny a wink and turns around to look at Billy. 'Ah now, go ta God, Billy. Is it yourself? The Mammy's doin' well I suppose?' Lizzie asks Billy one of Granny's questions, like she had been in the same class as Granny at school where they had learned to make capital letters fit where they shouldn't and had discovered magic questions that don't need any answers. Jenny wonders if this is a kind of trick. Billy nods and looks back down at the tiles.

'Mam, I'll have to go at four because the—' Eleanor's back in the kitchen with Saidhbhe.

Granny steps past her, into the hall, without letting Eleanor finish what she's saying. 'So, Let me Guess. You've got some kind of underwater yoga-aerobics or that feckin' Mindlessness that ya do and Saidhbhe has maths camp in feckin' Latin or Chinese, in someplace fancy like Harvard or Yale, no less and ya need to get goin' to beat the traffic!' Granny's voice stretches back in from the hall, sticks its head around the corner and pokes out Eleanor's eyes. So does the sound of her opening the door.

'No. Well yes. I'm heading up for late visiting. Sure, she won't have seen anyone today. And I want to get on the road before the rush.' But Eleanor's words don't make it out of the kitchen – they seem to get stuck in the strings of her pink Superdry hoodie, so it doesn't really matter that she has said them at all.

Jenny closes her eyes, as if she can blink away the sound of Eleanor's words. They don't count, Jenny decides.

'Come in. Come in. Aren't ya very good now for comin'?' Granny marches back into the kitchen with Frank, from the bus, marching behind her.

Frank isn't really marching. He's really just trying to keep up with Granny.

'Howya, Frank?' Da says. 'Thanks for comin'.'

Granny brushes some imaginary crumbs off the table into her open hand. She goes to the bin and drops them inside.

'Not at all. So where is the little man himself then?' This is another proper question. Frank asks it to the whole kitchen. Everyone's head moves around, like they are looking for something they know isn't there, but they still look for it anyway. Just in case.

'I'll go up and get him,' Jenny says to Granny, more than to anybody else.

Granny nods and without even asking she hands Frank a cup and a plate of buns.

When Jenny and Jacob arrive back in the kitchen Eleanor is the first one to give Jacob a present.

'Happy Birthday, my best boy,' she says.

Jacob picks it up, runs his hand across the top and places it back down on the counter again.

'Open it, Jacob! Your Auntie Ells got it just for you,' Da says with a smile and a quick look over at Eleanor.

Jacob walks over towards Granny. Da follows Jacob and hands him the present again. 'Go on, Jacob, open it. This is for you.' Jacob pulls the paper away from the box, like he's supposed to. 'What's this, Jacob?' Da says, trying to sound all excited. Jacob, without even looking at the box, moves his eyes across the kitchen and makes his way closer to the table where Granny is now putting crisps into a bowl.

'It's an iPad,' Eleanor says, as Jacob walks away.

'What in The Name of Jesus did ya get That Thing for? Isn't there already a computer in the house?' Granny says over her shoulder.

Lizzie's watching every word that flies past her. Jenny watches her trying to remember each one before even more come along to take their place instead. She's writing each word down in the notebook Jenny imagines her opening up inside her head so that she can change them around a bit later on and tell the story all over again tomorrow in the shop. And it will be even better then. Jenny wonders what Lizzie will write about Mammy surprising them all. That will be the best bit of the whole story. Jenny just knows it. Frank looks frightened or embarrassed, Jenny's not sure which it is, but he turns to Billy for help. Billy just keeps on eating Rice Krispie buns, watching his own boots and drinking his tea.

'It's got a special app on it for Jacob, to help him with his words,' Eleanor tries to explain. 'He can use it to tell you what he—'

'And what does he need That for? Sure, isn't he gettin' on grand. Anyway, I'll Never manage That Thing!' Granny says, looking now at the iPad, like it's something really dangerous that could pull out a knife any minute and slit Granny's throat.

'The man in the shop says there's even—' Eleanor begins to say, but that's as far as she gets before Granny steps into the middle of her sentence again.

'I'm Sure He does and I'm Sure There is!' Granny's bottom lip seems to shuffle in and out with her teeth but then she makes herself straighter and taller again. She clears her throat.

Da looks at Eleanor. He makes new word shapes with his eyes. Eleanor makes more eye-word shapes back to Da. Then they nod at each other, like they are sharing some big, great invisible secret. Eleanor clears her throat too and tells Granny that she can return it to the shop, and that the man in the shop said that Jacob could try it out for a while, but that he'll take it back if Jacob or Granny don't like it. Da smiles at Eleanor. Eleanor throws her eyes up a little bit making her eyebrows look further apart than they really are but then she smiles back at Da. Her eyebrows come back down again to where they should be.

'Mam, I really have to go,' she says, pulling Saidhbhe away from the table.

'Where?' This is actually a real question, but Granny can't be bothered waiting for an answer.

Eleanor has already explained, and she looks like she can't be bothered explaining again.

'What is it, pet?' Granny asks Jacob. Jacob is pulling at Granny's cardigan. 'Hold on a minute, pet.' Granny puts the plate of sandwiches back down on the table. She bends down to Jacob. Jacob puts his hand into Granny's pocket and roots around, like Granny's pocket is some kind of lucky dip. Granny tells Jacob they'll do that later. But Jacob doesn't give up. He uses his other hand to hold Granny's cardigan while he tries to pull the pocket-hand back out. Granny tries to stand up again. Jacob holds on real tight. When he does manage to get his hand back out he is holding a pile of small, square cards. 'I'll take them for ya, pet!' Granny says, leaning back down again.

But Jacob's too quick for Granny and before she can grab them Jacob has spread them in a straight line all along the top of the table.

'What have ya got there, Jacob?' Da asks, peeping over Jacob's shoulder.

They are picture cards like the ones they sell in the Two Euro shop with the free chewing gum inside the silver packet. Each card has a different picture on it. Jacob looks at each one very carefully, like he's trying to find the answer to one of Granny's questions, and then, like he has found the right answer, he hands one of the cards back to Granny. Granny takes the card, holds it too close to her face and nods. Granny's face is very red.

'Over in me handbag, pet,' is all Granny needs to say.

Jacob turns and walks back to the counter. He opens Granny's bag and takes out a packet of coconut creams.

'Only one now, mind you! We've still to have some cake when all of your little friends arrive,' Granny says to the back of Jacob's head.

Granny looks at the clock on the oven. She checks her watch. Jacob takes two fluffy biscuits out of the packet. He hides one in his pocket and leaves the kitchen as quietly as he came, his little footsteps getting smaller and smaller as he goes back up the stairs.

CHAPTER 33

Jacob

Jacob sits on his bed looking at Granny's pink and white fluffy biscuits. The moon in the window is round like a biscuit is before taking a bite. The moon is not fluffy. Cat is fluffy. Cat is not round. The moon is round. So are the biscuits.

Today is Jacob's birthday. Tomorrow is not. Tomorrow is different. Not like today. Today is Saturday. Saturday is different to Birthday. So is Thursday. Today is Jacob's birthday. Today Jacob is six.

Pink is first. Jacob likes pink better. White is next. Jacob can taste the pink inside his mouth. Jacob likes pink more than the taste of any other colour. When pink is all gone Jacob likes white. White is not a colour. The moon is white like the white biscuit. It is not pink like the pink biscuit. The moon is round like the biscuits. It is not fluffy like Cat.

Jacob takes a white band out from under his pillow. Granny puts Jacob's stripy pyjamas under his pillow every morning. Socks are next in the morning. Then Jacob can put on his shoes.

Jacob takes another bite. Smaller bites are better than bigger bites.

Jenny put a tooth under her pillow. It was her tooth. It fell out of her mouth. That was for the fairies. That was a long time ago. Before today. Granny's teeth live in a glass on the toilet like fish. Lonely is a fish. He is not a fairy. Fairies can fly. Fish can't. Teeth can take pink bites. Teeth are white too like the moon.

Today is Jacob's birthday.

The white band smells yellow today. Like Mammy. Jacob puts the band around his wrist. Jacob knows legs go straight out and down for standing. They go straight out and back in again for swinging. This is not swinging. This is standing. Jacob can feel all the noises from the kitchen in the bottom of his feet. His socks look itchy. Jacob can hear the prickles scraping on his skin. Jacob holds his wrist up to his nose. He sniffs yellow out of the white band. Jacob lifts his feet off the floor to sit back on the bed again. He looks at his feet. Today Jacob is wearing birthday socks. Today is Jacob's birthday. Granny says Jacob's a *swank*. *Swank* is Granny's word. Tomorrow he will wear tomorrow's day socks. They will be different. Granny says different is good. Good is better than bad. Bad is not good. Granny and Jacob went to Tesco to buy Jacob's new socks. It was the night-time. The moon was round like Jacob's biscuit. White is next. Jacob takes a white bite. Granny puts Jacob's day socks on every morning. Granny says Jacob is her little pet. *Pet* is Granny's word. So is *Topper*. Granny says Jacob is a little *Topper*. The moon was yellow like Thursday.

Every day Jacob's socks are different. Different means not the same. Granny's words are not the same as Mammy's words. Granny's words are different.

Today the moon is white like Sunday.

Tuesday socks are green. Jacob is Mammy's little *Happy Cat*. Jacob can pet Cat if he is very gentle, Granny says. Friday socks are orange. Tigers are orange. Monday socks are red. Jacob cannot pet Lonely. Lonely is not Cat. Lonely is different. Today is different. Tigers are big cats. Tigers are orange. Today is Saturday. Saturday is purple. Today is Jacob's birthday. Today Jacob is six.

Tigers are not pets. Wednesday is blue. Yesterday Jacob was

five. Today Jacob is six. Today is the day Jacob came out of Mammy's tummy. Jacob was a bump and then he was Jacob and Mammy was happy. That was a long time ago. It was Sunday, Granny says. Sunday is white. Thursday is Jacob's favourite colour-day. Thursday is yellow. Today is not Thursday. Today is purple.

Jacob pulls the band open at the top of his head. Granny says this is Jacob's *Crown*. Jenny says this is Jacob's *Head*. The band is tight. Jacob feels little noises inside it. White noises pulling at his ears. Jacob has a pain. This is a red pain. Jacob can hear it all over his face. The white band is making the red pain. Jacob's head is growing bigger. The red pain feels purple. The purple pain thump-thumps behind Jacob's eyes. The white band is getting smaller like Jacob's clothes when Granny says he's getting big like a tree. Money does not grow on a tree, Granny says. Apples grow on a tree. Jacob pulls the band down over his face. Granny says *Puss*. Granny doesn't say face. *Puss* means Cat too. Granny calls Cat *Puss*. Puss is a pet. Jacob is Granny's little pet. The band snaps at Jacob's mouth. Jacob pushes his teeth in and out around all the white. Jacob hears white-ringing scratches inside his head. His skin sounds itchy again. Jacob closes his eyes. It is black behind Jacob's eyes. Jacob cannot see the moon. The moon is hiding. There are sparkles and white flashes in the black behind Jacob's eyes. Jacob's hands slide up and down his hair. Jacob's hair is sore hair today. Today is Jacob's birthday. The band is too tight around Jacob's neck. The biscuits are too big inside Jacob's mouth. The moon is back. There is a man in the moon, Mammy says. Jacob cannot see the man. Jacob rocks back and bang-bangs the wall. Jacob can taste the wee splashing his leg. It is warm. Jacob is too hot. Like fire is too hot. Jacob cannot see the fire but Jacob knows he is burning. The fire is inside Jacob and Jacob can't breathe. The smoke-clouds take the moon away.

Mammy. Jacob tries to make the word into a shout-sound.

He scratches his throat. Pulls at his skin. Mammy cannot hear Jacob. Jacob can see all Mammy's words up in the moon with the man.

'Jesus Christ, Jacob, what have ya done?' Granny is here but Jacob can't see her. 'Oh, pet. Oh, pet. Oh, pet. It's okay. It'sokay. Isokay, pet.'

Granny snaps the band open. Jacob's eyes roll around in his head. Granny pulls the band up over Jacob's nose. Jacob makes coughing noises. Granny's fingers root in Jacob's mouth. Granny's nails click-clack on Jacob's teeth. Granny pulls the biscuit away.

The moon is back.

Today is Jacob's birthday. Today Jacob is six.

CHAPTER 34

Annette

The bright yellow-light of the ward falls away. The clicking heels and squeaking trolley wheels fade into the receding walls. Annette sees herself. She's the same as she used to be before this.

'How are ya, love?' he is saying.

It is summer and they're having a picnic near a castle in a park. Annette doesn't know where it is, nor does she know how they got there. Annette is laughing at something the man has said. They are eating cold sausage rolls and ham and cheese sandwiches. They are sitting on a blue and white blanket. There are two children there, she can't remember their names, but that doesn't matter now because they are all together again. And there is a flask.

'Your mother sent up some clean stuff. I'll just put it here in the locker. Or should I give it to the nurse, do ya think?' he says.

Now they are playing chase. The girl with the pigtails is running so fast no one can catch her. The boy runs round in circles. Annette hears herself calling them and watches as she stoops down real low opening her arms out real wide. The boy and the girl run to her and she folds them up under her chin. She can smell them, and she feels their hair tickling her nose. She hears herself telling them a story about the Once Upon a Time Little Prince in the faraway land. She sees her own arm lift freely, her finger pointing at the castle hiding up there on the hill behind the trees.

'I went for the interview above in Bolger's. Went well too. I think. Said they'll let me know. I've a good feelin' about it though,' he says.

The man is asleep beside her and he's smiling in his sleep and his cheeks are shiny and pink. He's a very tired man.

'That's where he lived,' she listens to her own voice, remembering its sound, 'and as long as anybody could remember the little prince had been silent. His mammy was heartbroken, so she got into bed and she fell asleep for a hundred days.'

'I met the doctor on me way in here. I like him. He's a good, decent sort. Reminds me kinda of John Travolta, somehow. The Vincent Vega version of John Travolta. Not that poncey Danny, from *Grease*. Do you remember, love, the first time we saw *Pulp Fiction*? That was our first date. Best movie I'd ever seen. Still is!' he is saying.

They all look up at the tower. The boy moves in closer. Annette wobbles his little chin. The girl stands up, steps back. Her knees are all green.

'Nobody could wake up the Queen, so the King made a plan,' she tells them, 'and the King's plan was to find somebody who could help the little prince learn how to speak all the words that were inside his head so that then maybe the Queen could hear his voice for the first time and that would wake her up out of her big long sleep. And many brave knights on white horses and many fairies with purple sparkly dresses and matching wands tried to make the little prince talk. But they couldn't. The King had almost given up hope but then one day a little girl with ribbons in her hair knocked on the door of the castle.'

'What was her name?' the boy asks.

She strains to hear the boy's voice. 'Lola,' she says.

'That's a good name. Did she make him talk?' the boy asks.

'No,' Annette hears herself saying, 'but she taught him to sing like a bird!'

The boy's mouth makes a surprised O shape and so do his eyes. He snuggles himself even tighter up in under her arm. She can't see his face anymore.

'And did all the singing wake up the Queen?' the girl asks, still standing looking up at the castle.

'What happened at the end?' the boy asks.

Annette can't remember the end.

CHAPTER 35

Jenny

'Push the button.'

'What button? I can't see any button!' Granny says, like Jenny has just told her she's going to drive over the side of a cliff in a car if Granny doesn't find the right button to stop the disaster right now.

'That button. There. At the top!' Jenny says, like she's the one in the passenger seat and her life is now in Granny's hands.

'This button?'

'Yes!'

Granny puts her finger on the switch and presses it down waiting for something to explode any minute. 'Nothin's happenin'!'

'You just have to wait.'

'For what?'

'For it to turn on!' Jenny holds up the iPad to stop Granny's finger from pressing the button again.

'Oh. Hello! Look, Jenny, it's sayin, HELLO!'

'Don't tap the screen like that! Just wait a second.' Jenny pulls the iPad back over to her side of the table again. 'Now slide like this to unlock it.' Jenny moves her finger over to the right with a lovely soft stroke.

'What are all a them pictures?'

'They are just the different icons. The apps.'

'The what?'

'Apps! This is the one you want. Here. Look. Touch that one there.'

'Which one?'

'This one!'

'That one?'

'No. This one!'

Granny touches the little square, like it's going to bite off her finger or melt it. Her head is further back from her body than it should be, like she's trying to save it from the spitting out poison that's sure to burn off her face, once she presses the screen. Newer, sharper lines appear at the side of her eyes and her teeth seem to be about to fall out of her mouth on to her Good Clean Floor.

'HOW ARE YOU FEELING?' Granny reads the big white letters on the screen. 'Not so bad now, thank God!' Granny says to the screen, like she's just sat down beside it at bingo and it's offered her a cup of tea and a biscuit.

'Touch the icon!' Jenny says.

'The what?'

'Just touch one of the squares.'

'Which one?' Granny asks, hoping Jenny will know which one is the least dangerous.

'Whichever one you want!'

'Happy. Sad. Nervous. Surprised. Sickly. Hungry. Angry. Sleepy.' Granny reads each one out like they are all new words that she's never heard before and now she's trying the sounds out before she chooses her favourite new word from the list. 'I suppose I'm a bit tired.' Granny sits back in her chair to really think about the question. She thinks out loud. 'I wouldn't say now that I'm sleepy exactly, but I'm a bit the worse for wear. Jacob was up all night. He doesn't sleep so well sometimes, you see.' Granny seems quite delighted now with her new bingo friend.

Jenny shakes her head from side to side. She rolls her eyes round at the same time. She stands up. This makes her dizzy.

'I wouldn't mind a cup a tea but I'm not all that thirsty. Just, tea is great when you're a bit tired. You know yourself. And a biscuit. I like a biscuit with me tea.'

Jenny sits back and tries to steady the room in her head. 'Just pick one!' Jenny tells Granny.

'There's no picture here for tea!' Granny says, in her *I told you so* voice and she's not trying to hide the fact that she knows she was right all along about the iPad.

She sounds like she's just won the race back to the shop to return it and now she's cheering for herself because she's the winner. She starts to lift herself up from the chair as though there's nothing to keep her here now. Her work here is done.

'Sit back down!'

'Excuse Me, Young Lady?' Granny's capitals are back, looking more vicious than ever and she means to use them. 'Don't You Shout at Me!'

'I'm not shouting!' Jenny shouts up at the half-sitting half-standing figure beside her. 'All these pictures are about feelings. There's other ones for food and drinks. I'll show you them later.'

'Where's the one for tea?' Granny sits back down again but only on the condition that there is tea somewhere on this ridiculous contraption.

'Okay. Okay.' Jenny swipes the happy-sad coloured faces away. 'Look. This is for food. That one is for drinks.' More swiping. Another little tap. 'There.' Swipe. Tap. 'Look. Tea.'

'Jacob doesn't Like Tea. Sure, He won't be Needin' That One.' Granny is now the one shaking her head like she can't even believe just how stupid Jenny really is. She's not disappointed, exactly; she had suspected as much, but she must admit she had hoped for better. Granny looks out at Jenny with great pity from behind her glasses. It is such great pity, in fact, it seems to shine and glint on her lenses before offering its sympathies to Jenny. Granny stands up and puts water in the kettle.

'Granny, This Is Important.' Jenny didn't mean to free all the capitals, not yet anyway. But now they're out there's not too much she can do.

'I Have more Important Things to be Doin' Than Playin' Games on that Stupid Contraption!' Granny says, like she's a cowboy and this is a showdown of capitals in some little wooden town in the middle of the desert. Granny fills the kettle and places it back down on the counter.

Jenny imagines Granny in a big hat with a gun belt and a horse tied up behind her. Jenny stands opposite her, way down the street. There's a bit of a bush blowing down the street in the other direction, Granny's direction, and the sun is in Jenny's eyes.

'Do You Think That the Dinner is Not Important?' Bang. 'Or the Washing that's to be Hung out on that Line while There's such Good Dryin' outside? What about Jacob?' Bang. Bang. 'Isn't doin' His Words with him Important And Makin' his Lunch for Tomorrow? Isn't that Important? And gettin' the place ready for your Mammy for when she comes back home again? I Suppose That's not Important Either?' Bang. Bang. Bang. Granny's face is very red. Her eyes are very small. But she's not finished yet. 'And, to add insult to injury, I've an awful corn on me foot!'

'It's just that, well, this could really help Jacob,' Jenny says, looking at the little screen and counting to ten in her own head. She is only at five when Granny's back, sitting beside her again. 'Look, let's start again,' Jenny says and there's not a capital in sight.

'Okay!' Granny says, far from convinced.

'It's really very, very easy to use.' Jenny's not sure if she should repeat *really* or *very*. At the last minute she goes for *very*. *Really, really* might not work. Jenny doesn't know why exactly but something tells her Granny would prefer *very* twice, instead of *really*.

'Yes, I'm sure it really, really is!' Granny goes for *really*.

'These are the sections.' It says *categories* at the top of the screen, but Jenny doesn't think Granny will like *categories* so much.

Granny reads each square like now she's the host on a quiz show and she's offering the contestants a choice of questions. Jenny sees Granny in her going-to-Mass dress standing in the middle of the telly with cards in her hands. There are big blue lights behind her making her look a bit like an alien that's lost its way home and has had to stop at a garage somewhere on earth to ask for directions. 'Food and drink,' Granny says, like she knows this is definitely the right answer to whatever question is on her card.

'Okay, but if you press this one,' Jenny points at the Sentence Makers square, 'you can make a full sentence and ask for the things that you want to eat or drink.'

Granny taps. More new picture squares appear on the screen. 'I want,' Granny reads out loud. Tap. The *I want* square appears at the bottom of the screen.

'Okay. Now go back to categories. Here. At the top.'

Granny touches the word *categories* on the top left of the screen even though she doesn't really like the word *categories*.

'Now go into Food and Drink,' Jenny says, pointing to the funny-looking burger and the massive bar of chocolate in the square on the far right of the screen. Granny touches the icon and just like magic a whole load of food and drink pictures arrive on the screen. Granny scans them all twice before she settles on milk. She chooses the picture of the milk carton with the smiling cow on the front. Tap. The *milk* square turns up at the bottom of the screen beside the *I want* square.

'I want milk.' Granny reads the squares like a sentence she's taken great care to build.

'Now choose the arrow here. This one!' Jenny points to the two-way arrow at the bottom right of the screen.

Granny taps the arrow. All the other pictures just melt away and there is only the *I want* square and the *smiling-cow milk* square left on the screen. 'I want milk.' Granny reads the two squares again like she's learning a new language. She can read the words but she's not so sure she knows what they mean.

'Just click the X at the top to get back,' Jenny says to Granny's finger.

'Hold on there now just one minute!' Granny says, like she thinks Jenny has just stolen something from Tesco, and it's Granny's job to find out what it is. 'How do I say, "I'm sorry, pet, but there's not so much as a drop left in the house." Where's the pictures for that?'

'What?' Jenny asks, more confused now than she should be at this stage.

'Well, how do I tell Jacob there's no milk and that we'll have to go down to Lizzie's to get some, when there's no pictures for *no milk left* or for *Lizzie's*?'

'What?' Jenny asks, even though she's so bewildered now herself that she can't imagine any answer will be able to make the room stop spinning.

'Well, there isn't any milk left. Not a drop. I used the last of it in Jacob's scrambled eggs.' Granny speaks slowly and with more care than she normally does.

'But you don't have to use the app to say that. You can just tell Jacob yourself.' Jenny knows that what she is saying makes sense in her own head. It's when she puts the words out in the air that she starts to doubt their meaning.

'So, what do I need this thing for so? Amn't I killed tellin' ya we don't need it!'

'But Granny, this could give Jacob a voice!'

'And how could it ever do that? Sure, we only want to hear

his little voice. Just once. Isn't that all! No computer can do that, Jenny! I don't care what ya say. No fancy app or new-fangled gadget will ever be as powerful as the sound of a child's own little voice.'

CHAPTER 36

Jacob

Jacob spins the wheels round and round. Round and round. This is the engine. It is yellow like a round smiley face. The engine is first. Jacob puts the engine down on the track. A track is like a road. For trains.

Jacob picks up the carriage. It is red. This is for the people. They are going somewhere over the hill. Daddy made the hill. Jacob spins the wheels. Round and round. Jacob puts the red carriage on the track behind the yellow engine. Yellow is first. This is a rule. Red is next. This is another rule. The red carriage clicks on to the yellow engine. Click.

Jacob picks up the next carriage. Jacob spins the wheels round and round. This carriage is blue like Thomas is blue. Thomas is number one. Edward is number two. Edward is blue too. Henry is green. Henry is number three. Gordon is number four. Gordon is blue like Edward and Thomas. James is number five. James is not blue. James is red like Jacob's carriage is red. Percy is green like Henry is green. Percy is number six. Jacob is six. Jacob was five before. Now he is six like Percy. Toby is number seven. Toby is different. Granny says different is good. Toby is a tram. A tram is not an engine. A tram is different. Duck is number eight. Duck is green like Percy and Henry are green. Duck is not a tram. Duck is an engine like Thomas is an engine. Granny takes Jacob to feed the ducks sometimes. But not today. There is a picture of a duck in a book. The duck is yellow like Jacob's engine. The engine is first. A duck is not a train. A duck is different. A duck says quack-quack. Trains don't say quack-quack. This is a rule. Trains say choo-choo. Donald is number nine. Donald is black like Douglas. Douglas is number ten. Donald and Douglas are the same. Donald and Mickey are not the same. Donald is a duck. Mickey is a mouse. Jacob doesn't like black. Jacob puts the blue carriage down on the track behind the red carriage. The blue carriage clicks on to the red carriage.

Jacob picks up the next carriage. This is for the other people. This is for the people not in the red carriage. They are not in the blue carriage either. This carriage is green like Duck and Percy and Henry are green. Yellow is first. Red is next. Blue goes before green. Jacob spins the wheels round and round. Jacob puts the green carriage on the track after the blue carriage. Click. This is for the people. They are going somewhere over the hill and through the tunnel. Daddy made the tunnel and the trees. The trees are green like the carriage is green. Shrek is green. He is an ogre. The trees are very small. Jacob is very big. Jacob is six. Percy is number six. Six is bigger than five. James is number five. James was black like Donald and Douglas before he was red. The people in the green carriage are not in the red carriage or the blue carriage.

Jacob looks for the orange carriage. Orange is next. This is a rule. Yellow is first. Red is next. Blue is next before green. Green comes after blue. Gordon and Edward and Thomas are blue. Duck and Percy and Henry are green. Jacob cannot find the orange carriage.

'Is this what you're after, Jacob?'

Daddy has the orange carriage in his hand. He gives it to Jacob.

Jacob spins the wheels round and round. He places the orange carriage down on the track behind the green carriage. This is for more people. Click.

'Press the switch, Jacob.' Daddy points to the red button.

Jacob takes the train apart and puts it back down on the table again.

Jacob picks up the yellow engine again. The yellow engine is first. Jacob spins the wheels round and round. Round and round. The yellow engine is not blue. It is yellow like the sun. Thomas is blue. Like the sky is blue. Thomas is an engine. The engine is first. This is a rule. The engine pulls all the carriages. The carriages have all the people. Jacob puts the engine down on the track. The engine pulls the carriages.

'I'm goin' for that interview tomorrow, Jacob. Do ya remember I was tellin' ya about it? Up above in Bolger's. You know the hardware shop, where we go to get nails or paint?'

Jacob picks up the first carriage. It is red. Annie and Clarabel are red like Bertie the Bus is red. Annie and Clarabel are carriages. Bertie is not a carriage. Bertie is a bus. A bus is not a train. It is different. Different means not the same. The people on the bus are not going to the same place as the people on the train. The people on the bus are going somewhere different. The people on the train are going over the bridge. Daddy made the bridge. Jacob spins the wheels. Round and round. Jacob puts the red carriage on the track behind the yellow engine. Carriages are red. Red is the right colour for carriages. Annie and Clarabel are red. But yellow is first. This is a rule. Red is next. This is another rule. The red carriage fits on to the yellow engine. Click.

'Eleven fifteen in the mornin'! I don't know how many's in for it, but Larry O'Rourke says he'll put in a word for me. He's there this thirteen years or more. That's gotta count for somethin', doesn't it? I'll get there early. Make a good impression. Or would that look too desperate?'

Jacob picks up the next carriage. It is blue like Thomas is blue. Edward is blue too. Edward is number two. Edward delivered some trucks of milk, butter and cheese for Hiro to collect.

Hiro is black like Donald and Douglas are black. The waving-goodbye man is black. Jacob doesn't like black. Witches are black. But Jacob does like Hiro. When the Fat Controller opened the door of the milk truck the milk poured out.

'No, I will. I'll go early.'

Hiro is number fifty-one. Fifty-one is a big number. It is bigger than six. Jacob is six. He was five before. Now he is six like Percy. Percy is green like Henry. Percy fell into the water. Daddy made the water. It is blue like Thomas and Edward are blue. It goes under the bridge. The bridge goes over the water. Jacob puts the blue carriage down on the track after the red carriage. This is the next carriage. The blue carriage goes behind the red carriage. Blue comes after red. This is a rule. Click.

'What'll I wear, Jacob? Any suggestions?'

Jacob picks up the next carriage.

'Will I wear me striped shirt and black trousers or should I go the whole hog and put on me suit?'

This is for the other people. This is for the people not in the red carriage. Or in the blue carriage. This carriage is green like Duck and Percy and Henry are green. Yellow is first. Red is next before blue. Green is after blue.

'You reckon the suit? Ya know, I think you're right. Jesus, what about a tie?'

Jacob spins the wheels round and round. Jacob puts the green carriage on the track after the blue carriage. Click. This is for the people. They are going somewhere over the hill and through the tunnel away from the waving-goodbye man and past the shop. Daddy made the tunnel and the trees. Daddy made the waving-goodbye man. Daddy made the shop. The trees are green like the carriage is green. The shop is not green. The shop is pink. Jenny likes pink. There are lights in the shop. Daddy made the lights in the shop. Jacob and Granny go to the shop to get Smarties. There are no Smarties in Daddy's shop. The people in the green carriage are not the people in the red carriage. Or in the blue carriage. They are different. Different means not the same. Granny says different is good. Jacob puts the green carriage down on the track behind the blue carriage. Click.

'No tie? Are ya sure? Smart casual, ya reckon?'

Jacob picks up the orange carriage again. Jacob spins the wheels round and round. Round and round. Orange is next. This is a rule. Yellow is first. Red is next. Blue is next before green. Green comes after blue. Gordon and Edward and Thomas are blue. Duck and Percy and Henry are green. Jacob clicks the orange carriage on to the green carriage.

'Well, Jacob, are you goin' to turn it on this time? Now wouldn't you just make a fine health and safety inspector?' Daddy points to the switch.

Jacob waits. Daddy waits. Jacob checks all the colours again.

'Are ya sure about the tie?'

Jacob presses the little red button and watches the noise moving round the track. The yellow engine pulls the carriages up the hill and through the tunnel. Choo-choo. Daddy made the tunnel. The yellow engine pulls the carriages past all the trees and over the bridge away from the waving-goodbye man. Choo-choo. Daddy made the trees and the bridge. Daddy made the water under the bridge. Daddy made the waving-goodbye man. The yellow engine pulls the carriages past the shop with the light. Daddy made the light in the shop. Choo-choo. Daddy made the shop. The yellow engine pulls the carriages back past Jacob again. Yellow. Red. Blue. Green. Orange. All the colours go up the hill and through the tunnel again. They go past all the trees and over the bridge away from the waving-goodbye man again. They pass the shop with the light again and they pass Jacob again too. Yellow. Red. Blue. Green. Orange. Choo-choo. Up the hill. Over the tunnel. Past the trees. Over the bridge. Over the water. Away from the waving-goodbye man. Past the shop. Past Jacob. Past Daddy. Yellow. Red. Blue. Green.

Orange. Choo-choo. Up the hill. Over the tunnel. Past the trees. Over the bridge. Over the water. Away from the waving-goodbye man. Past the shop. Past Jacob. Past Daddy. Yellow. Red. Blue. Green. Orange. Choo-choo. Up the hill. Over the tunnel. Past the trees. Over the bridge. Over the water. Away from the waving-goodbye man. Past the shop. Past Jacob. Past Daddy. Yellow. Red. Blue. Green. Orange. Choo-choo. Up the hill. Over the tunnel. Past the trees. Over the bridge. Over the water. Away from the waving-goodbye man. Past the shop. Past Jacob. Past Daddy. Yellow. Red. Blue. Green. Orange. Choo-choo. Up the hill. Over the tunnel. Past the trees. Over the bridge. Over the water. Away from the waving-goodbye man. Past the shop. Past Jacob. Past Daddy. Yellow. Red. Blue. Green. Orange. Choo-choo. Up the hill. Over the tunnel. Past the trees. Over the bridge. Over the water. Away from the waving-goodbye man. Past the shop. Past Jacob. Past Daddy. Yellow. Red. Blue. Green. Orange. Choo-choo. Up the hill. Over the tunnel. Past the trees. Over the bridge. Over the water. Away from the waving-goodbye man. Past the shop. Past Jacob. Past Daddy. Yellow. Red. Blue. Green. Orange. Choo-choo. Up the hill. Over the tunnel. Past the trees. Over the bridge. Over the water. Away from the waving-goodbye man. Past the shop. Past Jacob. Past Daddy. Yellow. Red. Blue. Green. Orange. Choo-choo. Up the hill. Over the tunnel. Past the trees. Over the bridge. Over the water. Away from the waving-goodbye man. Past the shop. Past Jacob. Past Daddy. Yellow. Red. Blue. Green. Orange. Choo-choo. Up the hill. Over the tunnel. Past the trees. Over the bridge. Over the water. Away from the waving-goodbye man. Past the shop. Past Jacob. Past Daddy. Yellow. Red. Blue. Green. Orange. Choo-choo. Up the hill. Over the tunnel. Past the trees. Over the bridge. Over the water. Away from the waving-goodbye man. Past the shop. Past Jacob. Past Daddy. Yellow. Red. Blue. Green. Orange. Choo-choo. Up the hill. Over the tunnel. Past the trees. Over the bridge. Over the water. Away from the waving-goodbye man. Past the shop. Past Jacob. Past Daddy. Yellow. Red. Blue. Green. Orange. Choo-choo. Up the hill. Over the tunnel. Past the trees. Over the bridge. Over the water. Away from the waving-goodbye man. Past the shop. Past Jacob. Past Daddy. Yellow. Red. Blue. Green. Orange. Choo-choo. Up the hill. Over the tunnel. Past the trees. Over the bridge. Over the water. Away from the waving-goodbye man. Past the shop. Past Jacob. Past Daddy. Yellow. Red. Blue. Green. Orange. Choo-choo. Up the hill. Over the tunnel. Past the trees. Over the bridge. Over the water. Away from the waving-goodbye man. Past the shop. Past Jacob. Past Daddy. Yellow. Red. Blue. Green. Orange. Choo-choo. Up the hill. Over the tunnel. Past the trees. Over the bridge. Over the water. Away from the waving-goodbye man. Past the shop. Past Jacob. Past Daddy. Yellow. Red. Blue. Green. Orange. Choo-choo. Up the hill. Over the tunnel. Past the trees. Over the bridge. Over the water. Away from the waving-goodbye man. Past the shop. Past Jacob. Past Daddy. Yellow. Red. Blue. Green. Orange. Choo-choo. Up the hill. Over the tunnel. Past the trees. Over the bridge. Over the water. Away from the waving-goodbye man. Past the shop. Past Jacob. Past Daddy. Yellow. Red. Blue. Green. Orange. Choo-choo. Up the hill. Over the tunnel. Past the trees. Over the bridge. Over the water. Away from the waving-goodbye man. Past the shop. Past Jacob. Past Daddy. Yellow. Red. Blue. Green. Orange. Choo-choo. Up the hill. Over the tunnel. Past the trees. Over the bridge. Over the water. Away from the waving-goodbye man. Past the shop. Past Jacob. Past Daddy.

'I'll polish me shoes. Will ya remind me to polish me shoes, Jacob?'

This is the train. Daddy made the train for Jacob.

CHAPTER 37

Jenny

'So how are you, Jenny?'

Mrs French is watering a very sick-looking plant in the window when Jenny walks into the office in the wall. She doesn't look around so Jenny wonders how she knows that it's Jenny and not someone else standing there, looking at the heels of her purple boots.

'I'm okay,' Jenny says, and she thinks she means it.

When Dorcas told Jenny she had to go to see Mrs French, Jenny had nearly kissed her. This meant missing Irish. Jenny thinks about kissing Dorcas. Jenny doesn't think anybody would want to kiss Dorcas, not even her own mother on her birthday, if she ever even had one. Jenny tries to remember the last time she kissed Mammy. But she can't remember because she didn't know then that it would be the last time and that she'd have to try to remember it and imagine it again anyway.

Jenny sits down on the big chair in the corner without being told. She feels smaller than she is. And now she's not sure she really was sure about feeling okay a minute ago. She's still annoyed at Mrs French about the book. Mrs French sighs, like she's lost her keys or like she can hear what Jenny's thinking inside her own head and she's very sorry.

'I've tried everything I can think of to save Ophelia. But I just can't.' Mrs French sounds like she's in another room, somewhere else, that's not here. She has two white flowers in her hand when she turns around to Jenny, 'I think this is her final farewell.' Mrs French looks at Jenny for the first time. Then she looks back down at the sad-milky flowers in her hand.

Without having to ask, Jenny realises that the dying plant is Ophelia. Jenny looks over at Arthur, in the other corner, and she knows by the look on his tired old face that she is right.

'Why did you call it Ophelia?' Jenny asks because she can't really think of anything else to say.

'Oh, Jenny, just wait till you meet Ophelia!' Mrs French says, like she's remembering one of her most favourite people in the whole wide world and she's really sure Jenny will just love her too.

'Hello, Ophelia,' Jenny says, standing up and moving across the room.

She sticks out her hand as if to shake one of Ophelia's leaves. Ophelia's leaves are very green. There are six of them, close to the bottom, floating upwards, like a strange kind of upside-down skirt. They fan out, like wings, with the smallest ones nearest the strange-looking soil and the biggest ones at the top. Ophelia has a black stick tied to her stem, like the stick is talking Ophelia into standing up as tall as she can. Then, just near the top of the stick, Ophelia seems to find some courage and she creeps off a little bit on her own. In mid-air. Jenny wonders if maybe Ophelia should have stayed where she was – attached to her stick. Ophelia's flowers have all gone but still, Jenny thinks, Ophelia looks proud. Jenny smiles at the massive yellow cup and saucer Ophelia is sitting in and wonders if maybe this room is the room of a giant when Mrs French is not here. Jenny looks around for more signs but sees nothing else that is too big – only the chair and cup and saucer. Both Jenny and Mrs French look at Ophelia now, as if by staring alone the plant might just start repairing itself, if they wait long enough. It doesn't work.

'Why don't you google it?' Jenny says, like this is this first great idea anybody has ever had.

'I never thought of that. Okay. Come on. Help me!' Mrs French's voice is brighter now, bigger than it was when Jenny came in. 'Orchid care.' Mrs French says the words out loud while she's typing them into the computer. Jenny sits up on the stool beside her.

There's all sorts of information on soil and light and heat. Google says orchids are very easy to care for once you learn how to grow them properly. Mrs French doesn't agree. Mrs French runs her finger along under the words on the screen while she's reading. She mumbles the words, like she's really only making them up and then throwing them away again because they are not the right fit, but then when she's halfway down the second page, she reads clearly and out loud, 'Because they are now so abundant, many people treat *phalaenopsis* like cut flowers – they last a long time blooming, and when they're done, the plant can be discarded and replaced cheaply.' Mrs French looks very annoyed now with Google. 'I'm not going to just throw Ophelia away! Who writes this stuff anyway?' But Mrs French isn't really waiting for Jenny to answer. She scrolls down the page and picks another site. This one looks better. Mrs French reads out loud immediately. 'The good news is that *phalaenopsis* are among the easiest orchids to grow, as long as you follow a few basic rules. This is important because, like many flowers, *phalaenopsis* really only bloom once a year, so after your plant is done blooming you'll have to keep it alive and healthy until the next blooming season rolls around. So, she will come back!' Mrs French is so excited that suddenly Jenny feels excited too, like she can't wait for the new blooms when the next blooming season rolls around.

'Mammy loves daffodils,' Jenny says, like she has no control over the words falling out of her mouth.

'Oh, I do, too. The first real sign of spring,' Mrs French says, turning to Jenny. 'Does she grow them in the garden, at home?'

'Yes.' Jenny says, moving back over towards Ophelia, like she just wants to leave a big space between herself and the words she's just spoken. 'I think you should move her. She might get cold, when you're not here.'

'Good idea. Where will we put her though? It says she likes light and heat to feel happy.' Mrs French says, looking around the room like she suddenly doesn't know where she is, and she's checking each corner and new space like she's never even been in her own office before, or like the giant has moved things around while she was gone and she doesn't know where he has put them.

'And you need to water her more. But you are only here once every two weeks.'

'Now that could be a problem.'

Jenny and Mrs French both look around the room, like they are going to find something to fix this problem hidden somewhere behind the books or up on the shelves.

'How's the diary going?' Mrs French asks when there's no sign of a solution.

'Fine,' Jenny says, thinking about the one tiny entry she made in the little pink book with the lock on it that Granny bought her in Cut Price.

'Good. Oh, how did the party go?' Mrs French is rooting down behind the radiator now.

'Fine. But nobody came from Jacob's class.'

'I think I dropped the card that came stuck in Ophelia's pot down here.' Mrs French's cheek is pushed up against the wall and her arm has disappeared.

'And Jacob nearly choked himself with one of Mammy's hair bobbles while he was eating a coconut cream.'

'I think I can see it!' She stretches even further down. 'I love coconut creams. Is he okay?'

'And Granny had a fight with Auntie Eleanor because she changed her name and then she had a fight with Da because he said that Saidhbhe was a stupid name and Granny said that

Da's family is so lazy that they just call everyone by the same name. Yes, he's fine. Da built him a train set.'

Mrs French smiles, like she knew all along about Da's secret project and she's glad he's finally shown everybody what it is. 'You know, Jenny, sometimes we all say the wrong things. Out of love. Yuk. What's this?' Mrs French pulls up her arm and there's half-melted pink chewing gum glued to her sleeve. 'Oh no! Who would put chewing gum behind a radiator?'

Jenny lets a little surprised smile drift across her face.

'It's ruined!' Mrs French says, looking down at the mess on her arm.

'Put it in the freezer when you go home,' Jenny says, like this is something everybody knows.

'Does that work?' Mrs French asks, like nobody has ever heard this idea before.

'That's what Granny does!' Jenny thinks of all the times Granny's face got into a big scrunched-up mess when she had fished out something Jacob had stuffed down behind the radiator or between the cushions on the couch.

'Your granny sounds very wise, Jenny. It seems to run in your family. Is your mammy the same as you two?'

Jenny thinks about the question. She thinks about Mammy. 'She used to be. Before she got sick. So, I don't know anymore.'

'When was the last time you saw her?' Mrs French is picking at the stringy pink knitted into her dress.

'A hundred and eighty-five days ago.'

'That's a lot of days.'

Jenny shrugs, like the number doesn't matter. 'She didn't even come to Jacob's party.'

'You know, Jenny, when my brother died, my mother got into bed and I don't really think she ever got back out of it again. And I can remember hating her for that and I can remember thinking how she mustn't love the rest of us – I have one brother and one sister, too – and it's only really now I realise that she did get up, she did bring us to school, she did help us with homework, she did make our dinners and it was because she loved us so much that she managed to drag herself out of bed every morning, when really she would rather have been buried in the ground with Anthony.'

'But when will my mammy come back home again? When will Granny bring us to see her?' Jenny swallows back the tears that have been choking her for five months and sixteen days.

'I don't know, Jenny. But I do know that she will. When she is ready.'

Jenny turns away from Ophelia and throws her two arms around Mrs French's neck. She places her head into the space between Mrs French's ear and her shoulder. Mrs French's dangly earring catches in Jenny's hair, so she doesn't move her head. She can feel Mammy's two arms wrapping around her and holding her so tight they seem like one person shushing away everything that's not right and not happy. Jenny cries and cries with her whole body for the thing she has lost, and she thinks that maybe she is drowning.

On her way out of the office Jenny takes in a big breath. She tucks one of Ophelia's strange-looking roots back into the yellow cup under her arm and closes the door quietly, slotting it into the wall behind her, without looking back.

CHAPTER 38

Jenny

Thursday, 7th November, 2013

Dear Anne Frank,

I'm really sorry to hear you won't have any electricity for two whole weeks and that your granny is dead.

The electricity went out in our house too, one time, when Da did something with the Hoover that made it explode in our kitchen. The whole place went dark and nothing worked, not even the telly or the fridge, and there were even sparks coming out of the wall where the plug of the Hoover went on fire. And there was this terrible smell of things melting. Mammy went mental because she couldn't use the computer and Da started to curse about missing Neighbours. But after about an hour Da fixed the plug and our lights came back on, which was good, because Mammy said she was going to kill Da if we had to sit in the dark one minute longer.

My granny is not dead. She is alive, and she lives with us, too. But that's not because of Hitler, of course, it's because Mammy's not here anymore. Da says even Hitler would have gone into hiding had he got wind of Granny. Mammy went to the hospital ages ago and she didn't come home, not even for Jacob's birthday. Granny says Mammy has the flu. But she doesn't.

I think it is kinda funny that you spy on your neighbours because sometimes I do that too, when I'm bored. Crazy Billy and his mammy live next door to us. He calls her 'The Mammy' and not just 'Mammy'. Actually, and I don't know why this is, everybody calls her 'The Mammy', like she's the only mammy in the whole wide world. And that's why she's got 'The' in front of her name, that other mammies don't have, like she's more important. But she's not! Well, I don't think she is anyway, but I don't really know. But I did hear Da telling Granny that Billy tried to kill himself and The Mammy with fishing line, ten or maybe fifteen years ago. I suppose it must have been something really important for him to do that! But Da told Granny that the line broke and that botched up that job.

I've never ever seen The Mammy, even though she only lives next door and she's lived there my whole life. Da said she put Billy out in the coal hole for six weeks, and only let him out to go to confession every Saturday. Sometimes I try to imagine what she's like, and when I do, she's always sitting in a chair in the corner. It is a dark corner. It is a low chair. And she's been sitting in that chair so long now, that it looks like the two of them are joined together and sometimes Billy doesn't know if the chair is talking or if The Mammy has just grown into a chair. The chair is flat and shiny in patches and it feels greasy to touch, like a soggy-wet chip bag, and the springs scrape the carpet and there's lost bits of breakfast, dinner and tea going mouldy down the sides and at the back. And all around her there's dead daddy-long-legs and crunchy old bluebottles in bowls and cups and on windowsills. There's a sticky strip of yellow stuff hanging down from the ceiling over her head and it's almost furry with the half-moving legs of the blue-black flies stuck all the way down along it. I'm sure she has mad orange hair and her head is too big for her body and that's why she can't walk anymore. She doesn't let Billy past the front garden now, so he spends his days smoking and pretend fishing and, I bet, inventing new ways to kill The Mammy. She wears a long black dress, like a witch, and she sits spitting into the fire and thinking up ways to kill Billy.

My mammy had a stroke. The women in the shop were talking about it. I heard them.

'A stroke is the sudden death of brain cells due to lack of oxygen, caused by blockage of blood flow or rupture of an artery to the brain. Sudden loss of speech, weakness, or paralysis of one side of the body can be symptoms.'

I googled it. That's what it said.

I don't use 'field-glasses' like you do when you are looking at your neighbours and into their houses. I googled 'field-glasses' too. We call them binoculars now. I wonder what the couple you saw eating their dinner last night were talking about? Do you think that they were fighting about the man going out for a drink even though he doesn't have a job, and where did he think the money was going to come from because there isn't a money tree in the back garden, in case he didn't know, or were they fighting because the woman didn't get dressed yesterday or the day before that either and then there was nothing for the dinner because the woman forgot to go shopping because she was too busy looking up things about autism on the Internet? And was that dentist really going to take out the old lady's tooth, right there, in her sitting room? I wonder, if I got Da's binoculars out of the shed, would I be able to see where the old man from the broken house has gone – he's not there anymore. Why does Mr Dussel have to sleep in your room, Anne Frank? What did he think about the dentist across the road and the awfully scared woman?

Granny says that when she was small a dentist used to come to her school and take all their teeth out with a string tied to the door handle! Granny writes letters to me and she pretends that she's Mammy. Did your granny ever do that?

Mammy and me used to read every evening, too, just like you and your daddy do. We read two Harry Potters and loads of other books. I hope you enjoy Don Carlos! I asked Da about Don Carlos and he said that poor Don Carlos was in love with his father's wife, and I said that she must be his mother then, but Da said no, that, that was somebody called Oedipus, from Greece. Don Carlos was in love with the woman that Philip, his father the king, had married, but she wasn't Don's mother. When I asked Da what happened to Don's mother he said that she died when Don was very small. Da's mammy died when he was eight, but we didn't talk about that.

I read down through all the rules in your house, the ones you gave Dussel. My Auntie Eleanor would love the 'Special fat-free diet' rule. Granny wouldn't be able to stick with the 'Speak softly at all times, by order' rule, because Granny gives the orders around here and she never speaks softly. We have rules, too. Granny put our rules up on the fridge. There are ten of them and they scream at you and trip you up every time you get a yogurt or pass by, on your way somewhere else. Jacob would hate your 'Rest Hours' rule. Jacob loves rules but not rules about sleeping. And Da would never ever go to the doctor to get a pint! He would really hate that rule.

Anyway, Anne Frank, I think, really, that you discovered a kind of old-fashioned Facebook, last night, when you peeked out through your curtains. Granny says Facebook is like watching your neighbours putting all their washing out on the line, except they know you are watching. She says that's the whole point, like she's suddenly some kind of Facebook expert. Then she says that some people just love *to make an exhibition of themselves. I think that means they love showing off!*

On Wednesday 6th November, which was yesterday, Granny discovered Facebook, the new one that we have now. You don't need 'field-glasses' for it though. All you need is an iPad that Granny thought was a 'stupid new-fangled contraption' when Auntie Eleanor brought it here first. She loves it now though. She even asked Da to show her how to send an email and she's always checking to see if she's got any mail! Da says he doesn't know who in the name of God Granny would be emailing, but imagine finding Her sitting in your inbox!

'New statistics revealed that while more women die as a result of stroke across all age groups, in the younger age categories, men account for three-quarters of all strokes.'

And I really did think it was Mammy writing me those letters all the time. And then the last time she wrote, she said, 'That'll mean more cake for us!' But then she didn't come to Jacob's party, so she couldn't have written that, could she? Because Mammy would never, ever, not come to Jacob's party.

'Every four minutes, someone dies from a stroke.'

Da says that anybody who wants to sign up with Facebook should be made sit a test first. Anybody who thinks that their Christmas tree or dinner or IKEA bathroom is interesting to anybody else, anywhere, should be shot, just for being so stupid. Anybody sending virtual hugs and healing messages through some fancy pictures they've ripped off Buddah BrainyQuotes should be arrested for being so stupid and then locked away, all of them together, to suffer, forever, in the smell of their own bullshit. Da says that's the French word for nonsense. But it's not! And Da says that anybody who needs to tell the whole world just how lucky they are to be married to the most wonderful person in the whole wide world should be forced to do a special marriage course, somewhere where there's no Internet connection, like the moon, so as they can't send us all selfies of themselves and the most wonderful person in the whole fuckin' universe!

Mammy didn't even send Jacob a card.

I keep asking Granny to bring us up to see Mammy in the hospital. She keeps saying she will, but she never does. Mrs French says that Granny will bring us when she is ready or that Mammy will come home again when she is ready. I'm not really sure who she was talking about, but it seems like nothing is going to happen until somebody else is 'ready'. Me and Jacob are ready, which means we are 'willing or eager to do something'. I googled that too. Just to be sure. I wish I knew why Mammy or Granny are not 'eager or willing' to do the something we want them to do.

And now Granny's on Facebook, too! You should have seen Da's face!

'Emailin' is one thing,' Da said, 'but Jesus Christ, just think of the damage she could do on Facebook!'

Anne Frank, I really, really wish you had had Facebook, instead of just those field-glasses. Everything would be so much different for you then.

'There are 10,000 people affected by strokes every year in Ireland, and it's the leading cause of complex disability, as sufferers can be paralysed and unable to communicate. More people die from stroke than from breast cancer, prostate cancer and bowel cancer combined.'

I googled that too.

Love, Jenny

CHAPTER 39

Jenny

'Who's that?' Jenny says, to nobody really, when they walk into the front room.

She squints at a shape in the blue greyness of the fading evening light. She reaches her whole arm up in under the big tulip shade that's been standing on the top of the lamp in the corner her whole life. She blinks in the sudden yellow that falls into the room and quickly pushes Jacob behind her, so he won't have to see. There's some strange old woman wrapped in a blanket, sleeping on Mammy's chair in the corner. The air tastes bad. Like liver. Everything's a funny colour. Jenny scans the room looking for Granny. But she's not there.

The woman in the corner has a blue scarf piled round her head, with a knot at the back like she's a pirate. Jenny notices a small spit leaking from the side of her mouth. There are rattles in her throat. And coughs waiting to happen. Jenny sends her two arms round behind her, to fold over Jacob again.

Suddenly and without any warning, no stretching, no yawning, the woman's eyes suddenly flick open. Jenny presses Jacob tighter into her back. Then the eyes close again, just as quickly. But Jenny knows those eyes. She watches the mouth open, like it's got something really important to say, some story to tell. But then it just closes again, like it can't find the words, or it's lost the story, or like it just can't be bothered. She thinks she knows the mouth too from somewhere, but she can't be sure, or she just doesn't want to remember.

Jenny thinks about the witch in Hansel and Gretel who pretends to be all sleepy and floppy when she first sees Hansel and Gretel knocking at her front door. But that was a trick.

'That's Granny's friend Stella, from bingo,' she tells Jacob.

As soon as the lie is out of her mouth, her face burns with prickles and stings. Jacob's beside her again now, his head pressed into her ribs. Jenny holds his little hand real tight. Jacob doesn't like strangers he doesn't know very well.

But then, before Jenny realises what's happening, Jacob wriggles his fingers free and steps away from the safety of her leg. He moves towards the corner, like a sleepwalker going back to bed after many night-time adventures. He closes his eyes and stands straight in front of the strange woman in the corner, who is bundled up like the oldest baby in the whole wide world. But he's not afraid anymore. Very slowly Jacob reaches out and touches the old, old, white face with his thumb. He makes low little noises like he's talking to her in his own special, quiet way.

Jenny watches as the old head rolls heavily into the back of Mammy's chair, letting Jacob's fingertips slide along the top of her eyes, like he's a blind person trying to see her face with his hands. He puts his head right up against hers and takes in big breaths. Sniffing her. Breathing her in. Then he breathes the big breaths back out, his little chest pushing against his check shirt. He looks happy, like he's just found something very precious again. The best lost thing ever.

'Jacob. Come on. Let's go and find Granny.'

But Jacob doesn't move. Jenny doesn't move either.

'What are you two doin' here?' a voice says from the door. 'I didn't know you two were home.'

Granny stands looking in at them from the hall. Granny takes off her glasses and rubs them with the sleeve of her cardigan. When she puts them back up on her nose she nods at the children, like now her glasses are clean she can see everything better. Then she starts to fidget, like she's just been caught doing something she shouldn't have been doing and now she's been found out. She tries to make herself look far too busy to be guilty. And like she's in an awful hurry to get the things she thinks need doing done, she looks up at the wall and starts dusting down the door frame with her hankie, turning her back to the children. When she's finished with the door she moves into the room, bending down to pick up Jacob's hat and gathering other bits and pieces up from the floor.

'Look who's come back to us!' Granny says, looking down at the carpet.

'Who?' Jenny asks, looking at the top of Granny's head for the answer she's too terrified to hear.

'Why. It's your mammy, a course!'

Jenny looks into the corner and then back at Granny, who's still very busy looking for things to tidy away. Granny stands up frantically, searching the room for more clutter.

'I see ya didn't put those markers back in the drawer!' Granny says, watching Jenny looking back at her, in their double reflection, in the glass of the telly. Granny gathers up all the colours. She shoves them back in the tube. She picks up the tube and places it back in the drawer. 'Why are yas here anyway? You were supposed to be stayin' at Joyce's for the night,' Granny says into the telly.

'There was a smell of gas. She had to call some man to come to fix something.'

'Jesus Christ, I don't know what your father does be thinkin' sendin' yas round there. That one can't mind herself, let alone two children,' Granny says, putting Jacob's pictures in a pile, but still looking at Jenny in the telly.

'She says she'll come back and get us later. She was in a big hurry to get back for the man coming to fix the gas.'

'Well now, she needn't bother her backside. If that one had

minded her business she wouldn't have to go off gettin' in strangers to fix her gas. Imagine losin' your own husband behind the Specials in Aldi!' Granny shines up the screen till it squeals. 'He's not turned up since, I suppose?'

Jenny shakes her head. She blinks back the stinging at the side of her eyes.

'Did she give yas a proper dinner? Pizzas and chips, I suppose!'

'She couldn't make anything cos a the smell. She was afraid to even turn on the light,' Jenny says, glad to have something else to say now. In fact, she thinks she could talk about Auntie Joyce and the smell of gas and the no dinner all night.

'Yas must be starvin' so! Right, I'll get yas some dinner.'

Granny spits on her hankie and rubs the same spot on the telly so hard it's like she's trying to make a hole actually appear in the glass. Jenny just nods, like she has run out of words. Her eyes drift back to Mammy's chair in the corner. Jenny wishes she were blind, but then thinking better of it, she decides she would rather just rewind the story in her head, so that Granny flies back out of the room, Jenny and Jacob scoot back out the front door, where they stand on the step, waiting for Granny to answer. Granny is in the kitchen, making cupcakes and scones, and her hands are dusty white with flour when she opens the door.

'Ah, I wasn't expectin' you two back so soon, but never mind, cos you're just in time! There's a fresh batch just outta the oven!' Granny says, as they follow her down the hall, past the sitting room, and into the heavy-scone heat of the kitchen. The scones have raisins in them and the butter melts in little yellow puddles, before it soaks into the yummy soft middle, and Jenny and Jacob and Granny sit at the kitchen table, talking about lots of different things, happy things, between mouthfuls of warm, buttery scones.

Granny moves from the telly to the mantelpiece, destroying the scene in the kitchen. She shines the mirror hanging up on the wall and arranges the pictures of Mammy and Granddad again. She turns them both looking outwards, into the room.

'Now, that's better,' Granny says to Granddad with a nod.

Jacob curls up round Mammy's feet, petting her slippers.

Jenny feels like she is falling. She looks over at Granny again just to get her bearings. She knows where Granny is in the room. She knows where the telly is and where the mantelpiece is in the room. She knows where the lamp is and Mammy's chair. She just can't find herself anymore, like suddenly and for no reason at all she has disappeared into a hole in the floor. She thinks about Alice and the white rabbit. She looks over at Mammy's chair again. *Maybe Da was right all along about Granny being a witch and maybe she did this to Mammy when she sent her away to that hospital up there in Dublin!* Jenny thinks in the part of her brain that tries to hang on to something else, something that she can't find right now; the part that tries to figure things out on its own when there's no one else there to ask.

Jenny closes her eyes to blink away the story she's entered. She must have taken a very wrong turn somewhere between the lines or maybe, she thinks, she was eaten by a wolf or a troll under a bridge and now she's just left hovering somewhere between living and dying and that the sitting room is the place she's ended up before the doctors can save her and bring her back to life again in a hospital bed. Jenny looks for the bright light she's supposed to see or the tunnel. When she sees neither she looks back even further inside her own head again. This time she's searching for pictures of Mammy, the way she was before she got the flu. But Jenny can't find her. She's gone. All she can see is the chicken maggots eating her skin. Jenny takes in big breaths, so she won't cry.

Granny closes the curtains.

CHAPTER 40

Jacob

Mammy smells right. Like she should. Mammy smells happy. Like a smiling yellow face on the fridge. Jacob gives Mammy a sticker. It is a happy sticker. He puts it on the top of Mammy's bed. Mammy is in bed. Elaine gives Jacob a sticker when Jacob is good.

Mammy is sleeping under Jacob's sticker. Sleeping is not the same as waking up with eyes open. Sleeping is different. Sleeping is closing eyes. Sleeping is like a baby. Sleeping is not like blinking for a very long time. Sleeping and blinking are different. Sleeping and waking are different. Blinking is different too. Jacob doesn't like sleeping. Jacob likes waking. Jacob doesn't know about blinking. Jacob blinks. Open. Close. Jacob shows Mammy blinking. Open. Close. Open. Close. Open. Close. Open. Close. Open. Close. Open. Close. Open. Close. Open. Close.

Mammy is not blinking. Mammy is sleeping. Mammy smells happy. Like a smiling yellow face on the fridge. Jacob gives Mammy another sticker. It is a happy sticker. He puts it on the top of Mammy's bed. Mammy has two stickers now. One. Two. Mammy is in bed. Sleeping under two yellow stickers. One. Two. Elaine gives Jacob a sticker when Jacob is good. Elaine gives Jacob two yellow stickers when Jacob is very good. One. Two. Two happy stickers like two smiling yellow faces on the fridge.

Jacob's yellow marker doesn't work anymore. Jacob's black marker does. Jacob doesn't like black. Black is when all the colours are gone. Witches are black. So are spiders. Granny will get Jacob a new yellow marker tomorrow. Tomorrow Mammy will wake up. Mammy's face will be happy. Jacob doesn't like sad yellow faces. Jacob only likes happy yellow faces. Jacob gives Mammy another sticker. It is round like the sun. The sun is yellow. Yellow and black are different. Hiro is black like Donald and Douglas are black. Jacob doesn't like black. Witches are black. Black is when all the colours are gone. Gone means not here. Back means here. Here is not there, faraway. Here is beside Jacob. Jacob is here. So is Mammy. Mammy is here.

Jacob sits on Mammy's bed. Feet out is for sitting. Feet in and feet out is for swinging. Jacob is not swinging. Jacob is sitting. Beside Mammy. On Mammy's bed. Mammy is here. Mammy is here. Here is not there, faraway. Here is beside Jacob. Mammy is sleeping beside Jacob. Jacob is sitting beside Mammy. Jacob gives Mammy another sticker.

Mammy's arm moves up-ways. Jacob wriggles his fingers. One two three four. Thumb twiddle finger. One two three four. Twiddle. Touch. One two three four. Wriggle. Shake. One two three four.

Mammy's arm is on Mammy's pillow. Granny puts Jacob's pyjamas under his pillow.

Jacob's fingers move up and down up and down. Jacob's fingers close down on Jacob's thumb. Like a crocodile mouth. Crocodiles are green like Duck and Percy and Henry are green. Jacob's crocodile fingers snap-snap. Six. Seven. Eight. Nine. Open close open close open close.

Mammy's arm moves crossways.

Jacob's crocodile fingers snap-snap-snap. Open close open close open close. Ten. Snap. Open. Close.

Mammy's hand opens on Mammy's pillow.

Jacob's snapping crocodile fingers stop snapping. Mammy's fingers move. Jacob puts his hand into Mammy's hand. Mammy's hand is big. Mammy's fingers are long.

Jacob lifts Mammy's hand up to his hair. Mammy's hand is warm. Yellow is warm. Like the sun. The sun is round like a smiling yellow face on the fridge.

Mammy is here. Mammy is here. Here is not there. Here is here. Mammy is here. There is different. There is far away for a long time. Here is staying now. Mammy is staying here now. Jacob gives Mammy another yellow sticker.

CHAPTER 41

Jenny

Tuesday, 19th November, 2013

Dear Anne Frank,
Mammy came home a week ago, last Friday. And Da and
Jacob and Granny are so happy they don't really care or
maybe they haven't even noticed that the Mammy they sent
home from the hospital, up in Dublin, isn't really our same
Mammy at all. And she doesn't have any hair. And her face
is yellow-grey, like the bubbly paint on our front gate, and
it's too big. Too round. Like a ball. Her fingers and her
wrists are thin and brown, like the boiled chicken bones
Granny puts in the soup, and she's all crumpled up like old
paper and even though everyone's so glad she's home I
don't want to look at her.
Yours, Jenny

Jenny closes the little pink book. She doesn't like what she has
written down on the page but she's glad that she's written it
anyway. She fastens the hinge and clips on the tiny lock and
places it into her special drawer.

Then, for no reason really, she crosses the room and waits
at the door. Jenny is listening. She tiptoes outside, across the
landing, just to check. Always careful not to stand on the creaky
bit, just outside Mammy's door, she knows exactly where to

place her feet. Pushing the bedroom door gently open, she sits herself down halfway between the yellow lamp Granny always leaves on for Mammy and the blue-black of the rest of the house. With her pyjamaed back straight against the door frame and her legs lying the whole width of the saddle board she runs her finger around the patterns on Mammy's side; the multi-coloured carpet swirls make her think of adventures. She is counting them.

Raising her head from the floor map, Jenny lifts her eyes to look over at Mammy's shape in the bed. Mammy is facing the other way. Jenny is glad. Mammy looks strange, just lying there all wrong, like gravy on chocolate is wrong or forgetting some-body's birthday is wrong. Jenny hopes Mammy is not too cold. She always looks too cold. Then Jenny remembers something she didn't know she had forgotten. She closes her eyes and remembers how, when she was small, her door would open a little bit, every night, letting in a triangle of light where Mammy would stand, watching her for a minute, before crossing the room to her bed. Jenny sometimes kept her eyes closed, pretending to be asleep. She can see Mammy again now, like she was before, cosying her down under the quilt, pulling it up closely around her neck, just under her ears. And Jenny remem-bers the feel of Mammy's hand on her forehead first, then on her cheek. Two kisses follow; one on the top of her head, the other on the tip of her nose. Then the door clicks softly closed and Mammy's feet fade away, back down the landing again.

Jenny opens her eyes, but nothing has changed except Mammy's place in the bed. Where her cheek was on the pillow just a moment ago her good hand lies now, and her head falls backwards on to the sheet. Her mouth is open, like a black hole in the bottom of her face; her two lips the same blue-white as her skin. And she looks like she needs to be coloured in with some of Jacob's markers or she needs to be rubbed out completely and drawn all over again. The way she used to be.

Then, out of the sleeping darkness, Jenny hears slipper-shuffling feet closing in behind her. Granny stands towering above Jenny. Her hair is in rollers, so in the shadow on the opposite wall her head looks much bigger than it is in real life.

'Go on in outta that, pet. She'll be delighted to see ya,' Granny whispers down to Jenny, who has drawn her two legs up now, tight under her chin.

'Granny, why are you up? Mammy's asleep.'

'Ah, I know that. But I was just goin' out to the toilet, so I thought I'd check she's okay on me way. And, Young Lady, may I ask, what has you up anyway?'

'Toilet, too.'

'Why don't ya go on inside there and see her?'

'She's asleep.'

'No matter. She'll still know you're there.'

'No. I don't want to. I don't want to wake her.'

'Well, don't wake her so. Just don't step on that creaky bit inside the door.'

'No. I need to go back to bed. I've school tomorrow. I'm tired.'

'I'm tired, too, pet.'

Granny steps over Jenny into Mammy's room. The creaky bit creaks under Granny's slippered feet.

From her place on the floor Jenny watches Granny bend over Mammy's small shape in the bed. She puts her hand flat on Mammy's forehead and Mammy looks like she's shrinking under the duvet while Granny seems to grow bigger, as big as a tree. Standing back up and heading towards her own bedroom again, Jenny wonders if maybe Mammy is only pretending to be asleep after all.

CHAPTER 42

Jenny

Jenny looks at the big pulsing orange thing in the corner. It looks like the egg of a dinosaur except it's the wrong colour. Or it could be a heart. The heart of a giant.

'What's that?' Jenny asks, pointing her finger.

'Oh, that's my new Himalayan salt lamp,' Mrs French says, following the line of Jenny's pointing finger and clapping her two hands together.

'What's a Himalayan salt lamp?' Jenny asks, feeling no wiser now than she was before Mrs French's clapping explanation.

'Well, it's supposed to do all sorts of things, but I just really like it. It makes me feel safe,' Mrs French says, wrapping her two arms around her own body.

'Mammy's home,' Jenny says, without smiling.

'Yes. Mrs Nicholson told me. That's brilliant news, Jenny. I'm so glad. Do you want to sit down?' Mrs French asks. Her whole face is smiling.

For a moment there is nothing but the sound of a faraway bell. Jenny looks at the giant chair she's been offered but decides that over by the window would be a better place to be right now. The day outside the room is grey, like the giant has wrung all of the colours out of it and stored them up all together in his big warm heart in the corner but outside still doesn't know where all the colours have gone. The morning was grey. The afternoon is grey. Mammy is grey.

'She looks different. Granny didn't tell us.'

Jenny looks out at all the shadows behind the rain. Jenny doesn't want to watch the rain. Not today. She turns back to the room, nods over at Harry Potter up there on his shelf, and makes her way across to the biggest chair in the whole wide world. For no reason at all she picks a long white feather out of the pen holder on Mrs French's desk and then she sits down.

'So, it was a surprise?' Mrs French says but Mrs French doesn't seem surprised. Not at all.

Jenny nods slowly.

'You know, Jenny, sometimes surprises can shock us a little bit. Put us off kilter. My Summer was a surprise.'

'Did you not know you were going to have a baby?' Jenny looks at Mrs French's face and then her eyes move down to Mrs French's belly like Jenny's trying to make the connection.

'Oh no, I knew, of course I did. But she came early.'

'How did she do that?' Jenny imagines a tiny infant with a little suitcase ringing a doorbell. There's a little dog jumping and yapping. The telly in the sitting room is on. There's a radio playing somewhere.

'Well, she was supposed to come the following year.'

'What? She was a year too early?' Jenny watches the little child with the suitcase toddling back down the footpath and closing the gate behind her. The music fades with the child. Then Jenny looks at Mrs French like she's waiting for her to say something like *Ah, I'm only joking, come on inside.*

'Well, no. She was born at twenty-six weeks.'

Jenny tries to divide four into twenty-six. She doesn't know why she is doing that. But she is. She knows that four sixes are twenty-four but she doesn't know what to do with the leftover two weeks. She looks at Mrs French for the answer.

'You see she was due to arrive the following January, but she came at the end of October.'

Jenny squints up her eyes and tries to count up the months

Summer missed or gained in the middle. She's not sure if that was a good or a bad thing.

'And, Jenny, when I saw her for the first time I got a terrible shock. To be honest with you I was really very, very frightened. And it sounds awful, I know it does, when I say it out loud.' Mrs French puts all her fingers to her lips like she's trying to push the words back inside.

'Of Summer?' Jenny's not sure she understands.

'I wasn't ready, you see. She was so, so tiny. She was the only baby in the whole hospital with a sock on her head.' Mrs French looks at Jenny like she's only just realised that she is in fact saying all this out loud.

'Why was she wearing a sock on her head?' Jenny thinks about the baby picking through her suitcase to find something that fits and about how strange it must be to have nothing but a sock to wear on your head.

'Well, all the hats I'd bought were too big. And her head was so small. So very, very small.' Mrs French cups her two hands to make the tiny shape.

'What colour was the sock?' The picture in Jenny's head changes and she needs to know the colour before she can see this tiny baby in the sock hat.

'It was pink, with little love hearts on it, and it was very soft.' Jenny is glad.

'And, Jenny, I didn't want to look at her. I knew I should love her, but I didn't know how to. She looked like a little brown maggot with only a hint of a face. She was all squinched up and wrinkly.'

'What did you do?' Jenny suddenly feels such sadness for the tiny early baby that she's afraid she might cry.

'The only thing I could. I spent weeks sitting beside a plastic box looking in at her like she was something on show. Something I didn't know.'

'How long did you do that for?' Jenny sees herself standing

in the doorway at the edge of Mammy's room or sitting there sometimes at night.

'Six weeks. But it felt like so much longer.'

'Did she cry when you went away?'

'No. And I hated that she didn't.' Mrs French's hands join together in front of her mouth again, but this time she's praying small words into the tips of her fingers and she looks ashamed. Jenny knows that look of shame she sees in the mirror of Mrs French's face. 'But then one morning I stroked her little finger and she curled it around mine and I thought my heart would burst and for the first time I felt that she was mine. She was my baby. And I loved her with every inch of my body. And I realised then, in that moment, I had always loved her but that I had been too afraid.'

'Afraid of what?'

'Afraid of losing her. Afraid of touching her. Afraid of not being strong enough.'

'Strong enough for what?'

'I was afraid I wasn't strong enough to love her. I think really that's why I had called her Summer. Because I didn't actually believe she would live long enough to see her first summer and I wanted something to keep her warm, so I wrapped her up in her name.'

'Like a little present?'

'Yes. Exactly. Like a little present.'

'That was a good idea.' Jenny's eyes drift back to the big orange light in the corner behind Mrs French and she smiles for the first time since she's entered the room. She hopes it will push the choking tears back down into her throat again. It does. She holds the tip of the feather against her cheek.

'It's okay, you know,' Mrs French says, leaning slightly forward in her chair.

'What's this doing here?' Jenny asks, likes she's just realised she's got something in her hand, something very important and very, very interesting, but she doesn't know what it is or where it has come from.

'It's a swan feather.'

'Why is it on your desk?'

'Have you ever heard of *The Children of Lir*?'

'I don't think so,' Jenny says, though she can't be sure.

'Well, *The Children of Lir* is a story about four children; Aodh, Fionnula, Fiachra and Conn. They were turned into swans and it is one of the first stories I ever remember my father telling me.' Mrs French and Jenny both look over at Arthur at the same time as though it would be rude to talk about him behind his back. 'And it is a frightening story and it is lonely and terrible and magical and beautiful all at once. Well, the feather reminds me of them or at least it reminds me not to forget them.'

Jenny thinks about the two swans on the lake where they used to go with Mammy. But that was before. They would bring stale bread and sit on the seat and Mammy would tell them the story of the ugly duckling and how in the end he turned into a magnificent swan.

CHAPTER 43

Annette

The tick-tocks of the clock fall heavily from the locker beside Annette's bed. Steady, like a beating pulse and spreading beyond the bed itself, the tick-tocking stabs and stabs before blending and blurring with everything else around her – the silence, the smells – somehow changing the shape and patterns of things, making everything suddenly seem unfamiliar in a way Annette can't understand. The tick-tocking, tick-tocking, beats endlessly against the rawness inside her skull, until she feels buried beneath the stripes on the duvet. Or just buried.

It is too loud, too ceaselessly loud, counting and cutting away the minutes, the hours, the days. But the children's feet will soon break the silence, she thinks to herself, shattering it into millions of pieces, like the light that bursts into all the yellows, reds and indigos, after passing through the broken flower prism Kevin hung outside on the cherry-blossom tree somewhere out there. Somewhere before. The colours separating into shafts; all the rainbow names she'd tried to teach Jacob. She doesn't know them now. Or she does and she doesn't know. But Jacob doesn't like the rush of rainbows. Or he does. Jacob likes orange or blue or green. She can't remember the colour or the name of the colour. She remembers yellow.

His first Baby-gro was yellow. The door and the locker and the curtains around the bed in the ward had been yellow. The dado rail, dividing yellow-white from yellow-beige into upper wall and lower wall, was probably the first thing he'd seen from inside his little glass bed. His whole new little world was yellow; his face jaundiced, with creamy ochre eyes. Little yellow eyes. They'd looked past the white beam of the doctor's penlight. The doctor had turned the light off. He'd looked at Annette from the side. Then back to Jacob. He had said nothing, just smiled, pulled back the curtains and walked away.

Annette checks the clock. There's a big hand and a little hand. Ticking and tocking. Tocking and ticking. She remembers teaching Jenny the time.

The big hand is at two now. The small hand is at four. The hands will change, creeping from one number to another she may or she may not know. Scuttling spidery time. *Time will tell.* Her mother's phrase threatens and soothes all at once. *It always does.* Ticking, crawling-round hands, counting, counting, till they die. Some days she does know. Some days she doesn't. Some days she doesn't know if she does or she doesn't, so that the minutes and hours seem to creep backwards and forwards at the same time, keeping Annette in a strange foggy dreamtime, a faraway story, where she imagines, she reads herself young and old all at once, thinking about all the things she has done and all the things she will never do, all her efforts and failures rolling together as one, leaving her somewhere so enshrouded in confusion that sometimes she doesn't even know where she is anymore.

Time's a great healer. Is it? Is Time really the Great Healer?

Rubbing her nose against the pillow, she watches the afternoon light fading to grey, stealing its way round her body, creeping over the chair, the lamp, the mirror, the little glass bottles all in a row. The hand on the clock has changed again and then she hears them downstairs. They are late today, or they are early. Tick. Tick. Tocking.

The noises, small at first, fill up the house from the bottom, like water pouring into a jug, eventually surging their way furiously up to her room; the key in the front door is turning; school bags are thrown in a corner. Running feet follow little voices. Open presses close with a bang only to be reopened again. The telly talks behind all their sounds. Packets crackle and rustle. The kettle sings.

Annette waits in the failing light. It's not really light though. Not really. Not anymore. It's just something else mingling into the darkness that comes earlier and earlier now. But still there's a little line of something, white as a promise, streaking the sky. But it makes the darkness darker, because it's there, shining itself crossways beneath the Evening Star.

The brightest star of them all, he says.

It does not twinkle but instead glows with a steady, silvery light.

The Wandering Star, he calls it. *The Night Light of the Sky*, he whispers, pointing upwards, somewhere before now.

Annette tilts her neck slightly, lining her head up with the fall of her back, to see it more clearly.

That's Venus. The Shepherd's Guide, he says.

She remembers from somewhere far away inside.

The Wandering Star, he used to call it. *The Night Light of the Sky*, he would say, pointing upwards.

It's funny the things that stay with you. Their first steps. And the things that don't. Her last. All the firsts and all the lasts she didn't know she would never know again.

Jacob bounces into the room, skipping lightly on the balls of his feet. Jenny doesn't. Jacob places a yellow sticker on the headboard, tap-taps his fingers, rubs Annette's head.

'Ah, you're awake,' her mother says, stepping into the room. 'Jenny's a whole mountain a homework to do downstairs. She wanted to come up, but I made her do her tables before she starts that story she's gotta write for that competition in school. She's a great little writer altogether, ya know.'

Annette thinks she might be hungry but there's nothing for the dinner. She thinks she remembered at lunchtime but then she had forgotten again. Until now. She knows there's fish fingers fossilised somewhere in the bottom of the freezer. She'll have to root through scattered chips and curling waffles, old peas and lost Mr Freezes.

'Dinner time. Must make dinner. Getting late now. The children are hungry,' she says to her mother, trying to push back the cover on her bed.

'Ah musha, it's a bit early yet, love. You stay put. I'll do it today,' her mother says, in a steady, practised voice she remembers from before. Her mother moves closer. 'The kids are grand, love.'

'Fish fingers in the freezer. Need to go shopping. Now,' Annette says, trying to sit herself up in the bed.

'Now don't you be worryin' yourself about the shoppin'. Sure, it's all in hand. You can go tomorrow. Sure, isn't Tesco open all hours now?' Her mother passes her hand through the air, like a fairy godmother granting a wish, or else she's taking something away. Something important. Annette isn't sure.

'Have to get eggs. Milk. Eggs and sugar. For the cake.'

Her first birthday. Her last. Annette tries to push her good leg from under the covers.

Jacob places another yellow sticker on the headboard.

'There's plenty a eggs, love. We'll make a cake tomorrow. Now you stay in bed. Get a rest,' her mother says, tucking the quilt back around her and pushing Annette gently back against the pillows again.

Jacob tap-taps the walls.

'Flour. Sugar. For the cake! And eggs!' Annette's voice rises to something close to shouting. She pulls at the quilt with her good hand, her fingers trembling white.

Jacob puts his hands over his ears. He rocks backwards and forwards. Walks round in circles.

'It's okay, pet.' Her mother tries to soothe Jacob. 'Jenny! Can ya come up here a minute please?'

'More. Candles. More candles!' Annette stares at her fingers. She uses her good arm to lever herself up slowly again.

Jacob starts humming, tap-tap-tapping and louder humming, more tap-tap-tapping, more walking round in circles. Tapping. Humming. Circle walking. Tapping. Humming. Walking. Humming. Everything is faster now. Too fast. Too loud.

'For the cake! Candles. More. Candles for the cake.'

'Okay, Annette, you're just a bit confused, love. We'll get all a them candles. I promise ya. We will. As many a them as ya like. Jenny!'

Her mother stands between Jacob and the bed.

'Make a start. Now. I forgot. Present. Candles. Must start. Eggs. Sugar. Milk. Eggs. For the cake.' Annette, looking at the clock, pulls and pushes the covers away.

'Jenny, can ya come up and get Jacob? Jenny? Jenny? Don't worry, Annette. We've plenty a time yet, love.'

Annette checks the clock. She doesn't know any of the numbers.

Other feet thump up the stairs.

'It's okay, Jacob. Itsokay. Isokay,' her mother says, looking from Jacob to Annette, then back to Jacob again.

Jacob keeps tapping and walking and humming and shrieking and tapping and walking and screaming.

Annette checks the clock, kicks at the covers.

Jenny comes into the room. 'Granny, I'm watchin' telly!'

'Okay, pet. Will ya just take Jacob downstairs with ya now, please?'

'Jacob can come down the stairs on his own! Can't you, Jacob?'

'Chocolate. Sprinkles. Chocolate cake!' Annette shouts at her mother.

'Jenny, just take him down. Now. Okay, Annette, we'll get ya them sprinkles!' Her mother tries to guide Jacob towards Jenny, without actually touching him. She uses her whole body for this, blocking him off in little spaces.

Jacob scratches and pulls at his arms, picks and flicks the buttons on his shirt. He rocks backwards and forwards, his humming sounds different, like inside-sad crying that's leaking from every part of his small jerking body.

'What sprinkles?' Jenny looks at Mae-Anne.

'For the cake! The cake! Hurry. Hurry. No time! No time. Now. Not now,' Annette, screaming and half sobbing, checks the clock.

'What cake?' Jenny whispers to Mae-Anne.

'Jenny, please just take him downstairs now. Please, Jenny. Please?' Mae-Anne drops her head to her chest and takes in a big breath through her teeth.

Jenny reaches out to Jacob and sends a sad smile over to Annette. 'Come on, Jacob, let's go and see if Thomas is on the telly. I'll get you a cream cracker.'

Jacob stops all his noises. He tap-taps the walls. He tap-taps the mirror, the door, the door frame. Then, when he is ready, he takes Jenny's hand. 'Mammy remembered, Jacob. She remembered,' Jenny whispers into his ear. Jenny takes Jacob away.

'It's time. Look. Look. Now!' Annette is screaming. 'No. Now. Not now. Too late! It's too late!' Annette collapses back into the pillows again, her whole body crying and curling into the shape of a baby.

'It's never too late, love. Never!' Her mother sits down on the bed beside her. 'Sure, haven't we all the time in the world. When ya've nothin' else that's belongin' to you, not even so much as a penny in your pocket or a seat in your pants, sure ya've always got time, Annette. Time – the great healer and the greatest storyteller. Your daddy always said that. Do ya remember, love?'

The last time.

'Too late. Now. Too late. Too late now. Daddy,' Annette says the words over and over, like a machine made for recording.

CHAPTER 44

Jenny

'Come on you two. Let's get goin',' Granny says, standing at the kitchen door.

'Where are we goin?' Jenny asks.

'We're goin' up to that Chinese place up beyond the bank. They're doin' a special today. All haircuts for five euro. I saw it on Facebook. Now come on!'

'But we don't need our hairs cut,' Jenny says, putting her hand to her head like she's trying to measure the length of her hair just to make sure.

'Your fringe is gettin' too long. And meself and Jacob could do with a tidy-up, too.'

'No way. Jacob hates having his hair cut. Mammy always does it when he's asleep.'

'Sure, don't I know. But I made an awful hames of it the last time,' Granny says, looking strangely glad that the hames was of her doing.

'But, Granny, he'll go mental. He's never been to a hairdresser before.' Jenny pushes back her fringe, to see Granny better.

'But sure, now, don't I have me secret weapon with me,' Granny says, tapping her bag.

Jenny puts on her coat and gets Jacob's Spiderman jacket out from in under the stairs. Jacob will only wear his Spiderman coat this week, so it doesn't matter when Granny says there's a nasty stain on the front that she'll have to soak overnight. Jacob only wants Spiderman's blue body and red cobwebbed arms on him today and that's all there is to say about that. Granny buttons herself up, checks the plugs and the lights, throws her keys and a packet of coconut creams in her bag, and the three of them head out the door and off up the street to get their hair cut in the Chinese hair salon, with the Chinese takeaway out the back, where you don't need an appointment and where you know that whatever they do to you it will only cost five euro today. Well, that's according to Facebook anyway.

The children try to keep up with Granny. But she's fast. Too fast for little legs that want to stop and look in at the playground and in the Two Euro shop window. Jenny checks to see if the dancing Santa with the light-up flickering face is still in the window but it's all just a blur of colours and shapes as Granny marches them on. She's travelling too fast for them to catch the lovely warm smell of chips that's sticking in the air all round the front of Luigi's. Granny holds Jacob's hand, pulling him along beside her, race walking. Jenny's eyes start to go blurry in the wind she's sure is coming from Granny's hair that's stretching out so far behind her it has no chance of catching up with her head. Jenny tries to grab it. And Jacob's feet barely touch the ground as he does his hoppy-skip-toe-toddling jumping in double quick time for every one of Granny's determined, bulky strides.

'Are we late for somethin', Granny?' Jenny asks, running up beside them.

'We want to get in before the rush!'

Granny, a bit out of breath, steadies herself at the desk when they open the door and step into the claggy heat and fried-rice smells of Chin Chen Chung. There's a lady behind the desk, making strange sounds into the phone.

'Doo a clawalk? Yes? You com? Yes is okay?' Everything the

lady says seems to be a question. She does lots of head-nodding, too. 'Okay? Okay? You com?' Granny roots in her bag and her arm goes in so far and so deep even her elbow disappears. Jenny tries to remember if Mary Poppins ever brought the two Banks children into a Chinese hairdresser's. She remembers them flying across chimneys and feeding birds and singing under the sea, but she doesn't remember where they got their hair cut. Granny starts tapping her foot on the floor and her nail on the glass of the counter because she's nothing else to do while the lady is on the phone asking all them questions. Jenny wonders if Granny's going to burst into song, with cartoon birds sitting on her shoulders and flying round her head, just to get the lady's attention.

But the lady keeps nodding her head and asking questions into the phone. Granny keeps tap-tapping the glass counter. Then finally, after ages and ages of questions and millions of question marks, the lady puts the phone back down on her desk and asks if they need any help. Granny stands up real tall. Taller than she is in real life. She looks at the lady's head then she looks at her waist because she can't see her feet with the desk in the way and then she looks at the other lady cutting some-body's hair way off down in the back corner.

Granny shouts down to the corner lady while the desk lady chews the top off her pen. 'We all need a bit of a tidy-up. Do ya understand? Hair? Cut? Three?' Granny has taken all her question marks out of her bag and now she's throwing them across the room at the smiling lady. Granny uses her thumb to hold down her little finger and rams the three middle ones up in the air. 'Three?'

'One momeh pleeze, lady.'

Granny starts waving her hands around, making the first two fingers on her right hand into scissors. She lifts up her own hair and pretends to cut it with the finger scissors she has in her other hand. Then she points at the lady and shouts, 'You.'

Then she points at a red-faced Jenny's fringe and shouts, 'Cut. Good and short so as she'll get longer outta it.'

The lady looks at Granny like she's a bit mental. Then she sighs like she's just realised that these two children should really be taken away from Granny and put up for adoption somewhere in China and that it's her job to make sure that happens. But she really doesn't want to be the one to have to do it. The lady, frightened and confused and maybe a little bit annoyed, searches the room for another Chinese face to help her out, but like they've all decided they're looking the wrong way they all turn back around and continue cutting the heads sitting up on the chairs in front of them. So, alone with no one to help, she nods her head back at Granny and the two children.

'Ya'll have to be gentle now mind, Jacob's not too keen on strangers, specially foreign Chinese ones like yourself, touchin' his head,' Granny screams across the space between them.

'Pleeze, lady. Jus' one momeh pleeze, lady.'

Jenny looks down at the shiny magazines on the table. Granny puts one in her bag.

When the lady's finished drying the hair in front of her she holds a mirror up at the back of the head. The head nods and leaves.

Finally, it's time for them to be next. Granny sits down on the chair the lady points to and takes Jacob up into her lap.

'Now there's to be no dryers or spray things!' Granny says into the dark eyes looking back at her in the mirror. 'Now, Jacob, let's *Check In*.' Granny takes Jacob's iPad out of her bag. Jacob smiles as she flips back the cover. 'We need to go to *The Wall* bit first,' Granny announces to everyone in the place, like she's giving them all their first lesson in how to use Facebook, as she swipes her finger backwards and forwards again.

Jacob copies Granny's swiping finger, moving his own over and back through the air.

'Here, Jacob, press the *Check In* button, there.' This is part two of the lesson. Jacob *Checks In*! 'Now how's about a game a Candy Crush?' Granny asks Jacob, like this is something she's been doing for years.

Jacob's whole face lights up when he sees all the different-coloured sweets on the screen. He swipes and swaps, moving sweets into rows of three, matching colours and shapes, to the sound of the carnival music playing in the background.

When Jacob's hair is done, the desk lady sweeps up the floor around Granny's chair, and Jenny watches herself in the mirror next door as another Chinese lady cuts up her fringe.

'Good and short,' Granny had said.

The next-door lady looks like she remembers.

Granny is next. Granny puts Jacob down and he goes over to tap-tap on the big window that keeps the room separate from the takeaway out the back. Jenny can't believe it all happened so quickly, so quietly. Jacob seems fine.

Granny roots in her bag again. She pulls out the magazine she'd swiped off the low table out in the front and hands it back over her shoulder, 'Page fifty-nine please.'

The lady flicks through the pages. She stops, checks the page number, then she giggles, but it's a frightened little laugh, 'Ah yaa su, lady?'

Granny nods her head real slow and says, 'Yes,' with her mouth but not with her voice. Then the lady puts Granny's old, tired hair up in loads of ponytails. The lady cutting Jenny's hair lets out a little gasp. Jenny looks out from behind half a new fringe, wondering why Granny wants to look like Grammar Girl, and wondering who is on page fifty-nine anyway. The other heads in the room turn round to watch, too.

The lady lifts up each ponytail and then cuts each one off. She holds each of them in her hand for a minute, like she's sorry she has to do this but she has no choice, before throwing it in the bin at her feet. When the ponytails are all in the bin, she goes over to the drawer under the mirror and takes out a little machine. She gives Granny a quick squeeze on the shoulder and then moves her left hand to the top of Granny's head. Holding Granny's head, with her hand pressed out flat, the lady shaves all of Granny's hair off.

Jenny looks at Granny and thinks she might choke on the sudden, sharp laugh stuck in her throat. The lady standing in front of Jenny finishes cutting her fringe.

There are left-over small bits of Granny's hair in grey-blue, fluffy piles all round the floor, and now that it's not on her head anymore it looks like something else, something that doesn't belong anywhere because nobody wants it now. Something that's lost. The laugh falls and flops back down on to the floor of Jenny's stomach again. Granny looks at Jenny and winks. Jenny's eyes go a bit blurry.

All Jenny can see is Uncle Fester from *The Addams Family* and with her new short fringe that makes her face look gigantic, she feels a bit like Pugsley or the moon. *Oh no*, she thinks to herself, *wait till Jane-Anne Comerford Smyth sees me comin' like this.*

Granny pays the lady at the desk. She opens the door for the children and they step back out on to the street. They walk back the way that they came, and Jenny is sure she can definitely hear the dum-dad-a-dum. Click. Click. Dum-dad-a-dum. Click. Click – that's humming in everyone's head, as they pass by.

On the way home Granny brings the children into Dempsey's to get sweets. Jenny loves looking at all the big glass jars, full of colour, up on the ice-cream-pink shelves. They are always full, right up to the top, with perfect sweets that look too perfect to eat and Jenny wonders if maybe nobody ever buys the sweets from those jars because there's never any missing. None of the jars are ever empty or half-full or half-empty. There's blue raspberry fizzballs in one and orange barley twists in another. There's three more lined up beside them and they're full of different colour sherbets, all yellows and greens and reds. Next on the shelf are the black and white humbugs and then there's the apple drops and the kola cubes and the pineapple chunks. Jenny feels funny vinegar drips falling into her jaws. She swallows hard.

'Ah, how are ya there, Mae-Anne? How are things?' Mrs Dempsey enquires from the end of the counter.

'Ah sure, ya know yourself. Not so bad, I suppose.'

'That's a grand soft day out today,' Mrs Dempsey says, looking at Granny's head, but she pretends that she's not.

'Aye to be sure. Though there's to be a turn over the next few days.'

'How's your Annette doin' now, Mae-Anne? I heard she was home.'

'So she is, thanks be to God and His blessed mother.'

'Ah, it must be great for youse all. Will she have to go up and down for all the different therapies and things?' Mrs Dempsey stands straight across the counter now putting gold chocolate coins into little plastic bags. She crinkles them shut and ties little shiny-red bows on the top. 'Up to the hospital?'

'She will. Eventually. Couple a days a week. Just for a little while a course. No beds, ya see.' Granny's eyebrows move up her forehead. She looks out over the top of her glasses. 'But not yet.'

'Feckin' cutbacks!' Mrs Dempsey says. 'Absolute disgrace! Do ya know Martha Gleeson's mother died on one a them trollies out in the hall waitin' on a bed and all a them doctors and nurses walkin' up and down by her!'

'Well, now, for all that, they've been very good to her. She's on a waitin' list. So please God.'

'They say it was comin' on her a good while, Mae-Anne. The poor thing. That confusion. Someone said she used to take little Jacob to the playground in the dark.'

Granny sucks in her mouth and switches her eyes to the children real quick without even moving her head. Then her robotic eyes switch back to Mrs Dempsey again. 'She's fine again, thank God. Ya know yourself!' Granny pushes back an imaginary fringe and her eyes grow wider with every word she spits across the counter. The lights in the shop jump up and down on the top of her bald head. 'Time's a great healer!'

'He's said nothin' since, I suppose?' Mrs Dempsey says, looking down at Jacob. 'Isn't it true what they say? Some families are just born for tragedy. It doesn't seem fair.'

Granny grips the top of the counter until her knuckles go white. Jacob tap-taps on the glass.

'They say some of them can read two pages of a book at the same time. Some of them can even play whole piano concertos after hearin' the music only once – is he one a those ones? He certainly seems to have rhythm.'

'And now, tell me who'd be the *they* you'd be referrin' to exactly?' Granny asks Mrs Dempsey. 'Would *they* be the same ones talkin' about how your Johnny's got that young Brannighan one pregnant and him married with a lovely wife and four kids of his own?'

'I don't know what you're talkin' about and sure none of us can stand in glass houses, now can we, Mae-Anne?' Mrs Dempsey replies, with a stretch in her neck and a shake in her voice.

'No, he doesn't do any a that readin' or music stuff and would you kindly stop talkin' about Jacob as if he wasn't here or as if he was stupid without any brains!' Then there is nothing, only the crumple and crackle of plastic. 'Now pick out what youse want,' Granny says, more like it's a threat than a treat.

Jenny gets Rolos and they hope Jacob picks Monster Munch and not Smarties, because Smarties take ages, but Jacob decides he doesn't want Monster Munch, so Granny slams the money for Jenny's Rolos and Jacob's Smarties down on the counter and gets herself a paper because she knows Smarties take ages, so she may as well read the paper while they sit across the road in the park.

'I like your new look,' Mrs Dempsey says when Granny snaps her change back into her purse.

'Ah, would ya ever FUCK OFF,' Granny says, with the biggest clearest capitals Jenny's ever heard, on her way out the door.

The three walk to the park, in silence. They walk over to Jacob's bench, the one with the name of the man who died on it. Martin Gallagher was his name. Jacob traces the letters with his fingers and then touches the whole name with both his hands before they can sit down. Granny shakes the paper open with a flick and a rustle right in front of her face and Jenny sits down beside her and thinks about all the colours of the sweets in the jars up on the pink shelf behind Mrs Dempsey's head. She sucks the chocolate off the Rolo in her mouth and watches all the people in the park. There's always someone running in a bright orange T-shirt and there's always someone picking up dog poo in a bag and taking the bag off with them for a walk. Sometimes the man with the big silver metal detector is there sweeping the grass and listening for sounds, like he's trying to hear all the stories of the whole world coming up from the ground. And he's there today too, sweeping backwards and forwards, side to side. The old man from the steps of the dead house is back. He looks different today. Cleaner. Not so lonely. Jenny watches the old man watching the metal-detector man. The old man is waiting for all the stories too, she decides. All the stories of the world, buried like treasure or like old coins or cups, just waiting to be found and dug up, polished off a bit and given over like presents, wrapped in gold paper and tied up in silver bows for the rest of the world to read. He's going to take them back home in his pockets, together with all the sweets, to his children who will be there waiting. When he goes into the house he will call them all into the kitchen, where he will dig deep down into his pockets again and amaze them with the things he has brought home: stories of enchanted prisons and teddy-bear shops, of odd shoes and secret hurting rooms and trolls, frogs and witches and invisible trains. They will spread them all out on the white tablecloth, and they will spend the whole night eating the sweets and opening up all the adventures and fairy tales he has given them.

The mammies, pushing buggies and talking to their babies, are always there. Jenny likes watching them, most of all.

Jacob likes the shape of the Smarties box and he touches every side before he opens the top. He takes out the yellow ones first and lines them all up along Martin Gallagher's bench. Then he gets all the red ones and puts them behind the yellows. Then he finds all the green ones. They have to go behind the red ones. The orange ones come next. They go behind the green ones. The pink ones go at the back. Then he can eat them.

Granny folds up her paper, flattens it with open fingers pushing out to the sides.

'Granny, we have to wait till all the chocolate has melted off his teeth and then we'll have to search him for any lost bits a Smartie that might be stuck in his clothes. If Mammy sees the chocolatey teeth or the Smartie clothes she'll kill us. Mammy says she doesn't care what Nestle say on the box about no artificial colours or flavours, Mammy knows Smarties are *full* of Es,' Jenny says, with serious eyes.

Granny folds her arms across her chest and waits.

When they finally arrive home, Granny turns on the lights and closes the curtains even though it's not dark. 'Go on up there now and show your mammy your lovely new haircuts. I'll be up in a minute. Just let me put on the spuds.'

Jenny takes off Jacob's coat and hangs it back in under the stairs. She unbuttons her own, slips her arms out of the sleeves and places it on the same hook over Spiderman. Jacob bolts up the stairs. Jenny, not interested in winning this race, looks at the happy photographs that run up the walls at the same level as her head. When she takes a step up so does the next picture. Mammy made Da do it that way. There's the one of Mammy in a white dress holding a bunch of purple flowers. Next up is the one of Mammy in a pink jacket holding a ten-day-old Jenny up in the air. Straight up over step number five she sees Jacob's sleeping head flopped on to Da's shoulder. Then there's the picture of Jenny's first day at school. She's standing out in the garden holding Mammy's hand. Her school skirt is too long. But the best one of all is at the top where they are all there together on the wall. It is autumn inside the frame. Jenny and Jacob are throwing leaves up into the air. Da stands with his two arms stretched up past his ears, like a magic Y, and he's using his special powers to make all the yellows and golds blow up and over the two children. There are leaves in their hair and in the hoods of their jackets. Granny has stopped to look at something and is squatting slightly at the knees, rummaging in her bag. Mammy looks back at them all over her shoulder, one hand shading her eyes. Mammy is smiling. Jenny has seen these photographs so often she's forgotten just how much she needs to remember them now.

Jenny pushes open the bedroom door very quietly. Da's sitting up in the bed beside Mammy. He's telling her something about when they were young.

'Da, Mammy's asleep,' Jenny whispers, peeping on tiptoes at the rise and fall of the blankets on the bed.

Da doesn't hear her. He's laughing so hard his shoulders are shaking up and down but there's no sound of laughing in the room. Then Jenny watches the light catching some of the crying-laughing tears slipping down Da's cheeks and dropping from the end of his nose and there's a big awful mess gathering around his mouth. The type of mess Jenny knows Granny would just love to spit-wipe, with her hankie, off his top lip. Jacob tap-taps on the walls.

'Don't cry, Da,' Jenny says, with a wobbling lower lip. 'Granny says Mammy is just having a bad day today and that tomorrow she'll be better again. Granny says time is a great healer, like a doctor. Only slower!' She reaches out and pulls herself up round his neck. She stays wrapped up in Da while Jacob tap-taps on the mirror, making his way right round the room. Jenny often wonders if Jacob is trying to find a way in or a way out with his tapping fingers, always searching for something they can't seem to find. When she lets go of Da she notices a shiny elastic line of spit-snot left between her jumper and his nose like a string joining them together, 'Ah, Da!'

'Umbilical cord.'

'What?'

'Nothin'.'

They both laugh. Then Jenny, without even thinking, rubs Mammy's cheek very softly with the back of her hand.

Granny opens the door with a gentle push. The door rubs on the carpet. She stands at the end of the bed measuring all the tears and pain in the room. She says nothing. Da looks at Granny. His eyebrows do a dance. 'Jesus Christ, Kojak, what happened to your hair?'

Granny looks very surprised, like she's forgotten all about the Chinese lady and page fifty-nine in the magazine. Then she moves her fingers up to feel where her hair isn't, and she smiles to herself. 'Musha. Didn't like to think of her feelin' different. That's all.'

'Ya know what, Kojak? You're one in a million, so ya are.'

'Ah sure, ya know yourself. And I don't want no more a your snivellin' either! Do ya hear me? There's goin' to be bad days as well as good. You know that. She's just tired today. That's all. Sure, didn't I tell ya as much this mornin'! I knew by her. Bad times don't last. Give her time.'

Then there's a stirring under the cover. Da leans over and kisses Mammy on the top of her pirate head. Jenny sees a smile moving under Mammy's open eyes. Da pushes himself off the bed. He stands up like he's got something real important to do and moves towards Granny and kisses her on the top of her shiny bald head too.

'Would ya ever get away outta that, ya big feckin' poultice,' Granny says, swiping at Da with the tea towel she always seems to have in her hand.

'What's goin' to become of us at all?' Da says, to nobody really. 'I didn't get that job.'

'What job?' Granny says.

'There was a job goin' in Bolger's. Storeman's position. Really thought I was in with a chance.'

'Now, musha, don't you be worryin'. Do ya hear me? You mark my words. The future's surprised us plenty a times in the past,' Granny says, closing the door behind her.

CHAPTER 45

Jenny

Tuesday, 26th November, 2013

Dear Anne Frank,

You are not going to believe this, but Granny shaved all her hair off! I swear. She did! She's bald, like an egg. And it's like now she's no hair to think about she's got even more time for cleaning and sorting everybody out, especially poor Da. Da didn't get the job that he wanted in Bolger's, that's the big hardware shop out the road. He did get a letter though to say that they would keep his name in their computer and let him know if there are going to be any more jobs in the future. I said that was good but Da didn't seem to think so. He's very quiet now, mostly. But Granny says Da's not to worry, she has plenty of work lined up for him round here. She has given us all jobs to do, now that Mammy is home, and we all have to do these jobs, without any complaints, no matter what we're asked to do and even if we don't want to do it. Granny wrote that up as rule number eleven on the fridge.

'Jenny, come in here a minute, would ya, love?' Granny shouts across the landing.

'I can't. I have to finish my homework,' Jenny says, like it's true.

Granny doesn't hear her, or she does, but because Jenny's homework answer wasn't the one Granny wanted, she shouts across the landing again, louder this time, 'Jenny, love, would ya ever come in here a minute. It's important!'

Placing the little pink book down on her bed, Jenny lays her pen into the creased line between the page she's been writing on and the next one, which is blank for now, and closes the diary over. She picks up Anne Frank and slowly makes her way across to Mammy's door. It is open, but just a tiny bit open, so Jenny has to push it gently, to see into the room that is still so full of hospital plastic containers, basins and tablets in jars, that Jenny can hardly bear to go in.

'Ah, there she is now!' Granny says, like Jenny's been lost in a crowd somewhere, but now she's back, and Granny's the first one to recognise her. 'I have a little job for you.'

'What?' Jenny says, remembering rule number eleven, on the fridge.

'Listen, pet, I've a million and one things to do. I need to give Jacob his bath. I've a mountain of ironing needs doin' and I've not even started on those pots in the kitchen. So, will you read to your Mammy this evenin'? Won't it be good practice for you!'

'I can't. I haven't finished my Irish sentences yet,' Jenny says, again like it's true, and like doing Irish sentences is something she would look forward to doing if she did have to do them, 'and I have to do my reading and my sums, and I have to start my project on Pompeii, for history.'

Granny sees right through the lie. 'Ah, you can take a break from the homework, surely be to God. You've been at it all night. I wonder should I go in to see that teacher about all a this homework she's given ya? I could go in tomorrow.'

'No. It's fine. What do you want me to read?' Jenny says, knowing Granny's winning this round.

'Sure, can't ya just continue on with this one?' Granny says, folding a little triangle down on the top of the corner of the page she's been reading.

Jenny knows this book. She's heard it creeping across the landing every night since Mammy came home. Because this is the book, with the white porch on the cover, that Granny's been reading to Mammy. Jenny's not surprised that there are no people on the front. She would bet any money that all the characters left once they realised what was happening to them and how stupid the whole thing is. Because it is stupid, and Jenny doesn't need to read to the end to know that. It's a story about some old man reading a story to some old woman in a home for old people, and it's all about three thousand years in the life of this old woman and this old man and at first the old woman is young and so is the old man and she's rich but he's not rich. They're in love with each other but her da doesn't want her to marry him because he doesn't have a job. And he has to go to fight in a war, and she doesn't get to see him anymore after that. And it would be great if that was the end, but it isn't. The woman keeps getting older and older and she drinks lots of tea and grows lots of flowers and then one day she goes into a home for old people because she can't remember things, except the names of different kinds of birds and the colours of their feathers, and she meets the first man she was in love with in there, but she doesn't remember him either.

'Granny, Mammy doesn't like books like that. Mammy prefers Harry Potter!' Jenny says, still standing in the doorway and frowning down at the porch swing in Granny's hand.

Mammy smiles up at Jenny from her bed, like Jenny has just saved her life. Granny looks at Jenny, like she's just said a curse word.

Turning her head, Granny looks at Mammy. 'You like this, Annette?' But then, after waiting a couple of seconds, she adds, 'Don't you?' to the end of the question and for the first time ever, it actually sounds, to Jenny, like Granny is asking a real question, one that needs a real answer and not just the answer Granny wants to hear. Even Granny herself seems shocked.

Mammy nods her head slowly, but Jenny just knows it is one of them nods you do to keep someone happy and not because you agree with them at all. Jenny has lots of nodding experience. Mammy does too. Granny doesn't. But, Granny seems to know that this nod is different, somehow. She closes over the book. Granny looks like she's giving in.

'Granny, if that old woman doesn't die soon, Mammy will. Of boredom!'

This is the wrong thing to say. Jenny doesn't know why she let it change from a thought, which is one thing, into a sentence, which is another, without looking at it first. Granny's face changes from colour to black and white, like suddenly she's her own ghost and that frightens her. Mammy says nothing.

'Right so missy. In ya come. You can take over the readin' and pick whatever book you like. You bein' such an expert an all! Can't ya read your mammy that book about the prison you've been goin' on about? That'll surely cheer her up!'

'Granny, it's *The Prisoner of Azkaban*! And anyway, I had to bring that back to school,' Jenny says, even though the book is still hidden safely in her secret drawer. Because *The Prisoner of Azkaban* is for when Mammy is better and Mammy is not better yet.

'Well, no matter. What's that one you've got there?' Granny asks, pointing her head at the book in Jenny's hand.

Jenny looks down, like she doesn't know what Granny's talking about. She doesn't even remember taking Anne from her bed.

'Oh, just *The Diary of Anne Frank*,' Jenny says, because she can't think of a lie quick enough this time.

Granny nods, like people do when they've just made a big decision and there's no changing your mind after that.

'Ah, poor little Anne Frank,' Granny says, like Granny and

Anne are friends, great friends actually, and Granny knows
everything there is to know about Anne.

'How do *you* know Anne Frank?' Jenny says, pulling Anne's
small face into her jumper.

'Sure, didn't I read Anne Frank to them all when they were
young. Your mammy knows her too! Isn't that right, Annette?'

Jenny looks over at Mammy. Mammy is smiling again. A
proper smile this time. A proper mammy smile. Then she gives
a little nod, a little *Hello* nod, to Anne Frank. Granny gets up
from the bed, straightens the quilt till all the wrinkles are gone
and then she pats the space she's just left, for Jenny and Anne
to come in and sit down.

'Granny, I can't! I have to do my homework. I told you.'

'That can wait. This is more important.'

'But—'

'There'll be no Buts about it, Young Lady!'

'I can't. Not tonight. I'll read tomorrow night. I promise.'

'Ah now, Jenny, aren't promises just like babies; easy to make,
hard to deliver!'

'What? But I don't have time!'

'Jenny, mark my words, time is the best coin you have! Spend
it wisely!'

'What?'

Jenny looks from Granny to Mammy. Mammy's eyes seem
to be begging Jenny to come in and sit down before Granny
has second thoughts and opens the old-man-woman book again.
Mammy looks smaller now. Flatter. Her white face pasted onto
her white pillow is suddenly the face of a child. But her eyes
are just the same. Jenny sees that Mammy's eyes are just the
same as they always were. Mammy has these blue eyes that
change colour in the light and when they look at her, Jenny is
sure they're telling her the things Mammy can't say. They are
big eyes, reaching all the way to the edges of her face. They are
Mammy's eyes. Jenny has known them her whole life. They

belong to Mammy's face and her face could have no other eyes than those. But, they are Jenny's eyes too! And Granny's.

Jenny steps into the room and takes her place on the bed, beside her mammy.

Anne Frank, sorry I had to rush away and leave you earlier, but Granny had a job for me to do. Well a job for us both, really, Anne Frank, for you and me. Granny made me read your story to Mammy tonight because she had a hundred and one things to do! She always says that. And even though I've read all the way up to the end of your second November, hidden away in your Secret Annexe, I opened your diary on the very first page and it was your birthday all over again. And Mammy lay there listening and we laughed when I tried to say the names of some of your friends out loud because reading is very different when you hear your own voice outside your own head, speaking the words on the page for somebody else who is listening to a story, that it is now your job to make right. I think though, Anne Frank, that we are a good team. I explained the word 'unbosom-ings' to Mammy and I told her that I am now your real friend and that's why you don't mind me reading your diary and about how long you have waited for a friend to talk to. Jane-Anne Comerford Smyth used to be my friend but she's not anymore. We had a fight.

I told Mammy all about your family and about how you were not allowed to go to the cinema or play any tennis, but you were allowed to play ping-pong, and eat ice cream and have boyfriends. And I introduced her to Mr Van Daan and Miep, and showed her the wooden staircase and the storeroom and all the offices in your building, but by Thursday 9th July, 1942, Mammy was fast asleep.

I sat there with Mammy until Granny came back into the room again. Granny switched the big light off and turned the lamp on beside Mammy's bed. She pulled the quilt up around Mammy, closer to her head and in under her chin. She tucked the quilt down on both sides and I could see Mammy's small shape in the bed and I realised then that even though Mammy is my mammy, she's still really Granny's little girl, too.

'So how is Anne Frank?' Granny asked me, in a whisper.

I told Granny that you are okay for now, and then I saw something change in Granny's eyes, behind her glasses, and I wondered what it was they were or were not saying.

'Ya know, nobody gets to pick when or how they are born,' Granny whispered, taking your diary out of my hand and putting her own hand down softly on your face.

'The brightest sunshine is after the rain,' Granny said, closing her eyes.

Anne Frank, I hope my granny is right.

Love, Jenny

ps I think you would really like Harry Potter, Anne Frank, and I know Harry Potter would really like you.

CHAPTER 46

Annette

Annette is surrounded by pillows smelling of purple and white flowers. She knows the smell came from a bottle. It is a purple bottle with a blue lid, like a bowler hat. The bottle comes from the big shop where she used to take Jacob. Before. She remembers the shop with all the lights and the huge noises. She remembers the purple bottle sitting on a shelf beside other bottles in similar hats. Some were blue. Some yellow. Some colours she can't remember. Today. Tomorrow she might remember the name of the shop. Tomorrow she might remember the name of today. Yesterday she knew was Wednesday. Today is just today. For now. Tomorrow will just be tomorrow until she remembers its place on the list.

Jacob is sitting up beside Annette and all her flowery pillows. The telly is on. There are children making a snowman. The snowman is smiling. He's wearing a hat. A red engine with big eyes and cheeks passes the smiling children. A man's voice comes out of the telly but Annette cannot keep up with his words. They pass her by and run down along the track with the train. Then they are gone and more words take their place somewhere else far away from Annette.

Jacob is rocking and twiddling one of Annette's hair bands between his finger and thumb. The rubbing sound of the band is getting bigger.

There is another engine on the screen now. It is a different colour. It is the colour of grass. Annette cannot remember the colour. Just now. This is Percy.

'Percy is always very busy,' the man says.

Annette tries to say it too, 'Percy is always very busy. Percy is always very busy. Percy is very busy. Percy is always busy. Very busy. Always.'

Annette looks at Jacob. Jacob looks at Percy.

Percy is gone. There is a blue engine talking now. He has triangle eyebrows. They move up and down. Up and down. His eyes open and close. Open. Close. This is Thomas. Thomas is blue.

Annette says it slowly, 'Thomas is blue. Thomas. Is blue. Thomas is. Blue. Thomas is blue. Thomas is blue.'

Annette looks at Jacob. Jacob looks at Thomas. Jacob rocks backwards and forwards twiddling Annette's band.

The man is talking again. It is the next day on the telly. What day is it today? Annette knew this morning. Her mother tells her the name of the day every morning. Sometimes Annette can hold on to it and sometimes it just crumbles around her, like dust. Today is a dusty day.

The other engine is back though Annette does not remember his name. He is the colour of grass. He is smiling. The man is talking. Annette can only find the word *Christmas* in all the falling words coming out of the telly and landing at the end of her bed.

Christmas is one of the words she knows. Annette remembers Christmas. She was very young. There were carol singers at the door and a tree in the corner. Annette can still smell the tree and all the memories of it wrapped up, like presents, somewhere at the back of her mind. The taste of mince pies, sour and sweet baked in together – piping hot and with cream – brings them all into the kitchen where Mammy is wiping floury hands on a white apron. Daddy stands stirring mulled wine and spicing the air with a warmth only found in stories remembered. Daddy is whistling a tune. Annette listens. Now she can hear Daddy singing the words. Very softly, at first. Like a shy whisper.

O holy night, the stars are brightly shining . . . The whole kitchen stops what it is doing. There is only the sound of Daddy's growing voice. And it's all really only about that one note. The listening ears are only waiting on the *vine* of *Oh night di—*

Annette can feel it. In her spine. Low down in the deepest part of herself. She closes her eyes to see the notes better. And it is mesmerising. Annette can feel her bones shiver. She stands there, before herself, in flannel pyjamas. Daddy is singing and it is Christmas.

There are children giggling in the snow on the telly. They are still making snowmen. The grass engine is sad. He cannot think of a gift to give Reg for Christmas. Reg is yellow. Reg works in a scrapyard.

Annette tries to copy Reg; 'Merry Christmas. Merry Christmas. Percy. Merry Christmas, Percy.'

Annette looks at Jacob. Jacob looks at Reg.

'It was Christmas on the island of Sodor,' the man says, from the telly.

'It was Christmas on the island of Sodor.' Annette repeats what the man says from the telly.

'It was a very busy time,' the man says.

'It was a very busy time,' Annette repeats.

There's a woman at the station giving a pink present to a small girl wearing a pink coat and hat.

Duncan is yellow.

'He didn't like Christmas one bit,' the man says to Jacob and Annette.

'He didn't like Christmas one bit,' Annette says back to the man on the telly.

Annette loved Christmas. Before. She's not sure now. Not sure when it is or if she likes it. She remembers the Christmas story Daddy told them every Christmas Eve before bed. They are kneeling on the bed looking up at the night through the window. Daddy points to the star. The brightest one in the sky.

That's the star.

All their little heads follow Daddy's finger. *That's the Christmas star.* Daddy smiles up into the dark. *The same one the wise men followed from the east. The same star that guided the shepherds through the night. That's the star that lit up the world from over a little stable in Bethlehem. Mary and Joseph wrapped the baby in a blanket and laid him on a bed of straw. The animals' breath kept the little baby warm. The wise men brought gifts. The shepherds brought sheep and the angels' singing can still be heard tonight, if you listen very, very carefully.*

Annette watches each of their little heads turn ever so slightly to press a listening, little Christmas ear closer to the glass.

Ssssh. Listen.

Daddy's voice is soft, with the sounds of s fading to nothing, making more space for the angels.

'But the following day Duncan made his way to the steam works anyway,' the man tells Jacob and Annette.

'But the following day Duncan made his way to the steam works anyway,' Annette says back to the man.

It is the following day again. Annette wonders how many days have passed. How many days since before. How many days still to come. Sometimes Annette remembers the days. Sometimes she doesn't. Today is still just today until Annette remembers. Tomorrow Annette might remember today.

Jacob rocks backwards and forwards. He twiddles his fingers. He wiggles his toes. Annette watches Jacob. Jacob watches the telly. Annette looks at Jacob's feet and she smiles. Today is yellow. Today is Thursday. Annette moves her hand along the quilt, dusting it down.

CHAPTER 47

Jenny

Sunday, 1st December, 2013

Dear Anne Frank,

It was your birthday again, this evening, and Mammy stayed awake until Friday 10th September, 1943. That was good, wasn't it? My birthday is on the 13th of March. It was a Wednesday. But that was the day Mammy got sick. Lizzie, in the shop, gave me a Twix and I shared it with the old man on the step, who was waiting there for his children to come home from the cinema. He had brought them there, paid for their tickets and bought them all popcorn and a drink but then he left them to go back home again to talk to the doctor about his wife. His wife was very sick. Then I came home and me and Granny made muffins.

I really liked your birthday poem. Mammy did too. But do you really not have any knickers? I like the word 'clandestine', it sounds like a secret, like it should only be whispered, doesn't it? When I googled it, the dictionary said that it means 'to be kept secret'. I wonder is that just an accident or did the person who invented the word 'clandestine' know it sounds kinda sneaky and that's why they made it up? Da says that there is such things as words that sound like what they mean. Da says 'malevolence' is one of those words. I asked Da what it meant, and he said, 'Your

Granny is full of malevolence!' I said that it sounded like something bad and guess what, Anne Frank, when I googled it that's what it said. It said that 'malevolence' means 'hatred'. Imagine that. She's not, of course. Da just says things like that about Granny, but he doesn't really mean it. She says worse things about him!

There's nothing really happening here. Mammy still sleeps a lot, even during the day. Sometimes she gets up for a little while, but never for too long. She is very, very tired all the time. Sometimes I think she's just tired of being tired. But Granny says she's getting a bit better every day and that someday soon Mammy will be back to herself again. And I suppose she is much better than she was and she's probably only so tired because of all the work she's doing trying to get better. Granny does all the things now that Mammy used to do before. Granny's always very busy trying to make Jacob learn new things or else she's helping him with his words or she's helping Mammy with her words when Mammy's not sleeping.

Jacob is my little brother. He has Autism. Mammy used to say that Autism is like feeling the world screaming at you every minute of every day. And it is measured on A Spectrum. A spectrum is like a big long metre stick. The closer you are to 100 the more autistic you are. I think. Da says there was no such thing as Autism in his day but, Anne Frank, I think Mrs Van Daan is definitely at about fifty on the spectrum stick and I think Peter might be too. Dussel is. He might even be at sixty. But I think you already know that. So, I think Da is wrong. Granny says they only had feet and inches in her day so there was no measuring on spectrums or in metres either, but she says that there were always people who were a bit different. They've always been there. They were just called 'characters' back then though. Granny says we are destroying all the 'characters' nowadays, with so many new-fangled disorders and measuring sticks and tests and that there's no such thing anymore as honest to God good old-fashioned country 'characters' because nobody is allowed to be different anymore. They are all put on tablets and sent to therapists or into shelters and soon, Granny says, there'll be nobody left to write books or poems or songs about because we're all so bloody ordinary and afraid to be different and sure who wants to write about that!

Jacob is different. Jacob can't talk. The only word he has ever really said is 'fuck' and Mammy said it was the answer to all her prayers. But that was before. And he hasn't said anything since. Not even one word. And that was ages ago.

Granny says that all Jacob's words are right up there in heaven with Holy God, just waiting for Jacob to collect them and 'Mark my words,' Granny says, 'when he does, we'll have some party then!' My granny just loves parties.

Mammy used to make Jacob practise his words all the time except she doesn't any more. That was before she had to practise all her words all the time. But she never even seemed to notice that Jacob doesn't really have any real words at all. He just makes strange sounds – the same strange sounds he makes for everything. But Mammy still used to tell me and Da, every day, to listen to Jacob's new word. Then she used to throw her two hands out to the side and say 'Ta-daa', like she was a proper magician and Jacob was her new trick. But only one of Mammy's hands works properly now. The other one is too tired most of the time.

And at first me and Da used to get real excited about Jacob's new word and sit real quiet and real still so we could hear the new word real clear. But after days and days and weeks and weeks of being really quiet and sitting really still, me and Da still couldn't hear what Mammy could hear, *and Mammy did hear words in the sounds Jacob makes. She could even have little chats with Jacob that nobody else can have and only Mammy knew what Jacob wanted or needed and when he wanted it or needed it and only Mammy really knew if Jacob had a pain in his head or his belly or his ear or if he'd no pain at all and he was just crying because he can't talk. But that was before too.*

Sometimes I close my eyes real tight and hope Autism will just climb back out the kitchen window again, but sometimes I think maybe it's me gone instead. So, I understand what you mean, Anne Frank, about disappearing.

Granny says Jacob needs more minding than I do. She says I'm more like Mammy. I'm tough and strong but Jacob is more like Da and he needs more things done for him and he needs to be told what to do and when to do it and how to do it. But I think maybe Granny's wrong because I think Jacob's really more like Jack-Jack out of The Incredibles. *He's Violet's baby brother. Jack-Jack never needs gel in his hair either! It just sticks up away from his head anyway and at first it's like he's the only one in the family without any superpowers but really, he has a whole bunch of superpowers and really, he's the most powerful one of them all because he does molecular manipulation levitation and he has laser vision.*

I like the sound of your friends Elli and Miep, and of course Moffi the cat, but I'm sorry to hear about all the bombs and guns and shooting that you are so frightened of. Granny always says that if you are the only one who knows you are frightened, then you are brave. Granny also says she was born the year after you started writing your diary but Da says she's way older than that. Da says Granny can't even be carbon-dated, which is a very fancy way of finding out the age of old things. I googled that, too. Granny would have loved to help you and your daddy tidy up the 'Secret Annexe' when you arrived there too early and it was all, still, a big mess of boxes and bed sheets.

I want you to know that you are never alone, Anne Frank, no matter how far away you are. Mrs French is still reading you and so am I! I think you should try to stay happy and laugh if something is funny and you are not bothering me at all with your troubles. I will always be here to hear you. I like listening to your voice, Anne Frank, and so does Mammy.

On Friday, just before little break, I told Jane-Anne I was sorry about our fight. Well, I didn't tell her exactly, I just left a note on her desk. I told her all about Laura and Nellie and about how, even though they had a fight in a wheelchair, that really they were best friends and that Nellie had written a book about that and that maybe one day Jane-Anne would too.

And please don't worry, Anne Frank. There are lots of fights in my house as well, usually between Granny and Da. They are both on the spectrum, too.

Love, Jenny

CHAPTER 48

Jenny

On the second Wednesday of the month Dorcas nods her head in Jenny's direction. It's a big head, bigger than a normal head, but its nodding message is even bigger. Jenny can go. She moves quickly, in case Dorcas changes her mind and decides that Jenny needs to be fattened up with more capital letters or full stops, as if Jenny doesn't already know everything there is to know about capital letters and full stops. And Dorcas looked hungry!

Like she has just escaped from a spitting-flame oven, Jenny runs down the corridor as fast as she can. Head bent, eyes fixed, she follows the little glints in the tiles that today, for some reason, seem to glisten, like pieces of lost, secret silver. She stops at the end and looks back down the hall, half expecting Dorcas to come running after her. But Dorcas doesn't come. Jenny waits for her breathing to slow down or catch up. She's never sure which it is. When everything settles and feels okay in her head and her chest, she knocks on the little secret door in the wall. She stands and listens but hears nothing. She knocks again, a little louder now, in case Mrs French didn't hear her the first time. She looks back down the corridor once more, just to be sure, then back at the door. When there is nothing, except more silence, Jenny places her left ear and her right hand up against the door, like maybe she'll be able to feel Mrs French inside, even if she can't hear her. And strangely enough it works. Jenny's hand tells her that *yes* there is somebody in the room on the other side of the door. Gently she pushes the door forward, creating just enough space for her head to slip in and have a little look around. Mrs French is there! Jenny knew it. She smiles down at her right hand.

Mrs French, sitting at her desk, is slightly hunched over, so her head is lower down than it should be, her forehead looks wider than it is, and her chin seems like it's either missing or fading away. With her eyes fixed firmly on whatever is in front of her, she doesn't notice Jenny's smiling head or the rest of her body, slipping through the half-opened door. Jenny thinks she hears water everywhere, like it's flowing all over the room, under the floor, in through the windows, down from the ceiling. Looking up, down and then back at Mrs French again, she wonders if maybe it might just be a sound she thinks she can hear, like when she holds the big shell out in Da's shed up to her ear, to listen for the whispering ocean inside.

'Hi,' Jenny says quietly through the watery rushes in her head. She wants Mrs French to know she is here, but she doesn't want to disturb her either.

Mrs French's head moves upwards but it seems like the rest of her body doesn't know anything at all about her moving-upwards head and so it stays exactly as it was, close to the desk, and for a second only it looks like Mrs French doesn't know where she is or who Jenny is either and Jenny's face reflects the shock and surprise of suddenly being discovered, too. Jenny takes a tiny step backwards, as though this is actually the wrong room or the right room but on the wrong day or at the wrong time and she's sorry now she hadn't just left when the first knock went bouncing around the corridor unanswered.

'Ah, Jenny. Come in. Come in. I'm sorry, I was miles away there! How are you?'

Mrs French has three voices: understanding, excited and lost. This is somewhere between excited and lost.

'I'm fine, thanks,' Jenny says, and she almost believes it.

'Good. Come on in. Sit down,' Mrs French says, pointing to the big giant's chair.

But Jenny's not ready to sit yet.

'What's that noise?' Jenny asks, looking everywhere and nowhere really all at the same time.

Mrs French looks lost again, but she listens to the room with her whole face, as though that will help Jenny find what it is she's looking for.

'Oh! That's "The Lullaby of the Ocean",' Mrs French says, after a moment's searching, in a way that seems to make perfect sense, but only to herself.

'What?'

'It's just music I like to listen to, sometimes. It's on YouTube,' and she nods at her computer, like it's just another big old shell that has always been there too. 'Oh, I was meaning to ask you the last time, Jenny, how is Ophelia?'

'She's fine. Da says she's just resting. That's what they do, Da says. In wintertime they take a rest.'

'Like hedgehogs?' Mrs French asks, like she's trying to make the wrong jigsaw piece fit into a Lego building.

'Em, yea, I suppose so,' Jenny says, though she's not really sure how Ophelia is just like a hedgehog, but she'll happily help Mrs French look for the missing jigsaw space to stop the Lego house from falling over.

Jenny thinks about Hooch the Sleepy Hedgehog and how frightened he was when an apple got stuck in his spikes. Jacob loves when Jenny tells him about Hooch and his adventures.

The little hedgehog gathered all the lovely hedgehog food and he made a winter nest for himself. He piled up all his favourite snacks; coconut creams, cream crackers, Smarties, Monster Munch and licked his lips because this was the stuff he loved best. Hooch was just about to start eating when something fell down from the sky and on to his back. Slam. Bang. Wallop.

Hooch didn't know what had happened but he did know all about Henny Penny and Foxy Loxy so he guessed that it wasn't the sky that had fallen down with a whack. But still, there was something big and heavy stuck to the prickles on Hooch's back.

Sometimes Jenny puts Jacob into the story too and she lets him take the apple gently away. When this happens, Jenny makes Hooch so grateful that he offers to share all his winter food with Jacob. Happily, they crunch and they munch their way through all the goodies and then Jenny gives Jacob the job of snuggling Hooch into his winter nest.

Jacob tucks in the little blanket and tells Hooch the story about Biscuit Bear waking up in the middle of the night. 'Biscuit Bear was sad,' Jacob tells Hooch. 'Biscuit had no one to play with. Everyone else was asleep so Biscuit decided to make some friends for himself. He went into the kitchen and found milk, butter and flour. He mixed them all together in Mammy's big baking bowl and he cooked himself some friends, in the oven. When they were ready, Biscuit Bear and all his new friends, Gingerbread Girl, Cream Cracker Cat and Butterscotch Badger, had a night circus, right there in our kitchen.'

'So, Ophelia is kind of hibernating for the winter, then?' Mrs French says, just as Cream Cracker Cat is about to swing through the air.

'Yes,' Jenny says, freezing the swinging, trapezing cat, and trying to make sense of the *then* at the end of Mrs French's sentence. 'What are you doing?' she asks, tilting her head towards the page on Mrs French's desk and closing the curtains on Gingerbread Girl's disappearing act.

'Oh, I'm just colouring,' Mrs French says, like this is a perfectly normal thing to be doing.

'Oh,' Jenny says, trying to sound like she's not surprised. She's not really. 'What are you colouring?'

'Here, have a look. Do you like it?'

Mrs French slides the piece of paper across the desk which is really a table, Jenny decides. Mrs French would never have a *desk*.

Looking down at the picture, Jenny wishes she had more eyes. But she doesn't, so the two that she has open wider than they normally do, like they don't want to miss a line or a colour or a shape. Only after feasting on all the purples, blues, lilacs and greens does she actually try to figure out what it is. It could be a flower, she thinks, but the longer she looks at it, the more it seems like the sun. Or it could be the planets around the sun or the stars around the planets or it could be the earth or the moon or a whole new planet she's never even heard of. It could be all of space or an ocean or a shell. It could be a trick. But whatever it is, it's more than just a flower.

'It's beautiful,' Jenny says. 'What is it?'

'It's a mandala.'

'What's a mandala?'

'Well, the word *mandala* means circle. Mandalas start from the centre. You see, they move outwards but begin, always, with a dot in the middle.'

Mrs French's hands move around to make an imaginary circle. Then she points to the imaginary dot in the middle of the imaginary circle.

'Mandala. Mandala,' Jenny repeats the new word, wondering why it is she likes it so much.

It sounds like a good word; a quiet word with big muscles, its two arms folded across its chest. It is a word she can trust, like it could be used as a secret password to get into a cave full of diamonds and genies in lamps that need rubbing. She sees herself using it. *Mandala*. She likes the way it fits in her mouth and takes its time slowly coming out. 'Mandala.' She says it

again. The big man at the entrance, with the teal turban and
no feet, nods his head. He knows what it means, too, this strong
new word, because it is important to be able to know how
powerful a word is when you find it. The big-rock door slides
open . . .

'I have a spare one here, Jenny, if you'd like to give it a go?'
Mrs French says, taking another page from a drawer, like
Gingerbread Girl making a coin appear from behind Badger's
ear. Alakazam!

Jenny pulls the giant's chair closer and sits down.

'It looks very difficult,' Jenny says.

'It's not, Jenny. Just take each little bit at a time. Colour a
small area. Don't worry about the rest of it until you get there,'
Mrs French says, sliding a long, flat packet of markers across
the table and smiling.

'Sharpies!' Jenny says.

'Do you like Sharpies, Jenny?'

'I've never used them. Granny says you'd want to be mental
to pay thirty feckin' euro for a packet a markers! She says the
ones in Cut Price are just as good! But they're not.'

Jenny picks out an orange marker from the pack. Pulling the
orange lid away from the grey pen, she sees FINE POINT
written in big black capital letters. She knows that this is a
serious marker, not like the JUMBO ones they have at home.
JUMBO couldn't mean serious. Not ever. Sausages and breakfast rolls are all JUMBO on the signs behind Lizzie's head in
the shop. Things that are bigger than they should be are called
JUMBO, like Dorcas's head. Jenny decides the word JUMBO
is a stupid word. It tries too hard to be seen, when really, it's
just too fat for itself.

Starting in the centre she fills the small dot with colour. Jenny
is amazed at how easy it is, as though the marker itself knows
just where to go and where not to go. *THIS IS BECAUSE IT
IS A FINE POINT,* she says to herself in capital letters. Gliding

lightly around, in a perfect little circle, it touches nothing only the space it is supposed to be in, not like the fat JUMBOS at home that always spill over and leak into everything, everywhere. She places the lid back on the pen and puts the orange carefully into its own little, plastic place in the pack. Each marker lies in its own spot. It's so easy to pick the colour and lift the pen that Jenny thinks these are the best markers in the whole wide world, ever. The JUMBOS at home stand up straight in their tube but they're jammed in so tight that most of the time it's impossible to get one out at all. The trick is to pull up the one in the middle because it's only when that one's gone that the rest have enough room to be wriggled free. But it takes so much poking and gripping that usually Jenny just uses whatever colour she can get, which is never ever the colour she wants. But with the Sharpies there is a system. All the pinks lie together; the darker pink is first then the salmon pink, then the lipstick pink, then the baby pink. Then all the pinks are followed by all the reds, all the oranges and all the yellows. All the purples are next; dark first, then violet, then lilac. All the purples turn to blues and all the blues turn to greens and turquoises which come before all the browns and finally all the browns become blacks, light, dark and grey. Jenny thinks about Jacob as she reaches for the middle yellow. This is the yellow of the sun.

'Jacob would love these,' she says, as her yellow flows perfectly into the larger circle that runs around the orange dot in the centre.

'Does Jacob like to draw, then?'

'Yes. He does. He draws stories. And he loves yellow and making things into rows.'

'I think yellow is my favourite colour, too,' Mrs French says, looking faraway behind Jenny's head, like that's the place where all the wise things are. 'It's such a happy colour. He *draws* stories?' she says, like a soft echo of Jenny's own voice and not like a question at all.

'Yes. He writes in pictures.'

Now there is only the soft rubbing of colours on paper and the whispering wash of the waves in the air. Neither of them says a word, either because they don't have to or because maybe there's nothing that needs saying, for now. This quiet is easy, like it should be part of their conversation and not like a quiet that comes to pull panic words out of your mouth. Jenny likes not having to talk, just now. She thinks about Jacob again and about Mammy. She changes her marker; a deeper yellow this time. She tries to hear Jacob's voice. And what he would say. How he would say it. And then just behind all the yellows a voice appears growing up through the colours. It isn't Jacob's though. It's Mammy's.

'Words mean things. When you put them together, they speak. It's a bit like sending a flare up into the sky. It's a way of letting the world know that you're here – a kind of X Marks the Spot,' Mammy used to say. 'He *will* speak one day. He *will* have a first word and the whole world will stop, just to see it, to see Jacob's fireworks' display echoing through the dark!'

And Jenny can see Mammy's shape forming again, through her voice; her face as it used to be; her hair growing in all the colours and circles on the page. She fills it up. She's out of scale, larger than life, like she's in a story where size doesn't matter because it's just something you make up anyway. The way Gulliver was massive, or Alice in Wonderland when she drank the 'Drink Me' stuff, and either she grew too big or everything else grew too small. Jenny thinks about this for a minute. Then Mammy, straight, tall and enormous, holds out her two good arms to a tiny little Jenny.

When Jenny looks at her own moving right hand she realises she's filled the whole middle bit of her picture with many, many colours she doesn't even remember choosing. Other than that, they are both completely still at the table; Mrs French on one side, Jenny on the other, but for their moving-back-and-forward hands colouring swirls and spirals, petals, hearts, stars, moons and flowers.

'Da is left-handed too,' Jenny says, looking at Mrs French's colouring hand now.

'Is he? They say left-handed people are very creative. Is he good at drawing as well?'

'Granny says the only thing he's good at drawing is the dole.'

Jenny can feel Mrs French trying not to smile. Really trying, very hard, not to smile but when Jenny looks up she just catches the end of it. Then the waves fill up all the space around them again. Moving herself slightly, Jenny settles into the pull and push of the tide, her thoughts going in and out, like the ocean sounds in Da's shell.

'But he made the train set for Jacob?' Mrs French says, in a Granny question kind of way.

Mrs French is on Da's side now. Jenny just knows it.

'Yes. He did. He likes making things and fixing things.'

The waves ebb and flow. A lipstick-pink Sharpie glides along the line of a flower petal or maybe around one side of the world.

'Ah, he must be creative so. You must take after him, Jenny.'

'But I write with my right hand,' Jenny says, 'like Mammy.'

Jenny thinks about Mammy's right hand; how heavy it looks when she's trying to move it.

'Think left and think right and think low and think high—'

'Oh, the thinks you can think up if only you try,' Jenny finishes off Mrs French's rhyme, which really belongs to Da and not Mrs French at all because Da has it carved into a board, screwed to the wall, inside his shed.

'You know Dr Seuss!' Mrs French says, in her delighted-excited voice.

'Da does,' Jenny says, with a smile.

'Oh, I like your dad. Anyone who knows *The Cat in the Hat* is okay by me!'

'He used to read it to his sister Joyce, when she got sad. Da was an orphan.' Jenny doesn't know why she says this or why she doesn't include Auntie Joyce in the orphan bit, too. The words seem to come from Jenny's mouth without her even knowing at all and the hands pulling them out aren't her own. She swaps the pink marker for a deep purple-blue and gently lets it slide around the next band, a double band, separated into little boxes. Each box has a circle inside. The circles stay uncoloured, for now.

'An orphan? Really? Like Harry Potter!' Mrs French says, trying to seem not quite so delighted and excited by this news. But she is. Jenny knows that she is.

'Well, not really, but kind of, I suppose,' Jenny says, not sure where she should put her commas, at all, and lifting a lovely shell-coloured green from its place in the pack. 'His mother died when he was only eight. Then one day, they went to see *Bambi*, in the cinema, and when they came back his da was gone.'

Turquoise, she thinks. Turquoise is perfect. She takes the greeny-blue colour for the circles inside the boxes.

'Oh, no! Not *Bambi*!' Mrs French says, hiding her face behind her hands, like that's going to make something bad change into something better when she takes her hands away.

'Yes. I think it was *Bambi*,' Jenny says, wondering why *Bambi* seems to have been the most awful part of her last sentence and not the bit about Da's mother dying when he was eight, and his father going away.

'Oh, dear. Oh, no. What happened to him?'

'To Bambi?'

'No. No. To their father? Where did he go?' Mrs French says, taking her hands away from her eyes, as though she has now realised that bad things don't just disappear when you aren't looking at them.

Jenny shrugs.

Mrs French picks up her marker again. 'Did he have to go

and live with relatives, then?' she asks; now that there's nothing left to hide from, she's trying to find another lost piece of the jigsaw. The Lego house is long gone.

The soft scratching sounds swish-wish from one side of the table to the other. There is a quiet moment between their words, but it is not a silence. It's another pause, like a comma you know is right, in the middle of your mind, put there for thinking; for thinking about things or for feeling something about the things you are supposed to be thinking about. Jenny's not sure which one she should do, feeling or thinking, so she just listens instead to the washing waves, still crashing somewhere far away, but close enough to be heard. But then, and without her permission, she thinks about Da on a doorstep somewhere, waiting to be let into a dark house, with orange curtains on the windows. He has a small brown suitcase at his side and a pair of old black boots, knotted together by their laces, hanging around his neck. His trousers are too short.

'No. They all looked after each other,' Jenny says, as she tears up the picture of Da knocking the stranger's door and throws it into a bin she's found somewhere outside their strange house.

The colours push more shapes up from the page. Jenny reaches out, like she could touch each one with her hand. She thinks about Da again, even though she doesn't want to, and the way he sometimes looks like he's trying to see something he's lost. Da's always losing things.

'Oh, did he have lots of brothers and sisters, then?' Mrs French asks, in her excited voice but she's trying to make it sound like her comforting one.

Then, what? Jenny wants to scream. *Then, they all lived happily ever after? Then, Da's story turned out well, like some of the stories, but not all of the stories, in all the books on your shelves? So then, Da grew up and then what? What happened then? What happened next? Then, he just became another character, someone else in the crowd, someone no one ever sees or hears because he is not so important? Because he didn't get that job? Because he wasn't found? Why did you need the then? Then what? What if there isn't any then? What then?*

Musha, Jenny, only time will tell, Jenny says to herself in Granny's voice.

Then, you look after the words, Jenny, she says to herself, doing Mrs French's voice now, in this imaginary bit of conversation. This seems to calm her.

The flower changes on the page before Jenny. It becomes a star. It is a big star behind the flower-world. It is a star that needs the deep red of the marker now in her hand. She sees Da and all his brothers and sisters. She counts to eleven. Six boys. Five girls. They are all sitting around a table, eating porridge. The tallest girl wears an apron, covered in pink and green cupcakes, and she stands at the top of the table. She's in charge of the porridge. She's in charge of the table. Her name is Paula. Auntie Paula. Jenny likes the name Paula. And it suits Paula because Paula is strong, like a boy, but pretty and clever, like a girl. Paula is in control. The youngest, a red freckled boy, is in a high chair, flinging porridge all round the kitchen. His name is John. He's just a baby, but of them all, John is the one she loves most. It is for him that she left school; for him she breathes in and out and forgets what the other girls her age are doing. And it is for him that her heart will break in two, years and years away from now, as she stands alone and shivering in the January rain, watching his coffin being lowered into the ground beside their mother. And it is him, more than any of the others, who reminds her so much of their father. There's porridge in everyone's hair and they are all laughing and singing. Then they are gone.

'Well, there's three of them. Da and Auntie Joyce and Uncle Michael. Uncle Michael is the eldest. He kinda looked after Da and Da looked after Auntie Joyce. She's the youngest. Granny says Da did too much for that one and that she still can't look after herself! She lost her husband in Aldi, you know!'

Mrs French's face fights off another smile.

The star-triangle shapes are different now. Jenny likes the change. She likes the up-and-down lines she is making. She likes that the colour is the same in every line. She likes that these markers aren't wasting. She likes that she doesn't have to go over the same spot again and again until the paper almost melts away and a hole appears. She doesn't have to lean heavily to squeeze the last bit of colour out.

'Did they ever see him again? Their father, I mean,' Mrs French asks, with her whole face, making sure Jenny stays with Da's story and not the story about how Uncle Maurice disappeared with the guard, behind the cheap pineapples and wetsuits, in Aldi.

Mrs French really wants a happy ending. Jenny knows this feeling only too well. She can almost taste it, like soupy air.

Picking up the light green, Jenny wonders how this will look when she's finished; if she ever gets it finished. It seems every circle is connected to every triangle and every triangle becomes part of the star that began as a spot in the middle. And everything is linked in some way to everything else. The shapes and lines move and change and grow into other lines going in other directions, into new shapes making new patterns, but they all seem to grow from that same little dot in the centre. The beginning. The eye.

'No. But Granny says she saw him. Once. At the railway station. She says she's sure it was him.'

'Really? At the railway station? When?' Mrs French asks, no longer trying to hide her excitement, her marker skipping hurriedly around the page.

Jenny watches the colours and shapes growing before her, like a story. Each point on the star stands beside or on top of a diamond. If Jenny makes the diamond shapes darker than the red or the star triangles, it will look better. It will read better.

'I don't know. A long time ago. He was gone when Da got there.'

When Jenny squints she sees a face somewhere beneath the stars. She searches the colours for the rest of the story. There is a man, an old waving man. He is waiting. With turquoise-blue eyes, like the turquoise sound of the sea. They are sad eyes, very old eyes. He is waiting for his children to come home. But they don't come. Jenny sighs and wonders why the railway man didn't wait for Da or come to find him. She's never wondered about that before.

'Oh, no! Does your dad talk about him at all?'

'No. Not to us. He used to talk to Mammy though and she would tell him that we are his family now. I used to hear them sometimes, whispering. Then Da would smile, like he was listening to the waves again inside his shell,' Jenny says to Mrs French, even though she doesn't know if Da smiled or not, but she likes to think that he did. And sometimes Jenny imagines the conversation Da would have had with his own father if he'd only got there on time. Sometimes they'd just stay at the station and sit down on the bench by the wall or sometimes Da would pick up his father's suitcase and they'd go off together for a walk, but only if it wasn't raining. When it was raining Jenny would make them find a warm corner in a pub or coffee shop.

'How have you been?' the old man would say to Da.

'Okay, I suppose,' Da would say back. 'Where have you been?'

'I waited,' he would tell Da, 'but you never came.'

'We missed each other,' Da would say, 'but you are back now and that's all that matters.'

Da would tell his father all about Michael and Joyce and about Mammy and me and Jacob and sometimes his father would tell him about sailing to America and hiking in China. Other times he would talk about living under a bridge, in a box big enough for him to sleep in. He was a shipbuilder or he had a factory that built cars or he held out a cup and fed biscuits to the pigeons that landed on his sleeping bag, depending on Jenny's mood and whether they were sitting down or taking a stroll. He would show Da some photographs and they would talk about all the things they had never talked about before and then he would tell Da about how he needed somebody to take over the business, now that he was too old.

'Are you working at the moment?' his father would ask.

'No,' Da would say, looking down at his hands, 'I lost my job a couple of years back, when Jimmy Smyth went bankrupt. They marched us off the site. Course he's operatin' again, under a different name now. But there's not much going round here at the moment. I've had a few jobs, on and off, here and there, labourin' mostly, but nothin' you could depend on and, you know, when you're out of work as long as I've been, well, you get kind of used to it, and you get kind of frightened of goin' back.'

Jenny sees Da and he's shrinking; getting smaller under all the colours, like he's disappearing inside his clothes, inside all the stories he never tells. He's standing at a corner in a train station, an orphan with a bundle of stories, wrapped up in a spotted handkerchief, tied to the end of a pole.

'There are stories in silence, Jenny,' Mrs French says.

'I'm never going to get this finished!' Jenny says, mostly to forget about Da and all his secret, missing, lost-silent stories.

'That's okay, Jenny. There's no hurry. Remember . . .' Mrs French turns slightly away and uses her right hand to draw Jenny's attention to the little funny chick up on the wall. He's yellow-green and fluffy and he seems to be balancing on one little orange leg as he tries to put the other little orange leg forward. Two tiny fluffy wings point out from each side of his roundy body, like the way the tightrope walker, in Jacob's night circus, uses his arms to stop himself falling, one way or the other, off the rope and into the crowd in the kitchen. Big white letters at the top of the poster say *Just take one step at a time* . . . and at the bottom, under the nervous chick, is written, *That's really all you can do* . . .'Is he frightened or brave, do you think?' Mrs French asks, although Jenny doesn't think Mrs French is looking for a proper-real answer at all.

'Both,' Jenny says, anyway, staring up at the little chick and although one part of her feels sorry for him, her other part feels happy for him too. 'Is he coming or going?'

'What?' Mrs French asks, still looking up at the chick. 'Coming or going? I don't know. Does it matter?'

They sit like that for a long time, just looking up at the wall. Jenny wonders where the chick might be going, why he is alone.

'Yes. Where has he been?' Jenny asks.

'Just away,' Mrs French's voice is sad now.

'Away? Where?'

'On a big adventure,' Mrs French says. She seems very sure.

'But he's only a chick! Look at him! Why did his parents let him go off on his own?' Jenny replies. 'He's so tiny.'

'Maybe he just needed a break?'

'A break? From what? From his own family?'

'Oh, no, Jenny. Just a little time away, on his own.'

'But why?'

'I don't know. Sometimes, Jenny, we just have to let people find their own way.'

'Where?'

'Back home, again.'

'But why did he go, in the first place? Why did he go away and leave them all behind?'

'Maybe he had to.'

'Maybe he had to, what?'

'Go away to come back?' Mrs French says with a question mark she's not really sure about.

'But is he going away now or coming back?' Jenny asks again.

'From where?'

'Home.'

'What do you think, Jenny?'

'Well, that depends on where the rest of his family are standing in the picture, I suppose. If they are behind him he's going. If they are in front of him he's coming.'

'That's very true!' Mrs French says. 'I hadn't really thought of it that way. But either way, Jenny, he's back now, isn't he? And that's good. Isn't it? He's had his big adventure but now he wants to see his family again. Doesn't he?' Mrs French says, gathering up as many question marks as she can find.

'So, you think he is *coming* home, then?' Jenny says *coming* kind of slantways. She doesn't know why she says *then*.

'Well, what do you think? *Coming* or *going?*' Mrs French uses slanty words, too.

'Well, I'm not sure. *Coming* or *going?*' Jenny borrows one of Mrs French's leftover question marks. 'If he is *coming*, that makes him brave, I think. But if he is *going*, well then, that means he's *frightened*.' Suddenly Jenny can see his whole family, standing somewhere outside the picture, waiting. She can hear them chirping and chucking as they watch him coming down the road. 'Granny says, "It's not the size of the chicken in the fight, it's the size of the fight in the chicken!"'

'That is very true, Jenny. Very true,' Mrs French says. 'Your granny is brilliant!'

'He is definitely *coming* home. He is safe now. He is coming home,' Jenny says, easily, and without any doubt, this time.

'Yes. Yes, he is. Isn't he?' Mrs French says or asks. 'Are they going to have a party, for him, do you think?'

'Yes.' Jenny is sure about the party and surer still that the party will be great. 'Everybody will be there.'

'Well, they all missed him terribly, while he was away,' Mrs French says, smiling up at the little chick again.

'But, wait! Where are his stories?' Jenny searches the wall.

'What?' Mrs French searches too, even though she's not really sure what she's looking for.

'All the stories of his adventures!'

'Oh, they are all inside him, Jenny. We carry all our stories inside us. Just here,' Mrs French says, placing her palm over her heart. 'This is where we keep them.'

And just like they have both suddenly agreed not to talk anymore, they pick up their markers and get back to their colouring.

'But it doesn't seem to have any end. It just goes on and on and on,' Jenny says, breaking their agreement, after a long enough silence, but still keeping her eyes on the page on the table.

'Yes, it does seem a bit like that, I suppose,' Mrs French says.

Jenny looks into her mandala. She gazes at the sweeping lines and shapes, falls into the colours and swims in its patterns. She sees the words carved into the other sign, the one that's nailed to the back of the door in Da's shed and without meaning to, she says them out loud, 'You're on your own. And you know what you know. And you are the one who'll decide where to go.' Jenny's words float around the room and then join the whispering waves of the ocean lullaby song.

Mrs French smiles up at them as they pass over her head.

'Some people believe the mandala is like a story, the story of our lives. The story of ourselves,' Mrs French says, her voice coming on the next gentle wave, 'and that starts inside us, Jenny. In here. In the centre.'

'The beginning,' Jenny says.

'Yes, Jenny. The beginning.'

'I think I might know where Granddad is,' Jenny says and whatever it was she was expecting to say, it wasn't that!

Mrs French looks up from her page. She wasn't expecting that either. She drops her marker. 'What? Your dad's father? Have you seen him?'

'I think so. I think he might be the old man who sleeps on the steps of the cinema. He knows my name. He has Da's eyes. He collects stories in the park.'

Jenny sees the old man again now, walking behind the chick up there on the wall. He's coming home after many long adventures. He had waited for the children to come back from the cinema, to tell them that their mother was dead. The doctor had tried very hard, but he could not save her. And, somewhere along the way, the children got lost and they couldn't find their way home. It got darker and darker. The man waited and waited. The children walked and walked. Finally, the man stopped waiting. He decided to go to search for his lost children. The children did find their way back, eventually. But when they arrived home, their father had already gone. Da kept on looking for him but he didn't find him. He only found bits of him in half-remembered stories and strangers' faces. And, Jenny realises, Da is still waiting. Da has always been waiting, somewhere, outside the picture.

'Have you told anyone else about this? Have you told your granny? Your dad?'

'No, sure, I only realised now. Just this minute. I didn't know I thought it until I said it out loud. I saw him in my story.'

'What story?' Mrs French asks, like she's been out of the office all day and has just come back inside.

'This story. The mandala story,' Jenny says, taking her eyes away from the wall and back to the table. Then Jenny looks at Mrs French again, like she's waiting for her to understand.

'Why do you think it is him?' Mrs French asks, not even looking at Jenny's mandala.

'Well, nobody knows who he is, so he could be him. He often passes our house. He knows Jacob's name, too.'

'But, Jenny, if he is homeless he must pass lots of houses every day, the poor man. He could know your names from hearing them used on the street. He probably knows everyone's name, Jenny,' Mrs French says, repeating Jenny's name twice, like she's making sure Jenny knows she's talking to her and nobody else.

'I know,' Jenny says in a small voice. 'I just thought it would be great for Da. I think he's gone away again, now, anyway. He's not at the cinema or at the broken house anymore.'

On the wall Jenny sees Da and the old man with Da's eyes, looking at each other across a kitchen table. There is a white cloth on the table. The old man reaches into his pockets and takes out all the stories he has brought home for Da. But the best story of all is waiting inside the big shell that Granddad holds up to Da's ear.

'I know, Jenny, everybody loves a happy ending,' Mrs French interrupts. She reaches across the table and gives Jenny's hand a little squeeze. 'What do you want to be when you grow up?' she asks, sitting back into her chair again.

'I don't know,' Jenny says with a shrug.

'Jenny, I want you to do something for me, well for yourself, really. I want you to think about yourself in the future and I want you to sit down and write a letter to Jenny, to you, when you are older! It might be fun!'

'A letter to me? When I'm older?' Jenny says, confused about what exactly 'older' means here. 'When I'm how much older? Like, do I have to be twenty or thirty or what? How old do I have to be?'

'It doesn't matter how old you are. You can decide what age you want to be! I bet you'll be surprised at what you find! Jenny, you can be anything you want to be!'

'Can I?'

'You certainly can,' Mrs French says, looking off into the wise place again.

'Really?'

'Yes. Really. You could be anything! Anything at all. Believe in your own magic, Jenny, because if you don't believe, you will never find it! But you will. You will, and you must! And you must because you can!'

Jenny smiles at Mrs French's words, gathering together into a big crowd, clapping and cheering for her all over the place. Then she turns and watches Da and the old man hugging each other tightly, up on the wall, the little chick chirping at their feet.

CHAPTER 49

Annette

Annette, not sure if she is asleep or awake behind tired eyes, pulls herself up, almost. Half lying, half sitting, she looks at the clock: 3.03 a.m. The red numbers, too square really to be numbers at all, glow in the cube radio clock her mother has put beside her bed.

'Them numbers are easier to read,' she had told Annette. 'Ya know like if ya wake in the middle of the night and ya want to check the time. There's no messin' around with big hands and little hands, with this one. Ya'll know exactly where ya are in time!' she had said, like Annette is some kind of time traveller who needs reminding what time or year it is every time she opens her eyes.

Annette smiles at the idea. She remembers a book about a wife. She doesn't remember the name of the book.

In the middle of the night Annette can see more clearly than in the day. There are no questions coming too quickly at her from every corner of the room. There are no exercises to be done; no balls to be squished or kneaded by her bad hand; no walking up and down, trying stairs; no having to smile. When the day ends, when everything settles into night, then and only then does Annette feel like herself, like her old self, getting ready.

Sometimes when she wakes she forgets. Just for a moment. These are the moments she gathers up, like a small child collecting wishes from the stars before bedtime. These are the moments she strings together at night. These are the moments she attaches to the unexpected memories that sometimes creep into the dark, like cracks in broken glass. Her hair grows back thick and strong, so does her skin in these little gaps between all the noises of the day. She stretches herself out tall and long, wiggling her feet and treading her fingers, like she's just waking up from the longest sleep, in these moments. Then she remembers and her world crumbles again into a pile of broken-down memories and forgotten truths she can't recall.

3.06 a.m. Annette hears little feet tap-patting across the landing. Tap-pat. Tap-pat. The bedroom door swings open. The light, sharp and strong, startles her slightly. She blinks it away, the surprise of the light, and watches the little pyjamas move across the bottom of her bed and waddle up the side. With her good hand she pulls back the quilt. The sleeping little body finds its way in beside her. Snuggling in closer, curling herself up like a baby, Jenny and Annette fit together perfectly. They always have. Annette places her good hand, half cupped, around the back of Jenny's head. She smells her hair – coconut – and breathes her back inside herself once again. Jenny stirs slightly, only to push her little body tighter against Annette.

'I love you, my baby,' Annette whispers into Jenny's hair.

The words come easily, without any effort, like loving Jenny is the easiest thing in the world to say. Annette smiles as the words snuggle down on the pillow beside them. These were the first words Annette ever said to Jenny. She remembers it now. That first moment. She hadn't even had a name then. She was just *Baby, The Baby* or *My Baby* for the first forty-eight hours of her life. She had come early. Three weeks too early. Too early, for them to have agreed on a name.

'Ah, you'll know when you see its little face,' her mother had said, not knowing if she would be a girl or a boy.

'You are *my* Jenny,' Annette breathes the words into sounds. 'You always will be.'

Jenny curls her knees tighter into her lying-down body and inches her foot between Annette's knees. Annette lifts her good leg slightly to make room for the little foot and rubs Jenny's sleeping hair.

Then, like a flicker of light falling out of a crack in the ceiling, Annette thinks of a bedtime story from long, long ago. It was one of her favourites. She can remember her father's face, serious and smiling at the same time, as he whispered them warnings they'd never really understood. There was a boy, a prince. Some nights he was called Seamus, other nights he was Patrick or Terry, depending on which of her brothers her daddy had caught in his sights. Sometimes he was handsome and strong, clever and loved by all in the kingdom. But on other nights he was a bit puny and thick as a ditch, with two left feet and hands that couldn't scratch his own arse. They had loved hearing Daddy say 'arse' and the way he'd look around before saying it, to check that their mother wasn't listening.

'Though she'd hear it inside in me head anyway,' Daddy used to say with a wink.

But every night the prince grew up to be a bit too full of himself. 'Vain.' Daddy would say the word after providing the explanation first. He always did that with new words. Prince Seamus, or Terry, or Patrick, thought himself the only perfect one in all the land. But what the prince didn't know was that he had donkey's ears. And so when the royal barber was summoned or called – sometimes Daddy gave them two words that mean the same thing – to cut the prince's hair, both he and the prince were shocked, when the truth was revealed.

'But how could he not know?' Seamus asks Daddy.

'Nobody had told him!' Eleanor squeals at Seamus for interrupting Daddy's story. 'They'd made him wear a hat!'

'So what?' Seamus shouts back across the bed. 'I think even you would know if you had donkey ears, Eleanor! Even if we made you wear a hat!'

Annette smiles back at them all sitting there on the big double bed listening to Daddy.

Annette could never really see the prince with the ears of a donkey, but she could always see the barber down on his knees in the field telling the earth about the prince with donkey ears.

'The prince has donkey ears. The prince has donkey ears.' The words have a rhythm as they pass easily into the air. Annette says it again just to be sure she hasn't imagined the sounds, 'The prince has donkey ears!'

Annette feels the relief of the barber wash through her, like spring water. She hears the reeds hushing the wind with their whispers, *The prince has donkey ears! The prince has donkey ears!* Annette sings it too, 'The prince has donkey ears. The prince has donkey ears.'

Jenny moves her head on the pillow.

3.27 a.m. Tippy-toes move across the light and Jacob's face appears at the bottom of Annette's bed. Jacob waits. Annette takes her good hand away from Jenny's hair, moves it smoothly to the side, where it belongs, and pulls back the quilt. She straightens herself in the middle of the bed. Jacob waits at the bottom of the bed in his blue-striped pyjamas.

'Jacob,' she says, smiling.

Jacob's little shape moves to the left side of the bed even though the right side is Jacob's side. Not the left. But he comes anyway. Jacob climbs into the heat. Annette remains still. When he is ready, Jacob lies down with his head on the pillow. His fingers search for Annette's hand, under the quilt. When they find it they rub her skin with enough pressure to show they are happy fingers now. Annette counts the rubs. She counts to ten. Annette waits. The rubbing stops. The tapping begins. Jacob tap-taps the back of Annette's hand. Annette counts to ten. Waits. The rubbing begins again. Up to ten. Then ten more taps and back to rubs again.

4.01 a.m. The tapping stops. There is no more rubbing.

Jacob's little hand is curled under Annette's bigger one. Annette feels his soft flesh melting into her hands. She knows the rise and fall of each rib, each breath; the space between each freckle, the fall of downy hair on his spine and the dip between each shoulder where she rubs him to sleep. Jenny moves; her face now turned towards Annette looks smaller, younger, in the stolen landing light. Annette's weak hand lies on Jenny's knee. Annette thinks about the royal barber.

'I love you, my babies. I love you, my babies,' Annette whispers over and over into the reeds of night, hoping her children will hear her words forever.

CHAPTER 50

Jenny

Dear Older Me,

It's me, Jenny! You might not remember me, but I hope you do! I'm sure you must, because how could you forget yourself, and how could I forget me? Unless I had a stroke, in the future? Did I have a stroke? I hope you didn't. I am writing to you from the past, which means you are in the future, I think! Anyway, neither of us is here now. I don't think! Well I am, I suppose, but I won't be when you read this letter. You will be here then. I will be gone.

Jenny looks at the words, *I will be gone,* and she feels something empty opening up inside her. The empty thing is so big it fills her up completely.

You didn't have a stroke, did you? Because if you did you might not remember me. I hope I didn't have a stroke. I'm sitting here, in your past, in our bedroom. Do you remember our bedroom? What is your bedroom like, now? Does it have a balcony and a dressing table with big bright bulb lights all around the mirror? I bet it does. Do I like it there?

Jenny sees herself peeping into the fancy mirror, but she doesn't see herself peeping back.

Is Mammy okay? And Jacob and Da and Granny? Is every-body okay, where you are now? Mrs French made me write to you. She said I could be anything. Do you remember Mrs French? She gave us Ophelia and she gave us Anne Frank. She wears purple boots. I really, really, hope you and me have finished reading Harry Potter with Mammy by now. Did you like the ending? Was it a good end?

I hope you have a good job that I like. Will I need a briefcase for our job? Maybe you are a writer or a doctor. Maybe I have found a way to help people with Autism and strokes to get better and maybe you could write a story about the day we found out how to do that. That was a good day, wasn't it?

Jenny, confused with all this moving about from the past to the future and back again, from *then* to *now*, from *here* to *there*, from *you* to *I* and *I* to *you*, like there is no time at all, like she doesn't really exist at all, except in the letter, bites down hard on her lip.

I hope you have a car with heated seats and a radio that works but I hope you didn't let me get one with an annoy-ing-voice Sat Nav and Facebook. Da says they are putting Facebook into cars now and he says he can't even imagine anything more terrifying than being beeped about Granny's recent bingo win or seeing a close-up of her new profile picture, when he's driving.

Where do you live now? I hope I have a big, beautiful house up on a hill with 100 windows and big gates with peacock wings that open to the sides when I press the button in the wall and I hope there is a dog lying on the grass under a pink cherry-blossom tree.

Jenny can see the house so clearly, in her head, it's as though she has passed into the future herself. The dog is yellow, with brown eyes and a wet nose. There is a cat up the tree. The papery-pink cherry blossoms float down, like coloured snow. The dog is at the bottom, barking at the cat. The cat, called Sebastian Flea, won't come down until Crunkley Crunkley – that's the waiting dog with the folded-up face – gets bored enough to go and find something else to do. After a while, Jenny sees a girl coming out of the house, into the garden. Jenny recognises herself. She's calling out, 'Crunkley Crunkley.' The dog runs up the long driveway on his fat little legs after her voice. Jenny tells him that she's looking for Da and she only has to say, 'Crunkley Crunkley, where is Da?' and his tail starts to wag, his whole body seems to do a little waggling dance, and he runs round the side of the house, past the fish pond and the swings, past Mammy's daffodils and sweet peas and stops outside the door of Da's shed, sits down, snorts and barks twice. Then he is silent again, except for the scratch-scratching of his nails against his ear. He is waiting. Jenny watches herself opening the door to Da's shed, which is actually a workshop now, with benches and drills and machines made for sawing. And when she calls Da, he doesn't hear her with all the noise he's making, so she calls him again. When he does hear her, he seems shocked that she's still there, because Jenny is supposed to be going away on holiday.

'You still here, Jenny?' Da says, turning to look at her. 'What time is your flight?'

'Not till tonight,' Jenny says, 'we're meeting Summer at the airport.'

'Timbuktu! Ha! Can you believe it?'

'Da, will you give this to Jacob when he comes home? He said he's got to work late tonight. It's just a book I promised him,' Jenny hears herself saying, and she watches as she leaves *Anne Frank* on the nearest bench. 'Tell him to mind her for me, while I'm away!'

'Timbuktu! Can ya believe it! I will, of course. Now, listen to me, make sure you send us a text when you land. You know how your mother worries. Not to mention your granny! And I'll not hear the end of it until they know you've arrived safely.'

'Don't I always, Da?'

'To be fair, love, ya do!'

'I'm on my way over to see Granny now. Do you need anything while I'm out?'

'No. Actually, check the milk situation before you go. Your mother will go mental if she comes home from that book club of hers and discovers there's none!'

'Okay.'

'Oh, and listen, will you tell Twitter there's a programme on tonight called, *My Life Sucks Since Winning the Lottery*? Tell her to watch it! It's very important! There was this one woman who was kidnapped for her fortune. Oh, can ya imagine the poor kidnapper if he took Mae-Anne? Imagine how much he'd pay to give her back!'

Jenny smiles as she hears her older self telling Da to stop giving out about Granny and about how granny's already googled it and that Google told her all about the ten steps to take when you win the lottery jackpot. She tells Da that Granny has each step, one to ten, written out and stuck up on her fridge!

'What are ya up to, there, Jenny?' Granny's voice bounces off the white page, like sunlight that stings in Jenny's eyes and takes her back to the room, back into now.

Jenny blinks.

'I'm writing a letter. To myself. When I'm older!' she says, placing her pen down slantways across the page.

'Really?' Granny says, putting the messages up on the counter. 'A letter to YOURSELF?' She takes out the milk. 'When you're older?' She takes out the bread. 'So, how is she gettin' on?' She takes out the butter.

'How is who getting on?'

'YOU a course! How are YOU gettin' on?' Granny says, putting the bread into the press and then bustling, with the butter and milk, over to the fridge.

Jenny closes her eyes.

'Granny, is Mammy going to die?' Jenny asks, because the question is just so big she can't keep it inside her anymore. But she doesn't want to look at it either. The empty thing is going to swallow her up.

Jenny opens her eyes again.

'Go ta God, child, she is not!' Granny's face appears back from inside the fridge. She closes the door and moves towards Jenny in whispery shuffles. Granny squats down, her two knees wide apart, her back crumpled. She puts her two hands on Jenny's shoulders. 'Now, you listen to me, pet. YOUR MAMMY IS NOT GOING TO DIE! Do you hear me, now, Jenny? Do you hear me?'

Jenny nods.

'And when you are older, your mammy will still be here! You just ask that young lady in your letter! Herself, there, with all a them fancy degrees and big job. She'll tell ya! No better girl!' Granny winks so hard that one side of her head bobs down with her eye. 'Jesus me knee!'

'You win the lottery!' Jenny says, picking up her pen again.

'Of course I do! And didn't I know all along that I would! Sure, I've never felt luckier, pet!'

CHAPTER 51

Jenny

Jenny sits at the back of the room, listening. Dorcas stands at the top of the room, reading. She's using her acting voice and her acting face and she's reading a poem out loud to the class. It is a poem about a rabbit. The rabbit is in a trap and he's crying with the pain in his leg, and the man in the poem can't find him even though he looks all over the place and everything in the poem is frightened, even the air!

When Dorcas is finished reading, she tells them all about the man who wrote the poem. James Stephens was his name. He was brought up in an orphanage and he was a very small man. But all Jenny can see is the poor little rabbit's face, wrinkled up in pain. Jenny has never heard a rabbit make any sound really, but now, in this moment, inside the classroom, she can hear its shrieking and crying, and it is the saddest sound she thinks she has ever, ever heard – sadder even than the harp-girl's singing. The pain sounds are so clear, so awful and lonely, it's as though all that has ever been wrong and cruel in the world has found its way into the throat of the little trapped rabbit in the poem, and Jenny has to stop herself from looking under the desk or behind the bookcase in the corner.

'What do you think the poem is about?' Dorcas asks the class, moving her eyes this way and that, scanning heads and looking for eyes that don't want to look back. Jenny looks down at the book on her desk.

'Jennifer Augustt. What do you think this poem is about?'

Jenny looks up at the clock on the wall. It is half past ten, so there's no chance a bell anywhere can save her, unless someone lights a fire big enough to set off the alarm. A little fire would do, just big enough to create a small panic. But not big enough to burn somebody so badly on the face that they have to wear a hood or a mask for the rest of their life. Jenny hopes everybody will escape, unharmed, from the fire she's just lit inside her own head.

'It's about a rabbit,' Jenny says, like she can't believe this really is the question.

'But is it? *Really?*'

Dorcas pauses before *Really*, she gives it a capital R and she says it slowly, like she thinks there might be more to it than that; some secret somewhere in the poem that the word *Really* might unlock; some hidden message she knows about and she wants the children to discover too and *Really*, with a big R, said slowly, is the clue. The children, with faces more frightened and wrinkled now than the rabbit, look up at Dorcas, most of them hopeful that maybe they have misunderstood the poem and that *Really* it's not about a rabbit caught in a trap, with his little paw hanging off, at all.

'What do you think, Jane-Anne?'

'I agree with Jenny. I think it's about a rabbit, too,' Jane-Anne says to Dorcas but she's looking around at Jenny, like she's trying to say something more to Jenny, but with her eyes. Jane-Anne's face is different today. It is a nicer face than it used to be. Jenny remembers her note.

Jenny looks down at her hands, like she's just discovered them for the very first time and she's wondering what they are. She checks them both just to make sure they work. When she is satisfied and there's nothing left to examine, she looks back up at the clock. There are no alarm bells ringing, there's no smell of smoke. Jenny turns around to look at the door. If nothing happens soon she thinks she's just going to have to shout, 'Fire!' herself and hope for the best.

'Let's have another look at it,' Dorcas says, like this is a fun thing to do.

The second look isn't any better than the first. Jenny hurts all over again. In fact, it is worse this time round because she knows what's ahead, she knows how it's all going to end, and Jenny realises knowing that the man won't find the rabbit is worse than wondering if he will. Jenny decides she hates the man for not being able to find the little rabbit, but she hates James Stephens even more for making all this happen in the first place. *He* put the rabbit in the snare. *He* made everything afraid. *He* didn't let the man find the rabbit. Jenny wonders why on earth James Stephens decided to do it that way when it would have been so much easier just to let the man find the rabbit or not put the rabbit in the poem at all. Why couldn't *he* have written about something else, like having no parents or being so small that he couldn't be a soldier?

Marching in her class-line down the dark corridor, after little break, Jenny notices that Mrs French's door is open. It shouldn't be open. Not today. It's not the right Wednesday and Mrs French isn't supposed to be here this week. Slipping out of her line and making sure Dorcas doesn't notice, Jenny makes her way up to the office in the wall. She knocks twice on the door even though it's already open.

'Come in,' a voice says from inside. But it is the wrong voice. Jenny steps back to look at the door again. It is the only door there.

'Come in,' the wrong voice says again, just in case the knocker didn't hear properly the first time.

Jenny looks down at her hand. Nothing. But she pushes the door anyway and steps over a pile of books on the floor. The voice has a face. But it is the wrong face. Jenny looks around,

certain that she has, in fact, knocked on the wrong door and
now she's wondering why she knocked at all. There is a new
lady standing in the middle of the room where Mrs French
should be. There are new files and new folders up on the shelves
where the strange glass bottles stood in a row, like they were
guarding all the secrets of the room. Harry Potter has vanished.
The melting pottery people have melted away. Arthur is gone
and so is all the magic. The space feels colder, smaller, darker,
and it smells like it has been raining outside even though it
hasn't rained now for days. Even the idea of the giant is missing,
as well as his chair. It seems like a silly idea now anyway. The
ring-a-rosy children are still up on the wall, but they look older.
They look tired and fed up. Jenny feels tricked.

'Hello there!'

The voice is friendly and warm, but it is still the wrong voice.
Jenny looks at the strange lady's feet. She is wearing brown
shoes. The wrong shoes. Flat brown shoes. Shoes that are definitely not right. Not wrong because they are different. Wrong
because these shoes would never be on Mrs French's feet. Not
ever. Jenny looks up. The strange lady's hair is wrong; too big,
too thick, like you could lose your hand or at least a few fingers
in it if you tried to scratch your head. And her clothes are too
small – all wrong, with bulging bits of white blouse sticking
through gaps between where the buttons almost close on this
new lady's green cardigan.

'Are you looking for someone?' the strange lady asks, like
she must know by the look on Jenny's face that it certainly isn't
her Jenny has come to see.

'Where is Mrs French?' Jenny asks suspiciously, like maybe
this lady has taken Mrs French away to a strange place and
locked her up in a basement full of chickens.

'Mrs French has had to take some leave, I'm afraid. I'm
standing in for her. My name is Mrs O'Doherty.'

Jenny imagines watching telly, seventeen years from now, and seeing a frightened woman being helped from a dark hole underneath a house.

'When will she be back?'

'I'm not sure.'

The frightened woman on the telly looks around wildly, like she doesn't know where she is. Nobody knows who she is, but Jenny will know. She will recognise the purple boots, just barely visible, beneath the ragged dress.

'Are you Jenny?'

Jenny nods.

Are you Mrs French? Are you Aideen? Jenny will say.

'Ah, Jenny, Mrs French told me you would be calling. She left these here for you,' Mrs O'Doherty says, pointing to her desk.

Oh, Jenny, I'm so glad you found me, Mrs French will say.

Mrs O'Doherty hands Jenny a bag. It is a heavy bag. There's a yellow sticky square on the side.

To Jenny – for you and your mammy to read together. The words are scrawled across the sticker in black pen. There is a small, little smiling head drawn at the end of the line.

So am I, Jenny will say.

'Thank you,' Jenny says, to Mrs O'Doherty, before Mrs O'Doherty has a chance to say anything new.

Thank you, Jenny. Thank you for coming to find me, Mrs French will say, brushing the feathers off her purple boots.

I missed you, Jenny will say.

Oh, and I missed you, Jenny, Mrs French will say, squinting into the sun.

Is this the end of the story? Jenny will ask.

No. It is just the beginning, Mrs French will answer, taking an egg out of her pocket and handing it to Jenny.

Jenny and the seven Harry Potters march back out through the secret little door hidden away in the wall.

CHAPTER 52

Jenny

Thursday, 5th December, 2013

Dear Anne Frank,

I have great news today. First of all, Da is going to start up his own business. Granny says she'll buy him a van with his name on the side. Granny won €500 at bingo. Da is going to go round to people's houses fixing things and building things. Granny says she's going to put it all over Facebook.

And the other bit of good news is that me and Mammy are reading your story all the time now, and not just in the evenings after our dinner either, but any chance we get. Sometimes I sneak into her room at night and we just read a few more pages before I go back to bed. And sometimes I go in to Mammy in the mornings and we read a few more pages before I go off to school. And sometimes I just stay in Mammy's bed all night. And she's not sleeping as much as she was last week, and her voice is clearer, so are her words. Sometimes she still forgets the right word for something but then she remembers again and she's walking every day now, sometimes it's just around the room, but Granny says things like, Rome wasn't built in a day or Everything is difficult before it is easy or The slow horse reaches the mill or The apple won't fall till it's ripe, and they

all mean the same thing, Granny says. But my favourite one
is, Castles are built stone by stone, which means that
everything takes time to get right or to make. I love castles.

   Love, Jenny

CHAPTER 53

Jenny

'Kevin, what do ya think of this?' Granny says, looking at the screen, on the table. 'Look at all them *likes*! And I only put it up this mornin'!'

Granny reads out loud –

Kevin Augustt – The Handyman's Handyman.

Musha, there's nothing so bad that it could not be worse or fixed!

49 thumbs-up; 8 hearts; 12 smiley faces; 18 comments; 0 shares

---

'Hold on. Have a look at mine, Mae-Anne,' Da says. 'You too, Jenny. What do you think? Good, isn't it?

Da reads out loud –

Kevin Augustt & Son

No job too small. We fix them all!

25 thumbs-up; 0 hearts; 3 smiley faces; 6 comments; 1 share

'No. No. That'll never do,' Granny says, looking at Da's ad on Facebook. 'Too unoriginal. A bit of a cliché, and by cliché, I mean lazy, if ya don't mind my sayin', but I suppose there's no surprise there!'

Granny presses the 'share' button anyway, sending Da's ad off to everybody she knows, in the whole Facebook world.

'Well, Jesus Christ it's better than yours! This is just mental,' Da says, pointing to Granny's screen now. 'But, course, what else would ya expect! Ya can't go writin' that on the side of a van! It has to at least sound professional, Mae-Anne. And what's so wrong with clichés anyway? Clichés are good! They're familiar. Dependable. Like a caricature in the paper or a stereotype in a book or a film on the telly. A bit like your Eleanor, when ya think about it! She's exactly like a character in a book!'

Jenny thinks about Eleanor as a character in a book. Who would she be? And what would she be doing? Or wearing? She'd be funny, anyway, Jenny knows that much. And she'd be kind, with really cool clothes and make-up. But some of the other characters, like Granny – because Jenny can definitely imagine Granny as a character in the same book – wouldn't realise that Eleanor is really a superhero. Yes, Jenny can definitely see Eleanor as a superhero, or maybe she'd be a teacher, like Miss Honey in *Matilda*. Eleanor always says she'd love to have been a teacher, instead of just wasting her life away on a man. She always tells Jenny to work hard in school. Jenny makes Eleanor into a teacher who transforms into a superhero when there's trouble in the school! Granny could be the villain! Or Granny could be another superhero. Super Granny, she'd be called, and she'd be the one to save all the children from the evil nuns. And it would only be at the end of the story that Super Granny and Super Teacher Eleanor would realise that they are actually, both of them, on the same side.

'You know exactly what you're gettin' with a cliché,' Da says, 'and sure isn't that half the work?'

'I'm tellin' ya *cliché* sounds like it could be the French word for lazy!'

'It's not French for lazy!'

'Okay. So, tell me now, Kevin, what is the French word for lazy? You bein' a man a many tongues and all. You should know!'

'I don't know what it is, but I know it's not *cliché*.'

'But ya don't know. So, now I'll thank ya, very much, not to be makin' statements about things ya know nothin' about!'

'What?' Da says, looking even more confused than he usually does when he's talking to Granny.

'Eleanor is Not a Stereotype! She's. She's. Just a bit Eccentric!' Granny smiles at this new word, *Eccentric*, like she's happy she's got a little job for it to do. 'And I got more "likes" than you did!' Granny says, pointing to her screen.

'Sure, isn't Eccentric just a posh word for Mad?' Da says with a grin. 'And I don't care how many "likes" ya got. I AM NOT PUTTIN' THAT ON MY VAN! I got a share! And anyway, I didn't know we were in competition with each other!'

'A course ya got a share! I SHARED IT!' Granny says, like the competition is now over and she's getting ready to accept her gold medal. 'Okay, so, suit yourself! Course what would you know about advertising anyway! It's called a teaser, actually! It tells a story that gives people what they want! Everything in business is a competition, Kevin! You'd do well, now, to remember that. And you leave Eleanor alone!'

'It doesn't make any sense!' Da says with his whole face. 'Musha, there's nothing so bad that it could not be worse or fixed!' Da says, reading back over Granny's words again.

'It tells customers what you will do for them! The final word must be positive. "Fixed" is the happy endin' and sure isn't that what everybody wants? And That, Kevin, is what's called Effective Marketin'!'

'Since when did you become the expert?'

'Long before I made you into THE HANDYMAN'S HANDYMAN!'

'Actually, I have to admit it, Mae-Anne, I do like that bit! I like the way it looks.'

'Me too,' Jenny says, thinking there might just be a happy ending somewhere here too.

'Yes, well, I like the sound of the "& Son" bit of yours,' Granny says with a half little smile. 'Jacob will too! Won't he, Jenny?'

'Yes. He'll love that!' Jenny says, excited now about where this is going.

'He will, won't he? Accordin' to this *Paresseux* is French for Lazy,' Da says, looking at the words on his screen.

'Right. That's decided!' Granny says, rubbing her two hands together. 'Let's type up a new one so!'

Kevin Augustt & Son – The Handyman's Handyman!

Da clicks 'post' and 'share'. Granny clicks 'share' again. They wait.

'I see Eleanor has changed her profile picture, again!' Da says, scrolling down through all the new posts on his page.

'Ah, God love her, she's tryin' to reinvent herself all the time,' Granny says, in a different voice now. A voice that's looking back at something it finds kind of sad. 'She's been doin' that her whole life, really. She's never been what ya might call comfortable in her own skin. And she waited so long for that child, she's really only now gettin' to know herself proper, I suppose. Did she change her name on it?'

'No. No she didn't. She'll be okay, Mae-Anne, she will,' Da says, like he actually means it, and like he actually wants Granny to believe it. 'She'll find herself. Eventually. Anyway, that was all Karl, not Eleanor.'

'I know it was. She'll find her way, won't she? With little

Saidhbhe there beside her. She will, to be sure, she will. Eventually. Only it won't be with that Karl! And I'll tell you one thing, that child has made her, as God is my witness she has, and not the other way round at all. Anyway, I think we've got that slogan spot on! Would ya just look at all these likes!'

'It's perfect,' Da says, like he's looking at the imaginary words on the side of his imaginary van. 'It's got a good ring to it. It looks serious without bein' too proud.'

'And we'll need some kind of logo thing too! Like a hammer, maybe! It's important to have a good visual!' Granny says, spreading her fingers out like a fan.

'Will We now? And maybe a sickle too, while We're at it!' Da says, winking at Jenny.

'No,' Granny says, 'we'll just stick with the hammer for now. That'll do us.' Granny says 'we' and 'us' with such little fuss, like she's so used to using them that now, they don't need anything to make them bigger or louder. They're just two little words that don't need any notice at all. 'Paresseux, you say? Isn't that a lovely word, altogether! You keep your eye on Facebook. I need to check my emails!'

Jenny smiles at the scene in the kitchen. Da smiles at all the responses to their ad.

'Isn't Facebook great, really,' he says, and for the first time in ages Jenny hears hope in Da's voice.

103 thumbs-up; 16 hearts; 33 smiley faces; 31 comments; 9 shares.

CHAPTER 54

Jenny

Sunday, 8th December, 2013

Oh, Anne Frank, our heads started throbbing too, this evening, when we read about the burglars and the hole in the door and how Peter and Mr Van Daan had to pretend to be the robbers and by the time we got to the End of Part One, Granny was white in the face too.

The footsteps in the house and then on your stairs made us all very afraid, but then the rattling of the bookcase made us all want to crawl in under Mammy's bed and just stay there for the rest of the night.

'Oh, Jesus Christ,' Granny said, and then she blessed herself.

The strange light out on the landing was next, but before I could read anymore, Granny got up from Mammy's bed where she had been sitting, and she said how they were, 'Feckin' savages, them Nazis,' and she couldn't believe they'd do that on Easter Sunday. And I really thought Granny was going to have a meltdown, or worse – I thought she might cry. So, I stopped on page 170.

Granny comes in to clean and dust down Mammy's room most evenings now, when we're reading. But Granny has already read your story, so I asked her why she seemed so shocked at the footsteps on the stairs and the rattling of your secret bookcase door. She knows what's happening and what's going to happen, but still she arrives every evening, saying that she's really got to sort out the drawers or the tablets or the wardrobe and every evening she says, 'Don't mind me, child! I'm not stayin'. But she always does.

Anyway, when I thought it was safe to go on, I read about how you had to sleep on the floor between the table legs and about the smell from the pot and about how cold you were that night and then I read the bit about how the police rattled the cupboard door. Granny was up fixing the pleats in the curtains and then she checked Mammy's clock. When Miep and Henk arrived, I thought Granny was going to do a cartwheel, but she says she doesn't trust that greengrocer, one bit!

Then, she said that we don't know how lucky we are, but she didn't sound happy about all our good luck. She sounded sad.

'But, Granny, you know what's going to happen,' I said, but because I wasn't really sure if it was a question I was asking, or an answer I was giving, I didn't know where to put the question mark.

But Granny says that when she read your diary all those years ago, when she read it to Mammy and Auntie Eleanor, that really, all they wanted was to see what happened, to hear the story. But Granny says that this time it's different! She says that this time it's more special.

So, I asked her, how is it different or more special this time. And I definitely said it as a question, because I really did want to know what Granny meant by 'different' and 'special'.

Different and Special can mean so many things when Granny says them. Sometimes Granny says Jacob is different but not because he's not the same as everybody else. Granny says Jacob is different because he is himself

which makes him very, very special. So Special can mean
Different when Granny says it like that. But Granny says
Special means Better which is not the same as Different at
all and especially when it comes to Jacob, she says,
because he is better at bein' himself than anybody else is!
And that, she says, is Special!

'Well, Jenny, now it's like I'm hearin' the words for the first
time. I know the story. But it's little Anne's words and thoughts
and ideas that I'm listenin' for now. It's like now I can hear her
voice,' she said, after thinking about it for awhile.

And, Anne Frank, I really thought that something awful
was going to happen to you all tonight because Da says
them Nazi men were the most God-awful bastards ever to
walk the earth. Granny says you don't have to look too far
back in history to find monsters like them. Granny says it's
always Men destroying everything. She definitely uses a
capital M. She says you just have to turn on the telly any
evening at six o'clock and you'll see a whole clather of
them hacking each other to bits in the name of religion and
letting children starve because they're belonging to the
wrong group of people. Evil men will always be looking for
new ways to break apart the whole feckin' world: drowning
babies in buckets, blowing themselves up inside their own
jumpers, saying they're fighting for a cause or a belief,
when all they're actually doing is trying to kill the whole
goddamn lot of us. And they are Evil, Granny says, you can
see it in their faces; even the gates of hell are closed to
that class of evil. Once there's Evil Men in the world, Granny
says, then, the world will always be at war.

But I'm so glad everything is all right in your Secret
Annexe again, we all are, and that you didn't let them burn
your diary in the stove. I bet it was that Mrs Van Daan who
wanted it gone. I hate her. Granny does, too. She says Mrs
Van Daan's an awful auld sthreal of a yoke, and feckin'

useless too. She said that you all should have pegged that one out on the street, as soon as Mrs Van Daan opened her mouth this evening.

'I know she musta been frightened but it's when we're most frightened that we need to be at our best!' Granny says, like she was reading one of the posters on our classroom wall. Granny says it's called The Survival Instinct and she says that's when you dig down into the deepest part of yourself and find out exactly what you're made of and Granny says that you, Anne Frank, know that better than anybody she's ever met.

'That Dussel and his feckin' pillows should take a leaf outta little Anne's book!' Granny said, and she was really annoyed and then, Anne Frank, do you know what happened next? Mammy started to laugh, and it was a real belly laugh like I haven't seen Mammy do for so long now that I can't even remember hearing her so happy before. The whole bed was doing little laughing shakes and it felt like the whole room got brighter and warmer and that even the walls held out their arms to welcome back a sound they thought they'd never hug again.

But we weren't laughing at you, Anne Frank, especially not when your toilet is broken and your taps won't turn on, but I just want you to know how important you are to us all. I think that's why Mrs French introduced us. Mrs French knew how important you are, and she wanted me to know that too. But now Mrs French is gone. But she will be back – I just know it – when she is ready. There is a new lady in the secret office in the wall. Her name is Mrs O'Doherty. She seems nice, but she's not Mrs French. When I went in, to find Mrs French, Mrs O'Doherty handed me a bag full of Harry Potters that Mrs French had left there for me and Mammy to read. Granny says she doesn't think she'll much like Harry Potter though.

'Ah, all a that hocus-pocus jiggery-pokery stuff isn't really my cuppa tea. Sure, ya can't solve the world's problems with magic, Jenny. It'd be great, mind you, if we could!' Granny says, when I showed her all my new books.

But, Anne Frank, I heard Granny reading The Philosopher's Stone to Jacob this morning in the kitchen, and she was explaining to him about Mr Dursley and all the strange things that happened on his way to work and about Dumbledore being the head of wizardry at Hogwarts. And about Hagrid and Voldemort and about Harry's mammy and daddy and about how Harry was left in a basket on the Dursleys' front step.

'Sure, of course they took him in, Jacob!' Granny says. 'Nobody should be left sleepin' on a step. Man, woman or child – sure isn't everybody somebody's baby. Of course, they took him in. Of course, they did.'

Anne Frank, I hope you don't mind me telling you about all the stuff that goes on in my house, but I know that you can get very bored hidden away like that behind the book-case door and I hope that this will make you smile because you will know now that everybody's family is a bit mental really.

Love, Jenny

CHAPTER 55

Annette

Eleanor is *feng shuing* Annette's bedroom today. Today is Friday. Yesterday it was Thursday. Terry comes every Thursday. Seamus comes every Wednesday. Patrick comes when he can. Eleanor comes every Friday.

'Right, I've brought a wind chime and some *feng shui* crystals, for balance!' Eleanor says, standing up on a stool. She hangs a tinkling string on to the curtain pole.

Annette thinks of the fairies that used to come in with a bar of chocolate in the night-time, through one of the little doors Kevin had stuck on to the skirting boards in Jenny's room, and of all the little fairy letters they had left for Jenny when they had remembered to write them the night before.

The pure and perfect ring of the chime sounds like the magic music only made by the fairies; the little tinkles conjuring memories so clear Annette can almost reach out and touch them. There's Daddy telling her all about the fairies. He whispers quietly in case they may hear. *The farmer's wife was tricked by the fairies. Her husband was away, and she was left minding the farm. One morning the farmer's wife heard a voice somewhere inside her that told her the cattle were in distress. So, she left her infant son alone in his crib by the fire and while she was gone the fairies took her child away. When she returned, she checked on the boy. The fairies had left a replacement; a hideous child, deformed with strange features, under the little blue blanket she had crocheted herself. But the woman, refusing to believe this was a fairy child, continued to love him just the same. Because that's what you do, Daddy says, you love your children no matter what. But the child grew to be troublesome, solitary and was unable to talk.*

Annette closes her eyes again and listens to the lonely chimes of the fairies.

'I read all about it the other day while I was waiting to see the solicitor. All sounds lovely and kinda like common sense, really. So, with all the common sense we can muster between us, we need to get rid of all the negative chi in here. I'm leaving him, Annette. Let's build up your energy field. I've had enough of his shit. Always telling me I'm not good enough. Open your chakras somewhere around the meridian line or something like that! I've sorted it all out. Saidhbhe and I are moving into a new place, straight after Christmas!' Eleanor says, waving her arms around, like she's clearing smoke from the air. 'Today, everything changes!'

Today is Friday. Annette lists the days over and over, watching them roll from one into another inside her head, with plenty to spare. Annette has lots of hours to spare today. And tomorrow and the next day. She rummages further. Tomorrow is Saturday. Then it will be Sunday. Again. Plenty of time to figure out all the new words Eleanor has brought with her into the room. Plenty of time to think about the farmer's wife and the stolen child. Leaving. Moving. Everything changes. Another story.

'*Feng shui* means wind and water,' Eleanor says. 'I just like the sound of that. Don't you, Annette? The Chinese have special *feng shui* consultants, apparently. Wonder would they be any good at sorting out a cheating husband or a divorce! They probably would, you know. And everybody would be energised. And happy. And free,' Eleanor says, jamming herself between the headboard and the wall.

Monday will be next. There was a poker somewhere in the story.

'Jesus!' Eleanor says, like she's just about to pass out. 'Okay,

Annette. Sit tight!' she orders, as she sucks in her stomach and begins to heave and push.

Annette hears Eleanor's breath trapped in her ribs, the squeal of her runners hitting the back wall. Then she breathes out again and the whole bed begins to move around slowly. A slow half-circle, around to the right. The bed stops. Eleanor takes in another breath and braces herself once more. 'I found texts he'd sent. To Her! The Accountant!' She is at the left side of the bed now, digging the balls of her feet into the soles of her runners. Annette knows this by the fall of Eleanor's mouth, like she's moving the whole bed with her face. 'I saw her leaving his office.' With her arms at full stretch, Eleanor lies almost horizontal, as she shoves and skids across the floor. 'Course, he says there's nothing going on. Says she's looking to do business with them. And that he wouldn't touch her with a barge pole. That she reminds him of Jabba The Hut, with bad acne and cankles. He's not wrong there! Cunt. I hate that word. I really do. But it's the only word that comes anywhere near him. He says she just won't leave him alone!' She inches the bed bit by bit, heaving with her shoulder and everything else she's got, her cheeks getting redder all the time.

Then it will be Tuesday again. There was a poker and there was milk that soured in the farmer's kitchen. Leaving. Moving. Everything changes. Today. Cankles.

'Chakra zero,' Eleanor gasps between breaths. 'That's the one nobody knows about! We need your head at the wall. Lying under a window is, like, well, committing *feng shui* suicide!' she warns, 'and you need to be able to see the door, in case, like, someone tries to break in. This way, I'll see the cunt coming!' Eleanor's whole body moves up and down, her head lurching forward and back, like an agitated turtle, as she strains from her toes to her heels. Up and down. Up and down.

Annette thinks about the fairies sneaking in, taking the little boy away. Nobody had seen them.

'Now,' Eleanor says, sitting down on the newly positioned

bed, 'I bet you feel a whole lot better already! I know I do! Don't say anything to Mam. Not yet. I'm going to sign the separation papers this afternoon.'

There was an eggshell. Annette remembers the farmer's wife cooking the dinner in an eggshell. She doesn't know why. Annette touches the stubbly side of her head.

'See? I told you. The yin and the yang stuff. Positive energy! Sure, it's worth a go! The Communists made it illegal, you know. The Chinese even study *feng shui* in schools and they tore down some important building because it had bad *feng shui*! Imagine that. Imagine what they'd do to my marriage! He's been toxic for years! I am going to *feng shui* the shit out of my new place. Nothing dark or negative or controlling will ever cross my chakra again! Bastard!'

Tuesday will become Wednesday. Again. The farmer's wife tricked the fairy child.

Eleanor gets up from the bed, stands sideways, checking herself in the mirror and then facing herself once again, she fixes her hair. Satisfied, she takes the mirror down from its place on the wall. Placing it carefully on its side it makes a little triangle space between the frame and the skirting board.

'Mirrors are absolutely so forbidden in *feng shui* bedrooms! Recipe for disaster, apparently. You're only inviting trouble in. You may as well move Jabba The Hut into your marriage as have that mirror up there on the wall. I should know!'

'Will you be stoppin' for your lunch?' Mae-Anne's voice enters the room like a train.

Fairy babies could never be satisfied, no matter how much they ate! Annette remembers the farmer's wife trying to feed the child who cried endlessly.

'What?' Eleanor asks, looking more frightened, less brave than she was a moment ago.

'Do you want a toasted sandwich or an omelette or somethin' to eat? You know, Eleanor, like, food?'

'No. No thanks. I had some eggs earlier.'

'What day is it?' Mae-Anne asks.

'Friday,' Annette whispers in a voice that is dusty and too low to be heard.

'It's Friday,' Eleanor says.

'It's Friday a course!' Mae-Anne snaps back from her place in the doorway. 'Is it one a your fast days? The eggs, I suppose, will have to do ya now till, what? Sunday or Monday?'

'No. Mam, I'm just not hungry. Anyway, I can't stay long,' Eleanor says, looking at her phone. 'Christ and it's Friday the thirteenth. I hate Friday the thirteenth!'

'That's called friggatriskaidekaphobia!' Mae-Anne says, with a grin strangling her scowl. 'That's some word, isn't it? Probably more calories in that word than in your eggs!'

'What?'

'Jesus, Eleanor, don't make me say it again! Frigg-at-risk-aide-ka-phobia. It's some new feckin' stupid disorder them Yanks have dreamt up for people who are afraid of Friday the thirteenth!'

'No, I don't have that. Not yet anyway. It's just I have a . . . an appointment later,' Eleanor says, like she's really sorry, either about the appointment or about having to tell Mae-Anne about the appointment, but either way, she's sorry.

'Ah, sure don't be puttin' any auld pass on that kinda superstitious nonsense, love. Didn't I have our Patrick on a Friday the thirteenth?'

'I know, Mam. It's just, well it's important.'

'Sweet sufferin' Jesus! Eleanor, tell me! Please, for the love a God, tell me you are not on some other new fancy diet or goin' off to do something ridiculous, like changin' your name! What is wrong with you, in the name of God? You're never feckin' happy!' Mae-Anne says to Eleanor, but she's looking at Annette. 'Jesus Christ you should be ashamed a yourself, Eleanor!' Mae-Anne tut-tuts slowly.

'No, Mam, I'm l—'

'Changeling!' Annette remembers the name and throws it into the room with such force that everything else stops.

Eleanor looks at Annette.

'Changeling child!' Annette's voice forces itself into the space between her mother and her sister.

Mae-Anne moves into the room. 'Go on, love, we're listenin'.'

'Daddy's story. It was daybreak! The farmer went to help bury a dead neighbour!' Annette remembers every word and with every word spoken her voice grows stronger. 'And Thursday comes after Wednesday.'

'What? But today is Friday!' Eleanor looks at Annette. Looks at her mother. Back to Annette. Eleanor looks totally bewildered, like she doesn't know where she is anymore.

'It certainly does, love.' Mae-Anne sits down on the bed. 'What else do you remember, love?'

'The farmer's wife,' Annette says, searching Eleanor's eyes. 'What was her name?'

Eleanor curls her fingers round her chin and looks, into the wall, for an answer.

'Poor Sarah Flanaghan,' Mae-Anne says, like she's remembering an old friend she hasn't seen for such a long time.

'Jesus, yes! Sarah Flanaghan! That was her name and the fairies took the baby and she chased the child around the parlour with a knife or did she drown it in a bucket?' Eleanor says, looking up at the ceiling, like the answer might just be there.

'That was "The Stolen Child" story,' Mae-Anne says, placing her hand down over Annette's.

'No, it was a poker!' Annette says, remembering the old pictures Daddy had painted in her head: the child, frightened and small, running away from the woman holding the black poker up in the air. But they are frozen; the child not moving in his running position; the woman's poker never actually making contact with the child. But both of them are very afraid. No movement is needed to see that.

'And the child flew up the chimney!' Eleanor shouts, her arms moving up through the air.

Annette doesn't remember it that way.

'And then the real baby came back!' Eleanor says. Eleanor is very excited now.

'No—' Annette shakes her head.

'Jesus, when you think about it!' Eleanor has her thinking face on. She looks across the room trying to find the story, as if it had been told somewhere else, faraway in the distance.

'Jacob—' Annette starts to say.

'Don't you worry about Jacob. There's not a fairy in the land brave enough to take him away. Not with this old dragon looking after him!' Eleanor looks at her mother and smiles carefully.

The old dragon, looking out over the top of her glasses, waits just long enough to worry Eleanor, then nods and smiles back.

'Anyway, Annette, they all lived happily ever after in the end. Don't you remember it? The farmer came home, and the real baby was back, and Sarah made, like, an apple tart or Angel Delight or something. At least, that was the story Daddy told us on the train.' Eleanor smiles and sighs at the same time, as though she's not sure right now how she should be feeling. Then she sits down, across from Mae-Anne, on the opposite side of the bed. 'He told us that one on the train when we went on our holidays to Mosney. Mam, do you remember that holiday he won? When was that? We went on the train.' Eleanor, completely lost in time, now needs her mother to remember.

'Is it Butlins that ya mean? Course, it's Mosney now! Let me think. That was the summer before,' Mae-Anne says with the gleam of old stories in her eyes.

'Yes! It was Butlins then. The whole place smelled like sugar and chips! Do you not remember?'

'Do I remember it? Will I ever forget it! Sure, we weren't there so much as a wet day, when we all went down with food poisonin'! And your father got it the worst of us all. Sick for the whole week, he was. I can still see him lyin' with a bucket beside the bed, in one a them awful auld chalets with them Red Coats always knockin' on the door.'

'Were they not Yellow Coats, Mam?' Eleanor tilts her head and scrunches up her nose.

'No, they were the ones on the telly! They were the ones on *Hi-de-Hi!*'

'And the swimming pool with all the legs!' Annette says, piecing all the bits together again, 'on the street. We bought big, sticky soothers. We sucked them the whole week!'

'And the Kiss Me Quick hats! Do you remember, Annette? Do ya remember them? And the elephant teacups and the big bumpy slide and the disco?' Eleanor's eyes twinkle.

'Video arcade!' Annette shouts, triumphant.

'Oh, lord, and do ya remember the time Terry almost drowned in the boatin' lake? He fell outta one a them swan boats! Or was it Seamus?' Mae-Anne seems shocked by a vision she looks like she had forgotten and is suddenly entertained by its return.

'Was Seamus not run over by the little train? What was it called? Puffin' Billy!' Eleanor's excitement is growing with her laughter. Annette can feel the up-down jiggling of Eleanor's knee vibrating across the bed.

'No. I don't remember that! Course that doesn't mean it didn't happen!' Mae-Anne sweeps her hand through the air.

'I got lost!' Annette states clearly as rows of identical chalets grow up right there in the room; the twists and turns between them; high steps leading up to identical top storeys.

'Go ta God, so ya did!'

'I found Daddy!' Annette sees him so easily again.

'Ya did! Proppin' up the bar at Dan Lowry's, no doubt, and

him, sick as a dog he was, with the runs!' Mae-Anne's laughter shakes her whole body. Annette feels the mattress bob up and down.

'Oh, but it was magical!' Eleanor squeals, sounding just like the child that she was, sitting on that train, waiting for their stop to arrive.

Mae-Anne had brought sandwiches for the journey.

'Tell ya one thing for nothin'. We don't know how lucky we are! When ya think a them poor crathers stuck up there now. Like prisoners they are. And them poor little children doin' their bit a homework in the same place where we had our lunches served to us on trays!'

The three of them suddenly stop talking, needing the silence to see themselves again that summer. Annette, looking into all the yellows of memory, reaches out her good hand, as if to touch the faces of all those that she saw there in Butlins: Mammy, Seamus, Patrick, Terry, Eleanor, Daddy, before they are gone.

'What in the name of Jesus are ya doin' in here anyway, Eleanor?' Mae-Anne, breaking apart the stillness, looks around the room, like she's not sure where she is now either.

'Her bed was in the coffin position! She needs to see the sun rising! Mam, I'm leaving him.'

'And how, in the name a God, can she see the sun risin', when ya have her facin' in the wrong direction? Sure, the sun comes up in the east. Put her back against the other wall! You should have left a long time ago, ya know. You deserve a bit a love. Ya never got that from him.' Mae-Anne straightens up, heaving herself off the bed. 'But, better late than never, love!'

Together Eleanor and Mae-Anne push Annette around the room again.

'Thanks, Mam,' Eleanor whispers.

'Cunt!' Annette says, smiling up at them both.

Eleanor laughs.

'Coffin position! Over my dead body! There'll be no coffin

positions in this house!' Mae-Anne says, gasping a little breath. 'And you, watch your language!' she says, beaming at Annette.

'Jesus, what time is it?' Eleanor suddenly shouts, lifting her head up.

'It's almost one,' Mae-Anne says, without even looking at the clock. 'Why? Where's the fire?'

'No fire. But I'll have to go at half past! I'm signing the papers today, Mam. Makes it official. Is that toasted sandwich still on offer?'

'It surely is, and an eclair!' Mae-Anne rubs her two hands together and makes her way back to the door.

'We need a plant!' Eleanor reaches down to the floor and grabs her bag.

'You go outside if you're goin' to smoke!' Mae-Anne snaps, without looking back, and then she is gone.

'Jesus Christ, Annette, how do you put up with her?'

Annette smiles into Eleanor's grinning face and together they remember that summer, the last they'd had with their daddy.

CHAPTER 56

Jenny

Sunday, 15th December, 2013

Anne Frank, I saw you! I saw you! And it was like the whole world was shrinking into the tiniest little ball that I could fit inside The Child of Prague's head and time fell away, too, and it didn't matter anymore that you were there and I was here, because everything was rolling backwards and forwards, twirling and whirling; all the time that was inside the no time, inside the ball, inside The Child of Prague's head. And there you were! And here you were, too! Right here. And right there, all at once, in our kitchen! Anne Frank, you were there, and you were here, and I could see you! And you were looking out the window at the wedding. And you are so happy. Do you remember? Do you remember the wedding and the lady and the man and all the people in the street and all the music? The lady is wearing a white hat and a grey suit which is probably pink, or yellow, or maybe even light blue. I'm not sure, because it was all in black and white. But I saw you and you are happy and you are free, and you are smiling, and it is June and you are twelve. And the lady has a lovely bunch of flowers, tied with a ribbon. And there was music, lovely music, like a summer parade, soft and loud, the big and small sounds coming all at once, with no words to hear that were happy or sad, but only a song that I could feel inside me, deep down in my tummy, and outside across the back of my neck and all down my arms, too. And the man with the lady had a top hat and they are getting into a car.

Do you remember the wedding and the window and the sun in your eyes and the smile on your face? I saw you. I saw you! And so did Da and Granny did, too. And Granny kept saying your name over and over, 'Little Anne Frank. Little Anne Frank,' and touching your face with her thumb.

It was Da. Can you believe that, Anne Frank? It was Da. Da was the one who found you! He went searching for you on YouTube! And he found you, Anne Frank. Da found you! Imagine that! And I saw you and Granny saw you and you were right here, in our kitchen. And we made Da play it again and again. And we watched you again and again. We saw you and you were so happy. You looked around, over your shoulder, like you were talking to someone behind you.

Then Da said he had something else for us, too. Your diary! He had that, too! Da found all your words for us to hear. Can you believe that? I was so excited, Anne Frank, because this was the best of all the lost things. And I couldn't wait to meet your voice. Da found your diary on YouTube as well. And Da doesn't ever find anything! Not ever. He loses lots of things. He never finds things. Mammy finds all the things that Da loses, or Granny does, now. And we sat at our kitchen table, me, Granny and Da, and Da pressed play and we waited. And then, Anne Frank, we heard all your words, the same words you had written down in your secret diary, in your secret annexe, in your secret hiding house, and they flew all over our kitchen, like little birds just let out of a cage!

Jenny replays the scene in her head, like it's a movie she's watching on the telly –

The kitchen is very quiet. She watches Da pressing the button. She watches them listening with their whole bodies.

'Turn that off!' Granny says after about two minutes. 'That's not Anne Frank! That's Judy feckin' Garland!' she shouts, and then she stands up real quick, like she's trying to catch all Anne Frank's sentences and stuff them back into her pockets again. 'Turn it off!'

'It's an audiobook,' Da says, 'and it's not Judy Garland!'

'It's not Anne Frank!' Granny says, looking around in case she's missed a few stray words.

'I know that,' Da says, looking at Granny, looking up in the air. 'It's somebody reading her diary, like an actress or someone who reads books, out loud, for recordings. I thought it was a good idea!'

'Anne Frank WASN'T an IDEA!' Granny says, digging up all her capitals again. 'She Was a Child! And, sure now, Kevin, can't we read for ourselves, thank God! We Don't Need no Stranger readin' to us, even if it is feckin' Dorothy!'

'But I thought Jenny would like it?' Da says, looking now at Jenny, with different eyes.

'Granny's right, Da!' Jenny says, looking away from the computer and over at Granny. 'That's not Anne Frank's voice. It's just not. It doesn't sound right at all.'

And then Jenny remembers thinking that if she were a character in a story she was writing, that really, now would be the time she should or would remember what Granny had said on an earlier page. They were in the kitchen and Jenny was trying to show Granny the new app, for Jacob, on the newfangled gadget contraption thing that Auntie Eleanor had brought into the house. And Granny had said something like, *'I don't care what ya say. No fancy app or newfangled gadget will ever be as powerful as the sound of a child's own little voice.'*

'Granny IS right, Da!' Jenny says. 'You can't listen to Anne

Frank if it's not Anne Frank! And THAT IS NOT ANNE FRANK'S VOICE!'

Looking back, now, Jenny is sorry for Da.

She watches herself as she looks back over at Granny again, but Granny's too busy searching the imaginary pockets in her cardigan, like she's just remembered that she had forgotten where she'd put all Anne Frank's words. Then she turns away and says, 'Right so, I best put on the dinner!'

'But, Mae-Anne, it's only three o'clock!' Da says, still looking at Jenny, even though he is talking to Granny.

'Granny's right, Da. Turn it off. But it's okay because I can hear Anne Frank's voice, inside in my own head, anytime I want,' Jenny tells Da, 'like I do with Jacob.'

Da presses the pause button.

'Keep her safe, Jenny. Keep her safe in there,' is all Granny says.

CHAPTER 57

Jenny

Jenny presses the little button at the top and waits, like you are supposed to. A big round-faced Thomas smiles, his best-self-ever screensaver smile, and his googly eyes look even wider, even whiter, even bigger than they usually do.

'See you later, Thomas!' Jenny says with a swipe and then, just like he'd never been there at all, Thomas is gone. There's a page already open where Google should be, and Jenny is just about to X out of it when something catches her eye. It is a word – a word that is bigger, in every way, than all the other words on the page. That big word is MURDER! Jenny reads the email, even though she knows that she shouldn't.

From: Mae-Anne Greene [mailto:magreene@gmail.com]
Sent: 13 December 2013 23:10
To: Thomas Foley<tommyfTC@yahoo.co.uk>
Subject: The MURDER of F.S. Fitzgerald!

That's fine! And about fecking time you got round to it, too! This isn't a story, you know, this is real life!

Jenny checks the date. The thirteenth of December. *That was three days ago! And it was late. Very late, last Friday night.* Jenny tries to remember last Friday night, at ten past eleven. *Where was Granny last Friday night, on Friday the thirteenth?* She looks at the red letters, in the box at the side. Gmail. The big red M stands tracing the two sides and fold-down part of the envelope. She looks at MURDER again, then back to Gmail again. Jenny doesn't understand. There are stacks of other emails, too, lined up behind the MURDER one, like the library cards, in the box, at school. Jenny does the only thing she can think of doing. She taps the one behind it.

From: Thomas Foley<tommyfTC@yahoo.co.uk>
Sent: 12 December 2013 10:18
To: Mae-Anne Greene [mailto:magreene@gmail.com]
Subject: Mr Francis S. Fitzgerald

Dear Mrs Greene,
 I have, personally, set up a meeting for Mr Fitzgerald with Ms Marsha Lacey, our Housing Officer, as a matter of the utmost urgency, considering the severity of this unfortunate story.
 Ms Lacey has agreed to call to see Mr Fitzgerald at your home address, next Monday morning at 9.30 a.m.
 I trust this will be convenient?
 Regards,
 Thomas Foley

Who is Mr Fitzgerald? And what does Ms Lacey want to see him about? Jenny stares at the screen – at all the words and arrangements, dates and times – and suddenly her mind does one of those strange little shifty things.

'You are under arrest for the murder of Mr Francis S. Fitzgerald,' the Garda, with all the sweating hair, says, standing behind Granny as he clicks her two wrists into sharp, cold handcuffs, behind her cardiganed back. The blue lights of the siren make the little group that has gathered at the gate flicker, like they are being turned on and off, off and on.

'I'm not a bit surprised, ya know. She's feckin' mental so she is!' Da says to one of the people in the little blue circle.

Jenny's throat tightens. She looks at Granny, looking out the back window of the Garda car. The siren screeches strange blue light all over the road as the car pulls away.

'She's done it this time!' Da says, with his two hands jammed into his pockets. 'They'll give her life!'

The lady beside him nods her frowning head. She's got blue cauliflower hair. That must be Mrs Lacey, Jenny decides. She's very nice really.

'I was too late to help her,' Mrs Lacey says, wringing her hands. 'I was going to fix everything, on Monday.'

The scene bursts apart inside Jenny's head, just like Homer Simpson's heart did when he had the heart attack at Mr Burns' desk. Homer's heart turned to glass and shattered to pieces and then he floated up off the rug, out of his own body – every thought a new shape or shade of broken glass. Jenny sees Mammy, lying upstairs in bed, with no hair. There's Jacob, walking round in circles, tap-tapping the walls. There's Da running towards an old man looking up to say, 'No, I am your father.' And there is Granny, all alone, sitting on the side of a low bed, rocking backwards and forwards, locked into the dark.

There are too many questions now flying out of the blue light, questions with Jenny's imagined answers flying out behind them. Reading the story this way is a bit like starting with *Deathly Hallows* and working all the way back to *The Philosopher's Stone* with everybody and everything going in reverse. And it doesn't make any sense at all. Jenny's mind is too busy trying to tie together all the bits she's already missed or hasn't even read yet. She looks at the queue of emails again. With frightened, fascinated fingers, Jenny goes back to the start and clicks on the very first one.

From: Mae-Anne Greene [mailto:magreene@gmail.com]
Sent: 04 November 2013 11:02
To: Thomas Foley<tommyfTC@yahoo.co.uk>
Subject: Homeless Man

Dear Councillor Foley,

I hope you and the family are all well. I see the twins in the paper this week. Finalists in the school debating competition, no less! Isn't that great news, now, altogether. You must be very proud.

I am writing to complain about that poor man living rough on our streets. Now I'm not complaining about him, you understand, I'm complaining about the council and how they have let this happen. Surely something can be done to help this poor homeless man?

He is currently at my house, 15 Chapel Hill, but he can't stay there forever.

I do hope to hear from you soon. Isn't this email app great altogether!

Yours sincerely,

Mae-Anne Greene

'Ah!' Jenny says, relieved, but eager to read on. Click.

From: Mae-Anne Greene [mailto:magreene@gmail.com]
Sent: 04 November 2013 13:35
To: Thomas Foley<tommyfTC@yahoo.co.uk>
Subject: Homeless Man

Dear Councillor Foley,

I sent you an email this morning, about two hours ago, but there's nothing from you, yet, in my Inbox. My son-in-law tells me this email thing is instant, but I'm not so sure, so I'm not. It's nearly twenty-five to two now. Modern technology is great but there's so many passwords and secret codes and things that I wonder if half of it even works half the time. That Bank Link machine in Tesco never works! But I do like Facebook! Don't you?

Anyway, I'll be here all day if you want to send something into my Inbox.

Yours sincerely,

Mae-Anne Greene

Another click.

From: Mae-Anne Greene [mailto:magreene@gmail.com]
Sent: 04 November 2013 23:17
To: Thomas Foley<tommyfTC@yahoo.co.uk>
Subject: There's two more emails in your Inbox!

Dear Councillor,

So far today, I have sent you two emails into your inbox. Now, as I have already explained in my other two emails, I wish to talk to you about the poor man left destitute on the steps of the old cinema.

So, let me tell you what happened last Saturday night. I was walking back to Annette's after being round at my own house, just to put a bit of heat on, what with this cold snap and all. I am living at Annette's, for the moment, because she's not been too well recently, so I'm needed here to look after the children while she's away up above in the hospital. But, please God now and His blessed mother, she'll be back home with us again very soon. A house with no heat on in the winter crumbles in on itself come spring, don't you know. So anyway, there I was, minding my own business, on my way past the old cinema, and here what do I see – only a gang of young hooligans taunting and teasing the poor man. There he was, flat on his back, silver snail trails leaking out of his hair, and this little pup trying to set fire to the man's legs. Well, I took after them all with me umbrella and bag, especially that thug with the lighter, and just like the cowards they are, they all fecked off down the road, shouting and laughing and the divil knows what.

Jenny imagines Granny all covered up in her tan coat and hat, her umbrella and bag swinging and jabbing the air in slow motion.

The poor man was in an awful way altogether so between the two of us we bundled up all his things and I brought him back home to my house.

Now Jenny sees Granny tidying up the old man's things off the steps, flicking the bits of dirt from his shoulders and giving his face a rub with her hankie. Granny gets him up on his feet, checking to see what needs washing or ironing and then the two of them, their backs to her now, make their way along the dimly lit street, returning down the same road Granny had walked up alone. There is a strange yellow glow around Granny, probably from the street light in Jenny's mind.

Once I got him settled down, I gave the poor divil a cup of tea and some jam tarts. That was all I had in the house. I gave him an old pair of pyjamas that were in the hot press and a bed for the night. But come Sunday, sure what was I to do? I couldn't put him back out on the cinema steps for them young lads to go setting fire to him again! So, I am going to leave him stay there, for the moment, anyway, until I hear from you.

Thank you very much for your time and your service to the community. I especially liked all of them hanging baskets you put up round the town during the summer. It was lovely, so it was, just to see all them colours cheering up the place a bit.

Yours sincerely,

Mae-Anne Greene

Jenny clicks again.

From: Mae-Anne Greene [mailto:magreene@gmail.com]
Sent: 13 November 2013 23:51
To: Thomas Foley<tommyfTC@yahoo.co.uk>
Subject: JUST THINK OF YOUR POOR MOTHER!

Dear Mr Thomas Foley,

I dare say, Councillor, you must have you forgotten your promise to the people of this town? Well now, Councillor, although I have been up to my eyes these last few days getting our Annette settled back in home again and helping them all to adjust, I have not forgotten you or your promise to the people of this town!

In fact, I can remember back to the days before you were a councillor, when you first served this community as an altar boy, up above in the church. Do you know what, but I often thought your poor Mother, Lord have mercy on her, was going to have to be carted out of Mass some Sunday, before the communion would even be over. Weak she used to get at the sight of you, there, smiling down from the altar, ringleted like a little Apostle, so you were – those yellow curls of yours like a halo of light in her eyes and she'd say to me, 'You know, Mae-Anne, he's destined for greatness, so he surely is!'

Greatness indeed! Now don't you go making a liar out of your poor Mother, Thomas Foley!

You were supposed to be 'the one to be found when others weren't around'! That was according to all of them posters you nailed up on every pole and tree around the whole county before the last election anyway.

So where are you now? I have sent you four emails. I have a poor unfortunate man, with not a soul to look up nor down at him, still living in my house and there's not so much as a word from you in my Inbox! Do you not think now that I have enough to be doing without hunting you down?

Sincerely,

Mae-Anne Greene

Click.

From: Thomas Foley<tommyfTC@yahoo.co.uk>
Sent: 20 November 2013 11:07
To: Mae-Anne Greene [mailto:magreene@gmail.com]
Subject: Homeless Crisis

Dear Mrs Greene,

Thank you for your recent correspondence Re. Homeless Individual. And thank you for remembering my mother. As one of your local councillors I will endeavour to bring as much assistance as I possibly can to this case.

Please find attached our document policy Re Homeless Individuals.

Hoping this issue can be resolved promptly,

Best regards,

Thomas Foley

Jenny clicks again.

From: Mae-Anne Greene [mailto:magreene@gmail.com]
Sent: 21 November 2013 03:17
To: Thomas Foley<tommyfTC@yahoo.co.uk>
Subject: TALK IS CHEAP, SO IT IS!

Dear Mr Councillor Foley,

'Recent' indeed! I sent my first email letter on the 4th of November! Now, let me tell you, I was busy this morning when I found your correspondence in my Inbox and despite the fact that we've had a very trying day here altogether, I am now making the time to respond, as is only proper and right, as I'm sure you'll agree!

And don't you go giving me directions and opening times and what-not or any of your 'for further information' nonsense either! Sure, I don't need to go no further because you are as far as I'm going! Do you hear me now, Thomas Foley? I don't have the time to be reading your fancy initiatives and policies! Attachments indeed!

This man is not from around these parts, though he thinks he may have had a grandfather from here, away back. Anyway, the long and the short of it is, he has nowhere to go and no one to care about the fact that he has nowhere to go. That's where you come in, Councillor!

Well, you'll not miss the water till the well runs dry, young Thomas Foley or Foley, Thomas or whatever it is you're calling yourself these days! You mark my words! This time twelve months you'll be down on your hands and knees begging for votes.

Now, you have a choice to make here and there's no going back, once it's made, so choose wisely because many a ship is lost near the harbour, so it is!

Mrs Greene

Click.

From: Thomas Foley<tommyfTC@yahoo.co.uk>
Sent: 25 November 2013 09:05
To: Mae-Anne Greene [mailto:magreene@gmail.com]
Subject: Homeless Crisis

Dear Mrs Greene,

I understand your frustration, truly I do. However, there is a process and due to the current housing crisis, this may take some time.

Please find attached a list of voluntary organisations in receipt of government funding to provide temporary and permanent accommodation for homeless people and to provide advice and assistance to them. They may be of some assistance in the interim.

I have passed the details of this case, personally, to a colleague in the housing department and shall forward any relevant information directly and promptly to you.

I am thinking of you and your family at this difficult time.
Kindest regards,
T. Foley

Click.

From: Mae-Anne Greene [mailto:magreene@gmail.com]
Sent: 25 November 2013 23:33
To: Thomas Foley<tommyfTC@yahoo.co.uk>
Subject: MR FRANCIS S. FITZGERALD!

Thomas Foley, the person / persons / individual you referred to in your email this morning has a name! He is called Mr Francis S. Fitzgerald and he is STILL in my house. Now, mind you I'm not complaining about that, so I am not. He has somewhere to stay at least, no thanks to you, and sure it's peace of mind for me, having the place lived in while I'm residing here! I gave him a key so as he can come and go as he likes. Sure, it'd get awful lonely staying cooped up all day on your own. He says he likes watching the people. Makes him feel more connected, I suppose.

And thank you for thinking of us all here too but sure aren't we the lucky ones? We've a roof over our heads and we're all here together! We have each other! This man has nobody!

It's an absolute disgrace that anybody has to suffer like this, living like an animal out on the street and in this cold weather too. And, let me tell you, if Mr Fitzgerald had burned to death, that night, on the steps of the cinema, it wouldn't have been that young tinker, with the hare lip, I'd be accusing of murder, Thomas Foley. It would be YOU! And, like I always say, there's no use in crying when the funeral has gone. And there's no use looking for votes when there's blood on your hands!

Mrs M.A. Greene

PS. That new zebra crossing you put in at the corner, before the bank, is an absolute death trap. What were you thinking? Are you trying to kill us all stone dead or what? Fecking Yahoo is right!

Jenny laughs at the last bit and clicks again. But that's it. There are no more emails. She returns back to the MURDER letter, the one at the top of the pile. She reads it again. But the first one isn't the end either. Jenny knows that. There is more to be written, more to be said, but, either way, she understands the story now. Jenny thinks about this and smiles.

'Your granny is brilliant,' Mrs French had said.

CHAPTER 58

Jacob

Bath time is Jacob's favourite time of the day. Bath time is the time just after dinner and just before bed. It's in the middle of the other two times like yellow is in the middle of green and red on the traffic lights near the park. Bath time is a rule like red means hot and blue means cold. Red is the colour of stopping. Green is the colour of going. Blue is the colour of cold. Blue things are cold. Yellow is the colour of ducks and waiting.

Jacob is waiting. Granny is waiting too.

Granny says she's going to take off Jacob's clothes. But only when he is ready. Granny will wait for Jacob to be ready.

Jacob looks up at the men on the wall. Then he is ready. Shoes are first. This is rule number one. Right shoe. Left shoe. Socks are next – rule number two. Right sock. Left sock.

Granny opens the button on Jacob's jeans. She pulls at the zip and wriggles his jeans down over his bum and the tops of his legs. Sometimes Jacob's underpants come too at the same time. This is not a rule. Sometimes it just happens that way.

'It's okay, pet, don't worry,' Granny says.

Granny holds Jacob's hands. Jacob pulls his right leg up off the floor. His toes disappear into his jeans. Then they are back. Left leg is next.

Bye-bye toes.

'Peek-a-boo toes,' Granny says.

Jacob's jeans are in a lump on the floor.

Jumper is next.

'Let's get that jumper off,' Granny says.

Jacob pushes his two hands up to the sky and stands up real straight like a pencil. Yellow pencils don't work on white paper. Yellow markers do.

'Ready, steady, go,' Granny says.

Granny holds on to the bottom of Jacob's jumper and pulls it right up to his head. It is dark when his jumper gets stuck on his nose but then it is bright again.

Granny says, 'Boo.'

Jacob's arms are still stuck up in the air. Now there's a little bit of cold. Granny throws Jacob's jumper down on the floor. She moves his arms back down and takes a towel off the radiator. She wraps him up real tight like a present.

'My little pet.'

Granny's hand is on the top of Jacob's head.

The towel is soft and it is warm. Granny sits Jacob up on the closed-down seat of the toilet. This is rule number three because underpants and jeans isn't really a rule. Not really. Sometimes it just happens that way. If the toilet isn't closed Jacob will fall in.

Granny leans over the bath. Her hand goes in under the water. So does her arm.

'Perfect,' Granny says.

This is rule number four.

Granny's arm comes back, so does her hand. Granny is pink right up to her elbow. Pink is for girls. Blue is for boys. Jenny is a girl. Jacob is a boy. Mammy has pink shoes. Granny doesn't have pink shoes. Granny has a pink arm. Daddy doesn't have pink shoes or a pink arm. Daddy has colours and lines on his arm and a picture of a tiger. Jacob likes tigers. Tigers are not pink. Tigers are orange. Candyfloss is pink. Like Granny's arm.

Granny stands up straight like a pencil. Then she bends down lower and opens Jacob's towel like she's opening up the present again. Granny lifts Jacob up off the toilet.

'My little man.'

A man is not a boy. A boy is a boy. A boy gets big like a man. This is a rule.

Granny holds Jacob's two hands up in the air. 'Are you ready, Jacob?'

Granny is waiting. Jacob is waiting too. Yellow is the colour of ducks and waiting. The yellow man is in the middle. The yellow man is waiting. Granny is waiting. Jacob is waiting too. The green man is walking. The red man is not walking on the traffic lights near the park. The red man is stopping. Red is for stopping. Green is for walking. Pink is for girls. Blue is for boys. There are no boys on the traffic lights near the park.

'There's no hurry, pet. Whenever you are ready. Take your time.'

Jacob puts his right foot in first. Right foot first. This is a rule. This is rule number five. Right foot. Left foot. Left foot is after right foot. Right foot comes first. This is rule number five. Left foot is next. This is the rule. Rule number five.

Jacob stands up in the bath. The water covers his feet and the bottom of his legs. His toes look bigger. Jacob has to stay on the blue mat under the water. This is rule number six. Slipping is bad and he might get a bump. Jacob holds the two sides of the bath and slowly lowers himself down. At first the water is too hot on his bum. Then it is okay. Jacob sits into the warm suds. Suds are like sitting-down bubbles. Jacob is sitting down. Granny is not. Granny is kneeling on the floor beside the bath and Jacob can't see Granny's legs anymore.

'Ah Jesus, me knee is givin' me awful gyp altogether, Jacob. It's all this cold weather.'

Blue is the colour of cold. Blue things are cold. Hot things are red. These are the rules. Red. Hot. Blue. Cold.

Granny starts at Jacob's toes. The sponge tickles the bottom of Jacob's feet. Granny smells nice. Like a bun.

'This little piggy went to market. This little piggy stayed at home. This little piggy ate brown bread. This little piggy had none and this little piggy went wee-wee-wee all the way home.'

Jacob likes the little piggies. But he doesn't like the big bad wolf.

'A is for apple. AP-L'. Granny holds up the big red letter A that sticks to the side of the bath with the hand that isn't washing Jacob's feet. 'Can you say Apple, Jacob? AP-L.'

The black and white men are looking down from the wall. They are sitting on a grey line across the sky. Some of them have hats and big noses. Some of them don't. They all have feet. Jacob moves his finger through the air making little half-circles between finger-counting jumps.

One two three four five six seven eight nine ten eleven.

'They are *The Men at Lunch*, Jacob. Nobody knows who they are. Which is sad really. B is for ball.'

The big blue B is too close to Jacob's face.

'BA-BA-BALL,' Granny says.

Granny sticks B back on the bath but it slides down into the water. It's bigger now.

There are bubbles on Jacob's knees. Jacob likes bubbles. Granny slides them away. Man number five has no clothes on except for his pants and his hat. Jacob has no clothes on at all. Jacob wonders if the man is cold. He doesn't look cold. He is not blue. Blue is for cold. Jacob isn't cold. The water trickles out of the sponge from Jacob's neck all the way down to his belly button.

C is next. This is a rule. C is green like the walking man. Granny picks up the green letter C. Granny holds the green letter C up for Jacob.

C is for cold. Jacob is hot. His face feels bright red.

'C is for cat. C-AT. Meow.' Granny makes strange noises.

Granny puts the C back on the bath. Granny lifts up Jacob's arm and rubs it all over. She uses the sponge to spread the soft-fluffy white water.

Happy cats are good. Sad cats go in the bin. Sometimes the wolf tries to get in through the window.

Man number six has a box. It might be a present for man number five or it might be just a box. Granny warms Jacob's back again with water. Jacob has a box under his bed. It's not a present. It's just a box. Jenny takes it out every night before telling him the story about Hooch the Sleepy Hedgehog or The Three Little Pigs and she puts all Jacob's worries inside. Then she closes the lid and says, 'Don't worry, Jacob, there's nothing to worry about tonight.' Jacob can't see the worries because Jenny's hand catches them real quick and she squeezes them into a ball with her fingers. Then they are gone.

'Course now, you know, your daddy swears that the fella at the end there is his Great Uncle Mickey, a course! Himself there, with the big nose, swiggin' from that bottle. Him, at the end. Mind you, all a them Augustts did like a drink. Wouldn't a been too fond of the bit a work though. He does look a bit like him, mind you, now that I look at him, I suppose. Kinda lost up there on that girder. Musha, weren't they all.'

D is next. This is the rule. Granny takes D off the bath. D is purple.

'D is for Daddy, Jacob. DA-DEE. Can you say DA-DEE?'

D is for duck.

Jacob picks the yellow duck out of the water. There are tiny pink-blue bubbles falling back into the water like a rainbow. Jacob likes drawing rainbows. Red orange yellow green blue indigo – these are the colours of the rainbow.

'DA-DEE. Jacob, where is Daddy?'

Daddy's head peeps through the door. 'You lookin' for me, Mae-Anne?'

'No. Just doin' some words. Where's Jenny?'

'She's inside with Annette. Reading. I think they're coming to the end of *Anne Frank*.'

'Oh Jesus, she's nearly finished, you say?'

'I think so. She'll be all right, Mae-Anne. She will. Do you want me to take over there? I have ten minutes before I go and pick up the van. Jesus, I can't believe it. Goin' out on me own. Couldn't a done it without you.'

'Ah now, stop your mitherin' and go on round for the van. You're only gettin' in me way here. Mark my words, this time next year, you'll have a whole fleet a vans on the road! Me and Jacob are grand and sure we'll be doin' our readin' before ya know it! Won't we, Jacob?'

'Right so. If you're sure.'

Granny squeezes the sponge in under Jacob's chin. She puts a bubble on Jacob's nose. 'Jacob, everybody you'll ever meet will claim one a them poor divils up there is their great uncle or their great grandfather or in some way related to someone they know.'

Ears are next. Rule number seven. The man beside man number six is man number seven. He wants to know what's in the box. So does man number five. Man number three has a box too. Jacob wonders if they are playing pass the parcel up there in the sky. There are lots of buildings and windows under their boots. Small ones and big ones. But there's no music. Man number two has a box but he's looking at man number three's box. Man number eight with the black hat has opened his box.

'E is for elephant.' Granny holds up the red E.

Man number nine has a grey hat but he doesn't have a box. Man number ten doesn't have a hat or a box. Man number eleven has a box but no hat. Man number one doesn't have a box but he does have a bottle in his hand. There are lots and lots of windows under his feet.

'I suppose everyone just wants to be part of a story, Jacob. Your daddy's no different. We all need to feel connected in some way to somethin' and somebody, somewhere. Your daddy's never really had that, but, sure, isn't that all any of us wants, really, when it comes down to it? A feelin' a belonging. And that picture up there gives people a feelin' a connection, even if it's just imagined connection. And it means those men up there'll be remembered too, even if it's only through fanciful stories. Nobody wants to be forgotten or left behind. Can you say elephant, Jacob? El-eh-fant.' Granny pushes her nose into the top of her arm and swings her arm round in the air.

Jacob's fingers are wrinkled, so are his toes.

Jacob takes the yellow E from Granny. He turns it around so it looks like a three. When he turns the three up-ways with all its legs in the air it's a big W. Jacob doesn't know any W words. And when he turns the W downways it's a big M.

M is for Mammy.

CHAPTER 59

Jenny

Jenny closes the book. It is upside down on the table. She can't see Anne's face anymore.

'It is not going to end this way. I won't let it. Not this time,' Jenny says to herself, but out loud, so that Anne Frank might hear her too.

She turns the book over and looks at Anne's smiling face, her shiny black hair.

'I'm going to write you a new ending, Anne Frank. A better one, I promise.'

Anne Frank doesn't seem to have a problem with this. In fact, Jenny thinks her smile just got a little wider, making the lines at the side of her face a little deeper. Jenny thinks about Bruno and Schmuel.

Wednesday, 9th August, 1944

Dear Kitty,

I am free. We are free. Free from our clandestine attic at last. The smell of fresh air makes me feel clean again, like I've just had the longest, deepest bath ever, with bubbles. I don't have to look out at the world through old, scraggly curtains anymore, like I'm an awful dirty secret nobody wants to talk about. We are no longer secret or clandestine, Kitty. We are people again. We are free, Kitty. We are free.

The sky is big and blue over our heads and it seems to go on forever. The birds are singing up in the chestnut tree, and the daisies in the grass are swaying, like we are all at a big party. It is the biggest party ever and the best party ever. It is a welcome home party, just for us, because we have been away for such a long time, Kitty. And it's not like we have just been away on holiday, somewhere like Timbuktu, for two weeks or a month. It's like we were missing, but now we have found our way home, after many long adventures, and now the whole entire world is happy again.

Oh but, Kitty, it wasn't easy.

On Friday morning we were doing the things we always do on Friday mornings. The Van Daans were fighting, of course. Dussel was doing his exercises. Margot and I were shelling peas. Pim was upstairs helping Peter with his spellings. It was about ten thirty and everything was okay. But then, suddenly, out of nowhere, came the sound of boots, running and thumping and thudding up our secret stairs. The noise was so close that each of us froze like statues in the statue game. And we didn't know what to do. Before we could move our bodies, the door opened and there, right in front of us, were four men in uniforms. They were the Nazis and they were full of malevolence. I just knew by the way they looked at us. One Nazi had real bright, yellow-white hair and a purplish scar across his cheek. He pointed a gun straight at Margot and me. Then Mummy came out of nowhere, like a magical genie, and stood between us and the man with the gun. The gunman gave Mummy a wink, which we thought was weird, but we were too frightened to say anything. Then he left, but he told one of the other Nazis to stay and watch us. Then, Daddy and Peter were pushed in through the door. Mrs Van Daan was next, and she was so quiet that we felt even more afraid. Mrs Van

Daan is never quiet! Finally, Dussel and Mr Van Daan were sent in. The yellow-haired gunman marched in behind them.

'Get your things!' the yellow-haired man screamed, like the place was on fire. 'You have five minutes!'

Oh, Kitty, we were so scared. We gathered up whatever we could, like some knickers and socks and, of course, I took you. I hid you up under my jumper. They marched us down the stairs and out on to the street. They pushed us into a truck and we just sat there in the darkness, holding each other. It was a long drive. We didn't know where we were going to end up. After about fifteen hours the truck suddenly stopped. We could hear voices outside. We waited. We heard laughing. Then the doors were pulled open and the daylight stung our eyes, like cold ice. We had travelled all night. The yellow-haired man with the gun and the scar was standing in front of us again.

'I'm sorry we frightened you. Welcome to your new home,' he said, passing his hand through the air, like a prince showing off his kingdom to a princess with only one shoe.

We were so far away from everything we knew. The sky was bluer than it has ever been in any story book ever written. The bird song was louder. The trees bigger, greener. We stood outside the truck, Kitty, squinting into the brilliant light of the new day, our first day of freedom again. It was just brilliant, so it was.

We were on top of the world. And we actually were, not just like saying it when it means you are happy. We were so high up in the mountains that we could see for miles and miles and the war and the 'Secret Annexe' were gone away forever and ever. The mountains were like a big circle around us, keeping us safe.

We had to hike a long way up through the forest. We were hungry, and my feet got real sore, but I didn't mind.

We found two little boys, hiding up a tree, and they came with us.

Then after hours and hours of walking up the biggest mountain of them all, we finally came to a small village, where people were living quietly, in small houses made of wood and built in the shape of triangles and they glowed a bright fiery-orange, against the dark blue night sky. We could hear the ting-a-ling bells around the necks of the village goats and sheep, and the smallest whispers of children laughing. And it was just so perfect, like a little world inside a snow globe, except instead of snow falling, the sky was filled with a thousand glitter stars.

This is where we have made our lives now, with all these lovely people, in this little corner of heaven and it is so beautiful, it is like someplace you'd read about in a book, only it is better, Kitty, because it is real.

Yours, Anne Frank

Jenny rips the epilogue bit out and sellotapes the new entry into the back of the diary. She closes the book. She smiles at Anne Frank's smiling face on the front cover. She puts the Sellotape back in the drawer.

CHAPTER 60

Jenny

A Good Day

by Jennifer Augustt

The whole kitchen spits and sizzles and the windows get steamy, as Granny stirs all the sausage and rasher smells out of the pan and onto our plates.

'That'll put hairs on your chest!' Granny says, like that's a good thing, like it's something we would want to happen to us.

Jacob is at the table drawing our house, like a box we'd never fit into. He has put in an upstairs and a downstairs and crosses in all the windows. I can see myself wearing a triangle dress that Jacob has coloured in yellow. I have one short leg and one long leg and he has put me at the side, which probably means I'm out in the back garden again. Da's standing in the front door, which is round, like a plate.

'Where's Da?' I ask Granny.

'I sent him down to get milk. Didn't he use the last drop on his cornflakes last night, like he was gettin' a head start on today or somethin!' Granny says. 'As if!'

Jacob has given Da a square head on top of a crooked line-body with two stick-legs, sticking out in different directions like Da is a branch or maybe he is doing the splits. It's definitely Da though because he looks very confused, like he has just lost something he needs. There are two orange fish under the house. Jacob didn't give Da any clothes at all so he looks kinda cold. And he's blue. Mammy is at the other side of the house wearing a triangle dress, just like mine, only much bigger. She has a big smile on her face. But she doesn't have any arms or any hair. And Granny is there too, up on the roof, just like Santa, carrying a big bag of messages or presents.

'That's a great picture altogether, Jacob. Is that your school?' Granny says, standing over us, at the table, with the two plates she's holding up real high, like she doesn't want us to see what's on them at all. 'But would ya ever tidy it away, now, like a good child? Your breakfast is ready.'

Jacob pushes his markers back into the tube. He puts everything in the drawer and comes back to the table again. The sausages are hot, fat and crispy-brown on the outside, soft and delicious-pink inside. Exactly the way they should be. Jacob loves sausages. I look at a funny reflection of myself in the back of a spoon. If I move the spoon forwards, I have too much body and not enough head and I look much fatter than I am. When I stand it up straight, my head gets too long but my shoulders and arms look tiny, like a bird. I wonder how many different mes I can find, as I move the spoon around, but then all of me just slips off the back of it and down into the handle when I lie the spoon flat and there's only the lights on the ceiling left to see.

'Ah sure, isn't it the stones in the father's shoes that his children choke on!' Granny says, like she's having a whole other conversation with someone else we can't see.

I look all round the kitchen, just to be sure. 'Granny?' I say, making Granny's name sound like a question.

'Yes, pet?' Granny says, like she's just remembered we're

there. 'Musha, I was just thinkin' about your daddy. That's all, pet, that's all.'

After breakfast Granny shoos me and Jacob out to the back garden.

'The fresh air will crown yas,' she says.

'But, Granny, it's cold!' I tell her, thinking I just want to go back up to bed.

'Would ya go way outta that, Jenny, sure isn't it the bitterness a the winter that gives the summer its sweetness!' Granny says, like this makes any sense at all.

'What?'

'Nothin'! Now get your coats on. Sure, there's nothin' so bad that it could not be worse!'

Granny buttons up Jacob's coat. She pulls his hat so far down over his ears that his eyes disappear, too. Holding her two hands at the sides of his head, she uses her thumbs to push the front of Jacob's hat back up, so he can see again. I take Jacob by the hand and we go out the back door. Outside, the brightness makes me squint and the cold gets into my eyeballs but it isn't freezing cold. It feels clean.

'Swing or sandpit?' I ask Jacob, moving him away from the swing. I'm not in the mood for swinging today.

Sandpit.

'Okay. Sandpit it is! Let's make an island.'

No, let's make a castle for Mammy.

'A castle for Mammy? That's a very good idea, Jacob. Well done.'

We could make the biggest sandcastle ever!

'The biggest sandcastle ever? Mammy will love that. And we should make a miracle too, while we're at it, to make her better and bring back her hair.'

Jenny, there's no such things as miracles.

'No such thing as miracles? How do you know?'

I know things you don't know.

'You know things I don't? Like what?'

Like how to draw stories and write pictures.

'Jacob, we don't draw stories. We write stories. We draw pictures.'

Let's just make the castle for Mammy.

'Okay. Let's just make the castle for Mammy so,' I say back to Jacob, even though I don't really feel like doing anything now.

Jacob gets his yellow spade out of Da's shed. He puts it down in the sand. Then he goes back into the shed again. When he comes out again he's carrying his red spade. He puts it down beside the yellow spade. Jacob always uses the yellow spade first. He takes away the purple bucket, placing it to the side. He will not need the purple bucket until the green bucket, the one that looks like a perfect little castle with three steps up to the little front door, is half full - just past its window. Jacob always half-fills the green bucket first. Using his yellow spade, he puts some sand into the green bucket. He pats it down and checks his levels. He puts in more sand, pats it down, checks his levels again. When he is happy the halfway line has been reached, he picks up the red spade and half-fills the purple bucket, because that's the one that always comes next. The blue bucket behind him will be half-filled after the purple bucket. This is a rule. Then just out of the corner of my eye I see that the blue bucket still has its handle on even though blue buckets should never have handles. Only yellow buckets are allowed to have handles. These are Jacob's rules. So, I reach behind him and take the white handle off the blue bucket real quick before Jacob can see it.

'Let's sing a song, Jacob,' I say, to take his mind off buckets and handles and all the bucket-handle rules.

No. I don't want to sing today. Today's not a day for singing.

'Today's not a day for singing? Why not? Remember the Queen, Jacob, and how she taught the boy to sing, like a bird? In the story. We might be able to wake Mammy and then maybe she will get up and we could all go for a picnic.'

Singing won't work, Jenny. Not today. Not anymore. Not ever. Singing will only work in a story, and we're not in a story, Jenny, and I don't think there will be any picnic either, Jenny. Do you?

'I'm fed up making castles. It's freezing. Let's play hide-and-seek now. That'll warm us up! I'll count to ten. Jacob, you go and hide.'

Jacob's knees are all sandy when he stands up, but he doesn't brush the sand off, he just runs away to hide. I put my hands over my eyes, but I can still see the clouds floating up in the sky through the cracks in my fingers and for no reason at all I start thinking about how nice it must be to be a little swallow, living in a secret hidey-hole nest up in under the roof of our house, or better still, in Africa.

But the swallows are all gone now for the winter. They are gone somewhere warm. Probably Africa. I watched them getting ready to go, all the way back, in September. Mrs Swallow was very busy then. I can still see her flitting around. Her blue-black shiny head and the fork in her tail, like a little upside-down V, used to dart in and out all day.

'Swallows bring good luck to a house,' Granny always says. 'We'll never be hit be lightnin' so long as they're here. Don't ever disturb a swallow. The milk will turn sour and bad luck will pour in.'

I try to remember the swallow from the big blue book with my name on the front. *This book belongs to* was written in fancy letters on the first page. *Jenny Augustt* was scribbled, in my best earliest letters, along the line underneath. Apollo the Swallow. That was his name. He was learning how to fly to Africa, but his blackbird friend didn't believe him. The blackbird's name was Chack. And Chack said that the white blossom tree would be covered in tasty orange blossoms one day, but Apollo didn't believe him either. And I wonder now if Apollo and Chack ever existed at all or were they just characters I made up in my head. Did Mammy and I really sit together, reading, on my bed, every night, Mammy's finger slowly moving along and beneath every word, so I wouldn't lose my place in the sentence? Did Apollo really go to Africa? Why was Chack brown if he was supposed to be black? Was there even a tree or a dolphin or a camel? I want to go back and look at all the pictures again and tell the little me girl on the bed, reading with Mammy, to remember every word in the book, to never forget the story or the way Mammy reads it to her or how she helps her with the big words she thinks are too difficult. I want to get back in between the two of them, together in bed, take little bits of each one of us and make a perfect new Mammy and me. And I want to listen to the story once more just to be sure we ever read it at all.

I'm already at fifty when I hear myself counting again. I get up real quick to look for Jacob. I was supposed to start searching forty counts ago and I know Jacob doesn't like waiting, even though I keep telling him that when we play hide-and-seek the longer we have to wait to be found the better because it means we've got a really good hiding place that the seeker person can't find, which is good. But Jacob doesn't really like playing it like that. Jacob likes me to find him straight away.

The first place I look is in the shed, but I know as soon as I look in the door that he's not there, because when Jacob hides in the shed he just stands in the corner with his hands over his own face, like that's going to make him harder to find. So then I look under the bush at the back of the garden, because if Jacob's not in the shed then he is usually sitting under the bush. I look for his feet. But there are no feet under the bush. No Jacob there, either. I stand in the middle of the grass, looking for clues, and then I spot little bits of sand on the path, going back into the house. I follow the sand trail, like a detective, and just hope he hasn't gone into the house because Granny will go mental if he drags in sand, all over her Good Floors.

In the kitchen I look under the table. No Jacob. I open the door of the long press. Sometimes Jacob just sits inside the long press on his own even though we are not even playing hide-and-seek. He's not in the long press. I look behind the couch in the sitting room. No Jacob. He's not behind the curtains either.

'Jacob,' I say into the air, 'Jacob, where are you?'

I look under the coffee table even though I can see, standing up, that he's not there. I pull Mammy's chair away from the wall. I know Jacob wouldn't be able to fit behind it. But I look anyway. I open the press under the telly even though I know he's too big to even get in there. I go back out to the kitchen again. No Jacob. I check behind the ironing board and under the washing.

'Jacob, Jacob?' I call.

I run back out through the hall to the front door to see if he's out in the front garden. Jacob sometimes stands out there with Billy, from next door. They don't talk or laugh but they both seem to like each other enough to just stay there together, looking out at the world from behind the front wall. But there's no sign of Billy. And Jacob's not there either.

'He's not there. He's not there,' I say over and over, like I didn't believe myself the first time I said it. 'He's not there. He's not there.'

Then I run back into the house again and I try to remember where Jacob had put himself in the picture he was drawing before breakfast. Where was he? I go through the hall without seeing anything at all. The sitting room is empty. Da was in the round doorway, looking lost. There's nobody in the kitchen. Granny was up on the roof, with the shopping. Where was Jacob? I was out in the back garden in my triangle dress. Where was Jacob?

'Jacob, where are you?'

I am suddenly out in the back garden again, the real one. Not the one Jacob had put me in, at the side of the house. I check the shed and the bush again. But there's nobody there.

'Jacob, Jacob?'

I look back up at the house and somehow, I think I can see him running from one room to another. He's laughing and Mammy's running behind him. I squint harder.

'Can't catch me,' Jacob sings over his shoulder.

'Come back here, ya little monkey,' Mammy laughs, grabbing the empty space Jacob's just left behind him.

Jacob keeps running. Mammy keeps trying to catch him, but she can't. Then Mammy gets serious and ties her hair back with the bobble she always has on her wrist.

'For emergencies,' she used to say. 'Always keep a bobble on your wrist for the times you need to be able to see straight or if you need to tie up a bunch of daisies or if you just get too hot.'

Jacob looks back behind him to check if Mammy's running is as fast as his. He doesn't see the couch and just kind of flops into it sideways, laughing like he's never laughed before. And Mammy sees her chance. Mammy jumps on top of Jacob and starts tickling him and kissing him so much he's caught between laughing and crying. Then Mammy snuggles him up in under her and Jacob smiles in her smell.

'Let's make a cake!' Mammy says, and she runs back into the kitchen.

Jacob bounces up and down on the couch. And I can see myself, in there with them, in the kitchen, already stirring the flour and eggs in a bowl.

'That's my girl,' Mammy says. 'I'll get the milk.'

I watch myself and Mammy pour in the milk and everything sloshes round in the bowl. The mixing gets hard because the milk doesn't really want to be there. It sticks to the sides in big lumps, like it's running away from everything else in the world. The eggs and the flour sink down under the floating bits of milk, leaving it on its own at the top. There's a smell of something sour in the air.

'That milk's gone off,' Mammy says, and she starts crying.

'It's okay,' I hear myself saying. 'Granny's just sent Da down to the shop to get some. He'll be back in five minutes. Don't cry, Mammy. Mammy don't cry.'

'Five minutes? I don't have five minutes to wait for your Da. It's ruined!' she screams. 'It's wasted. It's all gone wrong. It's not supposed to be like this.' Then Mammy starts pulling her hair and she pulls so hard it starts coming out in big handfuls, all over the floor. Mammy's screaming gets louder and louder. I watch myself trying to hug Mammy and tell her that everything is going to be all right but no matter how hard I try I can't reach her and there's no sign of Da with the milk.

Suddenly, then, like all the things I've ever forgotten coming rushing back inside my head all at once, I remember Jacob. Jacob wasn't in the picture!

'You weren't there. You weren't there,' I say over and over, trying to understand.

Jacob is lost. I have to find him. I start shouting his name again but the more I shout it the more he seems missing and the more I feel like I'm the only person left in the whole wide world. Everybody else is gone. Lost out in the woods somewhere, following a trail of breadcrumbs the witch has left behind. Witches do that. They put things you want in places you shouldn't go. They make houses out of sweets and cakes to trick you and then they put you into cages to fatten you up. Then they eat you!

I call his name again and again. 'Jacob, Jacob!' There's nobody to hear me. Where's Da? Where's Granny? I run back into the house again, even though I'm afraid. I run through the kitchen, calling, calling, calling, 'Jacob, Jacob, Jacob!'

I go into the hall, the sitting room, and back out to the hall again. I go up the stairs, into the bathroom and into Jacob's bedroom. I remember all the crosses on all the windows. Nothing. I rush back down the stairs, not knowing what to do next, where to go, or how to find him. I go back out into the kitchen again. I open the drawer and throw everything out on the floor.

'Where is it? Where is it?'

But I can't find it. I can't find Jacob's picture. Jacob's picture is gone. Jacob is gone.

When the sound of my heart finally stops thump-thumping inside the front of my head I try to stop the crying noises that are growing in the back of my throat. Then I think I hear a small sound out in the hall. It is tiny, but it's there. I can hear it. As I move slowly, barely breathing now at all, the little sound gets a bit bigger, closer. I stop. I stand holding in my breath completely, to hear better.

'Ma-me. Ma-me.'

I hear it coming out softly from in under the stairs. The sounds slip out of the dark and up into the air. It's not just inside my head this time either. I didn't make it up or pretend to hear it. It is real. A real sound. A real word. And it floats around the hall and around me, like the first sound ever heard, the first word ever made.

'Jacob?' I whisper, sticking my head in through the door. 'Are you in there?'

At first, I can't see very well but then as the darkness clears I see a little shape, sitting way in at the back, in the smallest corner, like a little mouse hiding away and making himself as small as he can so that the fox won't get him.

'Ma-me. Mam-e. Mammy,' he keeps saying, like he's tasting the word, for the very first time, with his own little voice. Jacob's voice.

I can feel a strange coldness running along my arms and across the back of my shoulders. I give them a little shake, twitch my neck and without me doing it, a smile opens up on my face.

'Don't move, Jacob! I'll be back in a minute.'

I run out to the kitchen and get Mammy's big bottle of champagne, the one she's keeping for when Jacob says, 'Mammy,' for the first time, out of the back of the press. I blow the dust off the yellow-gold foil round the top. I give it a wipe with the end of my sleeve. Then I go back out to the hall.

'Jacob, come on! Come on!'

I reach in, stretching my right hand out to Jacob. Meeting his little fingers, I take Jacob by the hand and out of the dark. With the champagne in one hand and Jacob in the other, we make my way up the stairs to tell Mammy.

Jenny puts the lid back on her pen. She sits up very straight at the new desk Da made her, which isn't really new at all, because he made it out of an old desk he got from the second-hand shop, beside the bookie's, down the road. Granny said it would be riddled with woodworm and that they'd eat them all out of house and home and then the roof would fall in on their heads. Jenny, half-frightened at the idea of more worms, these ones wriggling and chomping their way through her desk and through the whole house, giggles now at the pictures she's drawing in her mind.

There's a whole army of them, gathering inside the desk. Two of the smaller ones are arguing about whether they are woodworm or woodworms and two of the bigger ones are screaming at each other because of what Da said.

You're wrong! We don't even exist. Sure, how could we when nobody's ever actually seen us! the fatter of the two shouts. *It's a well-known fact that we've just made each other up!*

Would ya go way outta that! says the thinner one. *Course we exist. Sure, hasn't Mae-Anne, there, seen the damage we can do!*

The thinner one wears green glasses and a spotted scarf.

When Da finally convinced Granny that the desk was a worm-free zone, she agreed that it could stay.

'Every writer needs a desk, I suppose!' Granny said, winking over at Jenny.

Jenny tries to imagine what it would be like to be a real writer, a proper one – a writer who writes whole books, all by themselves. Suddenly Jenny sees herself sitting at her desk, at the back of the class. Father Fennel is reading *her* story. The one she's just written. When he finishes, the whole room is silent. Then everybody in the whole class looks round at Jenny. Jenny can't work out if they all think she's stupid or brilliant. But once the clapping starts, she goes for brilliant. The children stand up, all around her, clap-clapping and smiling. Jane-Anne claps louder than the rest. Jenny, still sitting, looks up into all the smiling faces and she smiles back, like she imagines a brilliant person might smile at other people when the brilliant person knows they have just done something brilliant, but they don't want to boast about it too much. One of those smiles that don't make you look too sure of yourself but make you look calm and happy enough that things have worked out for you the way that they have.

Father Fennell places Jenny's story down on the desk, at the top of the class, and Dorcas looks like she's in love, as she stares back up at the voice, now replacing hers, in the room.

This is a fantastic piece of work. It really is. This made me sit up in my seat when I read it the first time. And I've read it many, many times since. I think we may have a writer, a real writer in our midst. In fact, I'm sure that we do! And so, it is with tremendous pleasure that I invite Jennifer Augustt up here, to accept this year's award for first place, Father Fennell says, like he really means it.

Jenny doesn't move. Dorcas stands up and with another nod of her jumbo head, she tells Jenny exactly what to do. This nod is a good nod. Jenny slips out from behind her desk at the back of the room. She starts to move slowly, up through the clapping children, towards the priest. Each child she passes smiles warmly, though none of them look quite as pleased as Grammar Girl, who is grinning and winking down at Jenny from her place high up there on the wall.

Jenny runs her hand along the smooth line at the front of her new desk. Da had cut the legs shorter and sanded it down, taken off the flat top bit and pushed the legs closer to each other, still leaving enough room though for Jenny's knees, and then he had nailed and glued it back together again. It was a sad, tired-looking desk when it first appeared out in Da's shed but now it's all painted pink, with stencilled blue flowers, and Jenny thinks it's the loveliest thing she's ever seen.

Looking down at the last page again, she tries to understand the thing that seems to be waking up inside her. She feels it stretch its arms wide and lengthen its neck, like the way she used to feel when she would wake up on a happy morning when there was nothing dark in her tummy from the night before and her head wasn't too hot either. Letting it uncurl itself, she sits back in the chair and something, she's not sure what it is, leaves her. She lets it go.

Looking out the window, she watches the twinkling of the little coloured Christmas lights. They flash on and off, off and on, bouncing reds, blues and greens against the glass and into her room, and when the lights inside are all off, the new outside colours make everything beat magically so that it seems there's a new happiness in the house now, a happiness that she can see even from the end of the street, when she turns the corner on to their road, on her way home from school. She thinks about Granny when they came home from Mass last week and saw Da up on the ladder.

'Did ya get that message I left for ya on the table? A Mary Hobbs rang the house, says she couldn't get you on the mobile,' Granny shouted up from the front gate.

'I did. Thanks. She's a whole list a things she needs me to do. I'm puttin' in that new kitchen for Luigi this week, so I told her I'd come round tomorrow and give her a price, but I won't be able to start till next week. You don't mind, Mae-Anne?'

'Ah course I don't mind! I keep tellin' ya to take every job you can get – word a mouth is worth more than any fancy advertisin. Work Christmas Day, if ya have to! I'll manage just fine here. But what in the name a God are ya doin' up there? It's not cleanin' the gutters ya are, I suppose!'

'Didn't I get a whole load a Christmas lights for half nothin' in Aldi!' Da shouts back, in a strange question-answer kind of way, down into the garden.

'And what, may I ask, in the name a God, are ya doin' coverin' the whole house in *more* fairy lights for? Jesus Christ, we'll be seen from feckin' Mars! You'll have it lookin' like a goddamn amusement arcade! Ya wouldn't see the likes of it in the tinkers' camp out the road! And a course, don't ya know, there'll not be a sign of a crib anywhere in the place. Mark my words, you'll blow us all into smithereens before you're finished!'

'Ah, I know, Mae-Anne, I got a bit carried away. I did. But sure, won't Annette love seein' all the lights out through the window?'

'Jenny, will ya run in next door, like a good girl, and ask Billy to come out and hold that ladder for Tenzing Norgay up there? True as God he's goin' to fall down and break both his legs!' Granny turns away from Jenny and looks back up into the air. 'And don't come runnin' to me when ya do!'

Jenny looks at the open copy on her desk again. She takes the lid back off her pen. 'THE END', she writes, in block letters, at the bottom of the page. Her shoulders drop as she lets out a big breath she doesn't remember taking in. She smiles as she closes it over. Now she's ready to begin something new.

Standing up, with a book in her hand, she moves across the room. She turns off the light and remains, for a moment, in the pulsing colours from outside, flashing though the darkness.

Jenny throws her right leg over the beast with the funny head that doesn't match its body, on the front cover of the book, and closes her arms around it.

'Come on, Harry Potter. You, too, Hermione! Mammy's been waiting far too long for us.'

Acknowledgements

Thank you to my earliest teachers – my grandmother, Eileen O'Reilly, and my great aunt, Maureen Murray – for all the stories you turned from black and white into colour. You were both there, at the very beginning.

Thank you to my mam and dad for everything; you continued with the stories, and continue every day to encourage my creative endeavours.

Thank you to my brother and sister, Colin and Eimear, for your indomitable belief in me and for living close enough so that you never have to stay with me for the whole weekend!

Thank you, Mr Tom Garry, for your interest, your patience, your wisdom and your endless early reading of my book.

Thank you, Aideen O'Toole, for your unfailing support, your creative advice, your sense of humour and your early reading. Thank you, Darragh O'Toole!

Thank you, Enda Rensing and Paul McCloskey, for saving my book, on more than one occasion!

Thank you, Nicholas Royle, for your brilliance, your tutorials, your perpetual correction of grammar and your militant stance on punctuation. Thank you to all the staff at MMU for your support and guidance.

Thank you, Claire Keegan, for your honesty, your integrity and your instruction.

Thank you, Vincent, Paul, Pat, Sean, Noel, Fintan, Joe,

Charlie, Kevin, Ger, Aoife, Stella, Paula, Kate, Mags, Edel, Peter, Susan and to all the staff of Gorey Community School, for lending me your words and often your names, too! You encouraged me, you made me laugh but more importantly you never failed to keep me grounded!

Thank you to everybody in the SEN Department for believing in me, and for sharing your experience and knowledge with me. A special thank you to Edel and Martina for reading key scenes. Thank you, Luke, for helping me to understand.

Thank you to all my students, past and present, for every day in Room 806! I would also like to thank Faber & Faber for permission to reproduce the extract from 'The Forge' by Seamus Heaney.

Thank you to my literary agent, Jennifer Hewson, of Rogers, Coleridge & White, for finding me and for finding a home for the Augustts. You allowed them to grow organically but remained watchful, astute and professional, at all times. You helped me to find my voice and you held my hand on that, often over-whelming, road to publication. For all that you have done, Jenny, I am eternally grateful.

Thank you, Lisa Highton and all at Two Roads. As my editor, Lisa, you brought me clarity, reassurance and confidence in my work. You showed me the future and gave me a team! You make it all feel easy, even when it is not.

Thank you, my dearest friend, Joyce Roche, for the long-distance walks and laughter and for just being you.

Brian Kelly, you gave me the space to write. You gave me your patience and never faltered in the faith you had in me. Ella Kelly, you made me see and you made me hear. You inspired, and you counselled me with the insight and wisdom that only an almost six-year-old can possess.

About the Author

Eleanor O'Reilly is a teacher of English and Classical Studies who has just completed an MA in Creative Writing at Manchester Metropolitan University. Having first started writing five years ago, she has received several literary prizes, including the 2015 RTE Francis McManus Radio Short Story Award and the 2013 William Trevor International Short Story Award, and has been shortlisted for several others, including the 2016 Colm Tóibín Literary Award. She lives in Ireland with her husband Brian Kelly, their daughter Ella Kelly, and a whole menagerie of pets. *M for Mammy* is her debut novel.